Rafael Sabatini, creator of some of the world's best-loved heroes, was born in Italy in 1875 and educated in both Portugal and Switzerland. He eventually settled in England in 1892, by which time he was fluent in a total of five languages. He chose to write in English, claiming that 'all the best stories are written in English'.

His writing career was launched in the 1890s with a collection of short stories, and it was not until 1902 that his first novel was published. His fame, however, came with *Scaramouche*, the much-loved story of the French Revolution, which became an international bestseller. *Captain Blood* followed soon after, which resulted in a renewed enthusiasm for his earlier work.

For many years a prolific writer, he was forced to abandon writing in the 1940s through illness and he eventually died in 1950.

Sabatini is best-remembered for his heroic characters and high-spirited novels, many of which have been adapted into classic films, including *Scaramouche, Captain Blood* and *The Sea Hawk* starring Errol Flynn.

TITLES BY THE SAME AUTHOR
ALL PUBLISHED BY HOUSE OF STRATUS

FICTION:

THE BANNER OF THE BULL
BARDELYS THE MAGNIFICENT
BELLARION
THE BLACK SWAN
CAPTAIN BLOOD
THE CAROLINIAN
CHIVALRY
THE CHRONICLES OF CAPTAIN BLOOD
COLUMBUS
FORTUNE'S FOOL
THE FORTUNES OF CAPTAIN BLOOD
THE GAMESTER
THE GATES OF DOOM
THE HOUNDS OF GOD
THE JUSTICE OF THE DUKE
THE LION'S SKIN
THE LOST KING
LOVE-AT-ARMS
THE MARQUIS OF CARABAS
THE MINION
THE NUPTIALS OF CORBAL
THE ROMANTIC PRINCE
SCARAMOUCHE
SCARAMOUCHE THE KING-MAKER
THE SEA HAWK
THE SHAME OF MOTLEY
THE SNARE
ST MARTIN'S SUMMER
THE STALKING-HORSE
THE STROLLING SAINT
THE SWORD OF ISLAM
THE TAVERN KNIGHT
THE TRAMPLING OF THE LILIES
TURBULENT TALES
VENETIAN MASQUE

NON-FICTION:

HEROIC LIVES
THE HISTORICAL NIGHTS' ENTERTAINMENT
KING IN PRUSSIA
THE LIFE OF CESARE BORGIA
TORQUEMADA AND THE SPANISH INQUISITION

Anthony Wilding

Rafael Sabatini

HOUSE OF
STRATUS

This edition published in 2001 by House of Stratus, an imprint of
Stratus Books Ltd., 21 Beeching Park, Kelly Bray,
Cornwall, PL17 8QS, UK.

www.houseofstratus.com

Typeset, printed and bound by House of Stratus.

A catalogue record for this book is available from the British Library
and the Library of Congress.

ISBN 07551-152-3-6

TO
RAFAEL-ANGELO

Contents

Contents (Contd)

Chapter 1

POT-VALIANCE

"Then drink it thus," cried the rash young fool, and splashed the contents of his cup full into the face of Mr Wilding even as that gentleman, on his feet, was proposing to drink to the eyes of the young fool's sister.

The moments that followed were full of interest. A stillness, a brooding expectant stillness, fell upon the company – and it numbered a round dozen – about Lord Gervase's richly appointed board. In the soft candlelight the oval table shone like a deep brown pool, in which were reflected the gleaming silver and sparkling crystal that seemed to float upon it.

Blake sucked in his nether-lip, his florid face a thought less florid than its wont, his prominent blue eyes a thought more prominent. Under its golden periwig old Nick Trenchard's wizened countenance was darkened by a scowl, and his fingers, long, swarthy, and gnarled, drummed fretfully upon the table. Portly Lord Gervase Scoresby – their host, a benign and placid man of peace, detesting turbulence – turned crimson now in wordless rage. The others gaped and stared – some at young Westmacott, some at the man he had so grossly affronted – whilst in the shadows of the hall a couple of lacqueys looked on amazed, all teeth and eyes.

1

Mr Wilding stood, very still and outwardly impassive, the wine trickling from his long face, which, if pale, was no paler than its habit, a vestige of the smile with which he had proposed the toast still lingering on his thin lips, though departed from his eyes. An elegant gentleman was Mr Wilding, tall, and seeming even taller by virtue of his exceeding slenderness. He had the courage to wear his own hair, which was of a dark brown and very luxuriant; dark brown too were his sombre eyes, low-lidded and set at a downward slant. From those odd eyes of his, his countenance gathered an air of superciliousness tempered by a gentle melancholy. For the rest, it was scored by lines that stamped it with the appearance of an age in excess of his thirty years.

Thirty guineas' worth of Mechlin at his throat was drenched, empurpled and ruined beyond redemption, and on the breast of his blue satin coat a dark patch was spreading like a stain of blood.

Richard Westmacott, short, sturdy, and fair complexioned to the point of insipidity, watched him sullenly out of pale eyes, and waited. It was Lord Gervase who broke at last the silence – broke it with an oath, a thing unusual in one whose nature was almost woman-mild.

"As God's my life!" he spluttered wrathfully, glowering at Richard. "To have this happen in my house! The young fool shall make apology!"

"With his dying breath," sneered Trenchard, and the old rake's words, his tone, and the malevolent look he bent upon the boy increased the company's *malaise*.

"I think," said Mr Wilding, with a most singular and excessive sweetness, "that what Mr Westmacott has done he has done because he apprehended me amiss."

"No doubt he'll say so," opined Trenchard with a shrug, and had caution dug into his ribs by Blake's elbow, whilst Richard made haste to prove him wrong by saying the contrary.

"I apprehended you exactly, sir," he answered, defiance in his voice and wine-flushed face.

"Ha!" clucked Trenchard, irrepressible. "He's bent on self-destruction. Let him have his way, in God's name."

But Wilding seemed intent upon showing how long-suffering he could be. He gently shook his head. "Nay, now," said he. "You thought, Mr Westmacott, that in mentioning your sister, I did so lightly. Is it not so?"

"You mentioned her, and that is all that matters," cried Westmacott. "I'll not have her name on your lips at any time or in any place – no, nor in any manner." His speech was thick from too much wine.

"You are drunk," cried indignant Lord Gervase with finality.

"Pot-valiant," Trenchard elaborated.

Mr Wilding set down at last the glass which he had continued to hold until that moment. He rested his hands upon the table, knuckles downward, and leaning forward he spoke impressively, his face very grave; and those present – knowing him as they did – were one and all lost in wonder at his unusual patience.

"Mr Westmacott," said he, "I do think you are wrong to persist in affronting me. You have done a thing that is beyond forgiveness, and yet, when I offer you this opportunity of honourably retrieving…" He shrugged his shoulders, leaving the sentence incomplete.

The company might have spared its deep surprise at so much mildness. There was but the semblance of it. Wilding proceeded thus of purpose set, and under the calm mask of his long white face his mind worked wicked and deliberately. The temerity of Westmacott, whose nature was notoriously timid, had surprised him for a moment. But anon, reading the boy's mind as readily as though it had been a scroll unfolded for his instruction, he saw that Westmacott, on the strength of his position as his sister's brother conceived himself immune. Mr Wilding's avowed courtship of the lady, the hopes he still entertained of winning her, despite the aversion she was at pains to show him, gave Westmacott assurance that Mr Wilding would never elect to shatter his all too slender chances by embroiling himself in a quarrel with her brother. And – reading him, thus, aright – Mr Wilding put on that mask of patience, luring the boy into greater conviction of the security of his position.

And Richard, conceiving himself safe in his entrenchment behind the bulwarks of his brothership to Ruth Westmacott, and heartened further by the excess of wine he had consumed, persisted in insults he would never otherwise have dared to offer.

"Who seeks to retrieve?" he crowed offensively, boldly looking up into the other's face. "It seems you are yourself reluctant." And he laughed a trifle stridently, and looked about him for applause, but found none.

"You are over-rash," Lord Gervase disapproved him harshly.

"Not the first coward I've seen grow valiant at a table," put in Trenchard by way of explanation, and might have come to words with Blake on that same score, but that in that moment Wilding spoke again.

"Reluctant to do what?" he questioned amiably, looking Westmacott so straightly between the eyes that the boy shifted uneasily on his high-backed chair.

Nevertheless, still full of confidence in the unassailability of his position, the mad youth answered, "To cleanse yourself of what I threw at you."

"Fan me, ye winds!" gasped Nick Trenchard, and looked with expectancy at his friend Wilding.

Now there was one factor with which, in basing with such craven shrewdness his calculations upon Mr Wilding's feelings for his sister, young Richard had not reckoned. He was not to know that Wilding, bruised and wounded by Miss Westmacott's scorn of him, had reached that borderland where love and hate are so merged that they are scarce to be distinguished. Embittered by the slights she had put upon him – slights which his sensitive, lover's fancy had magnified a hundredfold – Anthony Wilding's frame of mind was grown peculiar. Of his love she would have none; his kindness she seemingly despised. So be it; she should taste his cruelty. If she scorned his wooing and forbade him to pursue it, at least it was not hers to deny him the power to hurt; and in hurting her that would not be loved by him, some measure of fierce and bitter consolation seemed to await him.

He realised, perhaps, not quite all this – and to the unworthiness of it all he gave no thought. But he realised enough as he toyed, as cat with mouse, with Richard Westmacott, to know that in striking at her through the worthless person of this brother whom she cherished – and who persisted in affording him this opportunity – a wicked vengeance would be his.

Peace-loving Lord Gervase had heaved himself suddenly to his feet at Westmacott's last words, still intent upon saving the situation.

"In Heaven's name…" he began, when Mr Wilding, ever calm and smiling, though now a trifle sinister, waved him gently into silence. But that persisting calm of Mr Wilding's was too much for old Nick Trenchard. He rose abruptly, drawing all eyes upon himself. It was time, he thought, he took a hand in this.

In addition to his affection for Wilding and his contempt for Westmacott, he was filled with a fear that the latter might become dangerous if not crushed at once. Gifted with a shrewd knowledge of men, acquired during a chequered life of much sour experience, old Nick instinctively mistrusted Richard. He had known him for a fool, a weakling, a babbler, and a bibber of wine. Out of such elements a villain is soon compounded, and Trenchard had cause to fear the form of villainy that lay ready to Richard's hand. For it chanced that Mr Trenchard was second cousin to that famous John Trenchard, so lately tried for treason and acquitted to the great joy of the sectaries of the West, and still more lately – but yesterday, in fact – fled the country to escape the re-arrest ordered in consequence of that excessive joy. Like his more famous cousin, Nick Trenchard was one of the Duke of Monmouth's most active agents; and Westmacott, like Wilding, Vallancey, and one or two others at that board, stood, too, committed to the cause of the Protestant Champion.

Out of his knowledge of the boy Trenchard was led to fear that if he were leniently dealt with now, tomorrow, when, sober, he came to realise the grossness of the thing he had done and the unlikelihood of its being forgiven him, there was no saying but that to protect himself he might betray Wilding's share in the plot that was being hatched. That in itself would be bad enough; but there might be worse, for he could scarcely betray Wilding without betraying others and – what mattered most – the Cause itself. He must be dealt with out of hand, Trenchard opined, and dealt with ruthlessly.

"I think, Anthony," said he, "that we have had words enough. Shall you be disposing of Mr Westmacott tomorrow, or must I be doing it for you?"

With a gasp of dismay young Richard twisted in his chair to confront this fresh and unsuspected antagonist. What danger was this that he had overlooked? Then even as he turned, Wilding's voice fell on his ear, and each word of the few he spoke was like a drop of icy water on Westmacott's overheated brain.

"I protest you are vastly kind, Nick. But I intend, myself, to have the pleasure of killing Mr Westmacott." And his smile fell now in mockery upon the disillusioned lad. Crushed by that bolt from the blue, Richard sat as if stunned, the flush receding from his face until his very lips were livid. The shock had sobered him, and, sobered, he realised in terror what he had done. And yet even sober he was amazed to find that the staff upon which with such security he had leaned should have proved rotten. True he had put much strain upon it; but then he had counted that it would stand much strain.

He would have spoken, but he lacked words, so stricken was he. And even had he done so it is odds none would have heard him, for the late calm was of a sudden turned to garboil. Every man of that company – with the sole exception of Richard himself – was on his feet, and all were speaking at once, in clamouring, excited chorus.

Wilding alone – the butt of their expostulations – stood quietly smiling, and wiped his face at last with a kerchief of finest lawn. Dominating the others in the babel rose the voice of Sir Rowland Blake – impecunious Blake; Blake lately of the Guards, who had sold his commission as the only thing remaining him upon which he could raise money; Blake, that other suitor for Miss Westmacott's hand, the suitor favoured by her brother.

"You shall not do it, Mr Wilding," he shouted, his face crimson. "No, by God! You were shamed forever. He is but a lad, and drunk."

Trenchard eyed the short, powerfully built man beside him, and laughed unpleasantly. "You should get yourself bled one of these days, Sir Rowland," he advised. "There may be no great danger yet; but a man can't be too careful when he wears a narrow neckcloth."

Blake – a short, powerfully built man – took no heed of him, but looked straight at Mr Wilding, who, smiling ever, calmly returned the gaze of those prominent blue eyes.

"You will suffer me, Sir Rowland," said he sweetly, "to be the judge of whom I will and whom I will not meet."

Sir Rowland flushed under that mocking glance and caustic tone. "But he is drunk," he repeated feebly.

"I think," said Trenchard, "that he is hearing something that will make him sober."

Lord Gervase took the lad by the shoulder, and shook him impatiently. "Well?" quoth he. "Have you nothing to say? You did a deal of prating just now. I make no doubt but that even at this late hour if you were to make apology…"

"It would be idle," came Wilding's icy voice to quench the gleam of hope kindling anew in Richard's breast. The lad saw that he was lost, and he is a poor thing indeed who cannot face the worst once that worst is shown to be irrevocable. He rose with some semblance of dignity.

"It is as I would wish," said he, but his livid face and staring eyes belied the valour of his words. He cleared his huskiness from his throat. "Sir Rowland," said he, "will you act for me?"

"Not I!" cried Blake with an oath. "I'll be no party to the butchery of a boy unfledged."

"Unfledged?" echoed Trenchard. "Body o me! 'Tis a matter Wilding will amend tomorrow. He'll fledge him, never fear. He'll wing him on his flight to heaven."

Of set purpose did Trenchard add this fuel to the blazing fire. It was no part of his views that this encounter should be avoided. If

Richard Westmacott were allowed to live after what had passed, there were too many tall fellows might go in peril of their lives.

Richard, meanwhile, had turned to the man on his left – young Vallancey, a notorious partisan of the Duke of Monmouth's, a harebrained gentleman who was his own worst enemy.

"May I count on you, Ned?" he asked.

"Aye – to the death," said Vallancey magniloquently.

"Mr Vallancey," said Trenchard with a wry twist of his sharp features, "you grow prophetic."

Chapter 2

SIR ROWLAND TO THE RESCUE

From Scoresby Hall, near Weston Zoyland, young Westmacott rode home that Saturday night to his sister's house in Bridgwater, a sobered man and an anguished. He had committed a folly which was like to cost him his life tomorrow. Other follies had he committed in his twenty-five years – for he was not quite the babe that Blake had represented him, although he certainly looked nothing like his age. But tonight he had contrived to set the crown to all. He had good cause to blame himself and to curse the miscalculation that had emboldened him to launch himself upon a course of insult against this Wilding, whom he hated with all the currish and resentful hatred of the worthless for the man of parts.

But there was more than hate in the affront that he had offered; there was calculation – to an even greater extent than we have seen. It happened that through his own fault young Richard was all but penniless. The pious, nonconformist soul of Sir Geoffrey Lupton – the wealthy uncle from whom he had had great expectations – had been so stirred to anger by Richard's vicious and besotted ways that he had left every guinea that was his, every perch of land, and every brick of edifice to Richard's half-sister Ruth. At present things were not so bad for the worthless boy. Ruth worshipped him. He was a sacred charge to her from their dead father, who, knowing the stoutness of her soul and the feebleness of Richard's, had in dying imposed on her the care and guidance of her graceless brother. But Ruth, in all things strong, was weak with Richard out of her very fondness for him. To what she had he might help himself, and thus it was that things were not so bad with him at present. But when Richard's calculating mind came to give thought to the future he found that this occasioned him some care. Rich ladies, even when they do not happen to be equipped in addition with Ruth's winsome beauty and endearing nature, are not wont to go unmarried. It would have pleased Richard best to have had her remain a spinster. But he well knew that this was a matter in which she might have a voice of her own, and it behoved him betimes to take wise measures where possible husbands were concerned.

The first that came in a suitor's obvious panoply was Anthony Wilding, of Zoyland Chase, and Richard watched his advent with foreboding. Wilding's was a personality to dazzle any woman, despite – perhaps even because of – the reputation for wildness that clung to him. That he was known as Wild Wilding to the countryside is true; but it were unfair – as Richard knew – to attach to this too much importance; for the adoption of so obvious an alliteration, the rude country minds needed but a slight encouragement.

From the first it looked as if Ruth might favour him, and Richard's fears assumed more definite shape. If Wilding married her – and he was a bold, masterful fellow who usually accomplished what he aimed at – her fortune and estate must cease to be a pleasant pasture land for bovine Richard. The boy thought at first of making terms with Wilding; the idea was old; it had come to him when first he had counted the chances of his sister's marrying. But he found himself hesitating to lay his proposal before Mr Wilding. And whilst he hesitated Mr Wilding made obvious headway. Still Richard dared not do it. There was a something in Wilding's eye that cried him danger. Thus, in the end, since he could not attempt a compromise with this fine fellow, the only course remaining was that of direct antagonism – that is to say, direct as Richard understood directness. Slander was the weapon he used in that secret duel; the countryside was well stocked with stories of Mr Wilding's many indiscretions. I do not wish to suggest that these were unfounded. Still, the countryside, cajoled by its primitive sense of humour into that alliteration I have mentioned, found that having given this dog its bad name, it was under the obligation of keeping up his reputation. So it exaggerated. Richard, exaggerating those exaggerations in his turn, had some details, as interesting and unsavoury as they were in the main untrue, to lay before his sister.

Now established love, it is well known, thrives wondrously on slander. The robust growth of a maid's feelings for her accepted suitor is but further strengthened by malign representations of his character. She seizes with joy the chance of affording proof of her great loyalty, and defies the world and its evil to convince her that the man to whom she has given her trust is not most worthy of it. Not so, however, with the first timid bud of incipient interest. Slander nips it like a frost; in deadliness it is second only to ridicule.

Ruth Westmacott lent an ear to her brother's stories, incredulous only until she remembered vague hints she had caught from this person and from that, whose meaning was now made clear by what Richard told her, which, incidentally, they served to corroborate. Corroboration, too, did the tale of infamy receive from the friendship that prevailed between Mr Wilding and Nick Trenchard, the old ne'er-do-well, who in his time – as everybody knew – had come so low, despite his gentle birth, as to have been one of a company of strolling players. Had Mr Wilding been other than she now learnt he was, he would surely not cherish an attachment for a person so utterly unworthy. Clearly, they were birds of a plumage.

And so, her maiden purity outraged at the thought that she had been in danger of lending a willing ear to the wooing of such a man, she had crushed this love which she blushed to think was on the point of throwing out roots to fasten on her soul, and was sedulous thereafter in manifesting the aversion which she accounted it her duty to foster for Mr Wilding.

Richard had watched and smiled in secret, taking pride in the cunning way he had wrought this change – that cunning which so often is given to the stupid by way of compensation for the intelligence that has been withheld them.

And now what time discountenanced, Wilding fumed and fretted all in vain, Sir Rowland Blake, fresh from London and in full flight from his creditors, flashed like a comet into the Bridgwater heavens. He dazzled the eyes and might have had for the asking the heart and hand of Diana Horton – Ruth's cousin. Her heart, indeed, he had without the asking, for Diana fell straightway in love with him and showed it, just as he showed that he was not without response to her affection. There were some tender passages between them; but Blake, for all his fine exterior, was a beggar, and Diana far from rich, and so he rode his feelings with a hard grip upon the reins. And then, in an evil hour for poor Diana, young Westmacott had taken him to Lupton House, and Sir Rowland had his first glimpse of Ruth, his first knowledge of her fortune. He went down before Ruth's eyes like a man of heart; he went down more lowly still before her possessions like a man of greed; and poor Diana might console herself with whom she could.

Her brother watched him, appraised him, and thought that in this broken gamester he had a man after his own heart; a man who would be ready enough for such a bargain as Richard had in mind; ready enough to sell what rags might be left him of his honour so that he came by the wherewithal to mend his broken fortunes.

The twain made terms. They haggled like any pair of traders out of Jewry, but in the end it was settled – by a bond duly engrossed and sealed – that on the day that Sir Rowland married Ruth he should make over to her brother certain values that amounted to perhaps a quarter of her possessions. There was no cause to think that Ruth would be greatly opposed to this – not that that consideration would have weighed with Richard.

But now that all essentials were so satisfactorily determined a vexation was offered Westmacott by the circumstance that his sister seemed nowise taken with Sir Rowland. She suffered him because he was her brother's friend; on that account she even honoured him with some measure of her own friendship; but to no greater intimacy did her manner promise to admit him. And meanwhile, Mr Wilding persisted in the face of all rebuffs. Under his smiling mask he hid the smart of the wounds she dealt him, until it almost seemed to him that from loving her he had come to hate her.

It had been well for Richard had he left things as they were and waited. Whether Blake prospered or not, leastways it was clear that Wilding would not prosper, and that, for the season, was all that need have mattered to young Richard.

But in his cups that night he had thought in some dim way to precipitate matters by affronting Mr Wilding, secure, as I have shown, in his belief that Wilding would perish sooner than raise a finger against Ruth's brother. And his drunken astuteness, it seemed, had been to his mind as a piece of bottle glass to the sight, distorting the image viewed through it.

With some such bitter reflection rode he home to his sleepless couch. Some part of those dark hours he spent in bitter reviling of Wilding, of himself, and even of his sister, whom he blamed for this awful situation into which he had tumbled; at other times he wept from self-pity and sheer fright.

Once, indeed, he imagined that he saw light, that he saw a way out of the peril that hemmed him in. His mind turned for a moment in the direction that Trenchard had feared it might. He bethought him of his association with the Monmouth Cause – into which he had been beguiled by the sordid hope of gain – and of Wilding's important share in that same business. He was even moved to rise and ride that very night for Exeter to betray to Albemarle the Cause itself, so that he might have Wilding laid by the heels. But if Trenchard had been right in having little faith in Richard's loyalty, he had, it seems, in fearing treachery made the mistake of giving Richard credit for more courage than was his endowment. For when, sitting up in bed, fired by his inspiration, young Westmacott came to consider the questions the Lord-Lieutenant of Devon would be likely to ask him, he reflected that the answers he must return would so incriminate himself that he would be risking his own neck in the betrayal. He flung himself down again with a curse and a groan, and thought no more of the salvation that might lie for him that way.

The morning of that last day of May found him pale and limp and all a-tremble. He rose betimes and dressed, but stirred not from his chamber till in the garden under his window he heard his sister's voice, and that of Diana Horton, joined anon by a man's deeper tones, which he recognised with a start as Blake's. What did the baronet here so early? Assuredly it must concern the impending duel. Richard knew no mawkishness on the score of eavesdropping. He stole to his window and lent an ear, but the voices were receding, and to his vexation he caught nothing of what was said. He wondered how soon Vallancey would come, and for what hour the encounter had been appointed. Vallancey had remained behind at Scoresby Hall last night to make the necessary arrangements with Trenchard, who was to act for Mr Wilding.

Now it chanced that Trenchard and Wilding had business – business of Monmouth's – to transact in Taunton that morning; business which might not be delayed. There were odd rumours afloat in the West; persistent rumours which had come fast upon the heels of the news of Argyle's landing in Scotland; rumours which maintained that Monmouth himself was coming over from Holland. These tales Wilding and his associates had ignored. The Duke, they knew, was to spend the summer in retreat in Sweden, with (it was alleged) the Lady Henrietta Wentworth to bear him company, and in the meantime his trusted agents were to pave the way for his coming in the following spring. Of late the lack of direct news from the Duke had been a source of mystification to his friends in the West, and now, suddenly, the information went abroad – it was something more than rumour this time – that a letter of the greatest importance had been intercepted. From whom that letter proceeded, or to whom it was addressed, could not yet be discovered. But it seemed clear that it was connected with the Monmouth Cause, and it behoved Mr Wilding to discover what he could. With this intent he rode with Trenchard that Sunday morning to Taunton, hoping that at the Red

Lion Inn – that meeting-place of dissenters – he might cull reliable information.

It was in consequence of this that the meeting with Richard Westmacott was not to take place until the evening, and therefore Vallancey came not to Lupton House as early as Richard thought he should expect him. Blake, however, – more no doubt out of a selfish fear of losing a valued ally in the winning of Ruth's hand than out of any excessive concern for Richard himself – had risen early and hastened to Lupton House, in the hope, which he recognised as all but forlorn, of yet being able to avert the disaster he foresaw for Richard.

Peering over the orchard wall as he rode by, he caught a glimpse through an opening between the trees of Ruth herself and Diana on the lawn beyond. There was a wicket gate that stood unlatched, and availing himself of this Sir Rowland tethered his horse in the lane and threading his way briskly through the orchard came suddenly upon the ladies. Their laughter reached him as he advanced, and told him they could know nothing yet of Richard's danger.

On his abrupt and unexpected apparition Diana paled and Ruth flushed slightly, whereupon Sir Rowland might have bethought him, had he been book-learned, of the axiom, "*Amour qui rougit, fleurette; amour qui pâlit, drame du coeur.*"

He doffed his hat and bowed, his fair ringlets tumbling forward till they hid his face, which was exceeding grave.

Ruth gave him good morning pleasantly. "You London folk are earlier risers than we are led to think," she added.

" 'Twill be the change of air makes Sir Rowland matutinal," said Diana, making a gallant recovery from her agitation.

"I vow," said he, "that I had grown matutinal earlier had I known what here awaited me."

"Awaited you?" quoth Diana, and tossed her head archly disdainful. "La! Sir Rowland, your modesty will be the death of you." Archness became this lady of the sunny hair, tip-tilted nose, and complexion that outvied the apple-blossoms. She was shorter by a half-head than her darker cousin, and made up in sprightliness what she lacked of

Ruth's gentle dignity. The pair were foils, each setting off the graces of the other.

"I protest I am foolish," answered Blake, a shade discomfited. "But I want not for excuse. I have it in the matter that brings me here." So solemn was his air, so sober his voice, that both ladies felt a premonition of the untoward message that he bore. It was Ruth who asked him to explain himself.

"Will you walk, ladies?" said Blake, and waved the hand that still held his hat riverwards, adown the sloping lawn. They moved away together, Sir Rowland pacing between his love of yesterday and his love of today, pressed with questions from both. He shaded his eyes to look at the river, dazzling in the morning sunlight that came over Polden Hill, and, standing thus, he unburdened himself at last.

"My news concerns Richard and – Mr Wilding." They looked at him, Miss Westmacott's fine level brows were knit. He paused to ask, as if suddenly observing his absence, "Is Richard not yet risen?"

"Not yet," said Ruth, and waited for him to proceed.

"It does credit to his courage that he should sleep late on such a day," said Blake, and was pleased with the adroitness wherewith he broke the news. "He quarrelled last night with Anthony Wilding."

Ruth's hand went to her bosom; fear stared at Blake from out her eyes, blue as the heavens overhead; a grey shade overcast the usual warm pallor of her face.

"With Mr Wilding?" she cried. "That man!" And though she said no more her eyes implored him to go on, and tell her what more there might be. He did so, and he spared not Wilding. The task, indeed, was one to which he applied himself with a certain zest; whatever might be the outcome of the affair there was no denying that he was by way of reaping profit from it by the final overthrow of an acknowledged rival. And when he told her how Richard had flung his wine in Wilding's face when Wilding stood to toast her, a faint flush crept to her cheeks.

"Richard did well," said she. "I am proud of him."

The words pleased Sir Rowland vastly; but he reckoned without Diana. Miss Horton's mind was illumined by her knowledge of herself. In the light of that she saw precisely what capital this tale-bearer sought to make. The occasion might not be without its opportunities for her; and to begin with, it was no part of her intention that Wilding should be thus maligned and finally driven from the lists of rivalry with Blake. Upon Wilding, indeed, and his notorious masterfulness did she found what hopes she still entertained of winning back Sir Rowland.

"Surely," said she, "you are a little hard on Mr Wilding. You speak as if he were the first gallant that ever toasted lady's eyes."

"I am no lady of his, Diana," Ruth reminded her, with a faint show of heat.

Diana shrugged her shoulders. "You may not love him, but you can't ordain that he shall not love *you*. You are very harsh, I think. To me it rather seems that Richard acted like a boor."

"But, mistress," cried Sir Rowland, half out of countenance, and stifling his vexation, "in these matters it all depends upon the manner."

"Why, yes," she agreed; "and whatever Mr Wilding's manner, if I know him at all, it would be nothing but respectful to the last degree."

"My own conception of respect," said he, "is not to bandy a lady's name about a company of revellers."

"Bethink you, though, you said just now, it all depended on the manner," she rejoined. Sir Rowland shrugged and turned half from her to her listening cousin. When all is said, poor Diana appears – despite her cunning – to have been short-sighted. Aiming at a defined advantage in the game she played, she either ignored or held too lightly the concomitant disadvantage of vexing Blake.

"It were perhaps best to tell us the exact words he used, Sir Rowland," she suggested, "that for ourselves we may judge how far he lacked respect."

"What signify the words!" cried Blake, now almost out of temper. "I don't recall them. It is the air with which he pledged Mistress Westmacott."

"Ah, yes – the manner," quoth Diana irritatingly. "We'll let that be. Richard threw his wine in Mr Wilding's face! What followed then? What said Mr Wilding?"

Sir Rowland remembered what Mr Wilding had said, and bethought him that it were impolitic in him to repeat it. At the same time, not having looked for this cross-questioning, he was all unprepared with any likely answer. He hesitated, until Ruth echoed Diana's question.

"Tell us, Sir Rowland," she begged him, "what Mr Wilding said."

Being forced to say something, and being by nature slow-witted and sluggish of invention, Sir Rowland was compelled, to his unspeakable chagrin, to fall back upon the truth.

"Is not that proof?" cried Diana in triumph. "Mr Wilding was reluctant to quarrel with Richard. He was even ready to swallow such an affront as that, thinking it might be offered him under a misconception of his meaning. He plainly professed the respect that filled him for Mistress Westmacott, and yet, and yet, Sir Rowland, you tell us that he lacked respect!"

"Madam," cried Blake, turning crimson, "that matters nothing. It was not the place or time to introduce your cousin's name."

"You think, Sir Rowland," put in Ruth, her air grave, judicial almost, "that Richard behaved well?"

"As I would like to behave myself, as I would have a son of mine behave on the like occasion," Blake protested. "But we waste words," he cried. "I did not come to defend Richard, nor just to bear you this untoward news. I came to consult with you, in the hope that we might find some way to avert this peril from your brother."

"What way is possible?" asked Ruth, and sighed. "I would not… I would not have Richard a coward."

"Would you prefer him dead?" asked Blake, sadly grave.

"Sooner than craven – yes," Ruth answered him, very white.

"There is no question of that," was Blake's rejoinder. "The question is that Wilding said last night that he would kill the boy, and what Wilding says he does. Out of the affection that I bear Richard is born my anxiety to save him despite himself. It is in this that I come to seek your aid or offer mine. Allied we might accomplish what singly neither of us could."

He had at once the reward of his cunning speech. Ruth held out her hands. "You are a good friend, Sir Rowland," she said, with a pale smile; and pale too was the smile with which Diana watched them. No more than Ruth did she suspect the sincerity of Blake's protestations.

"I am proud you should account me that," said the baronet, taking Ruth's hands and holding them a moment; "and I would that I could prove myself your friend in this to some good purpose. Believe me, if Wilding would consent that I might take your brother's place, I would gladly do so."

It was a safe boast, knowing as he did that Wilding would consent to no such thing; but it earned him a glance of greater kindliness from Ruth – who began to think that hitherto perhaps she had done him some injustice – and a look of greater admiration from Diana, who saw in him her beau-ideal of the gallant lover.

"I would not have you endanger yourself so," said Ruth.

"It might," said Blake, his blue eyes very fierce, "be no great danger, after all." And then dismissing that part of the subject as if, like a brave man, the notion of being thought boastful were unpleasant, he passed on to the discussion of ways and means by which the coming duel might be averted. But when they came to grips with facts, it seemed that Sir Rowland had as little idea of what might be done as had the ladies. True, he began by making the obvious suggestion that Richard should tender Wilding a full apology. That, indeed, was the only door of escape, and Blake shrewdly suspected that what the boy had been unwilling to do last night – partly through wine, and partly through the fear of looking fearful in the eyes of Lord Gervase Scoresby's guests – he might be willing enough to do today, sober and upon reflection. For the rest Blake was as far from suspecting Mr Wilding's peculiar frame of mind as had Richard been last night. This his words showed.

"I am satisfied," said he, "that if Richard were to go today to Wilding and express his regret for a thing done in the heat of wine,

Wilding would be forced to accept it as satisfaction, and none would think that it did other than reflect credit upon Richard."

"Are you very sure of that?" asked Ruth, her tone dubious, her glance hopefully anxious.

"What else is to be thought?"

"But," put in Diana shrewdly, "it were an admission of Richard's that he had done wrong."

"No less," he agreed, and Ruth caught her breath in fresh dismay.

"And yet you have said that he did as you would have a son of yours do," Diana reminded him.

"And I maintain it," answered Blake; his wits worked slowly ever. It was for Ruth to reveal the flaw to him.

"Do you not understand, then," she asked him sadly, "that such an admission on Richard's part would amount to a lie – a lie uttered to save himself from an encounter, the worst form of lie, a lie of cowardice? Surely, Sir Rowland, your kindly anxiety for his life outruns your anxiety for his honour."

Diana, having accomplished her task, hung her head in silence, pondering.

Sir Rowland was routed utterly. He glanced from one to the other of his companions, and grew afraid that he – the town gallant – might come to look foolish in the eyes of these country ladies. He protested again his love for Richard, and increased Ruth's terror by his mention of Wilding's swordsmanship; but when all was said, he saw that he had best retreat ere he spoiled the good effect which he hoped his solicitude had created. And so he spoke of seeking counsel with Lord Gervase Scoresby, and took his leave, promising to return by noon.

Chapter 3

DIANA SCHEMES

Notwithstanding the brave face Ruth Westmacott had kept during his presence, when he departed Sir Rowland left behind him a distress amounting almost to anguish in her mind. Yet though she might suffer, there was no weakness in Ruth's nature. She knew how to endure. Diana, bearing Richard not a tenth of the affection his sister consecrated to him, was alarmed for him. Besides, her own interests urged the averting of this encounter. And so she held in accents almost tearful that something must be done to save him.

This too appeared to be Richard's own view, when presently – within a few minutes of Blake's departure – he came to join them. They watched his approach in silence, and both noted – though with different eyes and different feelings – the pallor of his pale face, the dark lines under his colourless eyes. His condition was abject, and his manners, never of the best, – for there was much of the spoiled child about Richard – were clearly suffering from it.

He stood before his sister and his cousin, moving his eyes shiftily from one to the other, rubbing his hands nervously together.

"Your precious friend Sir Rowland has been here," said he, and it was not clear from his manner which of them he addressed. 'Not a doubt but he will have brought you the news." He seemed to sneer.

Ruth advanced towards him, her face grave, her sweet eyes full of pitying concern. She placed a hand upon his sleeve. "My poor Richard…" she began, but he shook off her kindly touch, laughing angrily – a mere cackle of irritability.

"Odso!" he interrupted her. "It is a thought late for this mock kindliness!"

Diana, in the background, arched her brows, then with a shrug turned aside and seated herself on the stone seat by which they had been standing. Ruth shrank back as if her brother had struck her.

"Richard!" she cried, and searched his livid face with her eyes. "Richard!"

He read a question in the interjection, and he answered it. "Had you known any real care, any true concern for me, you had not given cause for this affair," he chid her peevishly.

"What are you saying?" she cried, and it occurred to her at last that Richard was afraid. He was a coward! She felt as she would faint.

"I am saying," said he, hunching his shoulders, and shivering as he spoke, yet his glance unable to meet hers, "that it is your fault I am like to get my throat cut before sunset."

"My fault?" she murmured. The slope of lawn seemed to wave and swim about her. "My fault?"

"The fault of your wanton ways," he accused her harshly. "You have so played fast and loose with this fellow Wilding that he makes free of your name in my very presence, and puts upon me the need to get myself killed by him to save the family honour."

He would have said more in this strain, but something in her glance gave him pause. There fell a silence. From the distance came the melodious pealing of church bells. High overhead a lark was pouring out its song; in the lane at the orchard end rang the beat of trotting hoofs. It was Diana who spoke presently. Just indignation stirred her, and, when stirred, she knew no pity, set no limits to her speech.

"I think, indeed," said she, her voice crisp and merciless, "that the family honour will best be saved if Mr Wilding kills you. It is in danger while you live. You are a coward, Richard."

"Diana!" he thundered – he could be mighty brave with women – whilst Ruth clutched her arm to restrain her.

But she continued, undeterred: "You are a coward – a pitiful coward," she told him. "Consult your mirror. It will tell you what a palsied thing you are. That you should dare so speak to Ruth…"

"Don't!" Ruth begged her, turning.

"Aye," growled Richard, "she had best be silent."

Diana rose, to battle, her cheeks crimson. "It asks a braver man than you to compel my obedience," she told him. "La!" she fumed, "I'll swear that had Mr Wilding overheard what you have said to your sister, you would have little to fear from his sword. A cane would be the weapon he'd use on you."

Richard's pale eyes flamed malevolently; a violent rage possessed him and flooded out his fear, for nothing can so goad a man as an offensive truth. Ruth approached him again; again she took him by the arm, seeking to soothe his over-troubled spirit; but again he shook her off. And then to save the situation came a servant from the house. So lost in anger was all Richard's sense of decency that the mere supervention of the man would not have been enough to have silenced him could he have found adequate words in which to answer Mistress Horton. But even as he racked his mind, the footman's voice broke the silence, and the words the fellow uttered did what his presence alone might not have sufficed to do.

"Mr Vallancey is asking for you, sir," he announced.

Richard started. Vallancey! He had come at last, and his coming was connected with the impending duel. The thought was paralysing to young Westmacott. The flush of anger faded from his face; its leaden hue returned and he shivered as with cold. At last he mastered himself sufficiently to ask: "Where is he, Jasper?"

"In the library, sir," replied the servant. "Shall I bring him hither?"

"Yes – no," he answered. "I will come to him." He turned his back upon the ladies, paused a moment, still irresolute. Then, as by an effort, he followed the servant across the lawn and vanished through the ivied porch.

As he went Diana flew to her cousin. Her shallow nature was touched with transient pity. "My poor Ruth…" she murmured soothingly, and set her arm about the other's waist. There was a gleam of tears in the eyes Ruth turned upon her. Together they came to the granite seat and sank to it side by side, fronting the placid river. There Ruth, her elbows on her knees, cradled her chin in her hands, and with a sigh of misery stared straight before her.

"It was untrue!" she said at last. "What Richard said of me was untrue."

"Why, yes," Diana snapped, contemptuous. "The only truth is that Richard is afraid."

Ruth shivered. "Ah, no," she pleaded – though she knew how true was the impeachment. "Don't say it, Diana."

"It matters little that I say it," snorted Diana impatiently. "It is a truth proclaimed by the first glance at him."

"He is in poor health, perhaps," said Ruth, seeking miserably to excuse him.

"Aye," said Diana. "He's suffering from an ague – the result of a lack of courage. That he should so have spoken to you! Give me patience, Heaven!"

Ruth crimsoned again at the memory of his words; a wave of indignation swept through her gentle soul, but was gone at once, leaving an ineffable sadness in its room. What was to be done? She turned to Diana for counsel. But Diana was still whipping up her scorn.

"If he goes out to meet Mr Wilding he'll shame himself and every man and woman that bears the name of Westmacott," said she, and struck a new fear with that into the heart of Ruth.

"He must not go," she answered passionately. "He must not meet him!"

Diana flashed her a sidelong glance. "And if he doesn't, will things be mended?" she inquired. "Will it save his honour to have Mr Wilding come and cane him?"

"He'd not do that?" said Ruth.

"Not if you asked him – no," was Diana's sharp retort, and she caught her breath on the last word of it, for just then the devil dropped the seed of a suggestion into the fertile soil of her love-sick soul.

"Diana!" Ruth exclaimed in reproof, turning to confront her cousin. But Diana's mind started upon its scheming journey was now travelling fast. Out of that devil's seed there sprang with amazing rapidity a tree-like growth, throwing out branches, putting forth leaves, bearing already – in her fancy – bloom and fruit.

"Why not?" quoth she after a breathing space, and her voice was gentle, her tone innocent beyond compare. "Why should you not ask him?" Ruth frowned, perplexed and thoughtful, and now Diana turned to her with the lively eye of one into whose mind has leapt a sudden inspiration. "Ruth!" she exclaimed. "Why, indeed, should you not ask him to forgo this duel?"

"How…how could I?" faltered Ruth.

"He'd not deny you; you know he'd not."

"I do not know it," answered Ruth. "But if I did, how could I ask it?"

"Were I Richard's sister, and had I his life and honour at heart as you have, I'd not ask how. If Richard goes to that encounter he loses both, remember – unless between this and then he undergoes some change. Were I in your place, I'd go straight to Wilding."

"To him?" mused Ruth, sitting up. "How could I go to him?"

"Go to him, yes," Diana insisted. "Go to him at once – while there is yet time."

Ruth rose and moved away a step or two towards the water, deep in thought. Diana watched her furtively and slyly, the rapid rise and fall of her maiden breast betraying the agitation that filled her as she waited – like a gamester – for the turn of the card that would show her whether she had won or lost. For she saw clearly how Ruth

25

might be so compromised that there was something more than a chance that Diana would no longer have cause to account her cousin a barrier between herself and Blake.

"I could not go alone," said Ruth, and her tone was that of one still battling with a notion that is repugnant.

"Why, if that is all," said Diana, "then I'll go with you."

"I can't! I can't! Consider the humiliation."

"Consider Richard rather," the fair temptress made answer eagerly. "Be sure that Mr Wilding will save you all humiliation. He'll not deny you. At a word from you, I know what answer he will make. He will refuse to push the matter forward – acknowledge himself in the wrong, do whatever you may ask him. He can do it. None will question his courage. It has been proved too often." She rose and came to Ruth. She set her arm about her waist again, and poured shrewd persuasion over her cousin's indecision. "Tonight you'll thank me for this thought," she assured her. "Why do you pause? Are you so selfish as to think more of the little humiliation that may await you than of Richard's life and honour?"

"No, no," Ruth protested feebly.

"What, then? Is Richard to go out and slay his honour by a show of fear before he is slain, himself, by the man he has insulted?"

"I'll go," said Ruth. Now that the resolve was taken, she was brisk, impatient. "Come, Diana. Let Jerry saddle for us. We'll ride to Zoyland Chase at once."

They went without a word to Richard, who was still closeted with Vallancey, and riding forth they crossed the river and took the road that, skirting Sedgemoor runs south to Weston Zoyland. They rode with little said until they came to the point where the road branches on the left, throwing out an arm across the moor towards Chedzoy, a mile or so short of Zoyland Chase. Here Diana reined in with a sharp gasp of pain. Ruth checked, and cried to know what ailed her.

"It is the sun, I think," muttered Diana, her hand to her brow. "I am sick and giddy." And she slipped a thought heavily to the ground. In an instant Ruth had dismounted and was beside her. Diana was pale, which lent colour to her complaint, for Ruth was not to know that the pallor sprang from her agitation in wondering whether the ruse she attempted would succeed or not.

A short stone's-throw from where they had halted stood a cottage back from the road in a little plot of ground, the property of a kindly old woman known to both. There Diana expressed the wish to rest awhile, and thither they took their way, Ruth leading both horses and supporting her faltering cousin. The dame was all solicitude. Diana was led into her parlour, and what could be done was done. Her corsage was loosened, water drawn from the well and brought her to drink and bathe her brow.

She sat back languidly, her head lolling sideways against one of the wings of the great chair, and languidly assured them she would be better soon if she were but allowed to rest awhile. Ruth drew up a stool to sit beside her, for all that her soul fretted at this delay. What if in consequence she should reach Zoyland Chase too late – to find that Mr Wilding had gone forth already? But even as she was about to sit, it seemed that the same thought had of a sudden come to Diana. The girl leaned forward, thrusting – as if by an effort – some of her faintness from her.

"Do not wait for me, Ruth," she begged.

"I must, child."

"You must not," the other insisted. "Think what it may mean – Richard's life, perhaps. No, no, Ruth dear. Go on; go on to Zoyland. I'll follow you in a few minutes."

"I'll wait for you," said Ruth with firmness.

At that Diana rose, and in rising staggered. "Then we'll push on at once," she gasped, as if speech itself were an excruciating effort.

"But you are in no case to stand!" said Ruth. "Sit, Diana, sit."

"Either you go on alone or I go with you, but go at once you must. At any moment Mr Wilding may go forth, and your chance is lost. I'll not have Richard's blood upon my head."

Ruth wrung her hands in her dismay, confronted by a parlous choice. Consent to Diana's accompanying her in this condition she could not; ride on alone to Mr Wilding's house was hardly to be thought of, and yet if she delayed she was endangering Richard's life. By the very strength of her nature she was caught in the mesh of Diana's scheme. She saw that her hesitation was unworthy. This was no ordinary cause, no ordinary occasion. It was a time for heroic measures. She must ride on, nor could she consent to take Diana.

And so in the end she went, having seen her cousin settled again in the high chair, and took with her Diana's feeble assurances that she would follow her in a few moments, as soon as her faintness passed.

Chapter 4

TERMS OF SURRENDER

"Mr Wilding rode at dawn with Mr Trenchard, madam," announced old Walters, the butler at Zoyland Chase. Old and familiar servant though he was, he kept from his countenance all manifestation of the deep surprise occasioned him by the advent of Mistress Westmacott, unescorted.

"He rode…at dawn?" faltered Ruth, and for a moment she stood irresolute, afraid and pondering in the shade of the great pillared porch. Then she took heart again. If he rode at dawn, it was not in quest of Richard that he went, since it had been near eleven o'clock when she had left Bridgwater. He must have gone on other business first, and, doubtless, before he went to the encounter he would be returning home. "Said he at what hour he would return?" she asked.

"He bade us expect him by noon, madam."

This gave confirmation to her thoughts. It wanted more than half an hour to noon already. "Then he may return at any moment?" said she.

"At any moment, madam," was the grave reply.

She took her resolve. "I will wait," she announced, to the man's increasing if undisplayed astonishment. "Let my horse be seen to."

He bowed his obedience, and she followed him – a slender, graceful figure in her dove-coloured riding-habit laced with silver – across the stone-flagged vestibule, through the cool gloom of the great hall, into the spacious library of which he held the door.

"Mistress Horton is following me," she informed the butler. "Will you bring her to me when she comes?"

Bowing again in silent acquiescence, the white-haired servant closed the door and left her. She stood in the centre of the great room, drawing off her riding-gloves, perturbed and frightened beyond all reason at finding herself for the first time under Mr Wilding's roof. He was most handsomely housed. His grandfather, who had travelled in Italy, had built the Chase upon the severe and noble lines which there he had learnt to admire, and he had embellished its interior, too, with many treasures of art which with that intent he had there collected.

She dropped her whip and gloves on to a table, and sank into a chair to wait, her heart fluttering in her throat. Time passed, and in the silence of the great house her anxiety was gradually quieted, until at last through the long window that stood open came faintly wafted to her on the soft breeze of that June morning the sound of a church clock at Weston Zoyland chiming twelve. She rose with a start, bethinking her suddenly of Diana, and wondering why she had not yet arrived. Was the child's indisposition graver than she had led Ruth to suppose? She crossed to the windows and stood there drumming impatiently upon the pane, her eyes straying idly over the sweep of elm-fringed lawns towards the river gleaming silvery here and there between the trees in the distance.

Suddenly she caught a sound of hoofs. Was this Diana? She sped to the other window, the one that stood open, and now she heard the crunch of gravel and the champ of bits and the sound of more than two pairs of hoofs. She caught a glimpse of Mr Wilding and Mr Trenchard.

She felt the colour flying from her cheeks; again her heart fluttered in her throat, and it was in vain that with her hand she sought to repress the heaving of her breast. She was afraid; her every instinct bade her slip through the window at which she stood and run from Zoyland Chase. And then she thought of Richard and his danger and she seemed to gather courage from the reflection of her purpose in this house.

Men's voices reached her – a laugh, the harsh cawing of Nick Trenchard.

"A lady!" she heard him cry. " 'Od's heart, Tony! Is this a time for trafficking with doxies?" She crimsoned an instant at the coarse word and set her teeth, only to pale again the next. The voices were lowered so that she heard not what was said; one sharp exclamation she recognised to be in Wilding's voice, but caught not the word he uttered. There followed a pause, and she stirred uneasily, waiting. Then came swift steps and jangling spurs across the hall, the door opened suddenly, and Mr Wilding, in a scarlet riding-coat, his boots white with dust, stood bowing to her from the threshold.

"Your servant, Mistress Westmacott," she heard him murmur. "My house is deeply honoured."

She dropped him a half-curtsey, pale and tongue-tied. He turned to deliver hat and whip and gloves to Walters, who had followed him, then closed the door and came forward into the room.

"You will forgive that I present myself thus before you," he said, in apology for his dusty raiment. "But I bethought me you might be in haste, and Walters tells me that already have you waited nigh upon an hour. Will you not sit, madam?" And he advanced a chair. His long white face was set like a mask; but his dark, slanting eyes devoured her. He guessed the reason of her visit. She who had humbled him, who had driven him to the very borders of despair, was now to be humbled and to despair before him. Under the impassive face his soul exulted fiercely.

She disregarded the chair he proffered. "My visit…has no doubt surprised you," she began, tremulous and hesitating.

"I' faith, no," he answered quietly. "The cause, after all, is not very far to seek. You are come on Richard's behalf."

"Not on Richard's," she answered. "On my own." And now that the ice was broken, the suspense of waiting over, she found the tide of her courage flowing fast. "This encounter must not take place, Mr Wilding," she informed him.

He raised his eyebrows – fine and level as her own – his thin lips smiled never so faintly. "It is, I think," said he, "for Richard to prevent it. The chance was his last night. It shall be his again when we meet. If he will express regret…" He left his sentence there. In truth he mocked her, though she guessed it not.

"You mean," said she, "that if he makes apology…?"

"What else? What other way remains?"

She shook her head, and, if pale, her face was resolute, her glance steady.

"That is impossible," she told him. "Last night – as I have the story – he might have done it without shame. Today it is too late. To tender his apology on the ground would be to proclaim himself a coward."

Mr Wilding pursed his lips and shifted his position. "It is difficult, perhaps," said he, "but not impossible."

"It is impossible," she insisted firmly.

"I'll not quarrel with you for a word," he answered, mighty agreeable. "Call it impossible, if you will. Admit, however, that it is all I can suggest. You will do me the justice, I am sure, to see that in expressing my willingness to accept your brother's expressions of regret I am proving myself once more your very obedient servant. But that it is you who ask it – and whose desires are my commands – I should let no man go unpunished for an insult such as your brother put upon me."

She winced at his words, at the bow with which he had professed himself once more her servant.

"It is no clemency that you offer him," she said. "You leave him a choice between death and dishonour."

"He has," Wilding reminded her, "the chance of combat."

She flung back her head impatiently. "I think you mock me," said she.

He looked at her keenly. "Will you tell me plainly, madam," he begged, "what you would have me do?"

She flushed under his gaze, and the flush told him what he sought to learn. There was of course another way, and she had thought of it; but she lacked – as well she might, all things considered – the courage to propose it. She had come to Mr Wilding in the vague hope that he himself would choose the heroic part. And he, to punish for her scorn of him this woman whom he loved to hating-point, was resolved that she herself must beg it of him. Whether, having so far compelled her, he would grant her prayer or not was something he could not just then himself have told you. She bowed her head in silence, and Wilding, the faint smile, half friendliness, half mockery, hovering ever on his lips, turned aside and moved softly towards the window. Her eyes, veiled behind the long lashes of their drooping lids, followed him furtively. She felt that she hated him in very truth. She marked the upright elegance of his figure, the easy grace of his movements, the fine aristocratic mould of the aquiline face, which she beheld in profile; and she hated him the more for these outward favours that must commend him to no lack of women. He was too masterful. He made her realise too keenly her own weakness and that of Richard. She felt that just now he controlled the vice that held her fast – her affection for her brother. And because of that she hated him the more.

"You see, Mistress Westmacott," said he, his shoulder to her, his tone sweet to the point of sadness, "that there is nothing else."

She stood, her eyes following the pattern of the parquetry, her foot unconsciously tracing it; her courage ebbed, and she had no answer for him. After a pause he spoke again, still without turning.

"If that was not enough to suit your ends" – and though he spoke in a tone of ever-increasing sadness, there glinted through it the faintest ray of mockery – "I marvel you should have come to Zoyland – to compromise yourself to so little purpose."

She raised a startled face. "Com…compromise myself?" she echoed. "Oh!" It was a cry of indignation.

"What else?" quoth he, and turned abruptly to confront her.

"Mistress Horton was…was with me," she panted, her voice quivering as on the brink of tears.

" 'Tis unfortunate you should have separated," he condoled.

"But…but, Mr Wilding, I… I trusted to your honour. I accounted you a gentleman. Surely…surely, sir, you will not let it be known that… I came to you? You will keep my secret?"

"Secret!" said he, his eyebrows raised. " 'Tis already the talk of the servants' hall. By tomorrow 'twill be the gossip of Bridgwater."

Air failed her. Her blue eyes fixed him in horror out of her stricken face. Not a word had she wherewith to answer him.

The sight of her, thus, affected him oddly. His passion for her surged up, aroused by pity for her plight, and awakened in him a sense of his brutality. A faint flush stirred in his cheeks. He stepped quickly to her, and caught her hand. She let it lie, cold and inert, within his nervous grasp.

"Ruth, Ruth!" he cried, and his voice was for once unsteady. "Give it no thought! I love you, Ruth. If you'll but heed that, no breath of scandal can hurt you."

She swallowed hard. "As how?" she asked mechanically.

He bowed low over her hand – so low that his face was hidden from her.

"If you will do me the honour to become my wife…" he began, but got no further, for she snatched away her hand, her cheeks crimsoning, her eyes aflame with indignation. He stepped back, crimsoning too. She had dashed the gentleness from his mood. He was angered now and tigerish.

"Oh!" she panted. "It is to affront me! Is this the time or place…?"

He cropped her flow of indignant speech ere it was well begun. He caught her in his arms, and held her tight, and so sudden was the act, so firm his grip, that she had not the thought or force to struggle.

"All time is love's time, all places are love's place," he told her, his face close to her own. "And of all time and places the present ever preferable to the wise – for life is uncertain and short at best. I bring you worship, and you answer me with scorn. But I shall prevail, and you shall come to love me in very spite of your own self."

She threw back her head, away from his as far as the bonds he had cast about her would allow. "Air! Air!" she panted feebly.

"Oh, you shall have air enough anon," he answered with a half-strangled laugh, his passion mounting ever. "Hark you, now – hark you, for Richard's sake, since you'll not listen, for my own nor yours. There is another course by which I can save both Richard's life and honour. You know it, and you counted upon my generosity to suggest it. But you overlooked the thing on which you should have counted. You overlooked my love. Count upon that, my Ruth, and Richard shall have naught to fear. Count upon that, and when we meet this evening, Richard and I, it is I who will tender the apology, I who will admit that I was wrong to introduce your name into that company last night, and that what Richard did was a just and well-deserved punishment upon me. This will I do if you'll but count upon my love."

She looked up at him fearfully, yet with flutterings of hope. "What is't you mean?" she asked him faintly.

"That if you'll promise to be my wife…"

"Your wife!" she interrupted him. She struggled to free herself, released one arm and struck him in the face. "Let me go, you coward!"

He was answered. His arms melted from her. He fell back a pace, very white and even trembling, the fire all gone from his eye, which was now turned dull and deadly.

"So be it," he said, and strode to the bell-rope. "I'll not offend again. I had not offended now," he continued, in the voice of one offering an explanation cold and formal; "but that when first I came into your life you seemed to bid me welcome." His fingers closed upon the crimson bell-cord. She guessed his purpose.

"Wait!" she gasped, and put forth her hand. He paused, the rope in his, his eye kindling anew. "You…you mean to kill Richard now?" she asked him.

A swift lifting of his brows was his only answer. He tugged the cord. From the distance the peal of the bell reached them faintly.

"Oh, wait, wait!" she begged, her hands pressed against her cheeks. He stood impassible – hatefully impassible. "If…if I were to consent to…this…how…how soon…?" He understood the unfinished question. Interest warmed his face again. He took a step towards her, but by a gesture she seemed to beg him come no nearer.

"If you will promise to marry me within the week, Richard shall have no cause to fear either for his life or his honour at my hands."

She seemed now to be recovering her calm. "Very well," she said, her voice singularly steady. "Let that be a bargain between us. Spare Richard's life and honour – both, remember! – and on Sunday next…" For all her courage her voice quavered and faltered. She dared add no more, lest it should break altogether.

Mr Wilding drew a deep breath. Again he would have advanced. "Ruth!" he cried, and some repentance smote him, some shame shook him in his purpose. At that moment it was in his mind to capitulate unconditionally; to tell her that Richard should have naught to fear from him, and yet that she should go free as the winds. Her gesture checked him. It was so eloquent of aversion. He paused in his advance, stifled his better feelings, and turned once more, relentless. The door opened, and old Walters stood awaiting his commands.

"Mistress Westmacott is leaving," he informed his servant, and bowed low and formally in farewell before her. She passed out without another word, the old butler following, and presently through the door that remained open came Trenchard, in quest of Mr Wilding, who stood bemused.

Nick sauntered in, his left eye almost hidden by the rakish cock of his hat, one hand tucked away under the skirts of his plum-coloured coat, the other supporting the stem of a long clay pipe, at which he was pulling thoughtfully. The pipe and he were all but inseparable; indeed, the year before in London he had given appalling scandal by appearing with it in the Mall, and had there remained him any character to lose, he must assuredly have lost it then.

He observed his friend through narrowing eyes – he had small eyes, very blue and very bright, in which there usually abode a roguish gleam.

"My sight, Anthony," said he, "reminds me that I am growing old. I wonder did it mislead me on the score of your visitor?"

"The lady who left," said Wilding with a touch of severity, "will be Mistress Wilding by this day se'night."

Trenchard took the pipe from his lips, audibly blew out a cloud of smoke, and stared at his friend. "Body o' me!" quoth he. "Is this a time for marrying? – with these rumours of Monmouth's coming over."

Wilding made an impatient gesture. "I thought to have convinced you they are idle," said he, and flung himself into a chair at his writing-table.

Nick came over and perched himself upon the table's edge, one leg swinging in the air. "And what of this matter of the intercepted letter from London to our Taunton friends?"

"I can't tell you. But of this I am sure, His Grace is incapable of anything so rash. Certain is it that he'll not stir until Battiscomb returns to Holland, and Battiscomb is still in Cheshire sounding the Duke's friends."

"Yet were I you, I should not marry just at present."

Wilding smiled. "If you were me, you'd never marry at all."

"Faith, no!" said Trenchard. "I'd as soon play at 'hot-cockles,' or 'Parson-has-lost-his-cloak.' 'Tis a mort more amusing and the sooner done with."

Chapter 5

THE ENCOUNTER

Ruth Westmacott rode back like one in a dream, with vague and hazy notions of what she saw or did. So overwrought was she by the interview from which she came, her mind so obsessed by it, that never a thought had she for Diana and her indisposition until she arrived home to find her cousin there before her. Diana was in tears, called up by the reproaches of her mother, Lady Horton – the relict of that fine soldier Sir Cholmondeley Horton, of Taunton.

The girl had arrived at Lupton House a half-hour ahead of Miss Westmacott, and upon her arrival she had expressed surprise, either feigned or real, at finding Ruth still absent. Detecting the alarm that Diana was careful to throw into her voice and manner, her mother questioned her, and elicited the story of her faintness and of Ruth's having ridden on alone to Mr Wilding's. So outraged was Lady Horton that for once in a way this woman, usually so meek and ease-loving, was roused to an energy and anger with her daughter and her niece that threatened to remove Diana at once from the pernicious atmosphere of Lupton House and carry her home to Taunton. Ruth found her still at her remonstrances, arrived, indeed, in time for her share of them.

"I have been sore mistaken in you, Ruth!" the dame reproached her. "I can scarce believe it of you. I have held you up as an example to Diana, for the discretion and wisdom of your conduct, and you do this! You go alone to Mr Wilding's house – to Mr Wilding's of all men!"

"It was no time for ordinary measures," said Ruth, but she spoke without any of the heat of one who defends her conduct. She was, the slyly watchful Diana observed, very white and tired. "It was no time to think of nice conduct. There was Richard to be saved."

"And was it worth ruining yourself to do that?" quoth Lady Horton, her colour high.

"Ruining myself?" echoed Ruth, and she smiled never so weary a smile. "I have indeed done that, though not in the way you mean."

Mother and daughter eyed her, mystified. "Your good name is blasted," said her aunt, "unless so be that Mr Wilding is proposing to make you his wife." It was a sneer the good woman could not, in her indignation, repress.

"That is what Mr Wilding has done me the honour to propose," Ruth answered bitterly, and left them gaping. "We are to be married this day se'night."

A dead silence followed the calm announcement. Then Diana rose. At the misery, the anguish that could impress so strange and white a look on Ruth's winsome face, she was smitten with remorse, her incipient satisfaction dashed. This was her work; the fruit of her scheming. But it had gone further than she had foreseen; and for all that no result could better harmonize with her own ambitions and desires, for the moment – under the first shock of that announcement – she felt guilty and grew afraid.

"Ruth!" she cried, her voice a whisper of stupefaction. "Oh, I wish I had come with you!"

"But you couldn't; you were faint." And then – recalling what had passed – her mind was filled with sudden concern for Diana, even amid her own sore troubles. "Are you quite yourself again, Diana?" she inquired.

Diana answered almost fiercely, "I am quite well." And then, with a change to wistfulness, she added, "Oh, I would I had come with you!"

"Matters had been no different," Ruth assured her. "It was a bargain Mr Wilding drove. It was the price I had to pay for Richard's life and honour." She swallowed hard, and let her hands fall limply to her sides. "Where is Richard?" she inquired.

It was her aunt who answered her. "He went forth half an hour agone with Mr Vallancey and Sir Rowland."

"Sir Rowland had returned, then?" She looked up quickly.

"Yes," answered Diana. "But he had achieved nothing by his visit to Lord Gervase. His lordship would not intervene; he swore he hoped the cub would be flayed alive by Wilding. Those were his lordship's words, as Sir Rowland repeated them. Sir Rowland is in sore distress for Richard. He has gone with them to the meeting."

"At least, he has no longer cause for his distress," said Miss Westmacott with her bitter smile, and sank as one exhausted to a chair. Lady Horton moved to comfort her, her motherliness all aroused for this motherless girl, usually so wise and strong, and seemingly wiser and stronger than ever in this thing that Lady Horton had deemed a weakness and a folly.

Meanwhile, Richard and his two friends were on their way to the moors across the river to the encounter with Mr Wilding. But before they had got him to ride forth Vallancey had had occasion to regret that he stood committed to a share in this quarrel, for he came to know Richard as he really was. He had found him in an abject state, white and trembling, his coward's fancy anticipating a hundred times a minute the death he was anon to die. Vallancey had hailed him cheerily.

"The day is yours, Dick," he had cried, when Richard entered the library where he awaited him. "Wild Wilding has ridden to Taunton this morning and is to be back by noon. 'Odsbud, Dick! – twenty miles and more in the saddle before coming on the ground. Heard you ever of the like madness? He'll be stiff as a broom-handle – an easy victim."

Richard listened, stared, and finding Vallancey's eyes fixed steadily upon him, attempted a smile and achieved a horrible grimace.

"What ails you, man?" cried his second, and caught him by the wrist. He felt the quiver of the other's limb. "Stab me!" quoth he, "you are in no case to fight. What the plague ails you?"

"I am none so well this morning," answered Richard feebly. "Lord Gervase's claret," he added, passing a hand across his brow.

"Lord Gervase's claret?" echoed Vallancey in horror, as at some outrageous blasphemy. "Frontignac at ten shillings the bottle!" he exclaimed.

"Still, claret never does lie easy on my stomach," Richard explained, intent upon blaming Lord Gervase's wine – since he could think of nothing else – for his condition.

Vallancey looked at him shrewdly. "My cock," said he, "if you're to fight we'll have to mend your temper." He took it upon himself to ring the bell, and to order up two bottles of Canary and one of brandy. If he was to get his man to the ground at all – and young Vallancey had a due sense of his responsibilities in that connection – it would be well to supply Richard with something to replace the courage that had oozed out overnight. Young Richard, never loth to fortify himself, proved amenable enough to the stiffly-laced Canary that his friend set before him. Then, to divert his mind, Vallancey, with that rash freedom that had made the whole of Somerset know him for a rebel, set himself to talk of the Protestant Duke and his right to the crown of England.

He was still at his talk, Richard listening moodily what time he was slowly but surely befuddling himself, when Sir Rowland – returning from Scoresby Hall – came to bring the news of his lack of success. Richard hailed him noisily, and bade him ring for another glass, adding, with a burst of oaths, some appalling threats of how anon he should serve Anthony Wilding. His wits drowned in the stiff liquor Vallancey had pressed upon him, he seemed of a sudden to have grown as fierce and bloodthirsty as any scourer that ever terrorized the watch.

Blake listened to him and grunted. "Body o' me!" swore the town gallant. "If that's the humour you're going out to fight in, I'll trouble you for the eight guineas I won from you at Primero yesterday before you start."

Richard reared himself, by the help of the table, and stood a thought unsteadily, his glance laboriously striving to engage Blake's.

"Damn me!" quoth he. "Your want of faith dishgraces me – and 't 'shgraces you. Shalt ha' the guineas when we're back – and not before."

"Hum!" quoth Blake, to whom eight guineas were a consideration in these bankrupt days. "And if you don't come back at all upon whom am I to draw?"

The suggestion sank through Dick's half-fuddled senses, and the scare it gave him was reflected on his face.

"Damn you, Blake!" swore Vallancey between his teeth. "Is that a decent way to talk to a man who is going out? Never heed him, Dick! Let him wait for his dirty guineas till we return."

"Thirty guineas?" hiccoughed Richard. "It was only eight. Anyhow – wait 'll I've sli' the gullet of 's Mr Wilding." He checked on a thought that suddenly occurred to him. He turned to Vallancey with a ludicrous solemnity. " 'Sbud!" he swore. " 'S a scurvy trick I'm playing the Duke. 'S treason to him – treason no less." And he smote the table with his open hand.

"What's that?" quoth Blake so sharply, his eyes so suddenly alert that Vallancey made haste to cover up his fellow-rebel's indiscretion.

"It's the brandy-and-Canary makes him dream," said he with a laugh, and rising as he spoke he announced that it was high time they should set out. Thus he brought about a bustle that drove the Duke's business from Richard's mind, and left Blake without a pretext to pursue his quest for information. But the mischief was done, and Blake's suspicions were awake. He bethought him now of dark hints that Richard had let fall to Vallancey in the past few days, and of hints less dark with which Vallancey – who was a careless fellow at ordinary times – had answered. And now this mention of the Duke and of treason to him – to what Duke could it refer but Monmouth?

Blake was well aware of the wild tales that were going round, and he began to wonder now was aught really afoot, and was his good friend Westmacott in it?

If there was, he bethought him that the knowledge might be of value, and it might help to float once more his shipwrecked fortunes. The haste with which Vallancey had proffered a frivolous explanation of Richard's words, the bustle with which upon the instant he swept Richard and Sir Rowland from the house to get to horse and ride out from Bridgwater, were in themselves circumstances that went to heighten those suspicions of Sir Rowland's. But lacking all opportunity for investigation at the moment, he deemed it wisest to say no more just then, lest he should betray his watchfulness.

They were the first to arrive upon the ground – an open space on the borders of Sedgemoor, in the shelter of Polden Hill. But they had not long to wait before Wilding and Trenchard rode up, attended by a groom. Their arrival had an oddly sobering effect upon young Westmacott, for which Mr Vallancey was thankful. For during their ride he had begun to fear that he had carried too far the business of equipping his principal with artificial valour.

Trenchard came forward to offer Vallancey the courteous suggestion that Mr Wilding's servant should charge himself with the care of the horses of Mr Westmacott's party, if this would be a convenience to them. Vallancey thanked him and accepted the offer, and thus the groom – instructed by Trenchard – led the five horses some distance from the spot.

It now became a matter of making preparation, and leaving Richard to divest himself of such garments as he might deem cumbrous, Vallancey went forward to consult with Trenchard upon the choice of ground. At that same moment Mr Wilding lounged forward, flicking the grass with his whip in an absent manner.

"Mr Vallancey," he began, when Trenchard turned to interrupt him.

"You can leave it safely to me, Tony," he growled.

"But there is something I wish to say, Nick," answered Mr Wilding, his manner mild. "By your leave, then." And he turned again to Vallancey. "Will you be so good as to call Mr Westmacott hither?"

Vallancey stared. "For what purpose, sir?" he asked.

"For my purpose," answered Mr Wilding sweetly. "It is no longer my wish to engage with Mr Westmacott."

"Anthony!" cried Trenchard, and in his amazement forgot to swear.

"I propose," added Mr Wilding, "to relieve Mr Westmacott of the necessity of fighting."

Vallancey in his heart thought this might be pleasant news for his principal. Still, he did not quite see how the end was to be attained, and said so.

"You shall be enlightened if you will do as I request," Wilding insisted, and Vallancey, with a lift of the brows, a snort, and a shrug, turned away to comply.

"Do you mean," quoth Trenchard, bursting with indignation, "that you will let live a man who has struck you?"

Wilding took his friend affectionately by the arm. "It is a whim of mine," said he. "Do you think, Nick, that it is more than I can afford to indulge?"

"I say not so," was the ready answer; "but…"

"I thought you'd not," said Mr Wilding, interrupting him. "And if any does – why, I shall be glad to prove it upon him that he lies." He laughed, and Trenchard, vexed though he was, was forced to laugh with him. Then Nick set himself to urge the thing that last night had plagued his mind: that this Richard might prove a danger to the Cause; that in the Duke's interest, if not to safeguard his own person from some vindictive betrayal, Wilding would be better advised in imposing a reliable silence upon him.

"But why vindictive?" Mr Wilding remonstrated. "Rather must he have cause for gratitude."

Mr Trenchard laughed short and contemptuously. "There is," said he, "no rancour more bitter than that of the mean man who has offended you and whom you have spared. I beg you'll ponder it." He lowered his voice as he ended his admonition, for Vallancey and Westmacott were coming up, followed by Sir Rowland Blake.

Richard, although his courage had been sinking lower and lower in a measure as he had grown more and more sober with the approach of the moment for engaging, came forward now with a firm step and an arrogant mien; for Vallancey had given him more than a hint of what was toward. His heart had leapt, not only at the deliverance that was promised him, but out of satisfaction at the reflection of how accurately last night he had gauged what Mr Wilding would endure. It had dismayed him then, as we have seen, that this man who, he thought, must stomach any affront from him out of consideration for his sister, should have ended by calling him to account. He concluded now that upon reflection Wilding had seen his error, and was prepared to make amends that he might extricate himself from an impossible situation, and Richard blamed himself for having overlooked this inevitable solution and given way to idle panic.

Vallancey and Blake watching him, and the sudden meta-morphosis that was wrought in him, despised him heartily, and yet were glad – for the sake of their association with him – that things were as they were.

"Mr Westmacott," said Wilding quietly, his eyes steadily set upon Richard's own arrogant gaze, his lips smiling a little, "I am here not to fight, but to apologise." Richard's sneer was audible to all. Oh, he was gathering courage fast now that there no longer was the need for it. It urged him to lengths of daring possible only to a fool.

"If you can take a blow, Mr Wilding," said he offensively, "that is your own affair." And his friends gasped at his temerity and trembled for him, not knowing what grounds he had for counting himself unassailable.

"Just so," said Mr Wilding, as meek and humble as a nun, and Trenchard, who had expected something very different from him, swore aloud and with some circumstance of oaths. "The fact is," continued Mr Wilding, "that what I did last night, I did in the heat of wine, and I am sorry for it. I recognise that this quarrel is of my provoking; that it was unwarrantable in me to introduce the name of Mistress Westmacott, no matter how respectfully; and that in doing so I gave Mr Westmacott ample grounds for offence. For that I beg his pardon, and I venture to hope that this matter need go no further."

Vallancey and Blake were speechless in astonishment; Trenchard livid with fury. Westmacott moved a step or two forward, a swagger unmistakable in his gait, his nether-lip thrust out in a sneer.

"Why," said he, his voice mighty disdainful, "if Mr Wilding apologises the matter hardly can go further." He conveyed such a suggestion of regret at this that Trenchard bounded forward, stung to speech.

"But if Mr Westmacott's disappointment threatens to overwhelm him," he snapped, very tartly, "I am his humble servant, and he may call upon me to see that he's not robbed of the exercise he came to take."

Mr Wilding set a restraining hand upon Trenchard's arm. Westmacott turned to him, the sneer, however, gone from his face.

"I have no quarrel with you, sir," said he, with an uneasy assumption of dignity.

"It's a want that may be soon supplied," answered Trenchard briskly, and, as he afterwards confessed, had not Wilding checked him at that moment, he had thrown his hat in Richard's face. It was Vallancey who saved the situation, cursing in his heart the bearing of his principal.

"Mr Wilding," said he, "this is very handsome in you. You are of the happy few who may tender such an apology without reflection upon your courage."

Mr Wilding made him a leg very elegantly. "You are vastly kind, sir," said he.

"You have given Mr Westmacott the fullest satisfaction, and it is with an increased respect for you – if that were possible – that I acknowledge it on my friend's behalf."

"You are, sir, a very mirror of the elegancies," said Mr Wilding, and Vallancey wondered was he being laughed at. Whether he was or not, he conceived that he had done the only seemly thing. He had made handsome acknowledgment of a handsome apology, stung to it by the currishness of Richard.

And there the matter ended, despite Trenchard's burning eagerness to carry it himself to a different consummation. Wilding prevailed upon him, and withdrew him from the field. But as they rode back to Zoyland Chase the old rake was bitter in his inveighings against Wilding's folly and weakness.

"I pray Heaven," he kept repeating, "that it may not come to cost you dear."

"Have done," said Mr Wilding, a trifle out of patience. "Could I wed the sister having slain the brother?" And Trenchard, understanding at last, accounted himself a numskull that he had not understood before. But he none the less deemed it a pity Richard had been spared.

Chapter 6

THE CHAMPION

As vainglorious was Richard Westmacott's retreat from the field of unstricken battle as his advance upon it had been inglorious. He spoke with confidence now of the narrow escape that Wilding had had at his hands, of the things he would have done to Wilding had not that gentleman grown wise in time. Sir Rowland, who had seen little of Richard's earlier stricken condition, was in a measure imposed upon by his blustering tone and manner; not so Vallancey, who remembered the steps he had been forced to take to bolster up the young man's courage sufficiently to admit of his being brought to the encounter. Richard so disgusted him that he felt if he did not quit his company soon, he would be quarrelling with him himself. So, congratulating him in a caustic manner that Richard did not relish, upon the happy termination of the affair, Vallancey took his leave of him and Blake at the crossroads, pleading business with Lord Gervase, and left them to proceed without him to Bridgwater.

Blake, whose suspicions of some secret matter to which Vallancey and Richard were wedded had been earlier excited by Westmacott's indiscretions, was full of sly questions now touching the business which might be taking Vallancey to Scoresby. But Richard was too full of the subject of the fear he had instilled into Wilding to afford his companion much satisfaction on any other score. Thus they came to Lupton House, and as Richard swaggered down the lawn into the presence of the ladies – Ruth and her aunt were occupying the stone bench, Diana the circular seat about the great oak in the centre of the lawn – he was a very different person from the pale, limp creature they had beheld there some few hours earlier. Loud and offensive was he now in self-laudation, and so indifferent to all else that he left unobserved the little smile, half wistful, half scornful, that visited his sister's lips when he sneeringly told how Mr Wilding had chosen that better part of valour which discretion is alleged to be.

It needed Diana, who, blinded by no sisterly affection, saw him exactly as he was, and despised him accordingly, to enlighten him. It may also be that in doing so at once she had ends of her own to serve; for Sir Rowland was still of the company.

"Mr Wilding afraid?" she cried, her voice so charged with derision that it inclined to shrillness. "La! Richard, Mr Wilding was never afraid of any man."

"Faith!" said Rowland, although his acquaintance with Mr Wilding was slight and recent. "It is what I should think. He does not look like a man familiar with fear."

Richard struck something of an attitude, his fair face flushed, his pale eyes glittering. "He took a blow," said he, and sneered.

"There may have been reasons," Diana suggested darkly, and Sir Rowland's eyes narrowed at the hint. Again he recalled the words Richard had let fall that afternoon. Wilding and he were fellow-workers in some secret business, and Richard had said that the encounter was treason to that same business, whatever it might be. And of what it might be Sir Rowland had grounds upon which to found at least a guess. Had perhaps Wilding acted upon some similar feelings in avoiding the duel? He wondered; and when Richard dismissed Diana's challenge with a fatuous laugh, it was Blake who took it up.

"You speak, ma'am," said he, "as if you knew that there were reasons, and knew, too, what those reasons might be."

Diana looked at Ruth, as if for guidance before replying. But Ruth sat calm and seemingly impassive, looking straight before her. She was, indeed, indifferent how much Diana said, for in any case the matter could not remain a secret long. Lady Horton, silent too and listening, looked a question at her daughter.

And so, after a pause: "I know both," said Diana, her eyes straying again to Ruth; and a subtler man than Blake would have read that glance and understood that this same reason which he sought so diligently sat there before him. Richard, indeed, catching that sly look of his cousin's, checked his assurance, and stood frowning, cogitating. Then, quite suddenly, his voice harsh: "What do you mean, Diana?" he inquired.

Diana shrugged and turned her shoulder to him. "You had best ask Ruth," said she, which was an answer more or less plain to both the men. They stood at gaze, Richard looking a thought foolish. Blake, frowning, his heavy lip caught in his strong white teeth.

Ruth turned to her brother with an almost piteous attempt at a smile. She sought to spare him pain by excluding from her manner all suggestion that things were other than she desired.

"I am betrothed to Mr Wilding," said she. Sir Rowland made a sudden forward movement, drew a deep breath, and as suddenly stood still. Richard looked at his sister as she were mad and raving. Then he laughed, between unbelief and derision.

"It is a jest," said he, but his accents lacked conviction.

"It is the truth," Ruth assured him quietly.

"The truth?" His brow darkened ominously – stupendously for one so fair. "The truth, you baggage…?" He began and stopped in very fury.

She saw that she must tell him all.

"I promised to wed Mr Wilding this day se'night so that he saved your life and honour," she told him calmly, and added, "It was a bargain that we drove."

Richard continued to stare at her. The thing she told him was too big to be swallowed at a mouthful; he was absorbing it by slow degrees.

"So now," said Diana, "you know the sacrifice your sister has made to save you, and when you speak of the apology Mr Wilding tendered you, perhaps you'll speak of it in a tone less loud."

But the sarcasm was no longer needed. Already poor Richard was very humble, his make-believe spirit all snuffed out. He observed at last how pale and set was his sister's face, and he realised something of the sacrifice she had made. Never in all his life was Richard so near to lapsing from the love of himself; never so near to forgetting his own interests, and preferring those of Ruth. Lady Horton sat silent, her heart fluttering with dismay and perplexity. Heaven had not equipped her with a spirit capable of dealing with a situation such as this. Blake stood in make-believe stolidity dissembling his infinite chagrin and the stormy emotions waning within him, for some signs of which Diana watched his countenance in vain.

"You shall not do it!" cried Richard suddenly. He came forward and laid his hand on his sister's shoulder. His voice was almost gentle. "Ruth, you shall not do this for me. You must not."

"By Heaven, no!" snapped Blake before she could reply. "You are right, Richard. Mistress Westmacott must not be the scapegoat. She shall not play the part of Iphigenia."

But Ruth smiled wistfully as she answered him with a question, "Where is the help for it?"

Richard knew where the help for it lay, and for once – for just a moment – he contemplated danger and even death with equanimity.

"I can take up this quarrel again," he announced. "I can compel Mr Wilding to meet me."

Ruth's eyes, looking up at him, kindled with pride and admiration. It warmed her heart to hear him speak thus, to have his assurance that he was anything but the coward she had been so disloyal as to deem him; no doubt she had been right in saying that it was his health was the cause of the palsy he had displayed that morning; he was a little wild, she knew; inclined to sit overlate at the bottle; with advancing manhood, she had no doubt, he would overcome this boyish failing. Meanwhile it was this foolish habit – nothing more –

that undermined the inherent firmness of his nature. And it comforted her generous soul to have this proof that he was full worthy of the sacrifice she was making for him. Diana watched him in some surprise, and never doubted but that his offer was impulsive, and that he would regret it when his ardour had had time to cool.

"It were idle," said Ruth at last – not that she quite believed it, but that it was all-important to her that Richard should not be imperilled. "Mr Wilding will prefer the bargain he has made."

"No doubt," growled Blake, "but he shall be forced to unmake it." He advanced and bowed low before her. "Madam," said he, "will you grant me leave to champion your cause and remove this troublesome Mr Wilding from your path?"

Diana's eyes narrowed; her cheeks paled, partly from fear for Blake, partly from vexation at the promptness of an offer that afforded a fresh and so eloquent proof of the trend of his affections. Ruth smiled at him in a very friendly manner, but gently shook her head.

"I thank you, sir," said she. "But it were more than I could permit. This has become a family affair."

There was in her tone something which, despite its friendliness, gave Sir Rowland his dismissal. He was not at best a man of keen sensibilities; yet even so, he could not mistake the request to withdraw that was implicit in her tone and manner. He took his leave, registering, however, in his heart a vow that he would have his way with Wilding. Thus must he – through her gratitude – assuredly come to have his way with Ruth.

Diana rose and turned to her mother. "Come," she said, "we'll speed Sir Rowland. Ruth and Richard would perhaps prefer to remain alone."

Ruth thanked her with her eyes. Richard, standing beside his sister with bent head and moody gaze, did not appear to have heard. Thus he remained until he and his half-sister were alone together, then he flung himself wearily into the seat beside her, and took her hand.

"Ruth," he faltered, "Ruth!"

She stroked his hand, her honest, intelligent eyes bent upon him in a look of pity – and to indulge this pity for him, she forgot how much herself she needed pity. "Take it not so to heart," she urged him, her voice low and crooning – as that of a mother to her babe. "Take it not so to heart, Richard. I should have married some day, and, after all, it may well be that Mr Wilding will make me as good a husband as another. I do believe," she added, her only intent to comfort Richard, "that he loves me; and if he loves me, surely he will prove kind."

He flung himself back with an exclamation of angry pain. He was white to the lips, his eyes bloodshot. "It must not be – it shall not be – I'll not endure it!" he cried hoarsely.

"Richard, dear…" she began, recapturing the hand he had snatched from hers in his gust of emotion. He rose abruptly, interrupting her.

"I'll go to Wilding now," he cried, his voice resolute. "He shall cancel this bargain he had no right to make. He shall take up his quarrel with me where it stood before you went to him."

"No, no, Richard, you must not!" she urged him, frightened, rising too, and clinging to his arm.

"I will," he answered. "At the worst he can but kill me. But at least you shall not be sacrificed."

"Sit here, Richard," she bade him. "There is something you have not considered. If you die, if Mr Wilding kills you…" she paused. He looked at her, and at the repetition of the fate that would probably await him if he persevered in the course he threatened, his purely emotional courage again began to fail him. A look of fear crept gradually into his face to take the room of the resolution that had been stamped upon it but a moment since.

He swallowed hard. "What then?" he asked, his voice harsh, and, obeying her command and the pressure on his hand, he resumed his seat beside her.

She spoke now at length and very gravely, dwelling upon the circumstance that he was the head of the family, the last Westmacott of his line, pointing out to him the importance of his existence, the insignificance of her own. She was but a girl, a thing of small account where the perpetuation of a family was at issue. After all, she must marry somebody some day, she repeated, and perhaps she had been foolish in attaching too much importance to the tales she had heard of Mr Wilding. Probably he was no worse than other men, and after all he was a gentleman of wealth and position, such a man as half the women in Somerset might be proud to own for a husband.

Her arguments and his weakness – his returning cowardice, which made him lend an ear to those same arguments – prevailed with him; at least they convinced him that he was far too important a person to risk his life in this quarrel upon which he had so rashly entered. He did not say that he was convinced; but he said that he would give the matter thought, hinting that perhaps some other way might present itself of cancelling the bargain she had made. They had a week before them, and in any case he promised readily in answer to her entreaties – for her faith in him was a thing unquenchable – that he would do nothing without taking counsel with her.

Meanwhile Diana had escorted Sir Rowland to the main gates of Lupton House, in front of which Miss Westmacott's groom was walking his horse, awaiting him.

"Sir Rowland," said she at parting, "your chivalry makes you take this matter too deeply to heart. You overlook the possibility that my cousin may have good reason for not desiring your interference."

He looked keenly at this little lady to whom a month ago he had been on the point of offering marriage. His coxcombry might readily have suggested to him that she was in love with him, but that his conscience and inclinations urged him to assure himself that this was not the case.

"What shall that mean, madam?" he asked her.

Diana hesitated. "What I have said is plain," she answered, and it was clear that she held something back. Sir Rowland flattered himself upon the shrewdness with which he read her, never dreaming that he had but read just what she intended that he should.

He stood squarely before her, shaking his great head. "Not plain enough for me," he said. Then his tone softened to one of prayer. "Tell me," he besought her.

"I can't! I can't!" she cried in feigned distress. "It were too disloyal."

He frowned. He caught her arm and pressed it, his heart sick with jealous alarm. "What do you mean? Tell me, tell me, Mistress Horton."

Diana lowered her eyes. "You'll not betray me?" she stipulated.

"Why, no. Tell me."

She flushed delicately. "I am disloyal to Ruth," she said, "and yet I am loath to see you cozened."

"Cozened?" quoth he hoarsely, his egregious vanity in arms. "Cozened?"

Diana explained. "Ruth was at his house today," said she, "closeted alone with him for an hour or more."

"Impossible!" he cried.

"Where else was the bargain made?" she asked, and shattered his last doubt. "You know that Mr Wilding has not been here."

Yet Blake struggled heroically against conviction.

"She went to intercede for Richard," he protested.

Miss Horton looked up at him, and under her glance Sir Rowland felt that he was a man of unfathomable ignorance. Then she turned aside her eyes and shrugged her shoulders very eloquently. "You are a man of the world, Sir Rowland. You cannot seriously suppose that any maid would so imperil her good name in *any* cause?"

Darker grew his florid countenance; his bulging eyes looked troubled and perplexed.

"You mean that she loves him?" he said, between question and assertion.

Diana pursed her lips. "You shall draw your own inference," quoth she.

He breathed heavily, and squared his broad shoulders, as one who braces himself for battle against an element stronger than himself.

"But her talk of sacrifice?" he cried.

Diana laughed, and again he was stung by her contempt of his perceptions. "Her brother is set against her marrying him," said she. "Here was her chance. Is it not very plain?"

Doubt stared from his eyes. "Why do you tell me this?"

"Because I esteem you, Sir Rowland," she answered very gently. "I would not have you meddle in a matter you cannot mend."

"Which I am not desired to mend, say rather," he replied with heavy sarcasm. "She would not have my interference!" He laughed angrily. "I think you are right, Mistress Diana," he said, "and I think that more than ever is there the need to kill this Mr Wilding."

He took his departure abruptly, leaving her scared at the mischief she had made for him in seeking to save him from it, and that very night he sought out Wilding.

But Wilding was from home again. Under its placid surface the West Country was in a ferment. And if hitherto Mr Wilding had disdained the insistent rumours of Monmouth's coming, his assurance was shaken now by proof that the Government, itself, was stirring; for four companies of foot and a troop of horse had been that day ordered to Taunton by the Deputy-Lieutenant. Wilding was gone with Trenchard to White Lackington in a vain hope that there he might find news to confirm his persisting unbelief in any such rashness as was alleged on Monmouth's part.

So Blake was forced to wait, but his purpose suffered nothing by delay.

Returning on the morrow, he found Mr Wilding at table with Nick Trenchard, and he cut short the greetings of both men. He flung his hat – a black castor trimmed with a black feather – rudely among the dishes on the board.

"I have come to ask you, Mr Wilding," said he, "to be so good as to tell me the colour of that hat."

Mr Wilding raised one eyebrow and looked aslant at Trenchard, whose weather-beaten face was suddenly agrin with stupefaction.

"I could not," said Mr Wilding, "deny an answer to a question set so courteously." He looked up into Blake's flushed and scowling face with the sweetest and most innocent of smiles. "You'll no doubt disagree with me," said he, "but I love to meet a man halfway. Your hat, sir, is as white as virgin snow."

Blake's slow wits were disconcerted for a moment. Then he smiled viciously. "You mistake, Mr Wilding," said he. "My hat is black."

Mr Wilding looked more attentively at the object in dispute. He was in a trifling mood, and the stupidity of this runagate debtor afforded him opportunities to indulge it. "Why, true," said he, "now that I come to look, I perceive that it is indeed black." And again was Sir Rowland disconcerted. Still he pursued the lesson he had taught himself.

"You are mistaken again," said he, "that hat is green."

"Indeed?" quoth Mr Wilding, like one surprised, and he turned to Trenchard, who was enjoying himself. "What is your opinion of it, Nick?"

Thus appealed to, Trenchard's reply was prompt. "Why, since you ask me," said he, "my opinion is that it's a noisome thing not meet for a gentleman's table." And he took it up, and threw it through the window.

Sir Rowland was entirely put out of countenance. Here was a deliberate shifting of the quarrel he had come to pick, which left him all at sea. It was his duty to himself to take offence at Mr Trenchard's action. But that was not the business on which he had come. He became angry.

"Blister me!" he cried. "Must I sweep the cloth from the table before you'll understand me?"

"If you were to do anything so unmannerly I should have you flung out of the house," said Mr Wilding, "and it would distress me so to treat a person of your station and quality. The hat shall serve your purpose, although Mr Trenchard's concern for my table has removed it. Our memories will supply its absence. What colour did you say it was?"

"I said it was green," answered Blake, quite ready to keep to the point.

"Nay, I am sure you were wrong," said Wilding with a grave air. "Although I admit that, since it is your own hat, you should be the best judge of its colour, I am, nevertheless, of opinion that it is black."

"And if I were to say that it is white?" asked Blake, feeling mighty ridiculous.

"Why, in that case you would be confirming my first impression of it," answered Wilding, and Trenchard let fly a burst of laughter at sight of the baronet's furious and bewildered countenance. "And since we are agreed on that," continued Mr Wilding, imperturbable, "I hope you'll join us at supper."

"I'll be damned," roared Blake, "if ever I sit at table of yours, sir."

"Ah!" said Mr Wilding regretfully. "Now you become offensive."

"I mean to be," said Blake.

"You astonish me!"

"You lie! I don't," Sir Rowland answered him in triumph. He had got it out at last. Mr Wilding sat back in his chair, and looked at him, his face inexpressibly shocked.

"Will you of your own accord deprive us of your company, Sir Rowland," he wondered, "or shall Mr Trenchard throw you after your hat?"

"Do you mean…" gasped the other, "that you'll ask no satisfaction of me?"

"Not so. Mr Trenchard shall wait upon your friends tomorrow, and I hope you'll afford us then as felicitous entertainment as you do now."

Sir Rowland snorted, and, turning on his heel, made for the door.

"Give you a good night, Sir Rowland," Mr Wilding called after him. "Walters, you rascal, light Sir Rowland to the door."

Poor Blake went home deeply vexed; but it was no more than the beginning of his humiliation at Mr Wilding's hands – for what can be more humiliating to a quarrel-seeking man than to have his enemy refuse to treat him seriously? He and Mr Wilding met next morning, and before noon the tale of it had run through Bridgwater that Wild Wilding was at his tricks again. It made a pretty story how twice he had disarmed and each time spared the London beau, who still insisted – each time more furiously – upon renewing the encounter, till Mr Wilding had been forced to run him through the sword-arm and thus put him out of all case of continuing. It was a story that heaped ridicule upon Sir Rowland and did credit to Mr Wilding.

Richard heard it, and trembled, enraged and impotent. Ruth heard it, and was stirred despite herself to a feeling of gratitude towards Wilding for the patience and toleration he had displayed.

There for a while the matter rested, and the days passed slowly. But Sir Rowland's nature – mean at bottom – was spurred to find him some other way of wiping out the score that lay 'twixt him and Mr Wilding, a score mightily increased by the shame that Mr Wilding had put upon him in that encounter from which – whatever the issue – he had looked to cull great credit in Ruth's eyes.

He had been thinking constantly of the incautious words that Richard had let fall, thinking of them in conjunction with the startling rumours that were now the talk of the whole countryside. He laid two and two together, and the four he found them make, afforded him some hope. Then he realised – as he might have realised before had he been shrewder – that Richard's mood was one that made him ripe for any villainy. He thought that he was much in error if a treachery existed so black that Richard would quail before it, if it but afforded him the means of ridding himself and the world of Mr Wilding. He was considering how best to approach the subject, when it happened that one night when Richard sat at play with him in his own lodging, the boy grew talkative through excess of wine. It happened naturally enough that Richard sought an ally in Blake, just as Blake sought an ally in Richard. Indeed, their fortunes – so far as Ruth was concerned – were bound up together. The baronet saw that Richard, half fuddled, was ripe for any confidences that might aim at the destruction of his enemy. He questioned him adroitly, and drew from him the story of the rising that was being planned and of the share that Mr Wilding – one of the Duke of Monmouth's chief movement-men – bore in the business that was toward.

When, towards midnight, Richard Westmacott went home, he left in Sir Rowland's hands an instrument which the latter accounted potential not only for the destruction of Anthony Wilding, but perhaps also for laying the foundations to the building of his own fortunes anew.

Chapter 7

THE NUPTIALS OF RUTH WESTMACOTT

Here was Sir Rowland Blake in high fettle at knowing himself armed with a portentous weapon for the destruction of Anthony Wilding. Upon closer inspection of it, however, he came to realise – as Richard had realised earlier – that it was double-edged, and that the wielding of it must be fraught with as much danger for Richard as for their common enemy. For to betray Mr Wilding and the plot would scarce be possible without betraying young Westmacott, and that was unthinkable, since to ruin Richard – a thing he would have done with a light heart so far as Richard was himself concerned – would be to ruin his own hopes of winning Ruth.

Therefore, during the days that followed, Sir Rowland was forced to fret in idleness what time his wound was healing; but if his arm was invalided, his eyes and ears were sound, and he remained watchful for an opportunity to apply the knowledge he had gained. Richard mentioned the subject no more, so that Blake almost came to wonder whether the boy remembered what in his cups he had betrayed.

Meanwhile Mr Wilding moved serene and smiling on his way. Daily there were great armfuls of flowers deposited at Lupton House

– his lover's offering to his mistress – and no day went by but that some richer gift accompanied them. Now it was a collar of brilliants, anon a rope of pearls, again a priceless ring that had been Mr Wilding's mother's. Ruth received with reluctance these pledges of his undesired affection. It were idle to reject them, considering that she was to marry him; yet it hurt her sorely to retain them. On her side she made no dispositions for the marriage, but went about her daily tasks as though she were to remain a maid at Lupton House for a time as yet indefinite.

In Diana, Wilding had – though he was far from guessing it – an entirely exceptional ally. Lady Horton too was favourably disposed towards him. A foolish, worldly woman, who never probed beneath life's surface, nor indeed dreamed that anything existed in life beyond that to which her five senses testified, she was content placidly to contemplate the advantages that must accrue to her niece from this alliance.

And so mother and daughter pleaded in Mr Wilding's absence his cause with his refractory bride-elect. But they pleaded it to little real purpose. Something perhaps they achieved in that Ruth grew more or less resigned to the fate that awaited her. By repeating to herself the arguments she had employed to Richard – that she must wed some day, and that Mr Wilding would prove no doubt as good a husband as another – she came in a measure to believe them.

Richard meanwhile appeared to avoid her. Lacking the courage to adopt the heroic measures which at first he had promised, yet had he grace enough to take shame at his inaction. But if he was idle so far as Mr Wilding was concerned, there was no lack of work for him in other connections. The clouds of war were gathering in that summer sky, and about to loose the storm gestating in them upon that fair country of the West, and young Westmacott, committed as he stood to the Duke of Monmouth's party, was forced to take his share in the surreptitious bustle that was toward. He was away two days in that week, having been summoned to a meeting of the leading gentlemen of the party at White Lackington, where he was forced into the unwelcome company of his future brother-in-law, to meet with courteous, deferential treatment from that imperturbable gentleman.

Wilding, indeed, seemed to have forgotten that any quarrel had ever existed between them. For the rest, he came and went, supremely calm, as if he were, and knew himself to be, most welcome at Lupton House. Thrice in the course of that week of waiting he rode over from Zoyland Chase to pay his duty to Mistress Westmacott, and Ruth was persuaded on each occasion by her aunt and cousin to receive him. Indeed, how could she well refuse?

His manner was ever all that could be desired. Gallant, affectionate, deferential. He was in word and look and tone Ruth's most obedient servant. Had she been less prejudiced she must have admired the admirable restraint with which he kept all exultation from his manner, for, after all, it is difficult to force a victory as he had forced his, and not to triumph.

It is to be feared that during that week he neglected a good deal of his duty to the Duke, leaving Trenchard to supply his place, and undertake tasks of a seditious nature that should have been his own.

At heart, however, in spite of the stories current and the militia at Taunton, Wilding remained convinced – as did most of the other leading partisans of the Protestant Cause – that no such madness as this premature landing could be in contemplation by the Duke. Besides, were it so, they must unfailingly have definite word of it; and they had none.

Trenchard was less assured, but Wilding laughed at the old rake's forebodings, and serenely went about the business of his marriage.

On the eve of the wedding he paid Ruth his last visit in the quality of a lover, and was received by her in the garden. He found her looking paler than her wont, and there was a cloud of sadness on her brow, a haunting sadness in her eyes. It touched him to the soul, and for a moment he wavered in his purpose. He stood beside her – she seated on the old lichened seat – and a silence fell between them, during which Mr Wilding's conscience wrestled with his stronger passion. It was his habit to be glib, talking incessantly what time he was in her company, and seeing to it that his talk was shallow and touched at nothing belonging to the deeps of human life. Thus was it, perhaps, that this sudden and enduring silence affected her most oddly; it was as if she had absorbed some notion of what was passing in his mind. She looked up suddenly into his face, so white and so composed. Their eyes met, and he stooped to her suddenly, his long brown ringlets tumbling forward. She feared his kiss, yet never moved, staring up with fixed, dilated eyes as if fascinated by his dark, brooding gaze. He paused, hovering above her upturned face as hovers the hawk above the dove.

"Child," he said at last, and his voice was soft and winning from very sadness, "child, why do you fear me?"

The truth of it went home to her. She feared him; she feared the strength that lay behind that calm; she feared the masterfulness of his wild but inscrutably hidden nature; she was afraid to surrender to such a man as this, afraid that in the hot crucible of his love her own nature would be dissolved, transmuted, and rendered part of his. Yet, though the truth was now made plain to her, she thrust it from her.

"I do not fear you," said she, and her voice at least rang fearlessly.

"Do you hate me, then?" he asked. Her glance grew troubled and fell away from his; it sought the calm of the river, gleaming golden in the sunset. There was a pause. Wilding sighed heavily, and straightened himself from his bending posture.

"You should not have sought thus to compel me," she said presently.

"I own it," he answered a thought bitterly. "I own it. Yet what hope had I but in compulsion?" She returned him no answer. "You see," he said, with increasing bitterness, "you see, that had I not seized the chance that was mine to win you by compulsion I had not won you at all."

"It might," said she, "have been better so for both of us."

"Better for neither," he replied. "Ah, think it not! In time, I swear, you shall not think it. For you shall come to love me, Ruth," he added with a note of such assurance that she turned to meet again his gaze. He answered the wordless question of her eyes. "There is," said he, "no love of man for woman, so that the man be not wholly unworthy, so that his passion be sincere and strong, that can fail in time to arouse response." She smiled a little pitiful smile of unbelief. "Were I a boy," he rejoined, his earnestness vibrating now in a voice that was usually so calm and level, "offering you protestations of a callow worship, you might have cause to doubt me. But I am a man, Ruth – a tried, and haply a sinful man, alas! – a man who needs you, and who will have you at all costs."

"At all costs?" she echoed, and her lip took on a curl. "And you call this egotism by the name of love! No, doubt you are right," she continued with an irony that stung him, "for love it is – love of yourself."

"And is not all love of another founded upon the love of self?" he asked her, startling her with a question that revealed to her clear-sighted mind a truth undreamed of. "When some day – please Heaven – I come to find favour in your eyes, and you come to love me, what will it mean but that you have come to find me necessary to yourself and to your happiness? Would you deny me now your love if you felt that you had need of mine? I love you because I love myself, you say. I grant it you. But you'll confess that if you do not love me yet, it is for the same reason, and that when you do come to love me the reason will be still the same."

"You are very sure that I shall come to love you," said she, shifting woman-like the ground of argument now that she found insecure the place on which at first she had taken her stand.

"Were I not, think you I should compel you to the church tomorrow?"

She trembled at his calm assurance. It was as if she almost feared that what he said might come to pass.

"Since you bear such faith in your heart," said she, "were it not nobler, more generous, that you should set yourself to win me first and wed me afterwards?"

"It is the course I should, myself, prefer," he answered quietly. "But it is a course denied me. I was viewed here with disfavour, almost denied your house. What chance had I whilst I might not come near you, whilst your mind was poisoned against me by the idle, vicious prattle that goes round and round the countryside, increasing ever in bulk from constant repetition?"

"Do you say that these tales are groundless?" she asked, with a sudden lifting of her eyes, a sudden keen eagerness that did not escape him.

"I would to God I could," he cried, "since from your manner I see that would improve me in your sight. But there is just sufficient truth in them to forbid me, as I am, I hope, a gentleman, from giving them a full denial. Yet in what am I worse than my fellows? Are you of those who think a husband should come to them as one whose youth has been the youth of cloistered nun? Heaven knows, I am not one to draw parallels 'twixt myself and any other, yet you compel me. Whilst you deny me, you receive this fellow Blake – a London night-scourer, a broken gamester who has given his creditors leg-bail, and who woos you that with your fortune he may close the door of the debtor's gaol that's open to receive him."

"This is unworthy in you," she exclaimed, her tone indignant – so indignant that he experienced his first pang of jealousy.

"It would be were I his rival," he answered quietly. "But I am not. I have saved you from becoming the prey of such as he by forcing you to marry me."

"That I may become the prey of such as you, instead," was her retort.

He looked at her a moment, smiling sadly. Then, with pardonable self-esteem when we think of what manner of man it was with whom he now compared himself, "Surely," said he, "it is better to become the prey of the lion than the jackal."

"To the victim it can matter little," she answered, and he saw the tears gathering in her eyes.

Compassion moved him. It rose in arms to batter down his will, and in a weaker man had triumphed. Mr Wilding bent his knee and went down beside her.

"I swear," he said impassionedly, "that as my wife you shall never count yourself a victim. You shall be honoured by all men, but by none more deeply than by him who will ever strive to be worthy of the proud title of your husband." He took her hand and kissed it reverentially. He rose and looked at her. "Tomorrow," he said, and bowing low before her went his way, leaving her with emotions that found their vent in tears, but defied her maiden mind to understand them.

The morrow came – her wedding-day – a sunny day of early June, and Ruth – assisted by Diana and Lady Horton – made preparation for her marriage as spirited women have made preparation for the scaffold, determined to show the world a brave, serene exterior. The sacrifice was necessary for Richard's sake. That was a thing long since determined. Yet it would have been some comfort to her to have had Richard at her side; it would have lent her strength to have had his kiss of thanks for the holocaust which for him she was making of all that woman holds most dear and sacred. But Richard was away – he had been absent since yesterday, and none could tell her where he tarried.

With Lady Horton and Diana she took her way to St Mary's Church at noon, and there she found Mr Wilding – very fine in a suit of sky-blue satin, laced with silver – awaiting her. And with him was old Lord Gervase Scoresby, his friend and cousin, the very incarnation of benignity and ruddy health.

For a wonder Nick Trenchard was not at Mr Wilding's side. But Nick had definitely refused to be of the party, emphasising his refusal by certain choice reflections wholly unflattering to the married state.

Some idlers of the town were the only witnesses – and little did they guess the extent of the tragedy they were witnessing. There was no music, and the ceremony was brief and soon at an end. The only touch of joy, of festiveness, was that afforded by the choice blooms with which Mr Wilding had smothered nave and choir and altar-rails. Their perfume hung heavy as incense in the temple.

"Who giveth this woman to be married to this man?" droned the parson's voice, and Wilding smiled defiantly a smile which seemed to answer him, "No man. I have taken her for myself."

Lord Gervase stood forward as her sponsor, and as in a dream Ruth felt her hand lying in Mr Wilding's cool, firm grasp.

The ecclesiastic's voice droned on, his voice hanging like the hum of some great insect upon the scented air. It was accomplished, and they were welded each to the other until death should part them.

Down the festooned nave she came on his arm, her step unfaltering, her face calm; black misery in her heart. Behind followed her aunt and cousin and Lord Gervase. On Mr Wilding's aquiline face a pale smile glimmered, like a beam of moonlight upon tranquil waters, and it abode there until they reached the porch and were suddenly confronted by Nick Trenchard, red of face for once, perspiring, excited, and dust-stained from head to foot.

He had arrived that very instant; and, urged by the fearful news that brought him, he had come resolved to pluck Wilding from the altar be the ceremony done or not. But in that he reckoned without Mr Wilding – for he should have known him better than to have hoped to succeed. He stepped forward now, and gripped him with his dusty glove by the sleeve of his shimmering bridegroom's coat. His voice came harsh with excitement and smouldering rage.

"A word with you, Anthony!"

Mr Wilding turned placidly to regard him. "What now?" he asked, his bride's hand retained in the crook of his elbow.

"Treachery!" snapped Trenchard in a whisper. "Hell and damnation! Step aside, man."

Mr Wilding turned to Lord Gervase, and begged of him to take charge of Mistress Wilding. "I deplore this interruption," he told her, no whit ruffled by what he had heard. "But I shall rejoin you soon. Meanwhile, his lordship will do the honours for me." This last he said with his eyes moving to Lady Horton and her daughter.

Lord Gervase, in some surprise, but overruled by his cousin's calm, took the bride on his arm and led her from the churchyard to the waiting carriage. To this he handed her, and after her her aunt and cousin. Then, mounting himself, they drove away, leaving Wilding and Trenchard among the tombstones, whither the messenger of evil had meanwhile led his friend. Trenchard rapped out his story briefly.

"Shenke," said he, "who was riding from Lyme with letters for you from the Duke, was robbed of his dispatches late last night a mile or so this side Taunton."

"Highwaymen?" inquired Mr Wilding, his tone calm, though his glance had hardened.

"Highwaymen? No! Government agents belike. There were two of them, he says – for I have the tale from himself – and they met him at the 'Hare and Hounds' at Taunton, where he stayed to sup last night. One of them gave him the password, and he conceived him to be a friend. But afterwards, growing suspicious, he refused to tell them too much. They followed him, it appears, and on the road they overtook and fell upon him; they knocked him from his horse, possessed themselves of the contents of his wallet, and left him for dead – with his head broken."

Mr Wilding drew a sharp breath. His wits worked quickly. He was, he realised, in deadly peril. One thought he gave to Ruth. If the worst came to pass here was one who would rejoice in her freedom. The reflection cut through him like a sword. He would be loath to die until he had taught her to regret him. Then his mind returned to what Trenchard had told him.

"You said a Government agent," he mused slowly. "How would a Government agent know the password?"

Trenchard's mouth fell open. "I had not thought…" he began. Then ended with an oath. " 'Tis a traitor from inside."

Wilding nodded. "It must be one of those who met at White Lackington three nights ago," he answered.

Idlers – the witnesses of the wedding – were watching them with interest from the path, and others from over the low wall of the churchyard, as well they might, for Mr Wilding's behaviour was, for a bridegroom, extraordinary. Trenchard did not relish the audience.

"We had best away," said he. "Indeed," he added, "we had best out of England altogether before the hue and cry is raised. The bubble's pricked."

Wilding's hand fell on his arm, and its grasp was steady. Wilding's eyes met his, and their gaze was calm.

"Where have you bestowed this messenger?" quoth he.

"He is here in Bridgwater, in bed, at the Bell Inn, whence he sent for you to Zoyland Chase. Suspecting trouble, I rode to him at once myself."

"Come then," said Wilding. "We'll go talk with him. This matter needs probing ere we decide on flight. You do not seem to have sought to discover who were the thieves, nor other matters that it may be of use to know."

"Rat me!" swore Trenchard. "I was in haste to bring you news of it. Besides, there were other things to talk of. There is news that Albemarle has gone to Exeter, and that Sir Edward Phelips and Colonel Luttrell have been ordered to Taunton by the King."

Mr Wilding stared at him with sudden dismay.

"Odso!" he exclaimed. "Is King James taking fright at last?" Then he shrugged his shoulders and laughed.

"Pshaw!" he cried. "They are starting at a shadow."

"Heaven send," prayed Trenchard, "that the shadow does not prove to have a substance immediately behind it."

"Folly!" said Wilding. "When Monmouth comes, indeed, we shall not lack forewarning. Come," he added briskly. "We'll see this messenger and endeavour to discover who were these fellows that beset him." And he drew Trenchard from among the tombstones to the open path, and thus from the churchyard and the eyes of the gaping onlookers.

Chapter 8

BRIDE AND GROOM

And so the bridegroom, in all his wedding finery, made his way with Trenchard to the Bell Inn, in the High Street, whilst his bride, escorted by Lord Gervase, was being driven to Zoyland Chase, of which she was now the mistress.

But she was not destined just yet to cross its threshold. For scarcely were they over the river when a horseman barred their way and called upon the driver to pull up. Lady Horton, in a panic, huddled herself in the great coach and spoke of tobymen, whilst Lord Gervase thrust his head from the window to discover that the rider who stayed their progress was Richard Westmacott. His lordship hailed the boy who, thereupon, walked his horse to the carriage door.

"Lord Gervase," said he, "will you bid the coachman put about and drive to Lupton House?"

Lord Gervase stared at him in hopeless bewilderment. "Drive to Lupton House?" he echoed. The more he saw of this odd wedding, the less he understood of it. It seemed to the placid old gentleman that he was fallen among a parcel of Bedlamites. "Surely, sir, it is for Mistress Wilding to say whither she will be driven," and he drew in his head and turned to Ruth for her commands. But, bewildered herself, she had none to give him. It was her turn to lean from the carriage window to ask her brother what he meant.

"I mean you are to drive home again," said he. "There is something I must tell you. When you have heard me it shall be yours to decide whether you will proceed or not to Zoyland Chase."

Hers to decide? How was that possible? What could he mean? She pressed him with some such questions.

"It means, in short," he answered impatiently, "that I hold your salvation in my hands. For the rest, this is not the time or place to tell you more. Bid the fellow put about."

Ruth sat back and looked once more at her companions. But from none did she receive the least helpful suggestion. Lady Horton made great prattle to little purpose; Lord Gervase followed her example, whilst Diana, whose alert if trivial mind was the one that might have offered assistance, sat silent. Ruth pondered. She bethought her of Trenchard's sudden arrival at St Mary's, his dust-stained person and excited manner, and of how he had drawn Mr Wilding aside with news that seemed of moment. And now her brother spoke of saving her; it was a little late for that, she thought. Outside the coach his voice still urged her, and it grew peevish and angry, as was usual when he was crossed. In the end she consented to do his will. If she were to fathom this mystery that was thickening about her there seemed to be no other course. She turned to Lord Gervase.

"Will you do as Richard says?" she begged him.

His lordship blew out his chubby cheeks in his astonishment; he hesitated a moment, thinking of his cousin Wilding; then, with a shrug, he leaned from the window and gave the order she desired. The carriage turned about, and with Richard following lumbered back across the bridge and through the town to Lupton House. At the door Lord Gervase took his leave of them. He had acted as Ruth had bidden him; but he had no wish to be further involved in this affair, whatever it might portend. Rather was it his duty at once to go and acquaint Mr Wilding – if he could find him – with what was taking place, and leave it to Mr Wilding to take what measures might seem best to him. He told them so, and having told them, left them.

Richard begged to be alone with his sister, and alone they passed together into the library. His manner was restless; he trembled with excitement, and his eyes glittered almost feverishly.

"You may have thought, Ruth, that I was resigned to your marriage with this fellow Wilding," he began; "or that for other reasons I thought it wiser not to interfere. If you thought that you wronged me. I – Blake and I – have been at work for you during these last days, and I rejoice to say our labours have not been idle." His manner grew assertive, boastful as he proceeded.

"You know, of course," said she, "that I am married."

He made a gesture of disdain. "No matter," said he exultantly.

"It matters something, I think," she answered. "O, Richard, Richard, why did you not come to me sooner if you possessed the means of sparing me this thing?"

He shrugged impatiently; her remonstrance seemed to throw him out of temper. "Oons!" he cried; "I came as soon as was ever possible, and, depend upon it, I am not come too late. Indeed, I think I am come in the very nick of time." He drew a sheet of paper from an inside pocket of his coat and slapped it down upon the table. "There is the wherewithal to hang your fine husband," he announced in triumph.

She recoiled. "To hang him?" she echoed. With all her aversion to Mr Wilding it was plain she did not wish him hanged.

"Aye, to hang him," Richard repeated, and drew himself to the full height of his short stature in pride at the thing he had achieved. "Read it."

She took the paper almost mechanically, and for some moments she studied the crabbed signature before realising whose it was. Then she started.

"From the Duke of Monmouth!" she exclaimed.

He laughed. "Read it," he bade her again, though there was no need for the injunction, for already she was deciphering the crabbed hand and the atrocious spelling – for His Grace of Monmouth's education had been notoriously neglected. The letter, which was dated from The Hague, was addressed "To my good friend W, at Bridgwater." It began, "Sir," spoke of the imminent arrival of His Grace in the West, and gave certain instructions for the collection of arms and the work of preparing men for enlistment in his Cause, ending with protestations of His Grace's friendship and esteem.

Ruth read the epistle twice before its treasonable nature was made clear to her; before she understood the thing that was foreshadowed. Then she raised troubled eyes to her brother's face, and in answer to the question of her glance, he made clear to her the shrewd means by which they had become possessed of this weapon that should destroy their enemy, Mr Wilding.

Blake and he, forewarned – he said not how – of the coming of this messenger, had lain in wait for him at the "Hare and Hounds," at Taunton. They had sought at first to become possessed of the letter without violence. But, having failed in this through having aroused the messenger's suspicions, they had been forced to follow and attack him on a lonely stretch of road, where they had robbed him of the contents of his wallet. Richard added that the letter was, no doubt, one of several sent over by Monmouth to some friend at Lyme for distribution among his principal agents in the West. It was regrettable that they should have endeavoured to take gentle measures with the courier, as this had forewarned him, and he had apparently been led to remove the letter's outer wrapper – which, no doubt, bore Wilding's full name and address – against the chance of such an attack as they had made upon him. Nevertheless, as it was, that letter "to my old friend W," backed by Richard's and Blake's evidence of the destination intended for it, would be more than enough to lay Mr Wilding safely by the heels.

"I would to Heaven," he repeated in conclusion, "I could have come in time to save you from becoming his wife. But at least it is in my power to make you very speedily his widow."

"That," said Ruth, still retaining the letter, "is what you propose to do?"

"What else?"

She shook her head. "It must not be, Richard," she said. "I'll not consent to it."

Taken aback, he stared at her; then laughed unpleasantly. "Odds my life! Are you in love with the man? Have you been fooling us?"

"No," she answered. "But I'll be no party to his murder."

"Murder, quotha! Who talks of murder?"

Her shrewd eyes searched his face. "How came you by your knowledge that this courier rode to Mr Wilding?" she asked him suddenly, and the swift change that overspread his countenance showed her that she had touched him in a tender spot, assured her of the thing she had suddenly come to suspect – a suspicion which at the same time started from and explained much that had been mysterious in Richard's ways of late. "You had knowledge of this conspiracy," she pursued, answering her own question before he had time to speak, "because you were one of the conspirators."

"At least I am so no longer," he blurted out.

"I thank Heaven for that, Richard; for your life is very dear to me. But it would ill become you to make such use as this of the knowledge you came by in that manner. It were a Judas' act." He would have interrupted her, but her manner dominated him. "You will leave this letter with me, Richard," she continued.

"Damn me! No…" he began.

"Ah, yes, Richard," she insisted. "You will give it to me, and I shall thank you for the gift. It shall prove a weapon for my salvation, never fear."

"It shall, indeed," he cried, with an ugly laugh; "when I have ridden to Exeter to lay it before Albemarle."

"Not so," she answered him. "It shall be a weapon of defence – not of offence. It shall stand as a buckler between me and Mr Wilding. Trust me, I shall know how to use it."

"But there is Blake to consider," he expostulated, growing angry. "I am pledged to him."

"Your first duty is to me…"

"Tut!" he interrupted. "Blake feels that he owes it to his loyalty to lay this letter before the Lord-Lieutenant, and, for that matter, so do I."

"Sir Rowland would not cross my wishes in this," she answered him.

"Folly!" he cried, now thoroughly aroused. "Give me that letter."

"Nay, Richard," she answered, and waved him back. But he advanced nevertheless.

"Give it me," he bade her, waxing fierce. "Gad! It was folly to have told you of it. I had not done so but that I never thought you such a fool as to oppose yourself to the thing we intend."

"Listen, Richard…" she besought him. But he was grown insensible to pleadings.

"Give me that letter," he insisted, and caught her wrist. Her other hand, however – the one that held the sheet – was already behind her back.

The door was suddenly thrust open, and Diana appeared. "Ruth," she announced, "Mr Wilding is here."

At the mention of that name, Richard let her free. "Wilding!" he ejaculated, his fierceness all blown out of him. He had imagined that already Mr Wilding would be in full flight. Was the fellow mad?

"He is following me," said Diana, and, indeed, a step could be heard in the passage.

"The letter!" growled Richard in a frenzy, between fear and anger now. "Give it me! Give it me, do you hear?"

"Sh! You'll betray yourself," she cried. "He is here."

And at that same moment Mr Wilding's tall figure, still arrayed in his bridegroom's finery of sky-blue satin, loomed in the doorway. He was serene and calm as ever. Neither the discovery of the plot by the abstraction of the messenger's letter, nor Ruth's strange conduct – of which he had heard from Lord Gervase – had sufficed to ruffle, outwardly at least, the inscrutable serenity of his air and manner. He paused to make his bow, then advanced into the room, with a passing glance at Richard still spurred and booted and all dust-stained.

"You appear to have ridden far, Dick," said he, smiling, and Richard shivered in spite of himself at the mocking note that seemed to ring faintly at the words. "I saw your friend, Sir Rowland, in the garden," he added. "I think he waits for you."

Though Richard could not fail to apprehend the implied dismissal, he was minded at first to disregard it. But Mr Wilding, turning, held the door, addressing Diana.

"Mistress Horton," said he, "will you give us leave?" Diana curtsied and passed out, and Mr Wilding's eye falling upon the lingering Richard at that moment, Richard thought it best to follow her example. But he went with rage in his heart at being forced to leave that precious document behind him.

As Mr Wilding, his back to her a moment, closed the door, Ruth slipped the paper hurriedly into the bosom of her low-necked gown. He turned to her, calm but very grave, and his dark eyes seemed to reproach her.

"This is ill done, Ruth," said he.

"Ill done, or well done," she answered him, "done it is, and shall so remain."

He raised his brows. "Ah," said he, "I appear then to have misapprehended the situation. From what Gervase told me, I understood it was your brother forced you to return."

"Not forced, sir," she answered him.

"Induced, then," said he. "It but remains for me to induce you to repair what I think was a mistake."

She shook her head. "I have returned home for good," said she.

"You'll pardon me," said he, "that I am so egotistical as to prefer Zoyland Chase to Lupton House. Despite the manifold attractions of the latter, I do not intend to take up my abode here."

"You are not asked to."

"What then?"

She hated him for the smile, for his masterful air, which seemed to imply that he humoured her because he scorned to use authority, but that when he did use it, hers must it be to obey him. Again she felt that everlasting calm, arguing such latent forces, was the thing she hated most in him.

"I think I had best be plain with you," said she. "I have fulfilled my part of the bargain that we made. I intend to do no more. I promised that if you spared my brother, I would go to the altar with you today. I have carried out my contract to the letter. It is at an end."

"Indeed," said he; "I think it has not yet begun." He advanced towards her, and took her hand. She yielded it, unwilling though she was. "This is unworthy of you, madam," said he, his tone grave and deferential. "You think to escape fulfilling the spirit of your bargain by adhering to the letter of it. Not so," he ended, and shook his head, smiling gently. "The carriage is still at your door. You return with me to Zoyland Chase to take possession of your home."

"You mistake," said she, and tore her hand from his. "You say that what I have done is unworthy. I admit it; but it is with unworthiness that we must combat unworthiness. Was your attitude towards me less unworthy?"

"I'll make amends for it if you'll come home," said he.

"My home is here. You cannot compel me."

"I should be loath to," he admitted, sighing.

"You cannot," she insisted.

"I think I can," said he. "There is a law…"

"A law that will hang you if you invoke it," she cut in quickly. "This much can I safely promise you."

She had need to say no more to tell him everything. At all times half a word was as much to Mr Wilding as a whole sentence to another. She saw the tightening of his lips, the hardening of his eyes, beyond which he gave no other sign that she had hit him.

"I see," said he. "It is another bargain that you make. I do suspect there is some trader's blood in the Westmacott veins. Let us be clear. You hold the wherewithal to ruin me, and you will use it if I insist upon my husband's rights. Is it not so?"

She nodded in silence, surprised at the rapidity with which he had read the situation.

"I admit," said he, "that you have me between sword and wall." He laughed shortly. "Let me know more," he begged her. "Am I to understand that so long as I leave you in peace – so long as I do not insist upon your becoming my wife in more than name – you will not wield the weapon that you hold?"

"You are to understand so," she answered.

He took a turn in the room, very thoughtful. Not of himself was he thinking now, but of the Duke of Monmouth. Trenchard had told him some ugly truths that morning of how in his love-making he appeared to have shipwrecked the Cause ere it was well launched. If this letter got to Whitehall there was no gauging – ignorant as he was of what was in it – the ruin that might follow; but they had reason to fear the worst. He saw his duty to the Duke most clearly, and he breathed a prayer of thanks that Richard had chosen to put that letter to such a use as this. He knew himself checkmated; but he was a man who knew how to bear defeat in a becoming manner. He turned suddenly.

"The letter is in your hands?" he inquired.

"It is," she answered.

"May I see it?" he asked.

She shook her head – not daring to show it or betray its whereabouts lest he should use force to become possessed of it – a thing, indeed, that was very far from his purpose. He considered a moment, his mind intent now rather upon the Duke's interest than his own.

"You know," quoth he, "the desperate enterprise to which I stand committed. But it is a bargain between us that you do not betray me nor that enterprise so long as I leave you rid of my presence."

"That is the bargain I propose," said she.

He looked at her a moment with hungry eyes, and she found his glance almost more than she could bear, so strong was its appeal. Besides, it may be that she was a thought beglamoured by the danger in which he stood, which seemed to invest him with a certain heroic dignity.

"Ruth," he said at length, "it may well be that that which you desire may speedily come to pass; it may well be that in the course of this rebellion that is hatching you may be widowed. But at least I know that if my head falls it will not be my wife who has betrayed me to the axe. For that much, believe me, I am supremely grateful."

He advanced. He took her unresisting hand again and bore it to his lips, bowing low before her. Then, erect and graceful, he turned on his heel and left her.

Chapter 9

MR TRENCHARD'S COUNTERSTROKE

Now, however much it might satisfy Mr Wilding to have Ruth's word for it that so long as he left her in peace neither he nor the Cause had any betrayal to fear from her, Mr Trenchard was of a very different mind.

He fumed and swore and worked himself into a very passion. "Zoons, man!" he cried, "it would mean utter ruin to you if that letter reached Whitehall."

"I realise it; but my mind is easy. I have her promise."

"A woman's promise!" snorted Trenchard, and proceeded with great circumstance of expletives to damn "everything that daggled a petticoat."

"Your fears are idle," Wilding assured him. "What she says she will do."

"And her brother?" quoth Trenchard. "Have you bethought you of that canary-bird? He'll know the letter's whereabouts. He has cause to fear you more than ever now. Are you sure he'll not be making use of it to lay you by the heels?"

Mr Wilding smiled upon the fury provoked by Trenchard's concern and love for him. "She has promised," he said with an insistent faith that was fuel to Trenchard's anger, "and I can depend upon her word."

"So cannot I," snapped his friend.

"The thing that plagues me most," said Wilding, ignoring the remark, "is that we are kept in ignorance of the letter's contents at a time when we most long for news. Not a doubt but it would have enabled us to set our minds at ease on the score of these foolish rumours."

"Aye – or else confirmed them," said pessimistic Trenchard. He wagged his head. "They say the Duke has put to sea already."

"Folly!" Wilding protested.

"Whitehall thinks otherwise. What of the troops at Taunton?"

"More folly."

"Well – I would you had that letter."

"At least," said Wilding, "I have the superscription, and we know from Shenke that no name was mentioned in the letter itself."

"There's evidence enough without it," Trenchard reminded him, and fell soon after into abstraction, turning over in his mind a notion with which he had suddenly been inspired. That notion kept Trenchard secretly occupied for a couple of days; but in the end he succeeded in perfecting it.

Now it befell that towards dusk one evening early in the week Richard Westmacott went abroad alone, as was commonly his habit, his goal being the "Saracen's Head," where he and Sir Rowland spent many a night over wine and cards – to Sir Rowland's moderate profit, for he had not played the pigeon in town so long without having acquired sufficient knowledge to enable him to play the rook in the country. As Westmacott was passing up the High Street, a black shadow fell athwart the light that streamed from the door of the Bell Inn, and out through the doorway lurched Mr Trenchard a thought unsteadily to hurtle so violently against Richard that he broke the long stem of the white clay pipe he was carrying. Now Richard was not to know that Mr Trenchard – having informed himself of Mr Westmacott's evening habits – had been waiting for the past half-hour in that doorway hoping that Mr Westmacott would not depart this evening from his usual custom. Another thing that Mr Westmacott was not to know – considering his youth – was the singular histrionic ability which this old rake had displayed in those younger days of his when he had been a player, and the further circumstance that he had excelled in those parts in which ebriety was to be counterfeited. Indeed, we have it on the word of no less an authority on theatrical matters than Mr Pepys that Mr Nicholas Trenchard's appearance as Pistol in *Henry IV* in the year of the blessed Restoration was the talk alike of town and Court.

Mr Trenchard steadied himself from the impact, and, swearing a round and awful Elizabethan oath, accused the other of being drunk, then struck an attitude to demand with truculence, "Would ye take the wall o' me, sir?"

Richard hastened to make himself known to this turbulent roysterer, who straightway forgot his grievance to take Westmacott affectionately by the hand and overwhelm him with apologies. And that done, Trenchard – who affected the condition known as maudlin drunk – must needs protest almost in tears how profound was his love for Richard, and insist that the boy return with him to the Bell Inn, that they might pledge each other.

Richard, himself sober, was contemptuous of Trenchard so obviously obfuscated. At first it was his impulse to excuse himself, as possibly Blake might be already waiting for him; but on second thoughts, remembering that Trenchard was Mr Wilding's most intimate *famulus*, it occurred to him that by a little crafty questioning he might succeed in smoking Mr Wilding's intentions in the matter of that letter – for from his sister he had failed to get satisfaction.

So he permitted himself to be led indoors to a table by the window which stood vacant. There were at the time a dozen guests or so in the common-room. Trenchard bawled for wine and brandy, and for all that he babbled in an irresponsible, foolish manner of all things that were of no matter, yet not the most adroit of pumping could elicit from him any such information as Richard sought. Perforce young Westmacott must remain, plying him with more and more drink – and being plied in his turn – to the end that he might not waste the occasion.

An hour later found Richard much the worse for wear, and Trenchard certainly no better. Richard forgot his purpose, forgot that Blake waited for him at the "Saracen's Head." And now Trenchard seemed to be pulling himself together.

"I want to talk to you, Richard," said he, and, although thick, there was in his voice a certain impressive quality that had been absent hitherto. "'S a rumour current." He lowered his voice to a whisper almost, and, leaning across, took his companion by the arm. He hiccoughed noisily, then began again. "'S a rumour current, sweetheart, that you're disaffected."

Richard started, and his mind flapped and struggled like a trapped bird to escape the meshes of the wine, to the end that he might convincingly defend himself from such an imputation – so dangerously true.

"'S a lie!" he gasped.

Trenchard shut one eye and owlishly surveyed his companion with the other. "They say," he added, "that you're for forsaking 'Duke's party."

"Villainous!" Richard protested. "I'll sli' throat of any man 't says so." And draining the pewter at his elbow, he smashed it down on the table to emphasise his seriousness. Trenchard replenished it with the utmost promptness, then sat back in his tall chair and pulled a moment at the fresh pipe with which he had equipped himself.

"'I think I espy,'" he quoted presently, "'virtue and valour crouched in thine eye.' And yet…and yet…if I had cause to think it true, I'd… I'd run you through the vitals – jus' so," and he prodded Richard's waistcoat with the point of his pipe-stem. His swarthy face darkened, his eyes glittered fiercely. "Are ye sure ye're norrer foul traitor?" he demanded suddenly. "Are y' sure, for if ye're not…"

He left the terrible menace unuttered, but it was none the less understood. It penetrated the vinous fog that beset the brain of Richard, and startled him.

"'Swear I'm not!" he cried. "'Swear mos' solemnly I'm not."

"Swear?" echoed Trenchard, and his scowl grew darker still. "Swear? A man may swear and yet lie – 'a man may smile and smile and be a villain.' I'll have proof of your loyalty to us. I'll have proof, or as there's a heaven above and a hell below, I'll rip you up."

His mien was terrific, and his voice the more threatening in that it was not raised above a whisper. Richard sat back appalled, afraid.

"Wha'…what proof 'll satisfy you?" he asked.

Trenchard considered it, pulling at his pipe again. "Pledge me the Duke," said he at length. "Ther's truth 'n wine. Pledge me the Duke and confusion to his Majesty the goldfinch." Richard reached for his pewter, glad that the test was to be so light. "Up on your feet, man," grumbled Trenchard. "On your feet, and see that your words have a ring of truth in them."

Richard did as he was bidden, the little reason left him being concentrated wholly on the convincing of his fellow-tippler. He rose to his feet, so unsteadily that his chair fell over with a bang. He never heeded it, but others in the room turned at the sound, and a hush fell in the chamber. Dominating this came Richard's voice, strident with intensity, if thick of utterance.

"Down with Popery, and God save the Protestant Duke!" he cried. "Down with Popery!" And he looked at Trenchard for applause, and assurance that Trenchard no longer thought there was cause to quarrel with him.

Behind him there was a stir in the room that went unheeded by the boy. Men nudged their neighbours; some looked frightened and some grinned at the treasonable words.

A swift change came over Trenchard. His drunkenness fell from him like a discarded mantle. He sat like a man amazed. Then he heaved himself to his feet in a fury, and smashed down his pipe-stem on the wooden table, sending its fragments flying.

"Damn me!" he roared. "Have I sat at table with a traitor?" And he thrust at Richard with his open palm, lightly yet with sufficient force to throw Richard off his precarious balance and send him sprawling on the sanded floor. Men rose from the tables about and approached them, some few amused, but the majority very grave. Dodsley, the landlord, came hurrying to assist Richard to his feet.

"Mr Westmacott," he whispered in the rash fool's ear, "you were best away."

Richard stood up, leaning his full weight upon the arm the landlord had about his waist. He passed a hand over his brow, as if to brush aside the veil that obscured his wits. What had happened? What had he said? What had Trenchard done? Why did these fellows stand and gape at him? He heard his companion's voice, raised to address the company.

"Gentlemen," he heard him say, "I trust there is none present will impute to me any share in such treasonable sentiments as Mr Westmacott has expressed. But if there is any who questions my loyalty, I have a convincing argument for him – in my scabbard." And he struck his sword-hilt with his fist. Then he clapped on his hat, aslant over the locks of his golden wig, and, taking up his whip, he moved with leisurely dignity towards the door. He looked back with a sardonic smile at the ado he was leaving behind him, listened a moment to the voices that already were being raised in excitement, then closed the door and made his way briskly to the stable-yard, where he called for his horse. He rode out of Bridgwater ten minutes later, and took the road to Taunton as the moon was rising big and yellow over the hills on his left. He reached Taunton towards ten o'clock that night, having ridden hell-to-leather. His first visit was to the "Hare and Hounds," where Blake and Westmacott had overtaken the courier. His next to the house where Mr Edward Phelips and Colonel Luttrell – the gentlemen lately ordered to Taunton by His Majesty – had their lodging.

The fruits of Mr Trenchard's extraordinary behaviour that night were to be seen at an early hour on the following day, when a constable and three tything-men came with a Lord-Lieutenant's warrant to arrest Mr Richard Westmacott on a charge of high treason. They found the young man still abed, and most guilty was his panic when they bade him rise and dress himself – though little did he dream of the full extent to which Mr Trenchard had enmeshed him, or indeed that Mr Trenchard had any hand at all in this affair. What time he was getting into his clothes with a tything-man outside his door and another on guard under his window, the constable and his third myrmidon made an exhaustive search of the house. All they found of interest was a letter signed "Monmouth," which they took from the secret drawer of a secretaire in the library; but that, it seemed, was all they sought, for, having found it, they proceeded no further with their reckless and destructive ransacking.

With that letter and the person of Richard Westmacott, the constable and his men took their departure, and rode back to Taunton, leaving alarm and sore distress at Lupton House. In her despair poor Ruth was all for following her brother, in the hope that at least by giving evidence of how that letter came into his possession she might do something to assist him. But knowing, as she did, that he had had his share in the treason that was hatching, she had cause to fear that his guilt would not lack for other proofs. It was Diana who urged her to repair instead to the only man upon whose resource she might depend, provided he were willing to exert it. That man was Anthony Wilding, and whether Diana urged it from motives of her own or out of concern for Richard it would be difficult to say with certainty.

The very thought of going to him for aid, after all that had passed, was repugnant to Ruth. And yet what choice had she? Convinced by her cousin and urged by her affection and duty to Richard, she repressed her aversion, and, calling for a horse, rode out to Zoyland Chase, attended by a groom. Wilding by good fortune was at home, hard at work upon a mass of documents in that same library where she had talked with him on the occasion of her first visit to his home – to the home of which she remembered that she was now, herself, the mistress. He was preparing for circulation in the West a mass of libels and incendiary pamphlets calculated to forward the cause of the Protestant Duke.

Dissembling his surprise, he bade old Walters – who left her waiting in the hall whilst he went to announce her – to admit her instantly, and he advanced to the door to receive and welcome her.

"Ruth," said he, and his face was oddly alight, "you have come at last."

She smiled a wan smile of self-pity. "I have been constrained," said she, and told him what had happened; that her brother had been arrested for high treason, and that the constable in searching the house had come upon the Monmouth letter she had locked away in her desk.

"And not a doubt," she ended, "but it will be believed that it was to Richard the letter was indited by the Duke. You will remember that its only address was 'to my good friend W,' and that will stand for Westmacott as well as Wilding."

Mr Wilding was fain to laugh at the irony of this surprising turn of things of which she brought him news; for he had neither knowledge nor suspicion of the machinations of his friend Trenchard to which these events were due. But noting and respecting her anxiety for her brother, he curbed his natural amusement.

"It is a judgment upon you," said he, nevertheless.

"Do you exult?" she asked indignantly.

"No, but I cannot repress my admiration for the ways of Divine Justice. If you are come to me for advice, I can but suggest that you should follow your brother's captors to Taunton, and inform the lieutenants of how the letter came into your power."

She looked at him in anger almost at what seemed a callousness. "Would he believe me, think you?"

"Belike he would not," said Mr Wilding. "You can but try."

"If I told them it was addressed to you," she said, eyeing him sternly, "does it not occur to you that they would send for you to question you, and that if they did so, as you are a gentleman, you could not lie away my brother's life?"

"Why, yes," said he quite calmly, "it does occur to me. But does it not occur to you that by the time they came here they would find me gone?" He laughed at her dismay. "I thank you, madam, for this warning," he added. "I think I'll bid them saddle for me without delay. Too long already have I tarried."

"And must Richard hang?" she asked him fiercely.

Mr Wilding produced a snuffbox of tortoise-shell and gold. He opened it deliberately. "If he does, you'll admit that he will hang on the gallows that he has built himself – although intended for another. I'faith! He's not the first booby to be caught in his own springe. There is in this a measure of poetic justice. Poetry and justice! Do you know, Ruth, they are two things I have ever loved?" And he took a pinch of choice Burgamot.

"Will you be serious?" she demanded.

"Trenchard would tell you that it were to make an exception from the rule of my life," he assured her, smiling. "Yet even that might I do at your bidding."

"But this is a serious matter," she told him angrily.

"For Richard," he acknowledged, closing his snuffbox with a snap. "Tell me, what would you have me do?"

Since he asked her thus, she answered him in two words. "Save him."

"At the cost of my own neck?" quoth he. "The price is high," he reminded her. "Do you think that Richard is quite worth it?"

"And are you to save yourself at the cost of his?" she counter-questioned. "Are you capable of such a baseness?"

He looked at her thoughtfully a moment. "You have not reflected," said he slowly, "that in this affair is involved more than mine or Richard's life. There is a great cause weighing in the balance against all personal considerations. If I accounted Richard of more value to Monmouth than I am myself, I should not hesitate in riding to set him free by taking his place. As it is, however, I think I am of the greatest conceivable importance to His Grace, whilst if twenty Richards perished – frankly – their loss would be something of a gain, for Richard has played a traitor's part already. That is with me the first of all considerations."

"Am I of no consideration to you?" she asked him. And in an agony of terror for her brother she now approached him, and, obeying a sudden impulse, cast herself upon her knees before him. "Listen!" she cried.

"Not thus," said he, a frown between his eyes. He took her by the elbows and gently but very firmly brought her to her feet again. "It is not fitting you should kneel save at your prayers."

She was standing now, and very close to him, his hands still held her elbows, though their touch was so light that she scarce felt it. To release them was easy, and the next second her hands were on his shoulders, her brave eyes raised to him.

"Mr Wilding," she implored him, "you'll not let Richard be destroyed?"

He looked down at her with kindling glance, his arms slipped round her lissom waist. "It is hard to deny you, Ruth," said he. "Yet not my love of my own life compels me; but my duty, my loyalty to the cause to which I am pledged. I were a traitor were I now to place myself in peril."

She pressed against him, her face so close to his that her breath fanned his cheek, whither a faint colour crept in quick response. Despite herself almost, instinctively, unconsciously, she exerted the weapons of her sex to bend him to her will.

"You say you love me," she whispered. "Prove it me now, and I will believe you."

"Ah!" he sighed. "And believing me? What then?"

He had himself grimly in hand, yet feared he should not prove strong enough to hold himself for long.

"You…you shall find me your…dutiful wife," she faltered, crimsoning.

His arms tightened about her; he crushed her to him, he bent his head to hers and his lips burnt the lips she yielded to him as though they had been living fire.

Anon, she was to weep in shame – in shame and in astonishment – at that instant of surrender, but for the moment she had no thought save for her brother. Exultation filled her. She accounted that she had conquered, and she gloried in the power her beauty gave her, a power that had sufficed to melt to water the hard-frozen purposes of this self-willed man. The next instant, however, she was cold again with dismay and new-born terror. He unclasped her arms, he drew back, shaking off the hands she had rested upon his shoulders. His white face – the flush had faded from it again – smiled a thought disdainfully.

"You bargain with me," he said. "But I have some knowledge of your ways of trading. They are over-shrewd for an honest gentleman."

"You mean," she gasped, her hand pressed to her heart, her face a deathly white, "you mean that you'll not save him?"

"I mean," said he, "that I will have no further bargains with you."

There was such hard finality in his tone that she recoiled, beaten and without power, to return to the assault. She had played and lost. She had yielded her lips to his kisses, and – husband though he might be in name – shame was her only guerdon.

One look she gave him from out of that face so white and pitiful, then with a shudder turned from him and fled his presence. He sprang after her as the door closed, then checked and stood in thought, very grim for one who professed to bestow no seriousness on the affairs of life. Then he returned slowly to his writing-table, and rummaged there among the papers with which it was encumbered, seeking something of which he now had need. Through the open window he heard the retreating beat of her horse's hoofs. He sighed and sat down heavily, to take his long square chin in his hand and stare before him at the sunlight on the lawn outside.

And whilst he sat thus, Ruth made all haste back to Lupton House to tell of the failure that had attended her. There was nothing left her now but to embark upon the forlorn hope of following Richard to Taunton, to offer her evidence of how the incriminating letter had come to be locked in the drawer in which the constable had discovered it. Diana met her with a face as white as her own and infinitely more startled. She had just learnt that Sir Rowland Blake had been arrested also and that he had been carried to Taunton together with Richard, and, as a consequence, she was as eager now that Ruth should repair to Albemarle as she had erstwhile been earnest in urging her to seek out Mr Wilding; indeed, Diana went so far as to offer to accompany her, an offer that Ruth gladly, gratefully accepted.

Within an hour Ruth and Diana – in spite of all that poor, docile Lady Horton had said to stay them – were riding to Taunton, attended by the same groom who had so lately accompanied his mistress to Zoyland Chase.

Chapter 10

THEIR OWN PETARD

In a lofty spacious room of the town hall at Taunton sat Sir Edward Phelips and Colonel Luttrell to dispense justice, and with them, flanked by one of them on either side of him, sat Christopher Monk, Duke of Albemarle, Lord-Lieutenant of Devonshire, who had been summoned in all haste from Exeter that he might be present at an examination which promised to be of so vast importance. The three sat at a long table at the room's end, attended by two secretaries.

Before them, guarded by constable and tything-men, weaponless, their hands pinioned behind them – Blake's arm was healed by now – stood Mr Westmacott and his friend Sir Rowland to answer this grave charge.

Richard, not knowing who might have betrayed him and to what extent, was very fearful – having through his connection with the Cause every reason so to be. Blake, on the other hand, conscious of his innocence of any plotting, was impatient of his position, and a thought contemptuous. It was he who, upon being ushered by the constable and his men into the august presence of the Lord-Lieutenant, clamoured to know precisely of what he was accused that he might straightway clear himself.

Albemarle reared his great massive head, smothered in a mighty black peruke, and scowled upon the florid London beau. A black-visaged gentleman was Christopher Monk. His pendulous cheeks, it is true, were of a sallow pallor, but what with his black wig, black eyebrows, dark eyes, and the blue-black tint of shaven beard on his great jaw and upper lip, he presented an appearance sombrely sinister. His nether-lip was thick and very prominent; deep creases ran from the corners of his mouth adown his heavy chin; his eyes were dull and lacklustre, with great pouches under them. In the main, the air of this son of the great Parliamentarian general was stupid, dull, unprepossessing.

The creases of his mouth deepened as Blake protested against what he termed this outrage that had been done him; he sneered ponderously, thrusting further forward his heavily undershot jowl.

"We are informed, sir, of your antecedents," he staggered Blake by answering. "We have learnt the reason why you left London and your creditors, and in all my life, sir, I have never known a man more ready to turn his hand to treason than a broken gamester. Your kind turns by instinct to such work as this, as a last resource for the mending of battered fortunes."

Blake crimsoned from chin to brow. "I'm forejudged, it seems," he made answer haughtily, tossing his fair locks, his blue eyes glaring upon his judges. "May I, at least, know the name of my accuser?"

"You shall receive impartial justice at our hands," put in Phelips, whose manner was of a dangerous mildness. "Depend on that. Not only shall you know the name of your accuser, but you shall be confronted by him. Meanwhile, sirs," and his glance strayed from Blake's flushed and angry countenance to Richard's, pale and timid, "meanwhile, are we to understand that you deny the charge?"

"I have heard none as yet," said Sir Rowland insolently.

Albemarle turned to one of the secretaries. "Read them the indictment," said he, and sank back in his chair, his dull glance upon the prisoners, whilst the clerk in a droning voice read from a document which he took up. It impeached Sir Rowland Blake and Mr Richard Westmacott of holding treasonable communication with

James Scott, Duke of Monmouth, and of plotting against His Majesty's life and throne and the peace of His Majesty's realms.

Blake listened with unconcealed impatience to the farrago of legal phrases, and snorted contemptuously when the reading came to an end. Albemarle looked at him darkly. "I do thank God," said he, "that through Mr Westmacott's folly has this hideous plot, this black and damnable treason, been brought to light in time to enable us to stamp out this fire ere it is well kindled. Have you aught to say, sir?"

"I have to say that the whole charge is a foul and unfounded lie," said Sir Rowland bluntly. "I never plotted in my life against anything but my own prosperity, nor against any man but myself."

Albemarle smiled coldly at his colleagues, then turned to Westmacott. "And you, sir?" he said. "Are you as stubborn as your friend?"

"I incontinently deny the charge," said Richard, and he contrived that his voice should ring bold and resolute.

"A charge built on air," sneered Blake, "which the first breath of truth should utterly dispel. We have heard the impeachment. Will your Grace with the same consideration permit us to see the proofs that we may lay bare their falseness? It should not be difficult."

"Do you say there is no such plot as is here alleged?" quoth the Duke, and smote a paper sharply.

Blake shrugged his shoulders. "How should I know?" he asked. "I say I have no share in any, that I am acquainted with none."

"Call Mr Trenchard," said the Duke quietly, and an usher who had stood tamely by the door at the far end of the room departed on the errand. Richard started at the mention of that name. He had a singular dread of Mr Trenchard.

Colonel Luttrell – lean and wiry – now addressed the prisoners, Blake more particularly. "Still," said he, "you will admit that such a plot may indeed exist?"

"It may, indeed, for aught I know – or care," he added incautiously.

Albemarle smote the table with a heavy hand. "By God!" he cried in that deep booming voice of his, "there spoke a traitor! You do not care, you say, what plots may be hatched against His Majesty's life and crown! Yet you ask me to believe you a true and loyal subject."

Blake was angered; he was at best a short-tempered man. Deliberately he floundered further into the mire. "I have not asked your Grace to believe me anything," he answered hotly. "It is all one to me what your Grace believes me. I take it I have not been fetched hither to be confronted with what your Grace believes. You have preferred a lying charge against me; I ask for proofs, not your Grace's beliefs and opinions."

"By God, sir, you are a daring rogue!" cried Albemarle.

Sir Rowland's eyes blazed. "Anon, your Grace, when, having failed of your proofs, you shall be constrained to restore me to liberty, I shall ask your Grace to unsay that word."

Albemarle stared, confounded, and in that moment the door opened, and Trenchard sauntered in, cane in hand, his hat under his arm, a wicked smile on his wizened face. Leaving Blake's veiled threat unanswered, the Duke turned to the old rake. "These rogues," said he, pointing to the prisoners, "demand proofs ere they will admit the truth of the impeachment."

"Those proofs," said Trenchard, "are already in your Grace's hands."

"Aye, but they have asked to be confronted with their accuser."

Trenchard bowed. "Is it your wish, then, that I recite for them the counts on which I have based the accusation I laid before your Grace?"

"If you will condescend so far," said Albemarle.

"Blister me…!" roared Blake, when the Duke interrupted him.

"By God, sir!" he cried, "I'll have no such disrespectful language here. You'll observe the decency of speech and forbear from profanities, you damned rogue, or by God! I'll commit you forthwith."

"I will endeavour," said Blake, with a sarcasm lost on Albemarle, "to follow your Grace's lofty example."

"You will do well, sir," said the Duke, and was shocked that Trenchard should laugh at such a moment.

"I was about to protest, sir," said Blake, "that it is monstrous I should be accused by Mr Trenchard. He has but the slightest acquaintance with me."

Trenchard bowed to him across the chamber. "Admitted, sir," said he. "What should I be doing in bad company?" An answer this that set Albemarle bawling with laughter. Trenchard turned to the Duke. "I will begin, and it please your Grace, with the expressions used last night in my presence at the Bell Inn at Bridgwater by Mr Richard Westmacott, and I will confine myself strictly to those matters on which my testimony can be corroborated by that of other witnesses."

Colonel Luttrell interrupted him to turn to Richard. "Do you recall those expressions, sir?" he asked him.

Richard winced under the question. Nevertheless, he braced himself to make the best defence he could.

"I have not yet heard," said he, "what those expressions were; nor when I hear them must it follow that I recognise them as my own. I must admit to having taken more wine, perhaps, than…than…"

Whilst he sought the expression that he needed Trenchard cut in with a laugh, "*In vino veritas*, gentlemen," and His Grace and Sir Edward nodded sagely; Luttrell preserved a stolid exterior. He seemed less prone than his colleagues to forejudging.

"Will you repeat the expressions used by Mr Westmacott?" Sir Edward begged.

"I will repeat the one that, to my mind, matters most. Mr Westmacott, getting to his feet and in a loud voice, exclaimed, 'God save the Protestant Duke!'"

"Do you admit it, sir?" thundered Albemarle, his eyes glowering upon Richard from under his ponderous brows. Richard hesitated a moment, pale and trembling.

"You will waste breath in denying it," said Trenchard suavely, "for I have a drawer from the Bell Inn, and two gentlemen who overheard you waiting outside."

"I' faith, sir," cried Blake, "what treason was there in that? If he…"

"Silence!" thundered Albemarle. "Let Mr Westmacott speak for himself."

Richard, inspired by the defence Blake had begun, took the same line of argument. "I admit that in the heat of wine I may have used such words," said he. "But I deny their intent to be treasonable. There are many men who drink to the prosperity of the late King's son…"

"Natural son, sir; natural son," Albemarle amended. "It is treason to speak of him otherwise."

"It will be treason presently to draw breath," sneered Blake.

"If it be," said Trenchard, "it is a treason you'll not be long committing."

"Faith, you are right, Mr Trenchard," said the Duke with a laugh. Indeed, he found Mr Trenchard a most pleasant and facetious gentleman.

"Still," insisted Richard, endeavouring in spite of these irrelevancies to make good his point, "there be many men who drink daily to the prosperity of the late King's natural son."

"Ay, sir," answered Albemarle; "but not his prosperity in horrid plots against the life of our beloved sovereign."

"True, your Grace; very true," purred Sir Edward.

"It was not so I meant to toast him," cried Richard.

Albemarle made an impatient gesture, and took up a sheet of paper. "How, then," he asked, "comes this letter – this letter which makes plain the treason upon which the Duke of Monmouth is embarked, just as it makes plain your participation in it – how comes this letter to be found in your possession?" And he waved the letter in the air. Richard went the colour of ashes. He faltered a moment, then took refuge in the truth, for all that he knew beforehand that the truth was bound to ring more false than any lie he could invent.

"That letter was not addressed to me," he stammered.

Albemarle read the subscription, "To my good friend W, at Bridgwater." He looked up, a heavy sneer thrusting his heavy lip still further out. "What do you say to that? Does not 'W' stand for Westmacott?"

"It does not."

"Of course not," said Albemarle with heavy sarcasm. "It stands for Wilkins, or Williams, or…or… What-not."

"Indeed, I can bear witness that it does not," exclaimed Sir Rowland.

"Be silent, sir, I tell you," bawled the Duke at him again. "You shall bear witness soon enough, I promise you. To whom, then," he resumed, turning again to Richard, "do you say that this letter was addressed?"

"To Mr Wilding – Mr Anthony Wilding," Richard answered.

"I would have your Grace to observe," put in Trenchard quietly, "that Mr Wilding, properly speaking, does not reside in Bridgwater."

"Tush!" cried Albemarle; "the rogue but mentions the first name with a 'W' that occurs to him. He's not even an ingenious liar. And how, sir," he asked Richard, "does it come to be in your possession having been addressed, as you say, to Mr Wilding?"

"Aye, sir," said Sir Edward, blinking his weak eyes. "Tell us that."

Richard hesitated again, and looked at Blake. Blake, who by now had come to realise that his friend's affairs were not mended by his interruptions, moodily shrugged his shoulders, scowling.

"Come, sir," said Colonel Luttrell, engagingly, "answer the question."

"Aye," roared Albemarle; "let your invention have free rein."

Again poor Richard sought refuge in the truth. "We – Sir Rowland here and I – had reason to suspect that he was awaiting such a letter."

"Tell us your reasons, sir, if we are to credit you," said the Duke, and it was plain he mocked the prisoner. It was, moreover, a request that staggered Richard. Still, he sought to find a reason that should sound plausible.

"We inferred it from certain remarks that Mr Wilding let fall in our presence."

"Tell us the remarks, sir," the Duke insisted.

"Indeed, I do not call his precise words to mind, your Grace. But they were such that we suspicioned him."

"And you would have me believe that hearing words which awoke in you such grave suspicions, you kept your suspicions and straightway forgot the words. You're but an indifferent liar."

Trenchard, who was standing by the long table, leaned forward now.

"It might be well, and it please your Grace," said he, "to waive the point, and let us come to those matters which are of greater moment. Let him tell your Grace how he came by the letter."

"Ay," said Albemarle. "We do but waste time. Tell us, then, how came the letter into your hands?"

"With Sir Rowland, here, I robbed the courier as he was riding from Taunton to Bridgwater."

Albemarle laughed, and Sir Edward smiled. "You robbed him, eh?" said his Grace. "Very well. But how did it happen that you knew he had the letter upon him, or was it that you were playing the hightobymen, and that in robbing him you hoped to find other matters?"

"Not so, sir," answered Richard. "I sought but the letter."

"And how knew you that he carried it? Did you learn that too from Mr Wilding's indiscretion?"

"Your Grace has said it."

"'Slife? What an impudent rogue have we here!" cried the angry Duke, who conceived that Richard was purposely dealing in effrontery. "Mr Trenchard, I do think we are wasting time. Be so good as to confound them both with the truth of this matter."

"That letter," said Trenchard, "was delivered to them at the 'Hare and Hounds,' here at Taunton, by a gentleman who put up at the inn, and was there joined by Mr Westmacott and Sir Rowland Blake. They opened the conversation with certain cant phrases very clearly intended as passwords. Thus: the prisoners said to the messenger, as they seated themselves at the table he occupied, 'You have the air, sir, of being from overseas,' to which the courier answered, 'Indeed, yes. I am from Holland.' 'From the land of Orange,' says one of the prisoners. 'Aye, and other things,' replies the messenger. 'There is a fair wind blowing,' he adds; to which one of the prisoners, I believe it was Sir Rowland, makes answer, 'May it prosper the Protestant Duke and blow Popery to hell.' Thereupon the landlord caught some mention of a letter, but these plotters, perceiving that they were perhaps being overheard, sent him away to fetch them wine. A half-hour later the messenger took his leave, and the prisoners followed a very few minutes afterwards."

Albemarle turned to the prisoners. "You have heard Mr Trenchard's story. How do you say – is it true or untrue?"

"You will waste breath in denying it," Trenchard took it again upon himself to admonish them. "For I have with me the landlord of the 'Hare and Hounds,' who will corroborate, upon oath, what I have said."

"We do not deny it," put in Blake. "But we submit that the matter is susceptible to explanation."

"You can keep your explanations till your trial, then," snapped Albemarle. "I have heard more than enough to commit the pair of you to gaol."

"But, your Grace," cried Sir Rowland, so fiercely that one of the tything-men set a restraining hand upon his shoulder, "I am ready to swear that what I did, and what my friend Mr Westmacott did, was done in the interests of His Majesty. We were working to discover this plot."

"Which, no doubt," put in Trenchard slyly, "is the reason why, having got the letter, your friend Mr Westmacott locked it in a desk, and you kept silence on the matter."

"You see," exclaimed Albemarle, "how your lies do but serve further to bind you in the toils. It is ever thus with traitors."

"I do think *you* are a damned traitor, Trenchard," began Blake; "a foul…" But what more he would have said was checked by Albemarle, who thundered forth an order for their removal, and then, scarce were the words uttered, than the door at the far end of the hall was opened, and through it came a sound of women's voices. Richard started, for one was the voice of Ruth.

An usher advanced. "May it please your Grace, there are two ladies here beg that you will hear their evidence in the matter of Mr Westmacott and Sir Rowland Blake."

Albemarle considered a moment. Trenchard stood very thoughtful.

"Indeed," said the Duke, at last, "I have heard as much as I need hear," and Sir Edward Phelips nodded in token of concurrence.

Not so, however, Colonel Luttrell. "Still," said he, "in the interests of His Majesty, perhaps, we should be doing well to receive them."

Albemarle blew out his cheeks like a man wearied, and stared an instant at Luttrell. Then he shrugged his shoulders.

"Admit them, then," he commanded almost peevishly, and Ruth and Diana were ushered into the hall. Both were pale, but whilst Diana was fluttered with excitement, Ruth was calm and cool, and it was she who spoke in answer to the Duke's invitation. The burden of her speech was a clear, succinct recitation – in which she spared neither Wilding nor herself – of how the letter came to have remained in her hands, and silence to have been preserved regarding it. Albemarle heard her very patiently.

"If what you say is true, mistress," said he, "and God forbid that I should be so ungallant as to throw doubt upon a lady's word, it certainly explains – although most strangely – how the letter was not brought to us at once by your brother and his friend Sir Rowland. You are prepared to swear that this letter was intended for Mr Wilding?"

"I am prepared to swear it," she replied.

"This is very serious," said the Duke.

"Very serious," assented Sir Edward Phelips.

Albemarle, a little flustered, turned to his colleagues. "What do you say to this? Were it perhaps well to order Mr Wilding's apprehension, and to have him brought hither?"

"It were to give yourselves useless trouble, gentlemen," said Trenchard, with so much assurance that it was plain Albemarle hesitated.

"Beware of Mr Trenchard, your Grace," cried Ruth. "He is Mr Wilding's friend, and if there is a plot he is sure to be in it."

Albemarle, startled, looked at Trenchard. Had the accusation come from either of the men the Duke would have silenced him and abused him; but coming from a woman, and so comely a woman, it seemed to His Grace worthy at least of consideration. But nimble Mr Trenchard was easily master of the situation.

"Which, of course," he answered, with fine sarcasm, "is the reason why I have been at work for the past four-and-twenty hours to lay proofs of this plot before your Grace."

Albemarle was ashamed of his momentary hesitation.

"For the rest," said Trenchard, "it is perfectly true that I am Mr Wilding's friend. But the lady is even more intimately connected with him. It happens that she is his wife."

"His…his wife!" gasped the Duke, whilst Phelips chuckled, and Colonel Luttrell's face grew dark.

Trenchard's wicked smile flickered upon his mobile features. "There are rumours current of court paid her by Sir Rowland, there. Who knows?" he questioned most suggestively, arching his brows and tightening his lips. "Wives are strange kittle-kattle, and husbands have been known before to grow inconvenient. Upon reflection, your Grace will no doubt discern the precise degree of faith to attach to what this lady may tell you against Mr Wilding."

"Oh!" exclaimed Ruth, her cheeks flaming crimson. "But this is monstrous!"

" 'Tis how I should myself describe it," answered Trenchard without shame.

Spurred to it thus, Ruth poured out the entire story of her marriage, and so clear and lucid was her statement that it threw upon the affair a flood of light, whilst so frank and truthful was her tone, her narrative hung so well together, that the bench began to recover from the shock to its faith, and was again in danger of believing her.

Trenchard saw this and trembled. To save Wilding for the Cause he had resorted to this desperate expedient of betraying that Cause. It must be observed, however, that he had not done so save under the conviction that betrayed it was bound to be, and that since that was inevitable the thing had better come from him – for Wilding's sake – than from Richard Westmacott. He had taken the bull by the horns in a most desperate fashion, when he had determined to hoist Richard and Blake with their own petard, hoping that, after all, the harm would reach no further than the destruction of these two – a purely defensive scheme. But now, this girl threatened to wreck his scheme just as it was being safely steered to harbour. Suddenly he swung round, interrupting her.

"Lies, lies, lies!" he clamoured, and his interruption coming at such a time served to impress the Duke most unfavourably – as well it might.

"It is our wish to hear this lady out, Mr Trenchard," the Duke reproved him.

But Mr Trenchard was undismayed. Indeed, he had just discovered a hitherto neglected card, which should put an end to this dangerous game.

"I do abhor to hear your Grace's patience thus abused," he exclaimed with some show of heat. "This lady makes a mock of you. If you'll allow me to ask two questions – or perhaps three – I'll promise finally to prick this bubble for you. Have I your Grace's leave?"

"Well, well," said Albemarle. "Let us hear your questions." And his colleagues nodded.

Trenchard turned airily to Ruth. Behind her Diana sat – an attendant had fetched a chair for her – in fear and wonder at what she saw and heard, her eyes ever and anon straying to Sir Rowland's back, which was towards her.

"This letter, madam," said he, "for the possession of which you have accounted in so…so…picturesque a manner, was intended for and addressed to Mr Wilding, you say. And you are prepared to swear to it?"

Ruth turned indignantly to the bench. "Must I answer this man's questions?" she demanded.

"I think, perhaps, it were best you did," said the Duke, still showing her all deference.

She turned to Trenchard, her head high, her eyes full upon his wrinkled, cynical face. "I swear, then…" she began, but he – consummate actor that he was and versed in tricks that impress an audience – interrupted her, raising one of his gnarled, yellow hands.

"Nay, nay," said he. "I would not have perjury proved against you. I do not ask you to swear. It will be sufficient if you pronounce yourself *prepared to swear*."

She pouted her lip a trifle, her whole expression manifesting her contempt of him. "I am in no fear of perjuring myself," she answered fearlessly. "And I swear that the letter in question was addressed to Mr Wilding."

"As you will," said Trenchard, and was careful not to ask her how she came by her knowledge. "The letter, no doubt, was in an outer wrapper, on which there would be a superscription – the name of the person to whom the letter was addressed?" he half questioned, and Luttrell, who saw the drift of the question, nodded gravely.

"No doubt," said Ruth.

"Now you will acknowledge, I am sure, madam, that such a wrapper would be a document of the greatest importance, as important, indeed, as the letter itself, since we could depend upon it finally to clear up this point on which we differ. You will admit so much, I think?"

"Why, yes," she answered, but her voice faltered a little, and her glance was not quite so fearless. She, too, saw at last the pit he had dug for her. He leaned forward, smiling quietly, his voice impressively subdued, and launched the bolt that was to annihilate the credibility of the story she had told.

"Can you then explain how it comes that that wrapper has been suppressed? Can you tell us how – the matter being as you state it

– in very self-defence against the dangers of keeping such a letter, your brother did not also keep that wrapper?"

Her eyes fell away from his face, they turned to Albemarle, who sat scowling again, and from him they flickered unsteadily to Phelips and Luttrell, and lastly, to Richard, who, very white and with set teeth, stood listening to the working of his ruin.

"I… I do not know," she faltered at last.

"Ah!" said Trenchard, drawing a deep breath. He turned to the bench. "Need I suggest what was the need – the urgent need – for suppressing that wrapper?" quoth he. "Need I say what name was inscribed upon it? I think not. Your Grace's keen insight, and yours, gentlemen, will determine what was probable."

Sir Rowland now stood forward, addressing Albemarle. "Will your Grace permit me to offer my explanation of this?"

Albemarle banged the table. His patience was at an end, since he came now to believe – as Trenchard had earlier suggested – that he had been played upon by Ruth.

"Too many explanations have I heard already, sir," he answered. He turned to one of his secretaries. In his sudden access of choler he forgot his colleagues altogether. "The prisoners are committed for trial," said he harshly, and Trenchard breathed freely at last. But the next instant he caught his breath again, for a ringing voice was heard without demanding to see His Grace of Albemarle at once, and the voice was the voice of Anthony Wilding.

Chapter 11

THE MARPLOT

Mr Wilding's appearance produced as many different emotions as there were individuals present. He made the company a sweeping bow on his admission by Albemarle's orders, a bow which was returned by a stare from one and all. Diana eyed him in amazement, Ruth in hope; Richard averted his glance from that of his brother-in-law; whilst Sir Rowland met it with a scowl of enmity – they had not come face to face since the occasion of that encounter in which Sir Rowland's self-love had been so rudely handled. Albemarle's face expressed a sort of satisfaction, which was reflected on the countenances of Phelips and Luttrell; whilst Trenchard never thought of attempting to dissemble his profound dismay. And this dismay was shared, though not in so deep a measure, by Wilding himself. Trenchard's presence gave him pause; for he had been far indeed from dreaming that his friend had a hand in this affair. At sight of him all was made clear to Mr Wilding. At once he saw the rôle which Trenchard had assumed on this occasion, saw to the bottom of the motives that had inspired him to take the bull by the horns and level against Richard and Blake this accusation before they had leisure to level it against himself.

His quick wits having fathomed Trenchard's motive, Mr Wilding was deeply touched by this proof of friendship, and for a second, as deeply nonplussed, at a loss now how to discharge the task on which he came.

"You are very choicely come, Mr Wilding," said Albemarle. "You will be able to resolve me certain doubts which have been set on foot by these traitors."

"That," said Mr Wilding, "is the purpose for which I am here. News reached me of the arrest that had been made. May I beg that your Grace will place me in possession of the facts that have so far transpired."

It was one of his secretaries who, at Albemarle's bidding, gave Wilding the information that he craved. He listened gravely; then, before Albemarle had time to question him on the score of the name that might have been upon the enfolding wrapper of the letter, he begged that he might confer apart a moment with Mr Trenchard.

"But, Mr Wilding," said Colonel Luttrell, surprised not to hear the immediate denial of the imputation they had expected, "we should first like to hear…"

"By your leave, sirs," Wilding interrupted, "I should prefer that you ask me nothing until I have consulted with Mr Trenchard." He saw Luttrell's frown, observed Sir Edward shift his wig to scratch his head in sheer perplexity, and caught the foreshadowing of denial on the Duke's face. So, without giving any of them time to say him nay, he added quickly and very seriously, "I am begging this in the interests of justice. Your Grace has told me that some lingering doubt still haunts your mind upon the subject of this letter – the other charges can matter little, apart from that treasonable document. It lies within my power to resolve such doubts most clearly and finally. But I warn you, sirs, that not one word will I utter in this connection until I have had speech with Mr Trenchard."

There was about his mien and voice a firmness that forewarned Albemarle that to insist would be worse than idle. A slight pause followed his words, and Luttrell leaned across to whisper in His Grace's ear; from the Duke's other side Sir Edward bent his head forward till it almost touched those of his companions. Blake watched, and was most foolishly impatient.

"Your Grace will never allow this," he cried.

"Eh?" said Albemarle, scowling at him.

"If you allow those two villains to consort together we are all undone," the baronet protested, and ruined what chance there was of Albemarle's not consenting.

It was the one thing needed to determine Albemarle. Like the stubborn man he was, there was naught he detested so much as to have his course dictated to him. More than that, in Sir Rowland's anxiety that Wilding and Trenchard should not be allowed to confer apart, he smoked a fear on Sir Rowland's part, based upon the baronet's consciousness of his own guilt. He turned from him with a sneering smile, and without so much as consulting his associates he glanced at Wilding and waved his hand towards the door.

"Pray do as you suggest, Mr Wilding," said he. "But I depend upon you not to tax our patience."

"I shall not keep Mr Trenchard a moment longer than is necessary," said Wilding, giving no hint of the second meaning in his words. He stepped to the door, opened it himself, and signed to Trenchard to pass out. The old player obeyed him readily, if in silence. An usher closed the door after them, and in silence they walked together to the end of the passage.

"Where is your horse, Nick?" quoth Wilding abruptly.

"What a plague do you mean, where is my horse?" flashed Trenchard. "What midsummer frenzy is this? Damn you for a marplot, Anthony! What a pox are you thinking of to thrust yourself in here at such a time?"

"I had no knowledge you were in the affair," said Wilding. "You should have told me." His manner was brisk to the point of dryness. "However, there is still time to get you out of it. Where is your horse?"

"Damn my horse!" answered Trenchard in a passion. "You have spoiled everything!"

"On the contrary," said Mr Wilding tartly, "it seems you had done that very thoroughly before I arrived. Whilst I am touched by the regard for me which has misled you into turning the tables on Blake and Westmacott, yet I do blame you for this betrayal of the Cause."

"There was no help for it."

"Why, no; and that is why you should have left matters where they stood."

Trenchard stamped his foot; indeed, he almost danced in the excess of his vexation. "Left them where they stood!" he echoed. "Body o' me! Where are your wits? Left them where they stood! And at any moment you might have been taken unawares as a consequence of this accusation being lodged against you by Richard or by Blake. Then the Cause would have been betrayed, indeed."

"Not more so than it is now."

"Not less, at least," snapped the player. "You give me credit for no more wit than yourself. Do you think that I am the man to do things by halves? I have betrayed the plot to Albemarle; but do you imagine I have made no provision for what must follow?"

"Provision?" echoed Wilding, staring.

"Aye, provision. God lack! What do you suppose Albemarle will do?"

"Dispatch a messenger to Whitehall with the letter within an hour."

"You perceive it, do you? And where the plague do you think Nick Trenchard'll be what time that messenger rides?"

Mr Wilding understood. "Aye, you may stare," sneered Trenchard. "A letter that has once been stolen may be stolen again. The courier must go by way of Walford. I had in my mind arranged the spot, close by the ford, where I should fall upon him, rob him of his dispatches, and take him – bound hand and foot if necessary – to Vallancey's, who lives close by; and there I'd leave him until word came that the Duke had landed."

"That the Duke had landed?" cried Wilding "You talk as though the thing were imminent."

"And imminent it is. For aught we know he may be in England already."

Mr Wilding laughed impatiently. "You must forever be building on these crack-brained rumours, Nick," said he.

"Rumours!" roared the other. "Rumours? Ha!" He checked his wild scorn, and proceeded in a different key. "I was forgetting. You do not know the contents of that stolen letter."

Wilding started. Underlying his disbelief in the talk of the countryside and even in the military measures which by the King's orders were being taken in the West, was an uneasy dread lest they should prove to be well founded, lest Argyle's operations in Scotland should be but the forerunner of a rash and premature invasion by Monmouth. He knew the Duke was surrounded by such reckless, foolhardy counsellors as Grey and Ferguson – and yet he could not think the Duke would ruin all by coming before he had definite word that his friends were ready. He looked at Trenchard now with anxious eyes.

"Have you seen the letter, Nick?" he asked, and almost dreaded the reply.

"Albemarle showed it me an hour ago," said Trenchard.

"And it contains?"

"The news we fear. It is in the Duke's own hand, and intimates that he will follow it in a few days – in a few days, man – in person."

Mr Wilding clenched teeth and hands. "God help us all, then!" he muttered grimly.

"Meanwhile," quoth Trenchard, bringing him back to the point, "there is this precious business here. I had as choice a plan as could have been devised, and it must have succeeded, had you not come blundering into it to mar it all at the last moment. That fat fool Albemarle had swallowed my impeachment like a draught of muscadine. Do you hear me?" he ended sharply, for Mr Wilding stood bemused, his thoughts plainly wandering.

He let his hand fall upon Trenchard's shoulder. "No," said he, "I wasn't listening. No matter; for even had I known the full extent of your scheme I still must have interfered."

"For the sake of Mistress Westmacott's blue eyes, no doubt," sneered Trenchard. "Pah! Wherever there's a woman there's the loss of a man."

"For the sake of Mistress *Wilding's* blue eyes," his friend corrected him. "I'll allow no brother of hers to hang in my place."

"It will be interesting to see how you will rescue him."

"By telling the truth to Albemarle."

"He'll not believe it."

"I shall prove it," said Wilding quietly.

Trenchard swung round upon him in mingled anger and alarm for him. "You shall not do it!" he snarled. "It is nothing short of treason to the Duke to get yourself laid by the heels at such a time as this."

"I hope to avoid it," answered Wilding confidently.

"Avoid it? How?"

"Not by staying longer here in talk. That will ruin all. Away with you, Trenchard!"

"By my soul, no!" answered Trenchard. "I'll not leave you. If I have got you into this, I'll help to get you out again, or stay in it with you."

"Bethink you of Monmouth," Wilding admonished him.

"Damn Monmouth!" was the vicious answer. "I am here, and here I stay."

"Get to horse, you fool, and ride to Walford as you proposed, there to ambush the messenger. The letter will go to Whitehall none the less in spite of what I shall tell Albemarle. If things go well with me, I shall join you at Vallancey's before long."

"Why, if that is your intention," said Trenchard, "I had better stay, and we can ride together. It will make it less uncertain for you."

"But less certain for you."

"The more reason why I should remain."

The door of the hall was suddenly flung open at the far end of the corridor, and Albemarle's booming voice, impatiently raised, reached them where they stood.

"In any case," added Trenchard, "it seems there is no help for it now."

Mr Wilding shrugged his shoulders, but otherwise dissembled his vexation. Up the passage floated the constable's voice calling them.

Side by side they moved down, and side by side they stepped once more into the presence of Christopher Monk and his associates.

"Sirs, you have not been in haste," was the Duke's ill-humoured greeting.

"We have tarried a little that we might make an end the sooner," answered Trenchard dryly, and this was the first indication he gave Mr Wilding of how naturally – like the inimitable actor that he was – he had slipped into his new rôle.

Albemarle waved the frivolous rejoinder aside. "Come, Mr Wilding," said he, "let us hear what you may have to say. You are not, I take it, about to urge any reasons why these rogues should not be committed?"

"Indeed, your Grace," said Wilding, "that is what I am about to urge."

Blake and Richard looked at him suddenly, and from him to Trenchard; but it was only Ruth whose eyes were shrewd enough to observe the altered demeanour of the latter. Her hopes rose, founded upon this oddly assorted pair. Already in anticipation she was stirred by gratitude towards Wilding, and it was in impatient and almost wondering awe that she waited for him to proceed.

"I take it, sir," he said, without waiting for Albemarle to express any of the fresh astonishment his countenance manifested, "that the accusation against these gentlemen rests entirely upon the letter, which you have been led to believe was addressed to Mr Westmacott."

The Duke scowled a moment before replying. "Why," said he, "if it could be shown – irrefutably shown – that the letter was not

113

addressed to either of them, that would no doubt establish the truth of what they say – that they possessed themselves of the letter in the interests of His Majesty." He turned to Luttrell and Phelips, and they nodded their concurrence with his view of the matter. "But," he continued, "if you are proposing to prove any such thing, I think you will find it difficult."

Mr Wilding drew a crumpled paper from his pocket.

"When the courier whom they robbed, as they have correctly informed you," said he quietly, "suspected their design upon the contents of his wallet, he bethought him of removing the wrapper from the letter, so that in case the letter were seized by them it should prove nothing against any man in particular. He stuffed the wrapper into the lining of his hat, preserving it as a proof of his good faith against the time when he should bring the letter to its destination, or come to confess that it had been taken from him. That wrapper the courier brought to me, and I have it here. The evidence it will give should be more than sufficient to warrant your restoring these unjustly accused gentlemen their liberty."

"The courier took it to you?" echoed Albemarle, stupefaction in his glance. "But why to you?"

"Because," said Wilding, and with his left hand he placed the wrapper before Albemarle, whilst his right dropped again to his pocket, "the letter, as you may see, was addressed to me." The quiet manner in which he made the announcement conveyed almost as great a shock as the announcement itself.

Albemarle took up the wrapper; Luttrell and Phelips craned forward to join him in his scrutiny of it. They compared the two, paper with paper, writing with writing. Then Monk flung one and the other down in front of him.

"What lies have I been hearing, then?" he demanded furiously of Trenchard. " 'Slife I'll make an example of you. Arrest me that rogue – arrest them both," and he half rose from his seat, his trembling hand pointing to Wilding and Trenchard.

Two of the tything-men stirred to do his bidding, but in the same instant Albemarle found himself looking into the round nozzle of a pistol.

"If," said Mr Wilding, "a finger is laid upon Mr Trenchard or me I shall have the extreme mortification of being compelled to shoot your Grace." His pleasantly modulated voice was as deliberate and calm as if he were offering the bench a pinch of snuff. Albemarle's dark visage crimsoned; his eyes became at once wicked and afraid. Sir Edward's cheeks turned pale, his glance grew startled. Luttrell alone, vigilant and dangerous, preserved his calm. But the situation baffled even him.

Behind the two friends the tything-men had come to a terror-stricken halt. Diana had risen from her chair in the excitement of the moment and had drawn close to Ruth, who looked on with parted lips and bosom that rose and fell. Even Blake could not stifle his admiration of Mr Wilding's coolness and address. Richard, on the other hand, was concerned only with thoughts for himself, wondering how it would fare with him if Wilding and Trenchard succeeded in getting away.

"Nick," said Mr Wilding, "will you desire those catchpolls behind us to stand aside? If your Grace raises your voice to call for help, if, indeed, any measures are taken calculated to lead to our capture, I can promise your Grace – notwithstanding my profound reluctance to use violence – that they will be the last measures you will take in life. Be good enough to open the door, Nick, and to see that the key is on the outside."

Trenchard, who was by way of enjoying himself now, stepped briskly down the hall to do as his friend bade him, with a wary eye on the tything-men. But never so much as a finger did they dare to lift. Mr Wilding's calm was too deadly; they had seen a man in earnest before this, and they knew his appearance now. From the doorway Trenchard called Mr Wilding.

"I must be going, your Grace," said the latter very courteously, "but I shall not be so wanting in deference to His Majesty's august representatives as to turn my back upon you." Saying which, he walked backwards, holding his pistol level, until he had reached Trenchard and the door. There he paused and made them a deep bow, his manner the more mocking in that there was no tinge of mockery perceptible. "Your very obedient servant," said he, and stepped outside. Trenchard turned the key, withdrew it from the lock, and, standing on tiptoe, thrust it upon the ledge of the lintel.

Instantly a clamour arose within the chamber. But the two friends never stayed to listen. Down the passage they sped at the double, and out into the courtyard. Here Ruth's groom, mounted himself, was walking his mistress' and Diana's horses up and down whilst he waited: yonder one of Sir Edward's stableboys was holding Mr Wilding's roan. Two or three men of the Somerset militia, in their red and yellow liveries, lounged by the gates, and turned uninterested eyes upon these newcomers.

Wilding approached his wife's groom. "Get down," he said, "I need your horse – on the King's business. Get down, I say," he added impatiently, upon noting the fellow's stare, and, seizing his leg, he helped him to dismount by almost dragging him from the saddle. "Up with you, Nick," said he, and Nick very promptly mounted. "Your mistress will be here presently," Wilding told the groom, and, turning on his heel, strode to his own mare. A moment later Trenchard and he vanished through the gateway with a tremendous clatter, just as the Lord-Lieutenant, Colonel Luttrell, Sir Edward Phelips, the constable, the tything-men, Sir Rowland, Richard, and the ladies made their appearance.

Ruth pushed her way quickly to the front. She feared lest her horse and her cousin's being at hand might be used for the pursuit; so urging Diana to do the same, she snatched her reins from the hands of the dumfounded groom and leapt nimbly to the saddle.

"After them," roared Albemarle, and the constable with two of his men made a dash for the gateway to raise the hue and cry, whilst the militiamen watched them in stupid, inactive wonder. "Damnation, mistress!" thundered the Duke in ever-increasing passion, "hold your nag! Hold your nag, woman!" For Ruth's horse had become unmanageable, and was caracoling about the yard between the men and the gateway in such a manner that they dared not attempt to win past her.

"You have scared him with your bellowing," she panted, tugging at the bridle, and all but backed into the constable who had been endeavouring to get round behind her. The beast continued its wild prancing, and the Duke abated nothing in his furious profanity, until suddenly the groom, having relinquished to Diana the reins of the other horse, sprang to Ruth's assistance and caught her bridle in a firm grasp which brought the animal to a standstill.

"You fool!" she hissed at him, and half raised her whip to strike, but checked on the impulse, bethinking her in time that, after all, what the poor lad had done he had done thinking her distressed.

The constable and a couple of his fellows won through; others were rousing the stable and getting to horse, and in the courtyard all was bustle and commotion. Meanwhile, however, Mr Wilding and Trenchard had made the most of their start, and were thundering through the town.

Chapter 12

AT THE FORD

As Mr Wilding and Nick Trenchard rode hell-to-leather through Taunton streets they never noticed a horseman at the door of the Red Lion Inn. But the horseman noticed them. He looked up at the sound of their wild approach, started upon recognizing them, and turned in his saddle as they swept past him to call upon them excitedly to stop.

"Hi!" he shouted. "Nick Trenchard! Hi! Wilding!" Then, seeing that they either did not hear or did not heed him, he loosed a volley of oaths, wheeled his horse about, drove home the spurs, and started in pursuit. Out of the town he followed them and along the road towards Walford, shouting and clamouring at first, afterwards in a grim and angry silence.

Now, despite their natural anxiety for their own safety, Wilding and Trenchard had by no means abandoned their project of taking cover by the ford to await the messenger whom Albemarle and the others would no doubt be sending to Whitehall; and this mad fellow thundering after them seemed in a fair way to mar their plan. As they reluctantly passed the spot they had marked out for their ambush, splashed through the ford and breasted the rising ground beyond, they took counsel. They determined to stand and meet this rash pursuer. Trenchard calmly opined that if necessary they must shoot him; he was, I fear, a bloody-minded fellow at bottom, although, it is true, he justified himself now by pointing out that this was no time to hesitate at trifles. Partly because they talked and partly because the gradient was steep and their horses needed breathing, they slackened rein, and the horseman behind them came tearing through the water of the ford and lessened the distance considerably in the next few minutes.

He bethought him of using his lungs once more. "Hi, Wilding! Hold, damn you!"

"He curses you in a most intimate manner," quoth Trenchard.

Wilding reined in and turned in the saddle. "His voice has a familiar sound," said he. He shaded his eyes with his hand, and looked down the slope at the pursuer, who came on crouching low upon the withers of his goaded beast.

"Wait!" the fellow shouted. "I have news – news for you!"

"It's Vallancey!" cried Wilding suddenly. Trenchard too had drawn rein and was looking behind him. Instead of expressing relief at the discovery that this was not an enemy, he swore at the trouble to which they had so needlessly put themselves, and he was still at his vituperations when Vallancey came up with them, red in the face and very angry, cursing them roundly for the folly of their mad career, and for not having stopped when he bade them.

"It was no doubt discourteous," said Mr Wilding, "but we took you for some friend of the Lord-Lieutenant's."

"Are they after you?" quoth Vallancey, his face of a sudden very startled.

"Like enough," said Trenchard, "if they have found their horses yet."

"Forward, then," Vallancey urged them in excitement, and he picked up his reins again. "You shall hear my news as we ride."

"Not so," said Trenchard. "We have business here – down yonder at the ford."

"Business? What business?"

They told him, and scarce had they got the words out than he cut in impatiently, "That's no matter now."

"Not yet, perhaps," said Mr Wilding; "but it will be if that letter gets to Whitehall."

"Odso!" was the impatient retort, "there's other news travelling to Whitehall that will make small beer of this – and belike it's well on its way there already."

"What news is that?" asked Trenchard.

Vallancey told them. "The Duke has landed – he came ashore this morning at Lyme."

"The Duke?" quoth Mr Wilding, whilst Trenchard merely stared. "What Duke?"

"What Duke! Lord, you weary me! What Dukes be there? The Duke of Monmouth, man."

"Monmouth!" They uttered the name in a breath.

"But is this really true?" asked Wilding. "Or is it but another rumour?"

"Remember the letter your friends intercepted," Trenchard bade him.

"I am not forgetting it," said Wilding.

"It's no rumour," Vallancey assured them. "I was at White Lackington three hours ago when the news came to George Speke, and I was riding to carry it to you, going by way of Taunton that I might drop word of it for our friends at the 'Red Lion.' "

Trenchard needed no further convincing; he looked accordingly dismayed. But Wilding found it still almost impossible – in spite of what already he had learnt – to credit this amazing news. It was hard to believe the Duke of Monmouth mad enough to spoil all by this sudden and unheralded precipitation.

"You heard the news at White Lackington?" said he slowly. "Who carried it thither?"

"There were two messengers," answered Vallancey, with restrained impatience, "and they were Heywood Dare – who has been appointed paymaster to the Duke's forces – and Mr Chamberlain."

Mr Wilding was observed for once to change colour. He gripped Vallancey by the wrist. "You saw them?" he demanded, and his voice had a husky, unusual sound. "You saw them?"

"With these two eyes," answered Vallancey, "and I spoke with them."

It was true then! There was no room for further doubt.

Wilding looked at Trenchard, who shrugged his shoulders and made a wry face. "I never thought but that we were working in the service of a hare-brain," said he contemptuously.

Vallancey proceeded to details. "Dare and Chamberlain," he informed them, "came off the Duke's own frigate at daybreak today. They were put ashore at Seaton, and they rode straight to Mr Speke's with the news, returning afterwards to Lyme."

"What men has the Duke with him, did you learn?" asked Wilding.

"Not more than a hundred or so, from what Dare told us."

"A hundred! God help us all! And is England to be conquered with a hundred men? Oh, this is midsummer frenzy."

"He counts on all true Protestants to flock to his banner," put in Trenchard, and it was not plain whether he expressed a fact or sneered at one.

"Does he bring money and arms, at least?" asked Wilding.

"I did not ask," answered Vallancey. "But Dare told us that three vessels had come over, so that it is to be supposed he brings some manner of provisions with him."

"It is to be hoped so, Vallancey; but hardly to be supposed," quoth Trenchard, and then he touched Wilding on the arm and pointed with his whip across the fields towards Taunton. A cloud of dust was rising from between tall hedges where ran the road. "I think it were wise to be moving. At least, this sudden landing of James Scott relieves my mind in the matter of that letter."

Wilding, having taken a look at the floating dust that announced the oncoming of their pursuers, was now lost in thought. Vallancey, who, beyond excitement at the news of which he was the bearer, seemed to have no opinion of his own as to the wisdom or folly of the Duke's sudden arrival, looked from one to the other of these two men whom he had known as the prime secret agents in the West, and waited. Trenchard moved his horse a few paces nearer the hedge, whence he could the better survey the winding road to westward, and slightly below them. Wilding's thoughtful silence began to fret him, and he hummed a moment impatiently. At last: "Whither now, Anthony?" he asked suddenly.

"You may ask, indeed!" exclaimed Wilding, and his voice was as bitter as ever Trenchard had heard it. " 'S heart! We are in it now! We had best make for Lyme – if only that we may attempt to persuade this crack-brained boy to ship back to Holland again, and ship ourselves with him."

"There's sense in you at last," grumbled Trenchard. "But I misdoubt me he'll never turn back after having come so far. Have you any money?" he asked. He could be very practical at times.

"A guinea or two. But I can get money at Ilminster."

"And how do you propose to reach Ilminster with these gentlemen by way of cutting us off?"

"We'll double back as far as the crossroads," said Wilding promptly, "and strike south over Swell Hill for Hatch. If we ride hard we can do it easily, and have little fear of being followed. They'll naturally take it we have made for Bridgwater."

They acted on the suggestion there and then, Vallancey going with them; for his task was now accomplished, and he was all eager to get to Lyme to kiss the hand of the Protestant Duke. They rode hard, as Wilding had said they must, and they reached the junction of the roads before their pursuers hove in sight. Here Wilding suddenly detained them again. The road ahead of them ran straight for almost a mile, so that if they took it now they were almost sure to be seen presently by the messengers. On their right a thickly-grown coppice stretched from the road to the stream that babbled in the hollow. He gave it as his advice that they should lie hidden there until those who hunted them should have gone by. Obviously that was the only plan, and his companions instantly adopted it. They found a way through a gate into an adjacent field, and from this they gained the shelter of the trees. Trenchard, neglectful of his finery and oblivious of the ubiquitous brambles, left his horse in Vallancey's care and crept to the edge of the thicket that he might take a peep at the pursuers.

They came up very soon, six militiamen in lobster coats with yellow facings, and a sergeant, which was what Mr Trenchard might have expected. There was, however, something else that Mr Trenchard did not expect; something that afforded him considerable surprise. At the head of the party rode Sir Rowland Blake – obviously leading it – and with him was Richard Westmacott. Amongst them went a man in grey clothes, whom Mr Trenchard rightly conjectured to be the messenger riding for Whitehall. He thought with a smile of what a handful he and Wilding would have had had they waited to rob that messenger of the incriminating letter that he bore. Then he checked his smile to consider again how Sir Rowland Blake came to head that party. He abandoned the problem as the little troop swept unhesitatingly round to the left and went pounding along the road that led northwards to Bridgwater, clearly never doubting which way their quarry had sped.

As for Sir Rowland Blake's connection with this pursuit, the town-gallant had by his earnestness not only convinced Colonel Luttrell of his loyalty and devotion to King James, but had actually gone so far as to beg that he might be allowed to prove that same loyalty by leading the soldiers to the capture of those self-confessed traitors, Mr Wilding and Mr Trenchard. From his knowledge of their haunts he was confident, he assured Colonel Luttrell, that he could be of service to the King in this matter. The fierce sincerity of his purpose shone through his words; Luttrell caught the accent of hate in Sir Rowland's tense voice, and, being a shrewd man, he saw that if Mr Wilding was to be taken, an enemy would surely be the best pursuer to accomplish it. So he prevailed, and gave him the trust he sought, in spite of Albemarle's expressed reluctance. And never did bloodhound set out more relentlessly purposeful upon a scent than did Sir Rowland follow now in what he believed to be the track of this man who stood between him and Ruth Westmacott. Until Ruth was widowed, Sir Rowland's hopes of her must lie fallow; and so it was with a zest that he flung himself into the task of widowing her.

As the party passed out of view round the angle of the white road, Trenchard made his way back to Wilding to tell him what he had seen and to lay before him, for his enucleation, the problem of Blake's being the leader of it. But Wilding thought little of Blake, and cared little of what he might be the leader.

"We'll stay here," said he, "until they have passed the crest of the hill."

This, Trenchard told him, was his own purpose; for to leave their concealment earlier would be to reveal themselves to any of the troopers who might happen to glance over his shoulder.

And so they waited some ten minutes or so, and then walked their horses slowly and carefully forward through the trees towards the road. Wilding was alongside and slightly ahead of Trenchard; Vallancey followed close upon their tails. Suddenly, as Wilding was about to put his mare at the low stone wall, Trenchard leaned forward and caught his bridle.

"Ss!" he hissed. "Horses!"

And now that they halted they heard the hoof-beats clear and close at hand; the crackling of undergrowth and the rustle of the leaves through which they had thrust their passage had deafened their ears to other sounds until this moment. They checked and waited where they stood, barely screened by the few boughs that still might intervene between them and the open, not daring to advance, and not daring to retreat lest their movements should draw attention to themselves. They remained absolutely still, scarcely breathing, their only hope being that if these who came should chance to be enemies they might ride on without looking to right or left. It was so slender a hope that Wilding looked to the priming of his pistols, whilst Trenchard, who had none, loosened his sword in its scabbard. Nearer came the riders.

"There are not more than three," whispered Trenchard, who had been listening intently, and Mr Wilding nodded, but said nothing.

Another moment and the little party was abreast of those watchers; a dark brown riding-habit flashed into their line of vision, and a blue one laced with gold. At sight of the first Mr Wilding's eyelids flickered; he had recognized it for Ruth's, with whom rode Diana, whilst some twenty paces or so behind came Jerry, the groom. They were returning to Bridgwater.

They came along, looking neither to right nor to left, as the three men had hoped they would, and they were all but past, when suddenly Wilding gave his roan a touch of the spur and bounded forward. Diana's horse swerved so that it nearly threw her. Ruth, slightly ahead, reined in at once; so, too, did the groom in the rear, and so violently in his sudden fear of highwaymen that he brought his horse on to its hind legs and had it prancing and rearing madly about the road, so that he was hard put to it to keep his seat.

Ruth looked round as Mr Wilding's voice greeted her.

"Mistress Wilding," he called to her. "A moment, if I may detain you."

"You have eluded them!" she cried, entirely off her guard in her surprise at seeing him, and there echoed through her words a note of genuine gladness that almost disconcerted her husband for a moment. The next instant a crimson flush overspread her pale face, and her eyes were veiled from him, vexation in her heart at having betrayed the lively satisfaction it afforded her to see him safe when she feared him captured already or at least upon the point of capture.

She had admired him almost unconsciously for his daring at the town hall that day, when his strong calm had stood out in such strong contrast to the fluster and excitement of the men about him; of them all, indeed, it had seemed to her in those stressful moments that he was the only man, and she was – although she did not realise it – in danger of being proud of him. Then again the thing he had done. He had come deliberately to thrust his head into the lion's maw that he might save her brother. It was possible that he had done it in answer to the entreaties which she had earlier feared she had poured into deaf ears; or it was possible that he had done it spurred by his sense of right and justice, which would not permit him to allow another to suffer in his stead – however much that other might be caught in the very toils that he had prepared for Mr Wilding himself. Her admiration, then, was swelled by gratitude, and it was a compound of these that had urged her to hinder the tything-men from winning past her until he and Trenchard should have got well away.

Afterwards, when with Diana and her groom – on a horse which Sir Edward Phelips insisted upon lending them – she rode homeward from Taunton, there was Diana to keep alive the spark of kindness that glowed at last for Wilding in Ruth's breast. Miss Horton extolled his bravery, his chivalry, his nobility, and ended by expressing her envy of Ruth that she should have won such a man amongst men for her husband, and wondered what it might be that kept Ruth from claiming him for her own, as was her right. Ruth had answered little, but she had ridden very thoughtful; there was that in the past she found it hard to forgive Wilding. And yet she would now have welcomed an opportunity of thanking him for what he had done, of expressing to him something of the respect he had won in her eyes by his act of self-denunciation to save her brother. This chance it seemed was given her, for there he stood, with head bared before her; and already she thought no longer of seizing the chance, vexed as she was at having been surprised into a betrayal of feelings whose warmth she had until that moment scarce estimated.

In answer to her cry "You have eluded them!" he waved a hand towards the rising ground and the road to Bridgwater.

"They passed that way but a few moments since," said he, "and by the rate at which they were travelling they should be nearing Newton by now. In their great haste to catch me they could not pause to look for me so close at hand," he added with a smile, "and for that I am thankful."

She sat her horse and answered nothing, which threw her cousin out of all patience with her. "Come, Jerry," Diana called to the groom. "We will walk our horses up the hill."

"You are very good, madam," said Mr Wilding, and he bowed to the withers of his roan. Ruth said nothing; expressed neither approval nor disapproval of Diana's withdrawal, and the latter, with a word of greeting to Wilding, went ahead followed by Jerry, who had regained control by now of the beast he bestrode. Wilding watched them until they turned the corner, then he walked his mare slowly forward until he was alongside Ruth.

"Before I go," said he, "there is something I should like to say." His dark eyes were sombre, his manner betrayed some hesitation.

The diffidence of his tone proved startling to her by virtue of its unusualness. What might it portend, she wondered, and sought with grave eyes to read his baffling countenance; and then a wild alarm swept into her and shook her spirit in its grip; there was something of which until this moment she had not thought – something connected with the fateful matter of that letter. It had stood as a barrier between them, her buckler, her sole defence against him. It had been to her what its sting is to the bee – a thing which if once used in self-defence is self-destruction. Not, indeed, that she had used it as her sting; it had been forced from her by the machinations of Trenchard; but used it had been, and was done with; she had it no longer that with it she might hold him in defiance, and it did not occur to her that he was no longer in case to invoke the law.

Her face grew stony, a dry glitter came to her blue eyes; she cast a glance over her shoulder at Diana and her servant. Wilding observed it and read what was passing in her mind; indeed, it was not to be mistaken, no more than what is passing in the mind of the recruit who looks behind him in the act of charging. His lips half smiled.

"Of what are you afraid?" he asked her.

"I am not afraid," she answered in husky accents that belied her.

Perhaps to reassure her, perhaps, because he thought of his companions lurking in the thicket and cared not to have them for his audience, he suggested they should go a little way in the direction her cousin had taken. She wheeled her horse, and, side by side, they ambled up the dusty road.

"The thing I have to tell you," said he presently, "concerns myself."

"Does it concern me?" she asked him coldly, and her coolness was urged partly by her newborn fears, partly to counterbalance such impression as her ill-judged show of gladness at his safety might have made upon his mind. He flashed her a sidelong glance, the long white fingers of his right hand toying thoughtfully with a ringlet of the dark brown hair that fell upon the shoulders of his scarlet coat.

"Surely, madam," he answered dryly, "what concerns a man may well concern his wife."

She bowed her head, her eyes upon the road before her. "True," said she, her voice expressionless. "I had forgot."

He reined in and turned to look at her; her horse moved on a pace or two, then came to a halt, apparently of its own accord.

"I do protest," said he, "you treat me less kindly than I deserve." He urged his mare forward until he had come up with her again, and then drew rein once more. "I think that I may lay some claim to – at least – your gratitude for what I did today."

"It is my inclination to be grateful," said she. She was very wary of him. "Forgive me, if I am still mistrustful."

"But of what?" he cried, a thought impatiently.

"Of you. What ends did you seek to serve? Was it to save Richard that you came?"

"Unless you think that it was to save Blake," he said ironically. "What other ends do you conceive I could have served?" She made him no answer, and so he resumed after a pause. "I rode to Taunton to serve you for two reasons; because you asked me, and because I would have no innocent men suffer in my stead – not even though, as these men, they were but caught in their own toils, hoist with the petard they had charged for me. Beyond these two motives, I had no other thought in ruining myself."

"Ruining yourself?" she cried. Yes, it was true; but she had not thought of it until this moment; there had been so much to think of.

"Is it not ruin to be outlawed, to have a price set upon your head, as will no doubt a price be set on mine when Albemarle's messenger shall have reached Whitehall? Is it not ruin to have my lands and all I own made forfeit to the State, to find myself a beggar hunted and proscribed? Forgive me that I harass you with this catalogue of my misfortunes. You'll say, no doubt, that I have brought them upon myself by compelling you against your will to marry me."

"I'll not deny that it is in my mind," said she, and of set purpose stifled pity.

He sighed and looked at her again, but she would not meet his eye, else its whimsical expression might have intrigued her. "Can you deny my magnanimity, I wonder?" said he, and spoke almost as one amused. "All I had I sacrificed to do your will, to save your brother from the snare of his own contriving against me. I wonder do you yet realise how much I sacrificed today at Taunton! I wonder!" And he paused, looking at her and waiting for some word from her; but she had none for him.

"Clearly you do not, else I think you would show me if only a pretence of kindness." She was looking at him at last, her eyes less hard. They seemed to ask him to explain. "When you came this morning with the tale of how the tables had been turned upon your brother, of how he was caught in his own springe, and the letter found in his keeping was before the King's folk at Taunton with every appearance of having been addressed to him, and not a tittle of evidence to show that it had been meant for me, do you know what news it was you brought me?" He paused a second, looking at her from narrowing eyes. Then he answered his own question. "You brought me the news that you were mine to take whenso'er I pleased. Whilst that letter was in your hands it gave you the power to make me your obedient slave. You might blow upon me as you listed whilst you held it, and I was a vane that must turn to your blowing for my honour's sake and for the sake of the cause in which I worked. Through no rashness of mine must that letter come into the hands of the King's friends, else was I dishonoured. It was an effective barrier between us. So long as you possessed that letter you might pipe as you pleased, and I must dance to the tune you set. And then this morning what you came to tell me was that things were changed; that it was mine to call the tune. Had I had the strength to be villain, you had been mine now, and your brother and Sir Rowland might have hanged on the rope of their own weaving."

She looked at him in a startled, almost shamefaced manner. This was an aspect of the case she had not considered.

"You realise it, I see," he said, and smiled wistfully. "Then perhaps you realise why you found me so unwilling to do the thing you craved. Having treated me ungenerously, you came to cast yourself upon my generosity, asking me – though I scarcely think you understood – to beggar myself of life itself with all it held for me. God knows I make no pretence to virtue, and yet I think I had been something more than human had I not refused you and the bargain you offered – a bargain that you would never be called upon to fulfil if I did the thing you asked."

At last she interrupted him; she could bear it no longer.

"I had not thought of it!" she cried. It was a piteous wail that broke from her. "I swear I had not thought of that. I was all distraught for poor Richard's sake. Oh, Mr Wilding," she turned to him, holding out a hand; her eyes shone, filmed with moisture, "I shall have a kindness for you…all my days for your…generosity today." It was lamentably weak, far from the hot expressions which she forced it to replace.

"Yes, I was generous," he admitted. "We will move on as far as the crossroads." Again they ambled gently forward. Up the slope from the ford Diana and Jerry were slowly climbing; not another human being was in sight ahead or behind them. "After you left me," he continued, "your memory and your entreaties lingered with me. I gave the matter of our position thought, and it seemed to me that all was monstrously ill-done. I loved you, Ruth, I needed you, and you disdained me. My love was master of me. But 'neath your disdain it was transmuted oddly." He checked the passion that was vibrating in his voice and resumed after a pause, in the calm, slow tones, soft and musical, that were his own. "There is scarce the need for so much recapitulation. When the power was mine I bent you unfairly to my will; you did as much by me when the power suddenly became yours. It was a strange war between us, and I accepted its conditions. Today, when the power was mine again, mine to bring you at last to subjection, behold, I have capitulated at your bidding, and all that I held – including your own self – have I relinquished. It is perhaps fitting. Haply I am punished for having wed you before I had wooed you." Again his tone changed, it grew more cold, more matter-of-fact. "I rode this way a little while ago a hunted man, my only hope to reach home and collect what moneys and valuables I could carry, and make for the coast to find a vessel bound for Holland. I have been engaged, as you know, in stirring up rebellion to check the iniquities and persecutions that are toward in a land I love. I'll not weary you with details. Time was needed for this as for all things, and by next spring, perhaps, had matters gone well, this vineyard that so carefully and secretly I have been tending would have been, maybe, in condition to bear fruit. Even now, in the hour of my flight, I learn that others have come to force this delicate growth into sudden maturity. There! Soon ripe, soon rotten. The Duke of Monmouth has landed at Lyme this morning. I am riding to him."

"To what end?" she cried, and he saw in her face a dismay that amounted almost to fear, and he wondered was it for him.

"To place my sword at his service. Were I not encompassed by this ruin, I should not have stirred a foot in that direction – so rash, so foredoomed to failure is this invasion. As it is" – he shrugged and laughed – "it is the only hope – all forlorn though it may be – for me."

The trammels she had imposed upon her soul fell away at that like bonds of cobweb. She laid her hand upon his wrist, tears stood in her eyes; her lips quivered.

"Anthony, forgive me," she besought him. He trembled under her touch, under the caress of her voice, and at the sound of his name for the first time upon her lips.

"What have I to forgive?" he asked.

"The thing that I did in the matter of that letter."

"You poor child," said he, smiling gently upon her, "you did it in self-defence."

"Yet say that you forgive me – say it before you go!" she begged him.

He considered her gravely a moment. "To what end," he asked, "do you imagine that I have talked so much? To the end that I might show you that however I may have wronged you I have at the last made some amends; and that for the sake of this, the truest proof of penitence, I may have your forgiveness ere I go."

She was weeping softly. "It was an ill day on which we met," she sighed.

"For you – ay."

"Nay – for you."

"We'll say for both of us, then," he compromised. "See, Ruth, your cousin grows weary, and I have a couple of comrades who are no doubt impatient to be gone. It may not be good for us to tarry in these parts. Some amends I have made; but there is one crowning wrong which I have done you for which there is but one amend to make." He paused. He steadied himself before continuing. In his attempt to render his voice cold and commonplace he went near to achieving harshness. "It may be that this crack-brained rebellion of which the torch is already alight will, if it does no other good in England, at least make a widow of you. When that has come to pass, when I have thus repaired the wrong I did you, I hope you'll bear me as kindly as may be in your thought. Goodbye, my Ruth! I would you might have loved me. I sought to force it." He smiled ever so wanly. "Perhaps that was my mistake. It is an ill thing to eat one's hay while it is grass." He raised to his lips the little, gloved hand that still rested on his wrist. "God keep you, Ruth!" he murmured.

She sought to answer him, but something choked her; a sob was all she achieved. Had he caught her to him in that moment there is little doubt but that she had yielded. Perhaps he knew it; and knowing it kept the tighter rein upon desire. She was as metal molten in the crucible, to be moulded by his craftsman's hands into any pattern that he chose. But the crucible was the crucible of pity, not of love; that too he knew, and knowing it, forbore.

He dropped her hand, doffed his hat, and, wheeling his horse about, touched it with the spur and rode back towards the thicket where his friends awaited him. As he left her, she too wheeled about, as if to follow him. She strove to command her voice that she might recall him; but at that same moment Trenchard, hearing his returning hoofs, thrust out into the road with Vallancey following at his heels. The old player's harsh voice reached her where she stood, and it was querulous with impatience.

"What a plague do you mean, dallying here at such a time, Anthony?" he cried, to which Vallancey added: "In God's name, let us push on." At that she checked her impulse – it may even be that she mistrusted it. She paused, lingering undecided for an instant; then, turning her horse once more, she ambled up the slope to rejoin Diana.

Chapter 13

"PRO RELIGIONE ET LIBERTATE"

The evening was far advanced when Mr Wilding and his two companions descended to Uplyme Common from the heights whence as they rode they had commanded a clear view of the fair valley of the Axe, lying now under a thin opalescent veil of evening mist.

They had paused at Ilminster for fresh horses, and there Wilding had paid a visit to one of his agents, from whom he had procured a hundred guineas. Thence they had come south at a sharp pace, and with little said. Wilding was moody and thoughtful, filled with chagrin at this unconscionable rashness of the man upon whom all his hopes were centred. As they cantered briskly across Uplyme Common in the twilight they passed several bodies of countrymen, all heading for the town, and one group sent up a shout of "God save the Protestant Duke!" as they rode past him.

"Amen to that," muttered Mr Wilding grimly, "for I am afraid that no man can."

In the narrow lane by Hay Farm a horseman, going in the opposite direction, passed them at the gallop; but they had met several such since leaving Ilminster, for indeed the news was spreading fast, and the whole countryside was alive with messengers, some on foot and some on horseback, but all hurrying as if their lives depended on their haste.

They made their way to the Market Place where Monmouth's declaration – that remarkable manifesto from the pen of Ferguson – had been read some hours before. Thence, having ascertained where His Grace was lodged, they made their way to the George Inn.

In Coombe Street they found the crowd so dense that they could but with difficulty open out a way for their horses through the human press. Not a window but was open, and thronged with sightseers – mostly women, indeed, for the men were in the press below. On every hand resounded the cries of "A Monmouth! A Monmouth! The Protestant Religion! Religion and Liberty," which latter were the words inscribed on the standard Monmouth had set up that evening on the Church Cliffs.

In truth, Wilding was amazed at what he saw, and said as much to Trenchard. So pessimistic had been his outlook that he had almost expected to find the rebellion snuffed out by the time they reached Lyme-of-the-King. What had the authorities been about that they had permitted Monmouth to come ashore, or had Vallancey's information been wrong in the matter of the numbers that accompanied the Protestant Champion? Wilding's red coat attracted some attention. In the dusk its colour was almost all that could be discerned of it.

"Here's a militia captain for the Duke!" cried one, and others took up the cry, and if it did nothing else it opened a way for them through that solid human mass and permitted them to win through to the yard of the George Inn. They found the spacious quadrangle thronged with men, armed and unarmed, and on the steps stood a tall, well-knit, soldierly man, his hat rakishly cocked, about whom a crowd of townsmen and country fellows were pressing with insistence. At a glance Mr Wilding recognised Captain Venner – raised to the rank of colonel by Monmouth on the way from Holland.

Trenchard dismounted, and taking a distracted stable-boy by the arm, bade him see to their horses. The fellow endeavoured to swing himself free of the other's tenacious grasp.

"Let me go," he cried. "I am for the Duke!"

"And so are we, my fine rebel," answered Trenchard, holding fast.

"Let me go," the lout insisted. "I am going to enlist."

"And so you shall when you have stabled our nags. See to him, Vallancey; he is brainsick with the fumes of war."

The fellow protested, but Trenchard's way was brisk and short; and so, protesting still, he led away their cattle in the end, Vallancey going with him to see that he performed this last duty as a stable-boy ere he too became a champion militant of the Protestant Cause. Trenchard sped after Wilding, who was elbowing his way through the yokels about the steps. The glare of a newly-lighted lamp from the doorway fell full upon his long white face as he advanced, and Venner espied and recognised him.

"Mr Wilding!" he cried, and there was a glad ring in his voice, for though cobblers, tailors, deserters from the militia, pot-boys, stable-boys, and shuffling yokels had been coming in in numbers during the past few hours since the Declaration had been read, this was the first gentleman that arrived to welcome Monmouth. The soldier stretched out a hand to grasp the newcomer's. "His Grace will see you this instant, not a doubt of it." He turned and called down the passage. "Cragg!" A young man in a buff coat came forward, and to him Venner delivered Wilding and Trenchard that he might announce them to His Grace.

In the room that had been set apart for him above stairs, Monmouth still sat at table. He had just supped, with but an indifferent appetite, so fevered was he by the events of his landing. He was excited with hope – inspired by the readiness with which the men of Lyme and its neighbourhood had flocked to his banner – and fretted by anxiety that none of the gentry of the vicinity should yet have followed the example of the meaner folk, in answer to the messages dispatched at dawn from Seaton. The board at which he sat was still cumbered with some glasses and platters and vestiges of his repast. Below him on his right sat Ferguson – that prince of plotters – very busy with pen and ink, his keen face almost hidden by his great periwig; opposite were Lord Grey of Werke, and Andrew Fletcher, of Saltoun, whilst, standing at the foot of the table barely within the circle of candlelight from the branch on the polished oak, was Nathaniel Wade, the lawyer, who had fled to Holland on account of his alleged complicity in the Rye House plot and was now returned a major in the Duke's service. Erect and soldierly of figure, girt with a great sword and with the butt of a pistol protruding from his belt, he had little the air of a man whose methods of contention were forensic.

"You understand, then, Major Wade," His Grace was saying, his voice pleasant and musical. "It is decided that the guns had best be got ashore forthwith and mounted."

Wade bowed. "I shall set about it at once, your Grace. I shall not want for help. Have I your Grace's leave to go?"

Monmouth nodded, and as Wade passed out, Ensign Cragg entered to announce Mr Wilding and Mr Trenchard. The Duke rose to his feet, his glance suddenly brightening. Fletcher and Grey rose with him; Ferguson paid no heed, absorbed in his task, which he industriously continued.

"At last!" exclaimed the Duke. "Admit them, sir."

When they entered, Wilding coming first, his hat under his arm, the Duke sprang to meet him, a tall young figure, lithe and slender as a blade of steel, and of a steely strength for all his slimness. He was dressed in a suit of purple that became him marvellously well, and on his breast a star of diamonds flashed and smouldered like a thing of fire. He was of an exceeding beauty of face, wherein he mainly favoured that "bold, handsome woman" that was his mother, without, however, any of his mother's insipidity; fine eyes, a good nose, straight and slender, and a mouth which, if sensual and indicating a lack of strength, was beautifully shaped. His chin was slightly cleft, the shape of his face a delicate oval, framed now in the waving masses of his brown wig. Some likeness to his late Majesty was also discernible, in spite of the wart, out of which his uncle James made so much capital.

There was a slight flush on his cheeks, an added lustre in his eye, as he took Wilding's hand and shook it heartily before Wilding had time to kiss His Grace's. "You are late," he said, but there was no reproach in his voice. "We had looked to find you here when we came ashore. You had my letter?"

"I had not, your Grace," answered Wilding, very grave. "It was stolen."

"Stolen?" cried the Duke, and behind him Grey pressed forward, whilst even Ferguson paused in his writing to raise his piercing eyes and listen.

"It is no matter," Wilding reassured him. "Although stolen, it has but gone to Whitehall today, when it can add little to the news that is already on its way there."

The Duke laughed softly, with a flash of white teeth, and looked past Wilding at Trenchard. Some of the light faded out of his eyes. "They told me Mr Trenchard…" he began, when Wilding, half turning to his friend, explained.

"This is Mr Nicholas Trenchard – John Trenchard's cousin."

"I bid you welcome, sir," said the Duke very agreeably, "and I trust your cousin follows you."

"Alas!" said Trenchard, "my cousin is in France," and in a few brief words he related the matter of John Trenchard's home-coming on his acquittal and the trouble there had been connected with it.

The Duke received the news in silence. He had expected good support from old Speke's son-in-law. Indeed, there was a promise that when he came, John Trenchard would bring fifteen hundred men from Taunton. He took a turn in the room deep in thought, and there was a pause until Ferguson, rubbing his great Roman nose, asked suddenly had Mr Wilding seen the Declaration. Mr Wilding had not, and thereupon the plotting parson, who was proud of his composition, would have read it to him there and then, but that Grey sourly told him the matter would keep, and that they had other things to discuss with Mr Wilding.

This the Duke himself confirmed, stating that there were matters on which he would be glad to have their opinion.

He invited the newcomers to draw chairs to the table; glasses were called for, and a couple of fresh bottles of Canary went round the board. The talk was desultory for a few moments, whilst Wilding and Trenchard washed the dust from their throats; then Monmouth broke the ice by asking them bluntly what they thought of his coming thus, earlier than was at first agreed.

Wilding never hesitated in his reply. "Frankly, your Grace," said he, "I like it not at all."

Fletcher looked up sharply, his clear intelligent eyes full upon Wilding's calm face, his countenance expressing as little as did Wilding's. Ferguson seemed slightly taken aback. Grey's thick lips were twisted in a sneering smile.

"Faith," said the latter with elaborate sarcasm, "in that case it only remains for us to ship again, heave anchor and back to Holland."

"It is what I should advise," said Wilding slowly and quietly, "if I thought there was a chance of my advice being taken." He had a calm, almost apathetic way of uttering startling things which rendered them doubly startling. The sneer seemed to freeze on Lord Grey's lips; Fletcher continued to stare, but his eyes had grown more round; Ferguson scowled darkly. The Duke's boyish face – it was still very youthful despite his six-and-thirty years – expressed a wondering consternation. He looked at Wilding, and from Wilding to the others, and his glance seemed to entreat them to suggest an answer to him. It was Grey at last who took the matter up.

"You shall explain your meaning, sir, or we must hold you a traitor," he exclaimed.

"King James does that already," answered Wilding with a quiet smile.

"D'ye mean the Duke of York?" rumbled Ferguson's Scottish accent with startling suddenness, and Monmouth nodded approval of the correction. "If ye mean that bloody papist and fratricide, it were well so to speak of him. Had ye read the Declaration…"

But Fletcher cropped his speech in mid-growth. He was ever a short-tempered man, intolerant of irrelevancies.

"It were well, perhaps," said he, his accent abundantly proclaiming him a fellow-countryman of Ferguson's, "to keep to the matter before us. Mr Wilding, no doubt, will state the reasons that exist, or that he fancies may exist, for giving advice which is hardly worthy of the cause to which he stands committed."

"Aye, Fletcher," said Monmouth, "there is sense in you. Tell us what is in your mind, Mr Wilding."

"It is in my mind, your Grace, that this invasion is rash, premature, and ill-advised."

"Odds life!" cried Grey, and he swung angrily round fully to face the Duke, the nostrils of his heavy nose dilating. "Are we to listen to this milksop prattle?"

Nick Trenchard, who had hitherto been silent, cleared his throat so noisily that he drew all eyes to himself.

"Your Grace," Mr Wilding pursued, his air calm and dignified, and gathering more dignity from the circumstance that he proceeded as if there had been no interruption, "when I had the honour of conferring with you at The Hague two months ago, it was agreed that you should spend the summer in Sweden – away from politics and scheming, leaving the work of preparation to your accredited agents here. That work I have been slowly but surely pushing forward. It was not to be hurried; men of position are not to be won over in a day; men with anything to lose need some guarantee that they are not wantonly casting their possessions to the winds. By next spring, as was agreed, all would have been ready. Delay could not have hurt you. Indeed, with every day by which you delayed your coming you did good service to your cause, you strengthened its prospects of success; for every day the people's burden of oppression and persecution grows more heavy, and the people's temper more short; every day, by the methods that he is pursuing, King James brings himself into deeper hatred. This hatred is spreading. It was the business of myself and those others to help it on, until from the cottage of the ploughman the infection of anger should have spread to the mansion of the squire. Had your Grace but given me time, as I entreated you, and as you promised me, you might have marched to Whitehall with scarce the shedding of a drop of blood; had your Grace but waited until we were ready, England would have so trembled at your landing, that your uncle's throne would have toppled over 'neath the shock. As it is…" He shrugged his shoulders, sighed and spread his hands, leaving his sentence uncompleted.

Monmouth sat sobered by these sober words; the intoxication that had come to him from the little measure of success that had attended the opening of the listing on Church Cliffs deserted him now; he saw the thing stark and in its true proportions, and not even the shouting of the fold in the streets below, crying his name and acclaiming him their champion, served to lighten the gloom that Wilding's words cast like a cloud over his volatile heart. Alas, poor Monmouth! He was ever a weathercock, and even as Wilding's words seemed to strike the courage out of him, so did Grey's short contemptuous answer restore it.

"As it is, we'll thrust that throne over with our hands," said he after a moment's pause.

"Aye," cried Monmouth. "We'll do it, God helping us!"

"Our dependence and trust is in the Lord of Hosts, in Whose Name we go forth," boomed the voice of Ferguson, quoting from his precious Declaration. "The Lord will do that which seemeth good unto Him."

"An unanswerable argument," said Wilding, smiling. "But the Lord, I am told by the gentlemen of your cloth, works in His own good time, and my fears are all lest, finding us unprepared of ourselves, the Lord's good time be not yet."

"Out on ye, sir," cried Ferguson. "Ye want for reverence!"

"Common sense will serve us better at the moment," answered Wilding with a touch of sharpness. He turned to the frowning and perplexed Duke – whose mind was being tossed this way and that, like a shuttlecock upon the battledore of these men's words. "Your Grace," he said, "forgive me that I speak it if hear it you will, or forbid me to say it if your resolve is unalterable in this matter."

"It is unalterable," answered Grey for the Duke. But Monmouth gently overruled him for once.

"Nevertheless, speak by all means, Mr Wilding. Whatever you may say, you need have no fear that any of us can doubt your good intentions to ourselves."

"I thank your Grace. What I have to say is but a repetition of the first words I uttered at this table. I would urge your Grace even now to retreat."

"What? Are you mad?" It was Lord Grey who asked the impatient question.

"I doubt it's overlate for that," said Fletcher slowly.

"I am not so sure," answered Wilding. "But I am sure that to attempt it were the safer course – the surer in the end. I myself may not linger to push forward the task of stirring up the people, for I am already something more than under suspicion. But there are others who will remain to carry on the work after I have departed with your Grace, if your Grace thinks well. From the Continent by correspondence we can mature our plans. In a twelve-month things will be very different, and we can return with confidence."

Grey shrugged and turned his shoulder upon Wilding, but said no word. There was silence for some few moments. Andrew Fletcher leaned his elbow on the table and took his brow in his great bony hand. Wilding's words seemed an echo of those he himself had spoken a week or two ago, only to be overruled by Grey, who swayed the Duke more than did any other – and that he did not do so of fell purpose, and seeking deliberately to work Monmouth's ruin, no man will ever be able to say with certainty.

Ferguson rose, a tall, spare, stooping figure, and smote the board with his fist. "It is a good cause," he cried, "and God will not leave us unless we leave Him."

"Henry the Seventh landed with fewer men than did your Grace," said Grey, "and he succeeded."

"True," put in Fletcher. "But Henry the Seventh was sure of the support of not a few of the nobility, which does not seem to be our case."

Ferguson and Grey stared at him in horror; Monmouth sat biting his lip, more bewildered than thoughtful.

"O man of little faith!" roared Ferguson in a passion. "Are ye to be swayed like a straw in the wind?"

"I am no' swayed. Ye ken this was ever my own view. I feel, in my heart, that what Mr Wilding says is right. It is but what I said myself, and Colonel Matthews with me, before we embarked upon this expedition. We were in danger of ruining all by a needless precipitancy. Nay, man, never stare so," he said to Grey, "I am in it now and I am no' the man to draw back, nor do I go so far as Mr Wilding in counselling such a course. We've set our hands to the plough; let us go forward in God's name. Yet I would remind you that what Mr Wilding says is true. Had we waited until next year, we had found the usurper's throne tottering under him, and, on our landing, it would have toppled o'er of itself."

"I have said already that we'll overset it with our hands," Grey answered.

"How many hands have you?" asked a new voice, a crisp, discordant voice, much steeped in mockery. It was Nick Trenchard's.

"Have we anyone here of Mr Wilding's mind?" cried Grey, staring at him.

"I am seldom of any other," answered Trenchard.

"We shall no' want for hands," Ferguson assured him. "Had ye arrived earlier ye might have seen how readily men enlisted." He had risen and approached the window as he spoke; he pulled it open, to let in the full volume of sound that rose from the street below.

"A Monmouth! A Monmouth!" voices shouted.

Ferguson struck a theatrical posture, one long, lean arm stretched outward from the shoulder.

"Ye hear them, sirs," he cried, and there was a gleam of triumph in his eye. "That is answer enough to those who want for faith, to the feckless ones that think the Lord will abandon those that have set out to serve Him," and his glance comprehended Fletcher, Trenchard, and Wilding.

The Duke stirred in his chair, stretched a hand for the bottle and filled a glass. His mercurial spirits were rising again. He smiled at Wilding.

"I think you are answered, sir," said he; "and I hope that like Fletcher there, who shared your doubts, you will come to agree that since we have set our hands to the plough we must go forward."

"I have said that which I had it on my conscience to say. Your Grace may have found me over-ready with my counsel; at least you shall find me no less ready with my sword."

"Odso! That is better." Grey applauded, and his manner was almost pleasant.

"I never doubted it, Mr Wilding," His Grace replied; "but I should like to hear you say that you are convinced – at least in part," and he waved his hand towards the window. It was almost as if he pleaded for encouragement. In common with most men who came in contact with Wilding, he had felt the latent force of this man's nature, the strength that was hidden under that calm surface, and the acuteness of the judgment that must be wedded to it. He longed to have the word of such a man that his enterprise was not as desperate as Wilding had seemed at first to paint it. But Wilding made no concession to hopes or desires when he dealt with facts.

"Men will flock to you, no doubt; persecution has wearied many of the country-folk, and they are ready for revolt. But they are all untrained in arms; they are rustics, not soldiers. If any of the men of position were to rally round your standard they would bring the militia, and others in their train; they would bring arms, horses, and money, all of which your Grace must be sorely needing."

"They will come," answered the Duke.

"Some, no doubt," Wilding agreed; "but had it been next year, I would have answered for it that it would have been no handful had ridden in to welcome you. Scarce a gentleman of Devon or Somerset, of Dorset or Hampshire, of Wiltshire or Cheshire but would have hastened to your side."

"They will come as it is," the Duke repeated with an almost womanish insistence, persisting in believing what he hoped, all evidence apart.

The door opened and Ensign Cragg made his appearance. "May it please your Grace," he announced, "Mr Battiscomb has just arrived, and asks will your Grace receive him tonight?"

"Battiscomb!" cried the Duke. Again his cheek flushed and his eye sparkled. "Aye, in Heaven's name, show him up."

"And may the Lord refresh us with good tidings!" prayed Ferguson devoutly.

Monmouth turned to Wilding. "It is the agent I sent ahead of me from Holland to stir up the gentry from here to the Mersey."

"I know," said Wilding; "we conferred together some weeks since."

"Now you shall see how idle are your fears," the Duke promised him. And Wilding, who was better informed on that score, kept silence.

Chapter 14

HIS GRACE IN COUNSEL

Mr Christopher Battiscomb, that mild-mannered Dorchester gentleman, who, like Wade, was by vocation a lawyer, was ushered into the Duke's presence. He was dressed in black, and, like Ferguson, was almost smothered in a great periwig, which he may have adopted for purposes of disguise rather than adornment. Certainly he had none of that air of the soldier of fortune which distinguished his brother of the robe. He advanced, hat in hand, towards the table, greeting the company about it, and Wilding observed that he wore silk stockings and shoes, upon which there rested not a speck of dust. Mr Battiscomb was plainly a man who loved his ease, since on such a day he had travelled to Lyme in a coach. The lawyer bent low to kiss the Duke's hand, and scarce was that formal homage paid than questions poured upon him from Grey, from Fletcher, and from Ferguson.

"Gentlemen, gentlemen," the Duke entreated them, smiling; and remembering their manners they fell silent.

As Wilding afterwards told Trenchard, they reminded him of a parcel of saucy lacqueys who take liberties with an upstart master for whom they are wanting in respect.

"I am glad to see you, Battiscomb," said Monmouth, when quiet was restored, "and I trust I behold in you a bearer of good tidings."

The lawyer's full face was usually pale; tonight it was, in addition, solemn, and the smile that haunted his lips was a courtesy smile that expressed neither mirth nor satisfaction. He cleared his throat, as if nervous. He avoided the Duke's question as to the quality of the news he brought by answering that he had made all haste to come to Lyme upon hearing of His Grace's landing. He was surprised, he said; as well he might be, for the arrangement was that having done his work he was to return to Holland and report to Monmouth upon the feeling of the gentry.

"But your news, Battiscomb," the Duke insisted.

"Aye," put in Grey; "in Heaven's name, let us hear that."

Again there was the little nervous cough from Battiscomb. "I have scarce had time to complete my round of visits," he temporized. "Your Grace has taken us so by surprise. I... I was with Sir Walter Young at Colyton when the news of your landing came some few hours ago." His voice faltered and seemed to die away.

"Well?" cried the Duke. His brows were drawn together. Already he realised that Battiscomb's tidings were not good, else would he be hesitating less in uttering them. "Is Sir Walter with you, at least?"

"I grieve to say that he is not."

"Not?" It was Grey who spoke, and he followed the ejaculation by an oath. "Why not?"

"He is following, no doubt?" suggested Fletcher.

"We may hope, sirs," answered Battiscomb, "that in a few days – when he shall have seen the zeal of the countryside – he will be cured of his present lukewarmness." Thus, discreetly, did the man of law break the bad news he bore.

Monmouth sank back into his chair like one who has lost some of his strength. "Lukewarmness?" he repeated dully. "Sir Walter Young lukewarm!"

"Even so, your Grace – alas!" and Battiscomb sighed audibly.

Ferguson's voice boomed forth again to startle them. "The ox knoweth his owner," he cried, "the ass his master's crib; but Israel doth not know, my people doth not consider."

Grey pushed the bottle contemptuously across the table to the parson. "Drink, man, and get sense," said he, and turned aside to question Battiscomb touching others on the neighbourhood upon whom they had depended.

"What of Sir Francis Rolles?" he inquired.

Battiscomb answered the question, addressing himself to the Duke.

"Alas! Sir Francis, no doubt, would have been faithful to your Grace, but, unfortunately, Sir Francis is in prison already."

Deeper grew Monmouth's frown; his fingers drummed the table absently. Fletcher poured himself wine, his face inscrutable. Grey threw one leg over the other and in a voice that was carefully careless he inquired, "And what of Sidney Clifford?"

"He is considering," said Battiscomb. "I was to have seen him again at the end of the month; meanwhile, he would take no resolve."

"Lord Gervase Scoresby?" questioned Grey, carelessly.

Battiscomb half turned to him, then faced the Duke again as he made answer, "Mr Wilding, there, can tell you more concerning Lord Gervase."

All eyes swept round to Wilding, who sat in silence, listening; Monmouth's were laden with inquiry and some anxiety. Wilding shook his head slowly, sadly. "You must not depend upon him," he answered; "Lord Gervase was not yet ripe. A little longer and I think I must have won him for your Grace."

"Heaven help us!" exclaimed the Duke in petulant vexation. "Is no one coming in?"

Ferguson swung a hand towards the still open window, drawing attention to the sounds without.

"Does your Grace not hear, that ye can ask?" he cried, almost reproachfully; but they scarce heeded him, for Grey was inquiring if

Mr Strode might be depended upon to join, and that was a matter that claimed the greater attention.

"I think," said Battiscomb, "that he might have been depended upon."

"Might have been?" questioned Fletcher, speaking now for the first time since Battiscomb's arrival.

"Like Sir Francis Rolles, he is in prison," the lawyer explained.

Monmouth leaned forward, and his young face looked careworn now; he thrust a slender hand under the brown curls upon his brow. "Will you tell us, Mr Battiscomb, upon what friends you think that we may count?" he said.

Battiscomb pursed his lips a second, pondering. "I think," said he, "that you may count upon Mr Legge and Mr Hooper, and possibly upon Colonel Churchill, though I cannot say what following they will bring, if any. Mr Trenchard, upon whom we counted for fifteen hundred men of Taunton, has been obliged to fly the country to escape arrest."

"We have heard that from Mr Trenchard's cousin," answered the Duke. "What of Prideaux, of Ford? Is he lukewarm?"

"I was unable to elicit a definite promise from him. But he was favourably disposed to your Grace."

His Grace made a gesture that seemed to dismiss Prideaux from their calculations. "And Mr Hucker, of Taunton?"

Battiscomb's manner grew yet more ill at ease. "Mr Hucker himself, I am sure, would place his sword at your disposal. But his brother is a red-hot Tory."

"Well, well," sighed the Duke, "I take it we must not make certain of Mr Hucker. Are there any others besides Legge and Hooper upon whom you think that we may reckon?"

"Lord Wiltshire, perhaps," said Battiscomb, but with a lack of assurance.

"A plague of perhaps!" exclaimed Monmouth, growing irritable; "I want you to name the men of whom you are certain."

Battiscomb stood silent for a moment, pondering. He looked almost foolish, like a schoolboy who hesitates to confess his ignorance of the answer to a question set him. Fletcher swung round, his grey eyes flashing angrily, his accent more Scottish than ever.

"Is it that ye're certain o' none, Mr Battiscomb?" he exclaimed.

"Indeed," said Battiscomb, "I think we may be fairly certain of Mr Legge and Mr Hooper."

"And of none besides?" questioned Fletcher again. "Be these the only representatives of the flower of England's nobility that is to flock to the banner of the cause of England's freedom and religion?" Scorn was stamped on every word of his question.

Battiscomb spread his hands, raised his brows, and said nothing.

"The Lord knows I do not say it exulting," said Fletcher; "but I told your Grace yours was hardly the case of Henry the Seventh, as my Lord Grey would have you believe."

"We shall see," snapped Grey, scowling at the Scot. "The people are coming in hundreds – aye, in thousands – the gentry will follow; they must."

"Make not too sure, your Grace – oh, make not too sure," Wilding besought the Duke. "As I have said, these hinds have nothing to lose but their lives."

"Faith, can a man lose more?" asked Grey contemptuously. He disliked Wilding by instinct, which was but a reciprocation of the feeling with which Wilding was inspired by him.

"I think he can," said Mr Wilding quietly. "A man may lose honour, he may plunge his family into ruin. These are things of more weight with a gentleman than life."

"Odds death!" blazed Grey, giving a free rein to his dislike of this calm gentleman. "Do you suggest that a man's honour is imperilled in His Grace's service?"

"I suggest nothing," answered Wilding, unmoved. "What I think, I state. If I thought a man's honour imperilled in this service, you would not see me at this table now. I can make you no more convincing answer."

Grey laughed unpleasantly, and Wilding, a faint tinge on his cheekbones, measured him with a stern, intrepid look before which his lordship's shifty glance was observed to fall. Wilding's eye, having achieved that much, passed from him to the Duke, and its expression softened.

"Your Grace sees," said he, "how well founded were the fears I expressed that your coming has been premature."

"In God's name, what would you have me do?" cried the Duke, and petulance made his voice unsteady.

Mr Wilding rose, moved out of his habitual calm by the earnestness that pervaded him. "It is not for me to say again what I would have your Grace do. Your Grace has heard my views, and those of these gentlemen. It is for your Grace to decide."

"You mean whether I will go forward with this thing? What alternative have I?"

"No alternative," put in Grey with finality. "Nor is alternative needed. We'll carry this through in spite of timorous folk and birds of ill-omen that croak to affright us."

"Our service is the service of the Lord," cried Ferguson, returning from the window, in the embrasure of which he had been standing; "the Lord cannot but destine it to prevail."

"Ye said so before," quoth Fletcher testily. "We need here men, money, and weapons – not divinity."

"You are plainly infected with Mr Wilding's disease," sneered Grey.

"Ford," cried the Duke, who saw Wilding's eyes flash fire; "you go too fast. Mr Wilding, you will not heed his lordship."

"I should not be likely to do so, your Grace," answered Wilding, who had resumed his seat.

"What shall that mean?" quoth Grey, leaping to his feet.

"Make it quite clear to him, Tony," whispered Trenchard coaxingly; but Mr Wilding was not as lost as were these immediate followers of the Duke's to all sense of the respect due to His Grace.

"I think," said Wilding quietly, "that you have forgotten something."

"Forgotten what?" bawled Grey.

"His Grace's presence."

His lordship turned crimson, his anger swelled to think that the very terms of the rebuke precluded his allowing his feelings a free rein.

Monmouth leaned forward. "Sit down," he said to Grey, and Grey, so lately called to the respect he owed His Grace, obeyed him. "You will both promise me that this affair shall go no further. I know you will do it if I ask you, particularly when you remember how few are the followers upon whom I may depend. I am not in case to lose either of you through foolish words uttered in a heat which, in both your hearts, is born, I know, of your loyalty to me."

Grey's coarse, elderly face took on a sulky look, his heavy lips were pouted, his glance sullen. Mr Wilding, on the contrary, smiled across the table.

"For my part I very gladly give your Grace the undertaking," said he, and took care not to observe the sneer that altered the line of Lord Grey's lips. His lordship, too, was forced to give the same pledge, and he followed it up by inveighing sturdily against the suggestion that they should retreat.

"I do protest," he exclaimed, "that those who advise your Grace to do anything but go forward boldly now are evil counsellors. If you put back to Holland, you may leave every hope behind. There will be no second coming for you. Your influence will have been dissipated. Men will not trust you another time. I do not think that even Mr Wilding can deny the truth of this."

"I am by no means sure," said Wilding, and Fletcher looked at him with eyes that were full of understanding. This sturdy Scot, the only soldier worthy of the name in the Duke's following, who, ever since the project had first been mooted, had held out against it, counselling delay, was in sympathy with Mr Wilding.

Monmouth rose, his face anxious, his voice fretful. "There can be no retreat for me, gentlemen. Though many that were depended upon are not here to join us, yet let us remember that Heaven is on our side and that we are come to fight in the sacred cause of religion and a nation's emancipation from the thraldom of popery, oppression, and superstition. Let this dispel such doubts as yet may linger in our minds."

His words had a brave sound, but, when analysed, they but formed a paraphrase of what Grey and Ferguson had said. It was his destiny to be a mere echo of the minds of other men, just as he was now the tool of these two, one of whom plotted, seemingly, because plotting was a disease that had got into his blood; the other for reasons that may have been of ambition or of revenge – no man will ever know for certain.

In the chamber they shared, Trenchard and Mr Wilding reviewed that night the scene so lately enacted, in which one had taken an active part, the other been little more than a spectator. Trenchard had come from the Duke's presence entirely out of conceit with Monmouth and his cause, contemptuous of Ferguson, angry with Grey, and indifferent towards Fletcher.

"I am committed, and I'll not draw back," said he; "but I tell you, Anthony, my heart is not confederate with my hand in this. Bah!" he rallied. "We serve a man of straw, a Perkin, a very pope of a fellow."

Mr Wilding sighed. "He's scarce the man for such an undertaking," said he. "I fear we have been misled."

Trenchard was drawing off his boots. He paused in the act. "Ay," said he, "misled by our blindness. What else, after all, should we have expected of him?" he cried contemptuously. "The Cause is good; but its leader – Pshaw! Would you have such a puppet as that on the throne of England?"

"He does not aim so high."

"Be not so sure. We shall hear more of the black box anon, and of the marriage certificate it contains. 'Twould not surprise me if they were to produce forgeries of the one and the other to prove his father's marriage to Lucy Walters. Anthony, Anthony! To what a business are we wedded?"

Mr Wilding, already abed, turned impatiently. "Things cried aloud to be redressed; a leader was necessary, and none other offered. That is the whole story. But our chance is slender, and it might have been great."

"That rake-hell, Ford Lord Grey has made it so," grumbled Trenchard, busy with his stockings. "This sudden coming is his work. You heard what Fletcher said – how he opposed it when first it was urged." He paused, and looked up suddenly. "Blister me!" he cried, "is it his lordship's purpose, think you, to work the ruin of Monmouth?"

"What are you saying, Nick?"

"There are certain rumours current touching His Grace and Lady Grey. A man like Grey might well resort to some such scheme of vengeance."

"Get to sleep, Nick," said Wilding, yawning; "you are dreaming already. Such a plan would be over-elaborate for his lordship's mind. It would ask a villainy parallel with your own."

Trenchard climbed into bed, and settled himself under the coverlet.

"Maybe," said he, "and maybe not; but I think that were it not for that cursed business of the letter Richard Westmacott stole from us, I should be going my ways tomorrow and leaving His Grace of Monmouth to go his."

"Aye, and I'd go with you," answered Wilding. "I've little taste for suicide; but we are in it now."

" 'Twas a sad pity you meddled this morning in that affair at Taunton," mused Trenchard wistfully. "A sadder pity you were bitten with a taste for matrimony," he added thoughtfully, and blew out the rushlight.

Chapter 15

LYME OF THE KING

On the next day, which was Friday, the country-folk continued to come in, and by evening Monmouth's forces amounted to a thousand foot and a hundred and fifty horse. The men were armed as fast as they were enrolled, and scarce a field or quiet avenue in the district but resounded to the tramp of feet, the rattle of weapons, and the sharp orders of the officers who, by drilling, were converting this raw material into soldiers. On the Saturday the rally to the Duke's standard was such that Monmouth threw off at last the gloomy forebodings that had burdened his soul since that meeting on Thursday night. Wade, Holmes, Foulkes, and Fox were able to set about forming the first four regiments – the Duke's, and the Green, the White, and the Yellow. Monmouth's spirits continued to rise, for he had been joined by now by Legge and Hooper – the two upon whom Battiscomb had counted – and by Colonel Joshua Churchill, of whom Battiscomb had been less certain. Colonel Matthews brought news that Lord Wiltshire and the gentlemen of Hampshire might be expected if they could force their way through Albemarle's Militia, which was already closing round Lyme.

Long before evening, willing fellows were being turned away in hundreds for lack of weapons. In spite of Monmonth's big talk on landing, and of the rumour that had gone out, that he could arm thirty thousand men, his stock of arms was exhausted by a mere fifteen hundred. Trenchard, who now held a major's rank in the horse attached to the Duke's own regiment, was loud in his scorn of this state of things; Mr Wilding was sad, and his depression again spread to the Duke after a few words had passed between them towards evening. Fletcher was for heroic measures. He looked only ahead now, like the good soldier that he was; and, already, he began to suggest a bold dash for Exeter, for weapons, horses, and possibly the Militia as well, for they had ample evidence that the men composing it might easily be induced to desert to the Duke's side.

The suggestion was one that instantly received Mr Wilding's heartiest approval. It seemed to fill him suddenly with hope, and he spoke of it, indeed, as an inspiration which, if acted upon, might yet save the situation. The Duke was undecided as ever; he was too much troubled weighing the chances for and against, and he would decide upon nothing until he had consulted Grey and the others. He would summon a Council that night, he promised, and the matter should be considered.

But that Council was never to be called, for Andrew Fletcher's association with the rebellion was drawing rapidly to its close, and there was that to happen in the next few hours which should counteract all the encouragement with which the Duke had been fortified that day. Towards evening little Heywood Dare, the Taunton goldsmith, who had landed at Seaton and gone out with the news of the Duke's arrival, rode into Lyme with forty horse, mounted, himself, upon a beautiful charger which was destined to be the undoing of him.

News came, too, that the Dorset Militia were at Bridport, eight miles away, whereupon Wilding and Fletcher postponed all further suggestion of the dash for Exeter, proposing that in the meantime a night attack upon Bridport might result well. For once Lord Grey was in agreement with them, and so the matter was decided. Fletcher went down to arm and mount, and all the world knows the story of the foolish, ill-fated quarrel which robbed Monmouth of two of his most valued adherents. By ill-luck the Scot's eyes lighted upon the fine horse that Dare had brought from Ford Abbey. It occurred to him that nothing could be more fitting than that the best man should sit upon the best horse, and he forthwith led the beast from the stables and was about to mount, when Dare came forth to catch him in the very act. The goldsmith was a rude, peppery fellow, who did not mince his words.

"What a plague are you doing with that horse?" he cried.

Fletcher paused, one foot in the stirrup, and looked the fellow up and down. "I am mounting it," said he, and proceeded to do as he said. But Dare caught him by the tails of his coat and brought him back to earth.

"You are making a mistake, Mr Fletcher," he cried angrily. "That horse is mine."

Fletcher, whose temper was by no means of the most peaceful, kept himself with difficulty in hand at the indignity Dare offered him. "Yours?" quoth he.

"Ay, mine, I brought it from Ford Abbey myself."

"For the Duke's service," Fletcher reminded him.

"For my own, sir; for my own I would have you know," and brushing the Scot aside, he caught the bridle, and sought to wrench it from Fletcher's hand. But Fletcher maintained his hold.

"Softly, Mr Dare," said he, "Ye're a trifle o'er-true to your name, as you once told his late Majesty yourself."

"Take your hands from my horse," Dare shouted, very angry.

Several loiterers in the yard gathered round to watch the scene, culling diversion from it and speculating upon the conclusion it might have. One rash young fellow offered audibly to lay ten to one that Paymaster Dare would have the best of the argument.

Dare overheard, and was spurred on.

"I will, by God!" he answered. "Come, Mr Fletcher!" And he shook the bridle again.

There was a dull flush showing through the tan of Fletcher's skin. "Mr Dare," said he, "this horse is no more yours than mine. It is the Duke's, and I, as one o' the leaders, claim it in the Duke's service."

"Ay, sir," cried an onlooker, encouraging Fletcher, and did the mischief. It so goaded Dare to have his antagonist in this trifling matter supported that he utterly lost his head.

"I have said the horse is mine, and I repeat it. Let go the bridle – let it go!" Still, Fletcher, striving hard to keep his calm, clung to the reins. "Let it go, you damned, thieving Scot!" screamed Dare in a fury, and struck Fletcher with his whip.

It was unfortunate for them both that he should have had that switch in his hand at such a time, but more unfortunate still was it that Fletcher should have had a pistol in his belt. The Scot dropped the bridle at last; dropped it to pluck forth the weapon.

"Hi! I did not…" began Dare, who had stood appalled by what he had done in the second or two that had passed since he had delivered the blow. The rest of his sentence was drowned in the report of Fletcher's pistol, and Dare dropped dead on the rough cobbles of the yard.

Ferguson has left it on record – and, presumably, he had Fletcher's word for it – that it was no part of the Scot's intent to do Mr Dare a mischief. He had but drawn the pistol to intimidate him into better manners, but in his haste he accidentally pulled the trigger.

However that may be, there was Dare as dead as the stones on which he lay, and Fletcher with a smoking pistol in his hand.

After that all was confusion. Fletcher was seized by those who had witnessed the deed; there was none thought it an accident; indeed, they were all ready enough to say that Fletcher had received excessive provocation. He was haled to the presence of the Duke, with whom were Grey and Wilding at the time; and old Dare's son – an ensign in Goodenough's company – came clamouring for vengeance backed by such goodly numbers that the distraught Duke was forced to show at least the outward seeming of it.

Wilding, who knew the value of this Scottish soldier of fortune who had seen so much service, strenuously urged his enlargement. It was not a time to let the fortunes of a cause suffer through such an act as this, deplorable though it might be. The evidence showed that Fletcher had been provoked; he had been struck, a thing that might well justify the anger in the heat of which he had done this thing. Grey was stolid and silent, saying nothing either for or against the man who had divided with him under the Duke the honours of the supreme command.

Monmouth, white and horror-stricken, sat and listened first to Wilding, then to Dare, and lastly to Fletcher himself. But it was young Dare – Dare and his followers, who prevailed. They were too numerous and turbulent, and they must at all costs be conciliated, or there was no telling to what extremes they might not go. And so there was an end to the share of Andrew Fletcher of Saltoun in this undertaking – the end of the only man who was of any capacity to pilot it through the troubled waters that lay before it. Monmouth placed him under arrest and sent him aboard the frigate again, ordering her captain to sail at once. That was the utmost Monmouth could do to save him.

Wilding continued to plead with the Duke after Fletcher's removal, and to such good purpose that at last Monmouth determined that Fletcher should rejoin them later, when the affair should have blown over, and he sent word accordingly to the Scot. Even in this there were manifestations of antagonism between Mr Wilding and Lord Grey, and it almost seemed enough that Wilding should suggest a course for Lord Grey instantly to oppose it.

The effects of Fletcher's removal were not long in following. On the morrow came the Bridport affair, and Grey's shameful conduct when, had he stood his ground, victory must have been assured the Duke's forces instead of just that honourable retreat by which Colonel Wade so gallantly saved the situation. Mr Wilding did not mince his words in putting it that Grey had run away.

In his room at the George Inn, Monmouth, deeply distressed, asked Wilding and Colonel Matthews what action he should take in the matter – how deal with Grey.

"There is no other general in Europe would ask that, your Grace," answered Matthews gravely, and Mr Wilding added without an instant's hesitation that His Grace's course was plain.

"It would be an unwise thing to expose the troops to the chance of more such happenings."

Monmouth dismissed them and sent for Grey, and he seemed resolved to deal with him as he deserved. Yet an hour later, when Wilding, Matthews, Wade, and the others were ordered to attend the Duke in council, there was his lordship seemingly on as good terms as ever with His Grace.

They were assembled to discuss the next step which it might be advisable to take, for the militia was closing in around them, and to remain longer in Lyme would be to be caught there as in a trap. It was Grey who advanced the first suggestion, his assurance no whit abated by the shameful thing that had befallen, by the cowardice which he had betrayed.

"That we must quit Lyme we are all agreed," said he. "I would propose that your Grace marches north to Gloucester, where our Cheshire friends will assemble to meet us."

Colonel Matthews reminded the Duke of Andrew Fletcher's proposal that they should make a raid upon Exeter with a view to seizing arms, of which they stood so sorely in need. This Mr Wilding was quick to support.

"Not only that, your Grace," he said, "but I am confident that with very little inducement the greater portion of the militia will desert to us as soon as we appear."

"What assurance can you give of that?" asked Grey, his heavy lip protruded.

"I take it," said Mr Wilding, "that in such matters no man can give an assurance of anything. I speak with knowledge of the country and the folk from which the militia is enlisted. I offer it as my opinion that the militia is favourably disposed to your Grace. I can do no more."

"If Mr Wilding says so, your Grace," put in Matthews, "I have no doubt he has sound reasons upon which to base his opinion."

"No doubt," said Monmouth. "Indeed, I had already thought of the step that you suggest, Colonel Matthews, and what Mr Wilding says causes me to look upon it still more favourably."

Grey frowned. "Consider, your Grace," he said earnestly, "that you are in no case to fight at present."

"What fighting do you suggest there would be?" asked the Duke.

"There is Albemarle between us and Exeter."

"But with the militia," Wilding reminded him; "and if the militia deserts him for your Grace, in what case will Albemarle find himself?"

"And if the militia does not desert? If you should be proven wrong, sir? What then? What then?" asked Grey.

"Aye – true – what then, Mr Wilding?" quoth the Duke, already wavering. Wilding considered a moment, all eyes upon him. "Even then," said he presently, "I do maintain that in this dash for Exeter lies your Grace's greatest chance of success. We can deliver battle if need be. Already we are three thousand strong…"

Grey interrupted him rudely. "Nay," he insisted. "You must not presume upon that. We are not yet fit to fight. It is His Grace's business at present to drill and discipline his troops and induce more friends to join him."

"Already we are turning men away because we have no weapons to put into their hands," Wilding reminded them, and a murmur of approval ran round, which but served to anger Grey the more, to render more obstinate his opposition.

"But all that come in are not unprovided," was his lordship's retort. "There are the Hampshire gentry and their friends. They will come armed, and so will others if we have patience."

"Aye," said Wilding, "and if you have patience enough there will be troops the Parliament will send against us. They, too, will be armed, I can assure your lordship."

"In God's name let us keep from wrangling," the Duke besought them. "It is difficult enough to determine for the best. If the dash to Exeter were successful…"

"It cannot be," Grey interrupted again. The liberties he took with Monmouth and which Monmouth permitted him might well be a source of wonder to all who heard them. Monmouth paused now in his interrupted speech and looked about him a trifle wearily.

"It seems idle to insist," said Mr Wilding; "such is the temper of your Grace's counsellors, that we get no further than contradictions." Grey's bold eyes were upon Wilding as he spoke. "I would remind your Grace, and I am sure that many present will agree with me, that in a desperate enterprise a sudden unexpected movement will often strike terror."

"That is true," said Monmouth, but apparently without enthusiasm, and having approved what was urged on one side, he looked at Grey, as if waiting to hear what might be said on the other. His decision was pitiful – tragical, indeed, in the leader of so bold an enterprise.

"We should do better, I think," said Grey, "to deal with the facts as we know them."

"It is what I am endeavouring to do, your Grace," protested Wilding, a note of despair in his voice. "Perhaps some other gentleman will put forward better counsel than mine."

"Aye! In Heaven's name let us hope so," snorted Grey; and Monmouth, catching the sudden flash of Mr Wilding's eye, set a hand upon his lordship's arm as if to urge him to be gentler. But he continued, "When men talk of striking terror by sudden movements they build on air."

"I had hardly thought to hear that from your lordship," said Mr Wilding, and he permitted himself that tight-lipped smile that gave his face so wicked a look.

"And why not?" asked Grey, stupidly unsuspicious.

"Because I had thought you might have concluded otherwise from your own experience at Bridport this morning."

Grey got angrily to his feet, rage and shame flushing his face, and it needed Ferguson and the Duke to restore him to some semblance of calm. Indeed, it may well be that it was to complete this that His Grace decided there and then that they should follow Grey's advice and go by way of Taunton, Bridgwater, and Bristol to Gloucester. He was like all weak men, of conspicuous mental short-sightedness. The matter of the moment was ever of greater importance to him than any result that might attend it in the future.

He insisted that Wilding and Grey should shake hands before the breaking up of that most astounding council, and as he had done last night, he now again imposed upon them his commands that they must not allow this matter to go further.

Mr Wilding paved the way for peace by making an apology within limitations.

"If, in my zeal to serve your Grace to the best of my ability, I have said that which Lord Grey thinks fit to resent, I would bid him consider my motive rather than my actual words."

But when all had gone save Ferguson, the chaplain approached the preoccupied and distressed Duke with counsel that Mr Wilding should be sent away from the army.

"Else there'll be trouble 'twixt him and Grey," the plotting parson foretold. "We'll be having a repetition of the unfortunate Fletcher and Dare affair, and I think that has cost your Grace enough already."

"Do you suggest that I dismiss Wilding?" cried the Duke. "You know his influence, and the bad impression his removal would leave."

Ferguson stroked his long lean jaw. "No, no," said he; "all I suggest is that you find Mr Wilding work to do elsewhere."

"Elsewhere?" the Duke questioned. "Where else?"

"I have thought of that too. Send him to London to see Danvers and to stir up your friends there. And," he added, lowering his voice, "give him discretion to see Sunderland if he thinks well."

The proposition pleased Monmouth, and it seemed to please Mr Wilding no less when, having sent for him, the Duke communicated it to him in Ferguson's presence.

Upon this mission Mr Wilding set out that very night, leaving Nick Trenchard in despair at being separated from him at a time when there seemed to be every chance that such a separation might be eternal.

Monmouth and Ferguson may have conceived they did a wise thing in removing a man who was instinctively spoiling for a little swordplay with my Lord Grey. It is odds that had he remained, the brewing storm between the pair would have come to a head. Had it done so, it is more than likely, from what we know of Mr Wilding's accomplishments, that he had given Lord Grey his quietus. And had that happened, it is to be inferred from history that it is possible the Duke of Monmouth's rebellion might have had a less disastrous issue.

Chapter 16

PLOTS AND PLOTTERS

Mr Wilding left Monmouth's army at Lyme on Sunday, the 14th of June, and rejoined it at Bridgwater exactly three weeks later.

In the meanwhile a good deal had happened, yet the happenings on every hand had fallen far short of the expectations aroused in Mr Wilding's mind, now by one circumstance, now by another. In reaching London he had experienced no difficulty. Men travelling in that direction were not subjected to the scrutiny that fell to the share of those travelling from it towards the West, or rather, to the scrutiny ordained by the Government; for Wilding had more than one opportunity of observing how very lax and indifferent were the constables and tything-men – particularly in Somerset and Wiltshire – in the performance of this duty. Wayfarers were questioned as a matter of form, but in no case did Wilding hear of anyone being detained upon suspicion. This was calculated to raise his drooping hopes, pointing as it did to the general favouring of Monmouth that was toward. He grew less despondent on the score of the Duke's possible ultimate success, and he came to hope that the efforts he went to exert would not be fruitless.

But rude were the disappointments that awaited him in town. London, like the rest of the country, was not ready. There were not wanting men who favoured Monmouth; but no rising had been organized, and the Duke's partisans were not disposed to rashness.

Wilding lodged at Covent Garden, in a house recommended to him by Colonel Danvers, and there – an outlaw himself – he threw himself with a will into his task. He heard of the burning of Monmouth's Declaration by the common hangman at the Royal Exchange, and of the bill passed by the Commons to make it treason for any to assert that Lucy Walters was married to the late King. He attended meetings at the "Bull's Head," in Bishopsgate, where he met Disney and Danvers, Payton and Lock; but though they talked and argued at prodigious length, they did naught besides. Danvers, who was their hope in town, definitely refused to have a hand in anything that was not properly organized, and in common with the others urged that they should wait until Cheshire had risen, as was reported that it must.

Meanwhile, troops had gone West under Kirke and Churchill, and the Parliament had voted nearly half a million for the putting down of the rebellion. London was flung into a fever of excitement by the news that was reaching it. The position was not quite as – before coming over from Holland – Monmouth's advisers had represented that it would be. They had thought that, out of fear of tumults about his own person, King James would have been compelled to keep near him what troops he had, sparing none to be sent against Monmouth. This, King James had not done; he had all but emptied London of soldiery, and, considering the general disaffection, no moment could have been more favourable than this for a rising in London itself. The confusion that must have resulted from the recalling of troops would have given Monmouth not only a mighty grip of the West, but would have heartened those who – like Sunderland himself – were sitting on the wall, to declare themselves for the Protestant Champion. This Wilding saw, and almost frenziedly did he urge it upon Danvers that all that London needed at the moment was a resolute leader. But the Colonel still held back; indeed, he had neither truth nor valour; he was timid, and used deceit to mask his timidity; he urged frivolous reasons for inaction, and when Wilding waxed impatient with him, he suggested that Wilding himself should head the rising if he were so confident of its success. And Wilding would have done it but that, being unknown in London, he had no reason to suppose that men would flock to him if he raised the Duke's banner.

Later, when the excitement grew and rumours ran through town that Monmouth had now a following of twenty thousand men and that the King's forces were falling back before him, and discontent was rife at the commissioning of Catholic lords to levy troops, Wilding again pressed the matter upon Danvers. Surely no moment could be more propitious. But again he received the same answer, that Danvers had lacked time to organise matters sufficiently; that the Duke's coming had taken him by surprise.

Lastly came the news that Monmouth had been crowned at Taunton amid the wildest enthusiasm, and that there were now in England two men each of whom called himself King James the Second. This was the excuse that Danvers needed to be rid of a business he had not the courage to transact to a finish. He swore that he washed his hands of Monmouth's affairs; that the latter had broke faith with him and the promise he had made him in having himself proclaimed King. He protested that Monmouth had done ill, and prophesied that his act would alienate from him the numerous republicans who, like Danvers, had hitherto looked to him for the country's salvation. Wilding himself was appalled at the news – for Monmouth was indeed going further than men had been given to understand. Nevertheless, for his own sake, in very self-defence now, if out of no motives of loyalty to the Duke, he must urge forward the fortunes of this man. He had high words with Danvers, and the two might have quarrelled before long, but for the sudden arrest of Disney, which threw Danvers into such a panic that he fled incontinently, abandoning in body, as he already appeared to have abandoned in spirit, the Monmouth Cause.

The arrest of Disney struck a chill into Wilding. From his lodging at Covent Garden he had communicated cautiously with Sunderland a few days after his arrival, building upon certain information he had received from the Duke at parting as to Sunderland's attachment to the Cause. He had carefully chosen his moment for making this communication, having a certain innate mistrust of a man who so obviously as Sunderland was running with the hare and hunting with the hounds. He had sent a letter to the Secretary of State when London was agog with the Axminster affair, and the tale – of which Sir Edward Phelips wrote to Colonel Berkeley as "the shamefullest story that you ever heard" – of how Albemarle's forces and the Somerset Militia had run before Monmouth in spite of their own overwhelming numbers. This promised ill for James, particularly when it was perceived – as perceived it was – that this running away was not all cowardice, not all "the shamefullest story" that Phelips accounted it. It was an expression of good will towards Monmouth on the part of the militia of the West, and it was confidently expected that the next news would be that these men who had decamped before him would presently be found to have ranged themselves under his banner.

Sunderland had given no sign that he had received Wilding's communication. And Wilding drew his own contemptuous conclusions of the Secretary of State's cautious policy. It was a fortnight later – when London was settling down again from the diversion of excitement created by the news of Argyle's defeat in Scotland – before Mr Wilding attempted to approach Sunderland again. He awaited a favourable opportunity, and this he had when London was thrown into consternation by the alarming news of the Duke of Somerset's urgent demand for reinforcements. Unless he had them, he declared, the whole country was lost, as he could not get the militia to stand, whilst Lord Stawell's regiment were all fled and mostly gone over to the rebels at Bridgwater.

This was grave news, but it was followed in a few days by graver. The affair at Philips Norton was exaggerated by report into a wholesale defeat of the loyal army, and it was reported – on, apparently, such good authority that it received credence in quarters that might have waited for official news – that the Duke of Albemarle had been slain by the militia which had mutinied and deserted to Monmouth.

It was while this news was going round that Sunderland – in a moment of panic – at last vouchsafed an answer to Mr Wilding's letters, and he vouchsafed it in person, just as Wilding – particularly since Disney's arrest – was beginning to lose all hope. He came one evening to Mr Wilding's lodgings in Covent Garden, unattended and closely muffled, and he remained closeted with the Duke's ambassador for nigh upon an hour, at the end of which he entrusted Mr Wilding with a letter for the Duke, very brief but entirely to the point, expressing him Monmouth's most devoted servant.

"You may well judge, sir," he had said at parting, "that this is not such a letter as I should entrust to any man."

Mr Wilding had bowed gravely, and gravely he had expressed himself sensible of the exceptional honour his lordship did him by such a trust.

"And I depend upon you, sir, as you are a man of honour, to take such measures as will ensure against its falling into any but the hands for which it is intended."

"As I am a man of honour, you may depend upon me," Mr Wilding solemnly promised. "Will your lordship give me three lines above your signature that will save me from molestation; thus you will facilitate the preservation of this letter."

"I had already thought of that," was Sunderland's answer, and he placed before Mr Wilding three lines of writing signed and sealed which enjoined all, straitly, in the King's name to suffer the bearer to pass and repass and to offer him no hindrance.

On that they shook hands and parted, Sunderland to return to Whitehall and his obedience to the King James whom he was ready to betray as soon as he saw profit for himself in the act, Mr Wilding to return to Somerset to the King James in whom his faith was scant indeed, but with whom his fortunes were irrevocably bound up.

Meanwhile, Monmouth was back in Bridgwater, his second occupation of which town was not being looked upon with unmixed favour. The inhabitants had suffered enough already from his first visit; his return there, after the Philips Norton affair – of which such grossly exaggerated reports had reached London, and which, in point of fact, had been little better than a drawn battle – had been looked upon with dread by some, with disfavour by others, and with dismay by not a few, who viewed in this an augury of failure.

Now Sir Rowland Blake, who since his pursuit of Mr Wilding and Trenchard on the occasion of their flight from Taunton had – in spite of his failure on that occasion – been more or less in the service of Albemarle and the loyal army, saw in this indisposition towards Monmouth of so many of Bridgwater's inhabitants great possibilities of profit to himself.

He was at Lupton House, the guest of his friend Richard Westmacott, and the open suitor of Ruth, entirely ignoring the circumstance that she was nominally the wife of Mr Wilding – this to the infinite chagrin of Miss Horton, who saw all her scheming likely to go for nothing.

In his heart of hearts it was a matter of not the slightest consequence to Sir Rowland whether James Stuart or James Scott occupied the throne of England. His own affairs gave him more than enough to think of, and these disturbances in the West were very welcome to him, since they rendered difficult any attempt to trace him on the part of his London creditors. It happens, however, very commonly that enmity to an individual will lead to enmity to the cause which that individual espouses. Thus may it have been with Sir Rowland. His hatred of Wilding and his keen desire to see Wilding destroyed had made him a zealous partisan of the loyal cause. Richard Westmacott, easily swayed and overborne by the town rake, whose vices made him seem to Richard the embodiment of all that is splendid and enviable in man, had become practically the baronet's tool, now that he had abandoned Monmouth's Cause. Sir Rowland had not considered it beneath the dignity of his name and station to discharge in Bridgwater certain functions that made him more or less a spy. And so reliable had been the information he had sent Feversham and Albemarle during Monmouth's first occupation of the town, that he had won by now their complete confidence.

The second occupation, and its unpopularity with many of those who earlier – if lukewarm – had been partisans of the Duke, swelled the number of loyally inclined people in Bridgwater, and suddenly inspired Sir Rowland with a scheme by which at a blow he might snuff out the rebellion.

This scheme involved the capture of the Duke, and the reward of success should mean far more to Blake than the five thousand pounds at which the value of the Duke's head had already been fixed by Parliament. He needed a tool for this, and he even thought of Westmacott and Lupton House, but afterwards preferred a Mr Newlington, who was in better case to assist him. This Newlington, an exceedingly prosperous merchant and one of the richest men perhaps in the whole West of England, looked with extreme disfavour upon Monmouth, whose advent had paralysed his industries to an extent that was costing him a fine round sum of money weekly.

He was now in alarm lest the town of Bridgwater should be made to pay dearly for having harboured the Protestant Duke – he had no faith whatever in the Protestant Duke's ultimate prevailing – and that he, as one of the town's most prominent and prosperous citizens, might be amongst the heaviest sufferers in spite of his neutrality. This neutrality he observed because it was hardly safe in that disaffected town for a man to proclaim himself a loyalist.

To him Sir Rowland expounded his audacious plan. He sought out the merchant in his handsome mansion on the night of that Friday which had witnessed Monmouth's return, and the merchant, honoured by the visit of this gallant – ignorant as he was of the gentleman's fame in town – placed himself entirely and instantly at his disposal, though the hour was late. Sounding him carefully, and finding the fellow most amenable to any scheme that should achieve the salvation of his purse and industries, Blake boldly laid his plan before him. Startled at first, Mr Newlington, upon considering it, became so enthusiastic that he hailed Sir Rowland as his deliverer, and heartily promised his co-operation. Indeed, it was Mr Newlington who was himself to take the first step.

Well pleased with his evening's work, Sir Rowland went home to Lupton House and to bed. In the morning he broached the matter to Richard. He had all the vanity of the inferior not only to lessen the appearance of his inferiority, but to clothe himself in a mantle of importance; and it was this vanity urged him to acquaint Richard with his plans in the very presence of Ruth.

They had broken their fast, and they still lingered in the dining-room, the largest and most important room in Lupton House. It was cool and pleasant here in contrast to the heat of the July sun, which, following upon the late wet weather, beat fiercely on the lawn, the window-doors to which stood open. The cloth had been raised, and Diana and her mother had lately left the room. Ruth, in the window-seat, at a small oval table, was arranging a cluster of roses in an old bronze bowl. Sir Rowland, his stiff, short figure carefully dressed in a suit of brown camlet, his fair wig very carefully curled, occupied a tall-backed armchair near the empty fireplace. Richard, perched on the table's edge, swung his shapely legs idly backwards and forwards and cogitated upon a pretext to call for a morning-draught of last October's ale.

Ruth completed her task with the roses and turned her eyes upon her brother.

"You are not looking well, Richard," she said, which was true enough, for much hard drinking was beginning to set its stamp on Richard, and, young as he was, his insipidly fair face began to display a bloatedness that was exceedingly unhealthy.

"Oh, I am well enough," he answered almost peevishly, for these allusions to his looks were becoming more frequent than he savoured.

"Gad!" cried Sir Rowland's deep voice, "you'll need to be well. I have work for you tomorrow, Dick."

Dick did not appear to share his enthusiasm. "I am sick of the work you discover for us, Rowland," he answered ungraciously.

But Blake showed no resentment. "Maybe you'll find the present task more to your taste. If it's deeds of derring-do you pine for, I am the man to satisfy you." He smiled grimly, his bold grey eyes glancing across at Ruth, who was observing him, listening. Richard sneered, but offered him no encouragement to proceed.

"I see," said Blake, "that I shall have to tell you the whole story before you'll credit me. Shalt have it, then. But..." and he checked on the word, his face growing serious, his eye wandering to the door, "I would not have it overheard – not for a King's ransom," which was more literally true than he may have intended it to be. Richard looked over his shoulder carelessly at the door.

"We have no eavesdroppers," he said, and his voice bespoke his contempt of the gravity of this news of which Sir Rowland made so much in anticipation. He was acquainted with Sir Rowland's ways, and the importance of them. "What are you considering?" he inquired.

"To end the rebellion," said Blake, lowering his voice.

Richard laughed outright. "There are several others considering that – notably His Majesty King James, the Duke of Albemarle, and the Earl of Feversham. Yet they don't appear to achieve it."

"It is in that particular," said Blake complacently, "that I shall differ from them." He turned to Ruth, eager to engage her in the conversation, to flatter her by including her in the secret. Knowing the loyalist principles she entertained, he had no reason to fear that his plans could other than meet her approval. "What do you say, Mistress Ruth?" Presuming upon his friendship with her brother, he had taken to calling her by that name in preference to the other which he could not bring himself to give her. "Is it not an object worthy of a gentleman's endeavour?"

"If you can save so many poor people from encompassing their ruin by following that rash young man the Duke of Monmouth, you will be doing a worthy deed."

Blake rose, and made her a leg. "Madam," said he, "had aught been wanting to cement my resolve, your words would supply it to me. My plan is simplicity itself. I propose to capture Monmouth and his principal agents, and deliver them over to the King. And that is all."

"A mere nothing," croaked Richard.

"Could more be needed?" quoth Blake. "Once the rebel army is deprived of its leaders it will melt and dissolve of itself. Once the Duke is in the hands of his enemies there will be nothing left to fight for. Is it not shrewd?"

"You are telling us the object rather than the plan," Ruth reminded him. "If the plan is as good as the object…"

"As good?" he echoed, chuckling. "You shall judge." And briefly he sketched for her the springe he was setting with the help of Mr Newlington. "Newlington is rich; the Duke is in straits for money. Newlington goes today to offer him twenty thousand pounds; and the Duke is to do him the honour of supping at his house tomorrow night to fetch the money. It is a reasonable request for Mr Newlington to make under the circumstances, and the Duke cannot – dare not refuse it."

"But how will that advance your project?" Ruth inquired, for Blake had paused again, thinking that the rest must be obvious.

"In Mr Newlington's orchard I propose to post a score or so of men, well armed. Oh! I shall run no risk of betrayal by engaging Bridgwater folk. I'll get the fellows I need from General Feversham. We take Monmouth at supper, as quietly as may be, with what gentlemen happen to have accompanied him. We bind and gag the Duke, and we convey him with all speed and quiet out of Bridgwater. Feversham shall send a troop to await me a mile or so from the town on the road to Weston Zoyland. We shall join them with our captive, and thus convey him to the Royalist General. Could aught be simpler or more infallible?"

Richard had slipped from the table. He had changed his mind on the subject of the importance of the business Blake had in view. Excited by it, he clapped his friend on the back approvingly.

"A great plan!" he cried. "Is it not, Ruth?"

"It should be the means of saving hundreds, perhaps thousands of lives," said she, "and so it deserves to prosper. But what of the officers who may be with the Duke?" she inquired.

"There are not likely to be many – half a dozen, say. We shall have to make short work of them, lest they should raise an alarm." He saw her glance clouding. "That is the ugly part of the affair," he was quick to add, himself assuming a look of sadness. He sighed. "What help is there?" he asked. "Better that those few should suffer than that, as you yourself have said, there should be some thousands of lives lost before this rebellion is put down. Besides," he continued, "Monmouth's officers are far-seeing, ambitious men, who have entered into this affair to promote their own personal fortunes. They are gamesters who have set their lives upon the board against a great prize, and they know it. But these other poor misguided people who have gone out to fight for liberty and religion – it is these I am striving to rescue."

His words sounded fervent, his sentiments almost heroic. Ruth looked at him, and wondered had she misjudged him in the past. She sighed. Then she thought of Wilding. He was on the other side, but where was he? Rumour ran that he was dead; that he and Grey had quarrelled at Lyme, and that Wilding had been killed as a result. Had it not been for Diana, who strenuously bade her attach no credit to these reports, she would readily have believed them. As it was she waited, wondering, thinking of him always as she had seen him on that day at Walford when he had taken his leave of her, and more than once, when she pondered the words he had said, the look that had invested his drooping eyes, she found herself with tears in her own. They welled up now, and she rose hastily to her feet.

She looked a moment at Blake, who was watching her keenly, speculating upon this emotion of which she betrayed some sign, and wondering might not his heroism have touched her, for, as we have seen, he had arrayed a deed of excessive meanness, a deed worthy, almost, of the Iscariot, in the panoply of heroic achievement.

"I think," she said, "that you are setting your hand to a very worthy and glorious enterprise, and I hope, nay, I am sure, that success must attend your efforts." He was still bowing his thanks when she passed out through the open window-doors into the sunshine of the garden. Sir Rowland swung round upon Richard. "A great enterprise, Dick," he cried; "I may count upon you for one?"

"Ay," said Dick, who had found at last the pretext that he needed, "you may count on me. Pull the bell, we'll drink to the success of the venture."

Chapter 17

MR WILDING'S RETURN

The preparations to be made for the momentous *coup* Sir Rowland meditated were considerable. Mr Newlington was yet to be concerted with and advised, and, that done, Sir Rowland had to face the difficulty of eluding the Bridgwater guards and make his way to Feversham's camp at Somerton to enlist the General's co-operation to the extent that we have seen he looked for. That, done, he was to return and ripen his preparations for the business he had undertaken. Nevertheless, in spite of all that lay before him, he did not find it possible to leave Lupton House without stepping out into the garden in quest of Ruth. Through the window, whilst he and Richard were at their ale, he had watched her between whiles, and had lingered, waiting; for Diana was with her, and it was not his wish to seek her whilst Diana was at hand. Speak with her, ere he went, he must. He was an opportunist, and now, he fondly imagined, was his opportunity. He had made that day, at last, a favourable impression upon Richard's sister; he had revealed himself in a heroic light, and egregiously misreading the emotion she had shown before withdrawing he was satisfied that, did he strike now, victory must attend him. He sighed his satisfaction and pleasurable anticipation. He had been wary and he had known how to wait; and now, it seemed to him, he was to be rewarded for his patience. Then he frowned as another glance showed him that Diana still lingered with her cousin; he wished Diana at the devil. He had come to hate this fair-haired doll to whom he had once paid court. She was too continually in his way, a constant obstacle in his path, ever ready to remind Ruth of Anthony Wilding when Sir Rowland most desired Anthony Wilding to be forgotten; and in Diana's feelings towards himself such a change had been gradually wrought that she had come to reciprocate his sentiments – to hate him with all the bitter hatred into which love can be by scorn transmuted. At first her object in keeping Ruth's thoughts on Mr Wilding, in pleading his cause, and seeking to present him in a favourable light to the lady whom he had constrained to become his wife, had been that he might stand a barrier between Ruth and Sir Rowland to the end that Diana might hope to see revived – *faute de mieux*, since possible in no other way – the feelings that once Sir Rowland had professed for herself. The situation was rich in humiliations for poor, vain, foolishly crafty Diana, and these humiliations were daily rendered more bitter by Sir Rowland's unwavering courtship of her cousin in despite of all that she could do.

In the end the poison of them entered her soul, corroded her sentiments towards him, dissolved the love she had borne him, and transformed it into venom. She would not have him now if he did penitence for his disaffection by going in sackcloth and crawling after her on his knees for a full twelvemonth. But neither should he have Ruth if she could thwart his purpose. On that she was resolved.

Had she but guessed that he watched them from the windows, waiting for her to take her departure, she had lingered all the morning, and all the afternoon if need be, at Ruth's side. But, being ignorant of the circumstance – believing that he had already left the house – she presently quitted Ruth to go indoors, and no sooner was she gone than there was Blake replacing her at Ruth's elbow. Mistress Wilding met him with unsmiling but not ungentle face.

"Not yet gone, Sir Rowland?" she asked him, and a less sanguine man had been discouraged by the words.

"It may be forgiven me that I tarry at such a time," said he, "when we consider that I go, perhaps – to return no more." It was an inspiration on his part to assume the rôle of the hero going forth to a possible death. It invested him with noble, valiant pathos which could not, he thought, fail in its effect upon a woman's mind. But he looked in vain for a change of colour, be it never so slight, or a quickening of the breath. He found neither; though, indeed, her deep blue eyes seemed to soften as they observed him.

"There is danger in this thing that you are undertaking?" said she, between question and assertion.

"It is not my wish to overstate it; yet I leave you to imagine what the risk may be."

"It is a good cause," said she, thinking of the poor, deluded, humble folk that followed Monmouth's banner, whom Blake's fine action was to rescue from impending ruin and annihilation, "and surely Heaven will be on your side."

"We must prevail," cried Blake with kindling eye, and you had thought him a fanatic, not a miserable earner of blood-money. "We must prevail, though some of us may pay dearly for the victory. I have a foreboding…" he paused, sighed, then laughed and flung back his head, as if throwing off some weight that had oppressed him.

It was admirably played; Nick Trenchard, had he observed it, might have envied the performance; and it took effect with her, this adding of a prospective martyr's crown to the hero's raiment he had earlier donned. It was a master-touch worthy of one who was deeply learned – from the school of foul experience – in the secret ways that lead to a woman's favour. In a pursuit of this kind there was no subterfuge too mean, no treachery too base for Sir Rowland Blake.

"Will you walk, mistress?" he said, and she, feeling that it were an unkindness not to do his will, assented gravely. They moved down the sloping lawn, side by side, Sir Rowland leaning on his cane, bareheaded, his feathered hat tucked under his arm. Before them the river's smooth expanse, swollen and yellow with the recent rains, glowed like a sheet of copper, so that it blurred the sight to look upon it long.

A few steps they took with no word uttered, then Sir Rowland spoke. "With this foreboding that is on me," said he, "I could not go without seeing you, without saying something that I may never have another chance of saying; something that – who knows? – but for the emprise to which I am now wedded you had never heard from me."

He shot her a furtive, sidelong glance from under his heavy, beetling brows, and now, indeed, he observed a change ripple over the composure of her face like a sudden breeze across a sheet of water. The deep lace collar at her throat rose and fell, and her fingers toyed nervously with a ribbon of her grey bodice. She recovered in an instant, and threw up entrenchments against the attack she saw he was about to make.

"You exaggerate, I trust," said she. "Your forebodings will be proved groundless. You will return safe and sound from this venture, as indeed I hope you may."

That was his cue. "You hope it?" he cried, arresting his step, turning, and imprisoning her left hand in his right. "You hope it? Ah, if you hope for my return, return I will; but unless I know that you will have some welcome for me such as I desire from you, I think…" his voice quivered cleverly, "I think, perhaps, it were well if…if my forebodings were not as groundless as you say they are. Tell me, Ruth…"

But she interrupted him. It was high time, she thought. Her face he saw was flushed, her eyes had hardened somewhat. Calmly she disengaged her hand.

"What is't you mean?" she asked. "Speak, Sir Rowland, speak plainly, that I may give you a plain answer."

It was a challenge in which another man had seen how hopeless was his case, and, accepting defeat, had made as orderly a retreat as still was possible. But Sir Rowland, stricken in his vanity, went headlong on to utter rout.

"Since you ask me in such terms I will be plain indeed," he answered her. "I mean…" He almost quailed before the look that met him from her intrepid eyes. "Do you not see my meaning, Ruth?"

"That which I see," said she, "I do not believe, and as I would not wrong you by any foolish imaginings, I would have you plain with me."

Yet the egregious fool went on. "And why should you not believe your senses?" he asked her, between anger and entreaty. "Is it wonderful that I should love you? Is it…?"

"Stop!" She drew back a pace from him. There was a moment's silence, during which it seemed she gathered her forces to destroy him, and, in the spirit, he bowed his head before the coming storm. Then, with a sudden relaxing of the stiffness her lissom figure had assumed, "I think you had better leave me, Sir Rowland," she advised him. She half turned and moved a step away; he followed with lowering glance, his upper lip lifting and laying bare his powerful teeth. In a stride he was beside her.

"Do you hate me, Ruth?" he asked her hoarsely.

"Why should I hate you?" she counter-questioned, sadly. "I do not even dislike you," she continued in a more friendly tone, adding, as if by way of explaining this phenomenon, "You are my brother's friend. But I am disappointed in you, Sir Rowland. You had, I know, no intention of offering me disrespect; and yet it is what you have done."

"As how?" he asked.

"Knowing me another's wife…"

He broke in tempestuously. "A mock marriage! If it is but that scruple stands between us…"

"I think there is more," she answered him. "You compel me to hurt you; I do so as the surgeon does – that I may heal you."

"Why, thanks for nothing," he made answer, unable to repress a sneer. Then, checking himself, and resuming the hero-martyr posture, "I go, mistress," he told her sadly, "and if I lose my life tonight, or tomorrow, in this affair…"

181

"I shall pray for you," said she; for she had found him out at last, perceived the nature of the bow he sought to draw across her heart-strings, and, having perceived it, contempt awoke in her. He had attempted to move her by unfair, insidious means.

He fell back, crimson from chin to brow. He stifled the wrath that welled up, threatening to choke him. He was a short-necked man, of the sort – as Trenchard had once reminded him – that falls a prey to apoplexy, and surely he was never nearer it than at that moment. He made her a profound bow, bending himself almost in two before her in a very irony of deference; then, drawing himself up again, he turned and left her.

The plot which with some pride he had hatched and the reward he looked to cull from it were now to his soul as ashes to his lips. What could it profit him to destroy Monmouth so that Anthony Wilding lived? For whether she loved Wilding or not, she was Wilding's wife. Wilding, nominally, at least, was master of that which Sir Rowland coveted; not her heart, indeed, but her ample fortune. Wilding had been a stumbling-block to him since he had come to Bridgwater; but for Wilding he might have run a smooth course; he was still fool enough to hug that dear illusion to his soul. Somewhere in England – if not dead already – this Wilding lurked, an outlaw, whom any might shoot down at sight. Sir Rowland swore he would not rest until he knew that Anthony Wilding cumbered the earth no more – leastways, not the surface of it.

He went forth to seek Newlington. The merchant had sent his message to the rebel King, and had word in answer that His Majesty would be graciously pleased to sup at Mr Newlington's at nine o'clock on the following evening, attended by a few gentlemen of his immediate following. Sir Rowland received the news with satisfaction, and sighed to think that Mr Wilding – still absent, Heaven knew where – would not be of the party. It was reported that on the Monday Monmouth was to march to Gloucester, hoping there to be joined by his Cheshire friends, so that it seemed Sir Rowland had not matured his plan a day too soon. He got to horse, and, contriving to win out of Bridgwater, rode off to Somerton to concert with Lord Feversham concerning the men he would need for his undertaking.

That night Richard made free talk of the undertaking to Diana and to Ruth, loving, as does the pusillanimous, to show himself engaged in daring enterprises. Emulating his friend Sir Rowland, he held forth with prolixity upon the great service he was to do the State, and Ruth, listening to him, was proud of his zeal, the sincerity of which it never entered her mind to doubt.

Diana listened too, but without illusions concerning Master Richard and she kept her conclusions to herself.

During the afternoon of the morrow, which was Sunday, Sir Rowland returned to Bridgwater, his mission to Feversham entirely successful, and all preparations made. He completed his arrangements, and towards eight o'clock that night the twenty men sent by Feversham – they had slipped singly into the town – began to muster in the orchard at the back of Mr Newlington's house.

It was just about that same hour that Mr Wilding, saddle-worn and dust-clogged in every pore, rode into Bridgwater, and made his way to the sign of The Ship in the High Street, overlooking the Cross where Trenchard was lodged. His friend was absent – possibly gone with his men to the sermon Ferguson was preaching to the army in the Castle Fields. Having put up his horse, Mr Wilding, all dusty as he was, repaired straight to the Castle to report himself to Monmouth.

He was informed that His Majesty was in council. Nevertheless, urging that his news was of importance, he begged to be instantly announced. After a pause, he was ushered into a lofty, roomy chamber where, in the fading daylight, King Monmouth sat in council with Grey and Wade, Matthews, Speke, Ferguson and others. At the foot of the table stood a sturdy country-fellow, unknown to Wilding. It was Godfrey, the spy, who was to act as their guide across Sedgemoor that night; for the matter that was engaging them just then was the completion of their plans for the attack that was to be made that very night upon Feversham's unprepared camp – a matter which had been resolved during the last few hours as an alternative preferable to the retreat towards Gloucester that had at first been intended.

Wilding was shocked at the change that had been wrought in Monmouth's appearance during the few weeks since last he had seen him. His face was thin, pale and haggard, his eyes were more sombre, and beneath them there were heavy, dark stains of sleeplessness and care; his very voice, when presently he spoke, seemed to have lost the musical timbre that had earlier distinguished it; it was grown harsh and rasping. Disappointment after disappointment, set down to ill-luck, but in reality the fruit of incompetence, had served to sour him. The climax had been reached in the serious desertions after the Philips Norton fight, and the flight of Paymaster Goodenough with the funds for the campaign. The company sat about the long oak table, on which a map was spread, and Colonel Wade was speaking when Wilding entered.

On his appearance Wade ceased, and every eye was turned upon the messenger from London. Ferguson, fresh from his sermon, sat with elbows resting on the table, his long chin supported by his hands, his eyes gleaming sharply under the shadow of his wig, which was pulled down in front to the level of his eyebrows.

It was the Duke who addressed Mr Wilding, and the latter's keen ears were quick to catch the bitterness that underlay his words.

"We are glad to see you, sir; we had not looked to do so again."

"Not looked to do so, your Gr… Majesty!" he echoed, plainly not understanding, and it was observed that he stumbled over the Duke's new title.

"We had imagined that the pleasures of the town were claiming your entire attention."

Wilding looked from one to the other of the men before him, and on the face of all he saw a gravity that amounted to disapproval of him.

"The pleasures of the town?" said he, frowning, and again – "the pleasures of the town? There is something in this that I fear I do not understand."

"Do you bring us news that London has risen?" asked Grey suddenly.

"I would I could," said Wilding, smiling wistfully.

"Is it a laughing matter?" quoth Grey angrily.

"A smiling matter, my lord," said Wilding, nettled. "Your lordship will observe that I did but smile."

"Mr Wilding," said Monmouth darkly, "we are not pleased with you."

"In that case," returned Wilding, more and more irritated, "your Majesty expected of me more than was possible to any man."

"You have wasted your time in London, sir," the Duke explained. "We sent you thither counting upon your loyalty and devotion to ourselves. What have you done?"

"As much as a man could..." Wilding began, when Grey again interrupted him.

"As little as a man could," he answered. "Were His Grace not the most foolishly clement prince in Christendom, a halter would be your reward for the fine things you have done in London."

Mr Wilding stiffened visibly, his long white face grew set, and his slanting eyes looked wicked. He was not a man readily moved to anger, but to be greeted in such words as these by one who constituted himself the mouthpiece of him for whom Wilding had incurred ruin was more than he could bear with equanimity; that the risks to which he had exposed himself in London – where, indeed, he had been in almost hourly expectation of arrest and such short shift as poor Disney had – should be acknowledged in such terms as these, was something that turned him almost sick with disgust. To what manner of men had he leagued himself? He looked Grey steadily between the eyes.

"I mind me of an occasion on which such a charge of foolish clemency might indeed – and with greater justice – have been levelled against His Majesty," said he, and his calm was almost terrible. His lordship grew pale at the obvious allusion to Monmouth's mild treatment of him for his cowardice at Bridport, and his eyes were as baleful as Wilding's own at that moment. But before he could speak Monmouth had already answered Mr Wilding.

"You are wanting in respect to us, sir," he admonished him. Mr Wilding bowed to the rebuke in a submission that seemed ironical. The blood mounted slowly to Monmouth's cheeks.

"Perhaps," put in Wade, who was anxious for peace, "Mr Wilding has some explanation to offer us of his failure."

His failure! They took too much for granted. Stitched in the lining of his boot was the letter from the Secretary of State. To have achieved that was surely to have achieved something.

"I thank you, sir, for supposing it," answered Wilding, his voice hard with self-restraint; "I have indeed an explanation."

"We will hear it," said Monmouth, condescendingly, and Grey sneered, thrusting out his bloated lips.

"I have to offer the explanation that your Majesty is served in London by cowards; self-sufficient and self-important cowards who have hindered me in my task instead of helping me. I refer particularly to Colonel Danvers."

Grey interrupted him. "You have a rare effrontery, sir – ay, by God! Do you dare call Danvers a coward?"

"It is not I who so call him, but the facts. Colonel Danvers has run away."

"Danvers gone?" cried Ferguson, voicing the consternation of all.

Wilding shrugged and smiled; Grey's eye was offensively upon him. He elected to answer the challenge of that glance. "He has followed the illustrious example set him by other of your Majesty's devoted followers," said Wilding.

Grey rose suddenly. This was too much. "I'll not endure it from this knave!" he cried, appealing to Monmouth. Monmouth wearily waved him to a seat; but Grey disregarded the command.

"What have I said that should touch your lordship?" asked Wilding, and, smiling sardonically, he looked into Grey's eyes.

"It is not what you have said. It is what you have inferred."

"And to call me knave!" said Wilding in a mocking horror. The repression of his anger lent him a rare bitterness, and an almost devilishly subtle manner of expressing wordlessly what was passing in his mind. There was not one present but gathered from his utterance of those five words that he did not hold Grey worthy the honour of being called to account for that offensive epithet. He made just an exclamatory protest, such as he might have made had a woman applied the term to him.

Grey turned from him slowly to Monmouth. "It might be well," said he, in his turn controlling himself at last, "to place Mr Wilding under arrest."

Mr Wilding's manner quickened on the instant from passive to active anger.

"Upon what charge, sir?" he demanded sharply. In truth it was the only thing wanting that, after all that he had undergone, he should be arrested. His eyes were upon the Duke's melancholy face, and his anger was such that in that moment he vowed that if Monmouth acted upon this suggestion of Grey's he should not have so much as the consolation of Sunderland's letter.

"You have been wanting in respect to us, sir," the Duke answered him. He seemed able to do little more than repeat himself. "You return from London empty-handed, your task unaccomplished, and instead of a becoming contrition, you hector it here before us in this manner." He shook his head. "We are not pleased with you, Mr Wilding."

"But, your Grace," exclaimed Wilding, "is it my fault that your London agents had failed to organise the rising? That rising should have taken place, and it *would* have taken place had your Majesty been more ably represented there."

"You were there, Mr Wilding," said Grey with heavy sarcasm.

"Would it no' be better to leave Mr Wilding's affair until afterwards?" suggested Ferguson at that moment. "It is already past eight, your Majesty, and there be still some details of this attack to settle that your officers may prepare for it, whilst Mr Newlington awaits your Majesty to supper at nine."

"True," said Monmouth, ever ready to take a solution offered by another. "We will confer with you again later, Mr Wilding."

Wilding bowed, accepting his dismissal. "Before I go, your Majesty, there are certain things I would report…" he began.

"You have heard, sir," Grey broke in. "Not now. This is not the time."

"Indeed, no. This is not the time, Mr Wilding," echoed the Duke.

Wilding set his teeth in the intensity of his vexation.

"What I have to tell your Majesty is of importance," he exclaimed, and Monmouth seemed to waver, whilst Grey looked disdainful unbelief of the importance of any communication Wilding might have to make.

"We have little time, your Majesty," Ferguson reminded Monmouth.

"Perhaps," put in friendly Wade, "your Majesty might see Mr Wilding at Mr Newlington's."

"Is it really necessary?" quoth Grey.

This treatment of him inspired Mr Wilding with malice. The mere mention of Sunderland's letter would have changed their tone. But he elected by no such word to urge the importance of his business. It should be entirely as Monmouth should elect or be constrained by these gentlemen about his council-table.

"It would serve two purposes," said Wade, whilst Monmouth still considered. "Your Majesty will be none too well attended, your officers having this other matter to prepare for. Mr Wilding would form another to swell your escort of gentlemen."

"I think you are right, Colonel Wade," said Monmouth. "We sup at Mr Newlington's at nine o'clock, Mr Wilding. We shall expect you to attend us there. Lieutenant Cragg," said His Grace to the young officer who had admitted Wilding, and who had remained at attention by the door, "you may reconduct Mr Wilding."

Wilding bowed, his lips tight to keep in the anger that craved expression. Then, without another word spoken, he turned and departed.

"An insolent, overbearing knave!" was Grey's comment upon him after he had left the room.

"Let us attend to this, your lordship," said Speke, tapping the map. "Time presses," and he invited Wade to continue the matter that Wilding's advent had interrupted.

Chapter 18

BETRAYAL

Still smarting under the cavalier treatment he had received, Mr Wilding came forth from the Castle to find Trenchard awaiting him among the crowd of officers and men that thronged the yard.

Nick linked his arm through his friend's and led him away. They quitted the place in silence, and in silence took their way south towards the High Street, Nick waiting for Mr Wilding to speak, Mr Wilding's mind still in turmoil at the things he had endured. At last Nick halted suddenly and looked keenly at his friend in the failing light.

"What a plague ails you, Tony?" said he sharply. "You are as silent as I am impatient for your news."

Wilding told him in brief, disdainful terms of the reception they had given him at the Castle, and of how they had blamed him for the circumstance that London had failed to proclaim itself for Monmouth.

Trenchard snarled viciously. " 'Tis that mongrel Grey," said he. "O, Anthony, to what an affair have we set our hands? Naught can prosper with that fellow in it." He laid his hand on Wilding's arm and lowered his voice. "As I have hinted before, 'twould not surprise me if time proved him a traitor. Failure attends him everywhere, and so unfailingly that one wonders is not failure invited by him. And that fool Monmouth! Pshaw! See what it is to serve a weakling. With another in his place and the country disaffected as it is, we had been masters of England by now."

Two ladies passed them at that moment, cloaked and hooded, walking briskly. One of them turned to look at Trenchard, who, waving his arms in wild gesticulation, was a conspicuous object. She checked in her walk, arresting her companion.

"Mr Wilding!" she exclaimed. It was Lady Horton.

"Mr Wilding!" cried Diana, her companion. Wilding doffed his hat and bowed, Trenchard following his example.

"We had scarce looked to see you in Bridgwater again," said the mother, her mild, pleasant countenance reflecting the satisfaction it gave her to behold him safe and sound.

"There have been moments," answered Wilding, "when myself I scarce expected to return. Your ladyship's greeting shows me what I had lost had I not done so."

"You are but newly arrived?" quoth Diana, scanning him in the gloaming.

"From London, an hour since."

"An hour?" she echoed, and observed that he was still booted and dust-stained. "You will have been to Lupton House?"

A shadow crossed his face, his glance seemed to grow clouded, all of which watchful Diana did not fail to observe. "Not yet," said he.

"You are a laggard," she laughed at him, and he felt the blood driven back upon his heart. What did she mean? Was it possible she suggested that he should be welcome, that his wife's feelings towards him had undergone a change? His last parting from her on the road near Walford had been ever in his mind.

"I have had weighty business to transact," he replied, and Trenchard snorted, his mind flying back to the council-room at the Castle, and what his friend had told him.

"But now that you have disposed of that you will sup with us," said Lady Horton, who was convinced that, since Ruth had gone to the altar with him, he was Ruth's lover in spite of the odd things she had heard. Appearances with Lady Horton counted for everything, and all that glittered was gold to her.

"I would," he answered, "but that I am to sup at Mr Newlington's with His Majesty. My visit must wait until tomorrow."

"Let us hope," said Trenchard, "that it waits no longer." He was already instructed touching the night attack on Feversham's camp on Sedgemoor, and thought it likely Wilding would accompany them.

"You are going to Mr Newlington's?" said Diana, and Trenchard thought she had turned singularly pale. Her hand was over her heart, her eyes wide. She seemed about to add something, but checked herself. She took her mother's arm. "We are detaining Mr Wilding, mother," said she, and her voice quivered as if her whole being were shaken by some gusty agitation. They spoke their farewells briefly and moved on. A second later Diana was back at their side again.

"Where are you lodged, Mr Wilding?" she inquired.

"With my friend Trenchard – at the sign of The Ship, by the Cross."

She briefly acknowledged the information, rejoined her mother, and hurried away with her.

Trenchard stood staring after them a moment. "Odd!" said he; "did you mark that girl's discomposure?"

But Wilding's thoughts were elsewhere. "Come, Nick! If I am to render myself fit to sit at table with Monmouth, we'll need to hasten."

They went their way, but not so fast as went Diana, urging with her her protesting and short-winded mother.

"Where is your mistress?" the girl asked excitedly of the first servant she met at Lupton House.

"In her room, Madam," the man replied, and to Ruth's room went Diana breathlessly, leaving Lady Horton gaping after her and understanding nothing.

Ruth, who was seated pensive by her window, rose on Diana's impetuous entrance, and in the deepening twilight she looked almost ghostly in her gown of shimmering white satin, sewn with pearls about the neck of the low-cut bodice.

"Diana!" she cried. "You startled me."

"Not so much as I am yet to do," answered Diana, breathing excitement. She threw back the whimple from her head, and pulling away her cloak, tossed it on to the bed. "Mr Wilding is in Bridgwater," she announced.

There was a faint rustle from the stiff satin of Ruth's gown. "Then…" her voice shook slightly. "Then…he is not dead," she said, more because she felt that she must say something than because her words fitted the occasion.

"Not yet," said Diana grimly.

"Not yet?"

"He sups tonight at Mr Newlington's," Miss Horton exclaimed in a voice pregnant with meaning.

"Ah!" It was a cry from Ruth, sharp, as if she had been stabbed. She sank back to her seat by the window, smitten down by this sudden news.

There was a pause, which fretted Diana, who now craved knowledge of what might be passing in her cousin's mind. She advanced towards Ruth and laid a trembling hand on her shoulder, where the white gown met the ivory neck. "He must be warned," she said.

"But…but how?" stammered Ruth. "To warn him were to betray Sir Rowland."

"Sir Rowland?" cried Diana in high scorn.

"And…and Richard," Ruth continued.

"Yes, and Mr Newlington, and all the other knaves that are engaged in this murderous business. Well?" she demanded. "Will you do it, or must I?"

"Do it?" Ruth's eyes sought her cousin's white, excited face in the quasi-darkness. "But have you thought of what it will mean? Have you thought of the poor people that will perish unless the Duke is taken and this rebellion brought to an end?"

"Thought of it?" repeated Diana witheringly. "Not I. I have thought that Mr Wilding is here and like to have his throat cut before an hour is past."

"Tell me, are you sure of this?" asked Ruth.

"I have it from your husband's own lips," Diana answered, and told her in a few words of her meeting with Mr Wilding.

Ruth sat with hands folded in her lap, her eyes on the dim violet after-glow in the west, and her mind wrestling with this problem that Diana had brought her. "Diana," she cried at last, "what am I to do?"

"Do?" echoed Diana. "Is it not plain? Warn Mr Wilding."

"But Richard?"

"Mr Wilding saved Richard's life…"

"I know. I know. My duty is to warn him."

"Then why hesitate?"

"My duty is also to keep faith with Richard, to think of those poor misguided folk who are to be saved by this," cried Ruth in an agony. "If Mr Wilding is warned they will all be ruined."

Diana stamped her foot impatiently. "Had I thought to find you in this mind, I had warned him myself," said she.

"Ah! Why did you not?"

"That the chance of doing so might be yours. That you might thus repay him the debt in which you stand."

"Diana, I can't!" The words broke from her in a sob.

But whatever her interest in Mr Wilding for her own sake, Diana's prime intent was the thwarting of Sir Rowland Blake. If Wilding were warned of what manner of feast was spread at Newlington's, Sir Rowland would be indeed undone.

"You think of Richard," she exclaimed, "and you know that Richard is to have no active part in the affair – that he will run no risk. They have assigned him but a sentry duty that he may warn Blake and his followers if any danger threatens them."

"It is not of Richard's life I am thinking, but of his honour, of his trust in me. Ta warn Mr Wilding were…to commit an act of betrayal."

"And is Mr Wilding to be slaughtered with his friends?" Diana asked her. "Resolve me that. Time presses. In half an hour it will be too late."

That allusion to the shortness of the time brought Ruth an inspiration. Suddenly she saw a way. Wilding should be saved, and yet she would not break faith with Richard nor ruin those others. She would detain him, and, whilst warning him at the last moment, in time for him to save himself, not do so until it must be too late for him to warn the others. Thus she would do her duty by him, and yet keep faith with Richard and Sir Rowland. She had resolved, she thought, the awful difficulty that had confronted her. She rose suddenly, heartened by the thought.

"Give me your cloak and whimple," she bade Diana, and Diana flew to do her bidding. "Where is Mr Wilding lodged?" she asked.

"At the sign of The Ship – overlooking the Cross, with Mr Trenchard. Shall I come with you?"

"No," answered Ruth without hesitation. "I will go alone." She drew the whimple well over her head, so that in its shadows her face might lie concealed, and hid her shimmering white dress under Diana's cloak.

She hastened through the ill-lighted streets, never heeding the rough cobbles that hurt her feet, shod in light indoor wear, never heeding the crowds that thronged her way. All Bridgwater was astir with Monmouth's presence; moreover, there had been great incursions from Taunton and the surrounding country, the women-folk of the Duke-King's followers having come that day to Bridgwater to say farewell to father and son, husband and brother, before the army marched – as was still believed – to Gloucester.

The half-hour was striking from St Mary's – the church in which she had been married – as Ruth reached the door of the sign of The Ship. She was about to knock, when suddenly it opened, and Mr Wilding himself, with Trenchard immediately behind him, stood confronting her. At sight of him a momentary weakness took her. He had changed from his hard-used riding garments into a suit of roughly-corded black silk, which threw into relief the steely litheness of his spare figure. His dark brown hair was carefully dressed, diamonds gleamed in the cravat of snowy lace at his throat. He was uncovered, his hat under his arm, and he stood aside to make way for her, imagining that she was some woman of the house.

"Mr Wilding," said she, her heart fluttering in her throat. "May I... may I speak with you?"

He leaned forward, seeking to pierce the shadows of her whimple; he had thought he recognised the voice, as his sudden start had shown; and yet he disbelieved his ears. She moved her head at that moment, and the light streaming out from a lamp in the passage beat upon her white face.

"Ruth!" he cried, and came quickly forward. Trenchard, behind him, looked on and scowled with sudden impatience. Mr Wilding's philanderings with this lady had never had the old rake's approval. Too much trouble already had resulted from them.

"I must speak with you at once. At once!" she urged him, her tone fearful.

"Are you in need of me?" he asked concernedly.

"In very urgent need," said she.

"I thank God," he answered without flippancy. "You shall find me at your service. Tell me."

"Not here; not here," she answered him.

"Where else?" said he. "Shall we walk?"

"No, no." Her repetitions marked the deep excitement that possessed her. "I will go in with you." And she signed with her head towards the door from which he was barely emerged.

" 'Twere scarce fitting," said he, for being confused and full of speculation on the score of her need, he had for the moment almost overlooked the relations in which they stood. In spite of the ceremony through which they had gone together, Mr Wilding still mostly thought of her as of a mistress very difficult to woo.

"Fitting?" she echoed, and then after a pause, "Am I not your wife?" she asked him in a low voice, her cheeks crimsoning.

"Ha! 'Pon honour, I had almost forgot," said he, and though the burden of his words seemed mocking, their tone was sad.

Of the passers-by that jostled them a couple had now paused to watch a scene that had an element of the unusual in it. She pulled her whimple closer to her face, took him by the arm, and drew him with her into the house.

"Close the door," she bade him, and Trenchard, who had stood aside that they might pass in, forestalled him in obeying her. "Now lead me to your room," said she, and Wilding in amaze turned to Trenchard as if asking his consent, for the lodging, after all, was Trenchard's.

"I'll wait here," said Nick, and waved his hand towards an oak bench that stood in the passage. "You had best make haste," he urged his friend; "you are late already. That is, unless you are of a mind to set the lady's affairs before King Monmouth's. And were I in your place, Anthony, faith I'd not scruple to do it. For after all," he added under his breath, "there's little choice in rotten apples."

Ruth waited for some answer from Wilding that might suggest he was indifferent whether he went to Newlington's or not; but he spoke no word as he turned to lead the way above-stairs to the indifferent parlour which with the adjoining bedroom constituted Mr Trenchard's lodging – and his own, for the time being.

Having assured herself that the curtains were closely drawn, she put by her cloak and hood, and stood revealed to him in the light of the three candles burning in a branch upon the bare oak table, dazzlingly beautiful in her gown of ivory-white.

He stood apart, cogitating her with glowing eyes, the faintest smile between question and pleasure hovering about his thin mouth. He had closed the door, and stood in silence waiting for her to make known her pleasure.

"Mr Wilding…" she began, and straightway he interrupted her.

"But a moment since you did remind me that I have the honour to be your husband," he said with grave humour. "Why seek now to overcloud that fact? I mind me that the last time we met you called me by another name. But it may be," he added as an afterthought, "you are of opinion that I have broken faith with you."

"Broken faith? As how?"

"So!" he said, and sighed. "My words were of so little account that they have been, I see, forgotten. Yet, so that I remember them, that is what chiefly matters. I promised then – or seemed to promise – that I would make a widow of you, who had made a wife of you against your will. It has not happened yet. Do not despair. This Monmouth quarrel is not yet fought out. Hope on, my Ruth."

She looked at him with eyes wide open – lustrous eyes of sapphire in a face of ivory. A faint smile parted her lips, the reflection of the thought in her mind that had she indeed been eager for his death she would not be with him at this moment; had she desired it, how easy would her course have been.

"You do me wrong to bid me hope for that," she answered him, her tones level. "I do not wish the death of any man, unless…" She paused; her truthfulness urged her too far.

"Unless?" said he, brows raised, polite interest on his face.

"Unless it be His Grace of Monmouth."

He considered her with suddenly narrowed eyes. "You have not by chance sought me to talk politics?" said he. "Or…" and he suddenly caught his breath, his nostrils dilating with rage at the bare thought that leapt into his mind. Had Monmouth, the notorious libertine, been to Lupton House and persecuted her with his addresses? "Is it that you are acquainted with His Grace?" he asked.

"I have never spoken to him!" she answered, with no suspicion of what was in his thoughts. In his relief he laughed, remembering now that Monmouth's affairs were too absorbing just at present to leave him room for dalliance.

"But you are standing," said he, and he advanced a chair. "I deplore that I have no better hospitality to offer you. I doubt if I ever shall again. I am told that Albemarle did me the honour to stable his knackers in my hall at Zoyland."

She took the chair he offered her, sinking to it like one physically weary, a thing he was quick to notice. He watched her, his body eager, his soul trammelling it with a steely restraint. "Tell me, now," said he, "in what you need me."

She was silent a moment, pondering, hesitation and confusion seeming to envelop her. A pink flush rose to colour the beautiful pillar of neck and overspread the delicate half-averted face. He watched it, wondering.

"How long," she asked him, her whole intent at present being to delay him and gain time. "How long have you been in Bridgwater?"

"Two hours at most," said he.

"Two hours! And yet you never came to…to me. I heard of your presence, and I feared you might intend to abstain from seeking me."

He almost held his breath while she spoke, caught in amazement. He was standing close beside her chair, his right hand rested upon its tall back.

"Did you so intend?" she asked him.

"I told you even now," he answered with hard-won calm, "that I had made you a sort of promise."

"I… I would not have you keep it," she murmured. She heard his sharply indrawn breath, felt him leaning over her, and was filled with an unaccountable fear.

"Was it to tell me this you came?" he asked her, his voice reduced to a whisper.

"No…yes," she answered, an agony in her mind, which groped for some means to keep him by her side until his danger should be overpast. That much she owed him in honour if in nothing else.

"No – yes?" he echoed, and he had drawn himself erect again. "What is't you mean, Ruth?"

"I mean that it was that, yet not quite only that."

"Ah!" Disappointment vibrated faintly in his exclamation. "What else?"

"I would have you abandon Monmouth's following," she told him. He stared a moment, moved away and round where he could confront her. The flush had now faded from her face. This he observed and the heave of her bosom in its low bodice. He knit his brows, perplexed. Here was surely more than at first might seem.

"Why so?" he asked.

"For your own safety's sake," she answered him.

"You are oddly concerned for that, Ruth."

"Concerned – not oddly." She paused an instant, swallowed hard, and then continued. "I am concerned too for your honour, and there is no honour in following his banner. He has crowned himself King, and so proved himself a self-seeker who came dissembled as the champion of a cause that he might delude poor ignorant folk into flocking to his standard and helping him to his ambitious ends."

"You are wondrously well schooled," said he. "Whose teachings do you recite me? Sir Rowland Blake's?" At another time the sneer might have cut her. At the moment she was too intent upon gaining time. The means to it mattered little. The more she talked to no purpose, the more at random was their discourse, the better would her ends be served.

"Sir Rowland Blake?" she cried. "What is he to me?"

"Ah, what? Let me set you the question rather."

"Less than nothing," she assured him, and for some moments afterwards it was this Sir Rowland who served them as a topic for their odd interview. On the overmantel the pulse of time beat on from a little wooden clock. His eyes strayed to it; it marked the three-quarters. He bethought him suddenly of his engagement. Trenchard, below-stairs, supremely indifferent whether Wilding went to Newlington's or not, smoked on, entirely unconcerned by the flight of time.

"Mistress," said Wilding suddenly, "you have not yet told me in what you seek my service. Indeed, we seem to have talked to little purpose. My time is very short."

"Where are you going?" she asked him, and fearfully she shot a sidelong glance at the timepiece. It was still too soon, by at least five minutes.

He smiled, but his smile was singular. He began to suspect at last that her only purpose – to what end he could not guess – was to detain him.

" 'Tis a singularly sudden interest in my doings, this," said he quietly. "What is't you seek of me?" He reached for the hat he had cast upon the table when they had entered. "Tell me briefly. I may stay no longer."

She rose, her agitation suddenly increasing, afraid that after all he would escape her. "Where are you going?" she asked. "Answer me that, and I will tell you why I came."

"I am to sup at Mr Newlington's in His Majesty's company."

"His Majesty's?"

"King Monmouth's," he explained impatiently. "Come, Ruth. Already I am late."

"If I were to ask you not to go," she said slowly, and she held out her hands to him, her glance most piteous – and that was not acting – as she raised it to meet his own, "would you not stay to pleasure me?"

He considered her from under frowning eyes. "Ruth," he said, and he took her hands. "There is here something that I do not understand. What is't you mean?"

"Promise me that you will not go to Newlington's, and I will tell you."

"But what has Newlington to do with…? Nay, I am pledged already to go."

She drew closer to him, her hands upon his shoulders. "Yet if I ask you – I, your wife?" she pleaded, and almost won him to her will. But suddenly he remembered another occasion on which, for purposes of her own, she had so pled. He laughed softly, mockingly.

"Do you woo me, Ruth, who, when I wooed you, would have none of me?"

She drew back from him, crimsoning. "I think I had better go," said she. "You have nothing but mockery for me. It was ever so. Who knows?" she sighed as she took up her mantle. "Had you but observed more gentle ways, you…you…" She paused, needing to say no more. "Good night!" she ended, and made shift to leave. He watched her, deeply mystified. She had gained the door when suddenly he moved.

"Wait!" he cried. She paused, and turned to look over her shoulder, her hand apparently upon the latch. "You shall not go until you have told me why you besought me to keep away from

Newlington's. What is it?" he asked, and paused suddenly, a flood of light breaking in upon his mind. "Is there some treachery afoot?" he asked her, and his eye went wildly to the clock. A harsh, grating sound rang through the room. "What are you doing?" he cried. "Why have you locked the door?" She was tugging and fumbling desperately to extract the key, her hands all clumsy in her nervous haste. He leapt at her, but in that moment the key came away in her hand. She wheeled round to face him, erect, defiant almost.

"Here is some devilry!" he cried. "Give me that key." He had no need for further questions. Here was a proof more eloquent than words to his ready wit. Sir Rowland or Richard, or both, were in some plot for the Duke's ruin – perhaps assassination. Had not her very words shown that she herself was out of all sympathy with Monmouth? He was out of sympathy himself. But not to the extent of standing by to see his throat cut. She would have the plot succeed – whatever it might be – and yet that he himself be spared. There his thoughts paused; but only for a moment. He saw suddenly in this, not a proof of concern born of love but of duty towards him who had imperilled himself once – and for all time, indeed – that he might save her brother and Sir Rowland.

He told her what had been so suddenly revealed to him, taxing her with it. She acknowledged it, her wits battling to find some way by which she might yet gain a few moments more. She would cling to the key, and, though he should offer her violence, she would not let it go without a struggle, and that struggle must consume the little time yet wanting to make it too late for him to save the Duke, and – what imported more – thus save herself from betraying her brother's trust. Another fear leapt at her suddenly. If through deed of hers Monmouth was spared that night, Blake, in his despair and rage, might slake his vengeance upon Richard.

"Give me that key," he demanded, his voice cold and quiet, his face set.

"No, no," she cried, setting her hand behind her. "You shall not go, Anthony. You shall not go."

"I must," he insisted, still cold, but oh! so determined. "My honour's in it now that I know."

"You'll go to your death," she reminded him.

He sneered. "What signifies a day or so? Give me the key."

"I love you, Anthony!" she cried, livid to the lips.

"Lies!" he answered her contemptuously. "The key!"

"No," she answered, and her firmness matched his own. "I will not have you slain."

" 'Tis not my purpose – not just yet. But I must save the others. God forgive me if I offer violence to a woman," he added, "and lay rude hands upon her. Do not compel me to it." He advanced upon her, but she, lithe and quick, evaded him, and sprang for the middle of the room. He wheeled about, his self-control all slipping from him now. Suddenly she darted to the window, and with the hand that clenched the key she smote a pane with all her might. There was a smash of shivering glass, followed an instant later by a faint tinkle on the stones below, and the hand that she still held out covered itself all with blood.

"O God!" he cried, the key and all else forgotten. "You are hurt."

"But you are saved," she cried, overwrought, and staggered, laughing and sobbing, to a chair, sinking her bleeding hand to her lap, and smearing recklessly her spotless, shimmering gown.

He caught up a chair by its legs, and at a single blow smashed down the door – a frail barrier after all. "Nick!" he roared. "Nick!" He tossed the chair from him and vanished into the adjoining room to reappear a moment later carrying basin and ewer, and a shirt of Trenchard's – the first piece of linen he could find.

She was half fainting, and she let him have his swift, masterful way. He bathed her hand, and was relieved to find that the injury was none so great as the flow of blood had made him fear. He tore Trenchard's fine cambric shirt to shreds – a matter on which Trenchard afterwards commented in quotations from at least three famous Elizabethan dramatists. He bound up her hand, just as Nick made his appearance at the splintered door, his mouth open, his pipe, gone out, between his fingers. He was followed by a startled serving-wench, the only other person in the house, for everyone was out of doors that night.

Into the woman's care Wilding delivered his wife, and without a word to her he left the room, dragging Trenchard with him. It was striking nine as they went down the stairs, and the sound brought as much satisfaction to Ruth above as dismay to Wilding below.

Chapter 19

THE BANQUET

It was striking nine. Therefore, Ruth thought that she had achieved her object, Wilding imagined that all was lost. It needed the more tranquil mind of Nicholas Trenchard to show him the fly in madam's ointment, after Wilding, in half a dozen words, had made him acquainted with the situation.

"What are you going to do?" asked Trenchard.

"Run to Newlington's and warn the Duke – if still in time."

"And thereby precipitate the catastrophe? Oh, give it thought. It is all it needs. You are taking it for granted that nine o'clock is the hour appointed for King Monmouth's butchery."

"What else?" asked Wilding, impatient to be off. They were standing in the street under the sign of The Ship, by which Jonathan Edney – Mr Trenchard's landlord – distinguished his premises and the chandler's trade he drove there. Trenchard set a detaining hand on Mr Wilding's arm.

"Nine o'clock is the hour appointed for supper. It is odds the Duke will be a little late, and it is more than odds that when he does arrive the assassins will wait until the company is safely at table and lulled by good eating and drinking. You had overlooked that, I see. It asks an old head for wisdom, after all. Look you, Anthony. Speed to Colonel Wade as fast as your legs can carry you, and get a score of men. Then find some fellow to lead you to Newlington's orchard, and if only you do not arrive too late you may take Sir Rowland and his cut-throats in the rear and destroy them to a man before they realise themselves attacked. I'll reconnoitre while you go, and keep an eye on the front of the house. Away with you!"

Ordinarily Wilding was a man of a certain dignity, but you had not thought it had you seen him running in silk stockings and silver-buckled shoes at a headlong pace through the narrow streets of Bridgwater, in the direction of the Castle. He overset more than one, and oaths followed him from these and from others whom he rudely jostled out of his path. Wade was gone with Monmouth, but he came upon Captain Slape, who had a company of scythes and musketeers incorporated in the Duke's own regiment, and to him Wilding gasped out the news and his request for a score of men with what breath was left him.

Time was lost – and never was time more precious – in convincing Slape that this was no old wife's tale. At last, however, he won his way and twenty musketeers; but the quarter past the hour had chimed ere they left the Castle. He led them forth at a sharp run, with never a thought for the circumstance that they would need their breath anon, perhaps for fighting, and he bade the man who guided them take them by back streets that they might attract as little attention as possible.

Within a stone's throw of the house he halted them, and sent one forward to reconnoitre, following himself with the others as quietly and noiselessly as possible. Mr Newlington's house was all alight, but from the absence of uproar – sounds there were in plenty from the main street, where a dense throng had collected to see His Majesty go in – Mr Wilding inferred with supreme relief that they were still in time. But the danger was not yet past. Already, perhaps, the assassins were penetrating – or had penetrated – to the house; and at any moment such sounds might greet them as would announce the execution of their murderous design.

Meanwhile Mr Trenchard, having relighted his pipe, and set his hat rakishly atop his golden wig, strolled up the High Street, swinging his long cane very much like a gentleman taking the air in quest of an appetite for supper. He strolled past the Cross and on until he came to the handsome mansion – one of the few handsome houses in Bridgwater – where opulent Mr Newlington had his residence. A small crowd had congregated about the doors, for word had gone forth that His Majesty was to sup there. Trenchard moved slowly through the people, seemingly uninterested, but, in fact, scanning closely every face he encountered. Suddenly, out of the corner of his eye, he espied in the indifferent light Mr Richard Westmacott.

Trenchard passed him, jostling him as he went, and strolled on some few paces, then turned, and came slowly back, and observed that Richard had also turned and was now watching him as he approached. He was all but upon the boy when suddenly his wrinkled face lighted with recognition.

"Mr Westmacott!" he cried, and there was surprise in his voice.

Richard, conscious that Trenchard must no doubt regard him as a turn-tippet, flushed, and stood aside to give passage to the other. But Mr Trenchard was by no means minded to pass. He clapped a hand on Richard's shoulder. "Nay," he cried, between laughter and feigned resentment. "Do you bear me ill-will, lad?"

Richard was somewhat taken aback. "For what should I bear you ill-will, Mr Trenchard?" quoth he.

Trenchard laughed frankly, and so uproariously that his hat over-jauntily cocked was all but shaken from his head. "I mind me the last time we met I played you an unfair trick," said he. His tone bespoke the very highest good-humour. He slipped his arm through Richard's. "Never bear an old man malice, lad," said he.

"I assure you that I bear you none," said Richard, relieved to find that Trenchard apparently knew nothing of his defection, yet wishing that Trenchard would go his ways, for Richard's task was to stand sentry there.

"I'll not believe you till you afford me proof," Trenchard replied. "You shall come and wash your resentment down in the best bottle of Canary the 'White Cow' can furnish us."

"Not now, I thank you," answered Richard.

"You are thinking of the last occasion on which I drank with you," said Trenchard reproachfully.

"Not so. But…but I am not thirsty."

"Not thirsty?" echoed Trenchard. "And is that a reason? Why, lad, it is the beast that drinks only when he thirsts. And in that lies one of the main differences between beast and man. Come on" – and his arm effected a gentle pressure upon Richard's, to move him thence. But at that moment, down the street with a great rumble of wheels, cracking of whips, and clatter of hoofs, came a coach, bearing to Mr Newlington's King Monmouth escorted by his forty life-guards. Cheering broke from the crowd as the carriage drew up, and the Duke-King as he alighted turned his handsome face, on which shone the ruddy glow of torches, to acknowledge these loyal acclamations. He passed up the steps, at the top of which Mr Newlington – fat and pale and monstrously overdressed – stood bowing to welcome his royal visitor. Host and guest vanished, followed by some six officers of Monmouth's, among whom were Grey and Wade. The sightseers flattened themselves against the walls as the great lumbering coach put about and went off again the way it had come, the life-guards following after.

Trenchard fancied that he caught a sigh of relief from Richard, but the street was noisy at the time and he may well have been mistaken.

"Come," said he, renewing his invitation, "we shall both be the better for a little milk of the 'White Cow.' "

Richard wavered almost by instinct. The "White Cow," he knew, was famous for its sack; on the other hand, he was pledged to Sir Rowland to stand guard in the narrow lane at the back where ran the wall of Mr Newlington's garden. Under the gentle suasion of Trenchard's arm, he moved a few steps up the street; then halted, his duty battling with his inclination.

"No, no," he muttered. "If you will excuse me…"

"Not I," said Trenchard, drawing from his hesitation a shrewd inference as to Richard's business. "To drink alone is an abomination I'll not be guilty of."

"But…" began the irresolute Richard.

"Shalt urge me no excuses, or we'll quarrel. Come," and he moved on, dragging Richard with him. A few steps Richard took unwillingly under the other's soft compulsion; then, having given the matter thought – he was always one to take the line of least resistance – he assured himself that his sentryship was entirely superfluous, the matter of Blake's affair was an entire secret, shared only by those who had a hand in it. Blake was quite safe from all surprises; Trenchard was insistent and it was difficult to deny him; and the sack at the "White Cow" was no doubt the best in Somerset. He gave himself up to the inevitable and fell into step alongside his companion, who babbled aimlessly of trivial matters. Trenchard felt the change from unwilling to willing companionship, and approved it.

They mounted the three steps and entered the common-room of the inn. It was well thronged at the time, but they found places at the end of a long table, and there they sat, and discussed the landlady's canary for the best part of a half-hour, until a sudden spatter of musketry, near at hand, came to startle the whole room.

There was a momentary stillness in the tavern, succeeded by an excited clamouring, a dash for the windows and a storm of questions, to which none could return any answer. Richard had risen with a sudden exclamation, very pale and scared of aspect. Trenchard tugged at his sleeve.

"Sit down," said he. "Sit down. It will be nothing."

"Nothing?" echoed Richard, and his eyes were suddenly bent on Trenchard in a look in which suspicion was now blent with terror.

A second volley of musketry crackled forth at that moment, and the next the whole street was in an uproar. Men were running and shots resounded on every side, above all of which predominated the cry that His Majesty was murdered.

In an instant the common-room of the "White Cow" was emptied of every occupant save two – Trenchard and Westmacott. Neither of them felt the need to go forth in quest of news. They knew how idle was the cry in the streets. They knew what had taken place, and, knowing it, Trenchard smoked on placidly, satisfied that Wilding had been in time, whilst Richard stood stricken and petrified by dismay at realising, with even greater certainty, that something had supervened to thwart, perhaps to destroy, Sir Rowland. For he knew that Blake's party had gone forth armed with pistols only, and intent not to use even these save in the last extremity; to avoid noise they were to keep to steel. This knowledge gave Richard positive assurance that the volleys they had heard must have been fired by some party that had fallen upon Blake's men and taken them by surprise.

And it was his fault! He was the traitor to whom perhaps a score of men owed their deaths at that moment! He had failed to keep watch as he had undertaken. His fault it was – No! not his, but this villain's who sat there smugly taking his ease and pulling at his pipe.

At a blow Richard dashed the thing from his companion's mouth and fingers. Trenchard looked up startled.

"What the devil…?" he began.

"It is your fault, your fault!" cried Richard, his eyes blazing, his lips livid. "It was you who lured me hither."

Trenchard stared at him in bland surprise. "Now, what a plague is't you're saying?" he asked, and brought Richard to his senses by awaking in him the instinct of self-preservation.

How could he explain his meaning without betraying himself? – and surely that were a folly, now that the others were no doubt disposed of. Let him, rather, bethink him of his own safety. Trenchard looked at him keenly, with well-assumed intent to read what might be passing in his mind, then rose, paid for the wine, and expressed his intention of going forth to inquire into these strange matters that were happening in Bridgwater.

Meanwhile, those volleys fired in Mr Newlington's orchard had caused – as well may be conceived – an agitated interruption of the superb feast Mr Newlington had spread for his noble and distinguished guests. The Duke had for some days been going in fear of his life, for already he had been fired at more than once by men anxious to earn the price at which his head was valued; instantly he surmised that whatever that firing might mean, it indicated some attempt to surprise him with the few gentlemen who attended him.

The whole company came instantly to its feet, and Colonel Wade stepped to a window that stood open – for the night was very warm. The Duke turned for explanation to his host; the trader, however, professed himself entirely unable to offer any. He was very pale and his limbs were visibly trembling, but then his agitation was most natural. His wife and daughter supervened at that moment, in their alarm entering the room unceremoniously, in spite of the august presence, to inquire into the meaning of this firing, and to reassure themselves that their father and his illustrious guests were safe.

From the windows they could observe a stir in the gardens below. Black shadows of men flitted to and fro, and a loud, rich voice was heard calling to them to take cover, that they were betrayed. Then a sheet of livid flame blazed along the summit of the low wall, and a second volley of musketry rang out, succeeded by cries and screams from the assailed and the shouts of the assailers who were now pouring into the garden through the battered doorway and over the wall. For some moments steel rang on steel, and pistol-shots cracked here and there to the accompaniment of voices, raised some in anger, some in pain. But it was soon over, and a comparative stillness succeeded.

A voice called up from the darkness under the window to know if His Majesty was safe. There had been a plot to take him; but the ambuscaders had been ambuscaded in their turn, and not a man of them remained – which was hardly exact, for under a laurel bush, scarce daring to breathe, lay Sir Rowland Blake, livid with fear and fury, and bleeding from a rapier scratch in the cheek, but otherwise unhurt.

In the room above Monmouth had sunk wearily into his chair upon hearing of the design there had been against his life. A deep, bitter melancholy enwrapped his spirit. Lord Grey's first thoughts flew to the man he most disliked – the one man missing from those who had been bidden to accompany His Majesty, whose absence had already formed the subject of comment. Grey remembered his bearing before the council that same evening, and his undisguised resentment of the reproaches levelled against him.

"Where is Mr Wilding?" he asked suddenly, his voice dominating the din of talk that filled the room. "Do we hold the explanation of his absence?"

Monmouth looked up quickly, his beautiful eyes ineffably sad, his weak mouth drooping at the corners. Wade turned to confront Grey.

"Your lordship does not suggest that Mr Wilding can have a hand in this?"

"Appearances would seem to point in that direction," answered Grey, and in his wicked heart he almost hoped it might be so.

"Then appearances speak truth for once," came a bitter, ringing voice.

They turned, and there on the threshold stood Mr Wilding. Unheard he had come upon them. He was bareheaded and carried his drawn sword. There was blood upon it, and there was blood on the lace that half concealed the hand that held it; otherwise – and saving that his shoes and stockings were sodden with the dew from the long grass in the orchard – he was as spotless as when he had left Ruth in Trenchard's lodging; his face, too, was calm, save for the mocking smile with which he eyed Lord Grey.

Monmouth rose on his appearance, and put his hand to his sword in alarm. Grey whipped his own from the scabbard, and placed himself slightly in front of his master as if to preserve him.

"You mistake, sirs," said Wilding quietly. "The hand I have had in this affair has been to save your Majesty from your enemies. At the moment I should have joined you, word was brought me of the plot that was laid, of the trap that was set for you. I hastened to the Castle and obtained a score of musketeers of Slape's Company. With those I surprised the murderers lurking in the garden there, and made an end of them. I greatly feared I should not come in time; but it is plain that Heaven preserves your Majesty for better days."

In the revulsion of feeling, Monmouth's eyes shone moist. Grey sheathed his sword with an awkward laugh, and a still more awkward word of apology to Wilding. The Duke, moved by a sudden impulse to make amends for his unworthy suspicions, for his perhaps unworthy reception of Wilding earlier that evening in the council room, drew the sword on which his hand still rested. He advanced a step.

"Kneel, Mr Wilding," he said in a voice stirred by emotion. But Wilding's stern spirit scorned this all too sudden friendliness of Monmouth's as much as he scorned the accolade at Monmouth's hands.

"There are more pressing matters to demand your Majesty's attention," said Mr Wilding coldly, advancing to the table as he spoke, and taking up a napkin to wipe his blade, "than the reward of an unworthy servant." Monmouth felt his sudden enthusiasm chilled by that tone and manner.

"Mr Newlington," said Mr Wilding, after the briefest of pauses, and the fat, sinful merchant started forward in alarm. It was like a summons of doom. "His Majesty came hither, I am informed, to receive at your hands a sum of money – twenty thousand pounds – towards the expenses of the campaign. Have you the money at hand?" And his eye, glittering between cruelty and mockery, fixed itself upon the merchant's ashen face.

"It…it shall be forthcoming by morning," stammered Newlington.

"By morning?" cried Grey, who, with the others, watched Mr Newlington what time they all wondered at Mr Wilding's question and the manner of it.

"You knew that I march tonight," Monmouth reproached the merchant.

"And it was to receive the money that you invited His Majesty to do you the honour of supping with you here," put in Wade, frowning darkly.

The merchant's wife and daughter stood beside him watching him, and plainly uneasy. Before he could make any reply, Mr Wilding spoke again.

"The circumstance that he has not the money by him is a little odd – or would be were it not for what has happened. I would submit, your Majesty, that you receive from Mr Newlington not twenty thousand pounds as he had promised you, but thirty thousand, and that you receive it not as a loan, as was proposed, but as a fine imposed upon him in consequence of his lack of care in the matter of his orchard."

Monmouth looked at the merchant very sternly. "You have heard Mr Wilding's suggestion," said he. "You may thank the god of traitors it was made, else we might have thought of a harsher course. You shall pay the money by ten o'clock tomorrow to Mr Wilding, whom I shall leave behind for the sole purpose of collecting it." He turned from Newlington in plain disgust. "I think, sirs, that there is no more to be done. Are the streets safe, Mr Wilding?"

"Not only safe, your Majesty, but the twenty men of Slape's and your own life-guards are waiting to escort you."

"Then in God's name let us be going," said Monmouth, sheathing his sword and moving towards the door. Not a second time did he offer to confer the honour of knighthood upon his saviour.

Mr Wilding turned and went out to marshal his men. The Duke and his officers followed more leisurely. As they reached the door a woman's cry broke the silence behind them. Monmouth turned. Mr Newlington, purple of face and his eyes protruding horribly, was beating the air with his hands. Suddenly he collapsed, and crashed forward with arms flung out amid the glass and silver of the table all spread with the traitor's banquet to which he had bidden his unsuspecting victim.

His wife and daughter ran to him and called him by name, Monmouth paused a moment to watch them from the doorway with eyes unmoved. But Mr Newlington answered not their call, for he was dead.

Chapter 20

THE RECKONING

Ruth had sped home through the streets unattended, as she had come, heedless of the rude jostlings and ruder greetings she met with from those she passed; heedless, too, of the smarting of her injured hand, for the agony of her soul was such that it whelmed all minor sufferings of the flesh.

In the dining-room at Lupton House she came upon Diana and Lady Horton at supper, and her appearance – her white and distraught face and blood-smeared gown – brought both women to their feet in alarmed inquiry, no less than it brought Jasper, the butler, to her side with ready solicitude. Ruth answered him that there was no cause for fear, that she was quite well – had scratched her hand, no more; and with that dismissed him. When she was alone with her aunt and cousin, she sank into a chair and told them what had passed 'twixt her husband and herself, and most of what she said was Greek to Lady Horton.

"Mr Wilding has gone to warn the Duke," she ended, and the despair of her tone was tragical. "I sought to detain him until it should be too late – I thought I had done so, but…but… O, I am afraid, Diana!"

"Afraid of what?" asked Diana. "Afraid of what?" and she came to Ruth and set an arm in comfort about her shoulders.

"Afraid that Mr Wilding might reach the Duke in time to be destroyed with him," her cousin answered. "Such a warning could but hasten on the blow."

Lady Horton begged to be enlightened, and was filled with horror when – from Diana – enlightenment was hers. Her sympathies were all with the handsome Monmouth, for he was beautiful and should therefore be triumphant; poor Lady Horton never got beyond externals. That her nephew and Sir Rowland, whom she had esteemed, should be leagued in this dastardly undertaking against that lovely person horrified her beyond words. She withdrew soon afterwards, having warmly praised Ruth's action in warning Mr Wilding – unable to understand that it should be no part of Ruth's design to save the Duke – and went to her room to pray for the preservation of the late King's handsome son.

Left alone with her cousin, Ruth gave expression to the fears for Richard by which she was being tortured. Diana poured wine for her and urged her to drink; she sought to comfort and reassure her. But as moments passed and grew to hours and still Richard did not appear, Ruth's fears that he had come to harm were changed to certainty. There was a moment when, but for Diana's remonstrances, she had gone forth in quest of news. Bad news were better than this horror of suspense. What if Wilding's warning should have procured help, and Richard were slain in consequence? O, it was unthinkable! Diana, white of face, listened to and shared her fears. Even her shallow nature was stirred by the tragedy of Ruth's position, by dread lest Richard should indeed have met his end that night. In these moments of distress she forgot her hopes of triumphing over Blake, of punishing him for his indifference to herself.

At last, at something after midnight, there came a fevered rapping at the outer door. Both women started up, and with arms about each other, in their sudden panic, stood there waiting for the news that must be here at last.

The door of the dining-room was flung open; the women recoiled in their dread of what might come; then Richard entered, Jasper's startled countenance showing behind him.

He closed the door, shutting out the wondering servant, and they saw that though his face was ashen and his limbs all a-tremble, he showed no sign of any hurt or effort. His dress was as meticulous as when last they had seen him. Ruth flew to him, flung her arms about his neck, and pressed him to her.

"Oh, Richard, Richard!" she sobbed in the immensity of her relief. "Thank God! Thank God!"

He wriggled peevishly in her embrace, disengaged her arms, and put her from him almost roughly. "Have done!" he growled, and, lurching past her, he reached the table, took up a bottle, and brimmed himself a measure. He gulped the wine avidly, set down the cup, and shivered. "Where is Blake?" he asked.

"Blake?" echoed Ruth, her lips white. Diana sank into a chair, watchful, fearful and silent, taking now no glory in the thing she had encompassed.

Richard beat his hands together in a passion of dismay. "Is he not here?" he asked, and groaned, "O God!" He flung himself all limp into a chair. "You have heard the news, I see," he said.

"Not all of it," said Diana hoarsely, leaning forward. "Tell us what passed."

He moistened his lips with his tongue. "We were betrayed," he said in a quivering voice. "Betrayed! Did I but know by whom…" He broke off with a bitter laugh and shrugged, rubbing his hands together and shivering till his shoulders shook. "Blake's party was set upon by half a company of musketeers. Their corpses are strewn about old Newlington's orchard. Not one of them escaped. They say that Newlington himself is dead." He poured himself more wine.

Ruth listened, her eyes burning, the rest of her as cold as ice. "But…but oh, thank God that you at least are safe, Dick!"

"How did you escape?" quoth Diana.

"How?" He started as if he had been stung. He laughed in a high, cracked voice, his eyes wild and bloodshot. "How? Perhaps it is just as well that Blake has gone to his account. Perhaps…" He checked on the word, and started to his feet; Diana screamed in sheer affright. Behind her the windows had been thrust open so violently that one of the panes was shivered. Blake stood under the lintel, scarce recognisable, so smeared was his face with the blood escaping from the wound his cheek had taken. His clothes were muddied, soiled, torn and disordered.

Framed there against the black background of the night, he stood and surveyed them for a moment, his aspect terrific. Then he leapt forward, baring his sword as he came. An incoherent roar burst from his lips as he bore straight down upon Richard.

"You damned, infernal traitor!" he cried. "Draw, draw! Or die like the muckworm that you are."

Intrepid, her terror all vanished now that there was the need for courage, Ruth confronted him, barring his passage, a buckler to her palsied brother.

"Out of my way, mistress, or I'll be doing you a mischief."

"You are mad, Sir Rowland," she told him in a voice that did something towards restoring him to his senses.

His fierce eyes considered her a moment, and he controlled himself to offer an explanation. "The twenty that were with me lie stark under the stars in Newlington's garden," he told her, as Richard had told her already. "I escaped by a miracle, no less, but for what? Feversham will demand of me a stern account of those lives, whilst if I am found in Bridgwater there will be a short shift for me at the rebel hands – for my share in this affair is known, my name on every lip in the town. And why?" he asked with a sudden increase of fierceness. "Why? Because that craven villain there betrayed me."

"He did not," she answered in so assured a voice that not only did it give him pause, but caused Richard, cowering behind her, to raise his head in wonder.

Sir Rowland smiled his disbelief, and that smile, twisting his blood-smeared countenance, was grotesque and horrible. "I left him to guard our backs and give me warning if any approached," he informed her. "I knew him for too great a coward to be trusted in the fight; so I gave him a safe task, and yet in that he failed me – failed me because he had betrayed and sold me."

"He had not. I tell you he had not," she insisted. "I swear it."

He stared at her. "There was no one else for it," he made answer, and bade her harshly stand aside. Diana, huddled together, watched and waited in horror for the end of these consequences of her work.

Blake made a sudden movement to win past Ruth. Richard staggered to his feet intent on defending himself; but he was swordless; retreat to the door suggested itself, and he had half turned to attempt to gain it, when Ruth's next words arrested him, petrified him.

"There *was* someone else for it, Sir Rowland," she cried. "It was not Richard who betrayed you. It...it was I."

"You?" The fierceness seemed all to drop away from him, whelmed in the immensity of his astonishment. "You?" Then he laughed loud in scornful disbelief. "You think to save him," he said.

"Should I lie?" she asked him, calm and brave.

He stared at her stupidly; he passed a hand across his brow, and looked at Diana. "Oh, it is impossible!" he said at last.

"You shall hear," she answered, and told him how at the last moment she had learnt not only that her husband was in Bridgwater, but that he was to sup at Newlington's with the Duke's party.

"I had no thought of betraying you or of saving the Duke," she said. "I knew how justifiable was what you intended. But I could not let Mr Wilding go to his death. I sought to detain him, warning him only when I thought it would be too late for him to warn others. But you delayed overlong, and..."

A hoarse inarticulate cry from him came to interrupt her at that point. One glimpse of his face she had and of the hand half raised with sword pointing towards her, and she closed her eyes, thinking that her sands were run. And, indeed, Blake's intention was just then to kill her. That he should owe his betrayal to her was in itself cause enough to enrage him, but that her motive should have been her desire to save Wilding – Wilding of all men! – that was the last straw.

Had he been forewarned that Wilding was to be one of Monmouth's party at Mr Newlington's, his pulses would have throbbed with joy, and he would have flung himself into his murderous task with twice the zest he had carried to it. And now he learned that not only had she thwarted his schemes against Monmouth, but had deprived him of the ardently sought felicity of widowing her. He drew back his arm for the thrust; Diana huddled into her chair, too horror-stricken to speak or move; Richard – immediately behind his sister – saw nothing of what was passing, and thought of nothing but his own safety.

Then Blake paused, stepped back, returned his sword to its scabbard, and, bending himself – but whether to bow or not was not quite plain – he took some paces backwards, then turned and went out by the window as he had come. But there was a sudden purposefulness in the way he did it that might have warned them his withdrawal was not quite the retreat it seemed.

They watched him with many emotions, predominant among which was relief, and when he was gone Diana rose and came to Ruth.

"Come," she said, and sought to lead her from the room. But there was Richard now to be reckoned with, Richard from whom the palsy was of a sudden fallen, now that the cause of it had withdrawn. He had his back to the door, and his weak mouth was pursed up into a semblance of resolution, his pale eyes looked stern, his white eyebrows bent together in a frown.

"Wait," he said. They looked at him, and the shadow of a smile almost flitted across Diana's face. He stepped to the door and, opening it, held it wide. "Go, Diana," he said. "Ruth and I must understand each other."

Diana hesitated. "You had better go, Diana," said her cousin, whereupon Mistress Horton went.

Hot and fierce came the recriminations from Richard's lips when he and his sister were alone, and Ruth weathered the storm bravely until it was stemmed again by fresh fear in Richard. For Blake had suddenly reappeared. He came forward from the window; his manner composed and full of resolution. Young Westmacott recoiled, the heat all frozen out of him. But Blake scarce looked at him, his smouldering glance was all for Ruth, who watched him with incipient fear, despite herself.

"Madam," he said, " 'tis not to be supposed a mind holding so much thought for a husband's safety could find room for any concern as to another's. I will ask you, natheless, to consider what tale I am to bear Lord Feversham."

"What tale?" said she.

"Aye, that will account for what has chanced; for my failure to discharge the task entrusted me, and for the slaughter of an officer of his and twenty men."

"Why ask me this?" she demanded half angrily; then, suddenly bethinking her of how she had ruined his enterprise, and of the position in which she had placed him, she softened. Her clean mind held justice very dear. She approached. "Oh, I am sorry – sorry, Sir Rowland," she cried. He sneered. He had wiped some of the blood from his face, but still looked terrible enough.

"Sorry!" said he, and laughed unpleasantly. "You'll come with me to Feversham and tell him what you did," said he.

"I?" She recoiled in fear.

"At once," he informed her.

"Wha...what's that?" faltered Richard, calling up his manhood, and coming forward. "What are you saying, Blake?"

Sir Rowland disdained to heed him. "Come, mistress," he said, and putting forward his hand he caught her wrist and pulled her roughly towards him. She struggled to free herself, but he leered evilly upon her, no whit discomposed by her endeavours. Though short of stature, he was a man of considerable bodily strength, and she, though tall, was slight of frame. He released her wrist, and before she realised what he was about he had stooped, passed an arm behind her knees, another round her waist, and, swinging her from her feet, took her up bodily in his arms. He turned about, and a scream broke from her.

"Hold!" cried Richard. "Hold, you madman!"

"Keep off, or I'll make an end of you before I go," roared Blake over his shoulder, for already he had turned about and was making for the window, apparently no more hindered by his burden than had she been a doll. Richard sprang to the door. "Jasper!" he bawled. "Jasper!" He had no weapons, as we have seen, else it may be that he had made an attempt to use them.

Ruth got a hand free and caught at the window frame as Blake was leaping through. It checked their progress, but did not sensibly delay it. It was unfortunately her wounded hand with which she had sought to cling, and with an angry, brutal wrench Sir Rowland compelled her to unclose her grasp. He sped down the lawn towards the orchard, where his horse was tethered. And now she knew in a subconscious sort of way why he had earlier withdrawn. He had gone to saddle for this purpose.

She struggled now, thinking that he would be too hampered to compel her to his will. He became angry, and set her down beside his horse, one arm still holding her. "Look you, mistress," he told her fiercely, "living or dead, you come with me to Feversham. Choose now."

His tone was such that she never doubted he would carry out his threat. And so in dull despair she submitted, hoping that Feversham might be a gentleman and would recognise and respect a lady. Half fainting, she allowed him to swing her to the withers of his horse. Thus they threaded their way in the dim starlit night through the trees towards the gate. It stood open, and they passed out into the lane. There Sir Rowland put his horse to the trot, which he increased to a gallop when he was over the bridge and clear of the town.

Chapter 21

THE SENTENCE

Mr Wilding, as we know, was to remain at Bridgwater for the purpose of collecting from Mr Newlington the fine which had been imposed upon him. It is by no means clear whether Monmouth realised the fullness of the tragedy at the merchant's house, and whether he understood that, stricken with apoplexy at the thought of parting with so considerable a portion of his fortune, Mr Newlington had not merely fainted, but had expired under His Grace's eyes. If he did realise it he was cynically indifferent, and lest we should be doing him an injustice by assuming this, we had better give him the benefit of the doubt, and take it that in the subsequent bustle of departure, his mind filled with the prospect of the night attack to be delivered upon his uncle's army at Sedgemoor, he thought no more either of Mr Newlington or of Mr Wilding. The latter, as we know, had no place in the rebel army; although a man of his hands, he was not a trained soldier, and notwithstanding that he may fully have intended to draw his sword for Monmouth when the time came, yet circumstances had led to his continuing after Monmouth's landing the more diplomatic work of movement-man, in which he had been engaged for the months that had preceded it.

So it befell that when Monmouth's army marched out of Bridgwater at eleven o'clock on that Sunday night, not to make for Gloucester and Cheshire, as was generally believed, but to fall upon the encamped Feversham at Sedgemoor and slaughter the royal army in their beds, Mr Wilding was left behind. Trenchard was gone, in command of his troop of horse, and Mr Wilding had for only company his thoughts touching the singular happenings of that busy night.

He went back to the sign of The Ship overlooking the Cross, and, kicking off his sodden shoes, he supped quietly in the room of which shattered door and broken window reminded him of his odd interview with Ruth, and of the comedy of love she had enacted to detain him there. The thought of it embittered him; the part she had played seemed to his retrospective mind almost a wanton's part – for all that in name she was his wife. And yet, underlying a certain irrepressible nausea, came the reflection that, after all, her purpose had been to save his life. It would have been a sweet thought, sweet enough to have overlaid that other bitterness, had he not insisted upon setting it down entirely to her gratitude and her sense of justice. She intended to repay the debt in which she had stood to him since, at the risk of his own life and fortune, he had rescued her brother from the clutches of the lord-lieutenant at Taunton.

He sighed heavily as he thought of the results that had attended his compulsory wedding of her. In the intensity of his passion, in the blindness of his vanity, which made him confident – gloriously confident – that did he make himself her husband, she herself would make of him her lover before long, he had committed an unworthiness of which it seemed he might never cleanse himself in life. There was but one amend, as he had told her. Let him make it, and perhaps she would – out of gratitude, if out of no other feeling – come to think more kindly of him; and that night it seemed to him, as he sat alone in that mean chamber, that it were a better and a sweeter thing to earn some measure of her esteem by death than to continue in a life that inspired her hatred and resentment. From which it will be seen how utterly he disbelieved the protestations she had uttered in seeking to detain him. They were – he was assured – a part of a scheme, a trick, to lull him while Monmouth and his officers were being butchered. And she had gone the length of saying she loved him! He regretted that, being as he was convinced of its untruth. What cause had she to love him? She hated him, and because she hated him she did not scruple to lie to him – once with suggestions and this time with actual expression of affection – that she might gain her ends: ends that concerned her brother and Sir Rowland Blake. Sir Rowland Blake! The name was a very goad to his passion and despair.

He rose from the table and took a turn in the room, moving noiselessly in his stockinged feet. He felt the need of air and action; the weariness of his flesh incurred in his long ride from London was cast off or forgotten. He must go forth. He picked up his fine shoes of Spanish leather, but as luck would have it – little though he guessed the extent just then – he found them hardening, though still damp from the dews of Mr Newlington's garden. He cast them aside, and, taking a key from his pocket, unlocked an oak cupboard and withdrew the heavy muddy boots in which he had ridden from town. He drew them on and, taking up his hat and sword, went down the creaking stairs and out into the street.

Bridgwater had fallen quiet by now; the army was gone and the townsfolk were in their beds. Moodily, unconsciously, yet as if guided by a sort of instinct, he went down the High Street, and then turned off into the narrower lane that led in the direction of Lupton House. By the gates of this he paused, recalled out of his abstraction and rendered aware of whither his steps had led him by the sight of the hall door standing open, a black figure silhouetted against the light behind it. What was happening here? Why were they not abed like all decent folk?

The figure called to him in a quavering voice. "Mr Wilding! Mr Wilding!" for the light beating upon his face and figure from the open door had revealed him. The form came swiftly forward, its steps pattering down the walk, another slenderer figure surged in its place upon the threshold, hovered there an instant, then plunged down into the darkness to come after it. But the first was by now upon Mr Wilding.

"What is it, Jasper?" he asked, recognizing the old servant.

"Mistress Ruth!" wailed the fellow, wringing his hands. "She…she has been…carried off." He got it out in gasps, winded by his short run and by the excitement that possessed him.

No word said Wilding. He just stood and stared, scarcely understanding, and in that moment they were joined by Richard. He seized Wilding by the arm. "Blake has carried her off," he cried.

"Blake?" said Mr Wilding, and wondered with a sensation of nausea was it an ordinary running away. But Richard's next words made it plain to him that it was no amorous elopement, nor even amorous abduction.

"He has carried her to Feversham…for her betrayal of his tonight's plan to seize the Duke."

That stirred Mr Wilding. He wasted no time in idle questions or idler complainings. "How long since?" he asked, and it was he who clutched Richard now, by the shoulder and with a hand that hurt.

"Not ten minutes ago," was the quavering answer.

"And you were at hand when it befell?" cried Wilding, the scorn in his voice rising superior to his agitation and fears for Ruth. "You were at hand, and could neither prevent nor follow him?"

"I'll go with you now, if you'll give chase," whimpered Richard, feeling himself for once the craven that he was.

"If?" echoed Wilding scornfully, and dragged him past the gate and up towards the house even as he spoke. "Is there room for a doubt of it? Have you horses, at least?"

"To spare," said Richard as they hurried on.

They skirted the house and found the stable door open as Blake had left it. Old Jasper followed with a lamp which burned steadily, so calm was the air of that July night. In three minutes they had saddled a couple of nags; in five they were riding for the bridge and the road to Weston Zoyland.

"It is a miracle you remained in Bridgwater," said Richard as they rode. "How came you to be left behind?"

"I had a task assigned to me in the town against the Duke's return tomorrow," Wilding explained, and he spoke almost mechanically, his mind full of – anguished by – thoughts of Ruth.

"Against the Duke's return?" cried Richard, first surprised and then thinking that Wilding spoke at random. "Against the Duke's return?" he repeated.

"That is what I said."

"But the Duke is marching to Gloucester."

"The Duke is marching by circuitous ways to Sedgemoor," answered Wilding, never dreaming that at this time of day there could be the slightest imprudence in saying so much, indeed taking little heed of what he said, his mind obsessed by the other, to him, far weightier matter.

"To Sedgemoor?" gasped Westmacott.

"Aye – to take Feversham by surprise – to destroy King James's soldiers in their beds. He should be near upon the attack by now. But there! Spur on and save your breath if we are to overtake Sir Rowland."

They pounded on through the night at a breakneck pace which they never slackened until, when within a quarter of a mile or so of Penzoy Pound, where the army was encamped and slumbering by now, they caught sight of the musketeers' matches glowing in the dark ahead of them. An outpost barred their progress; but Richard had the watchword, and he spurred ahead shouting "Albemarle," and the soldiers fell back and gave them passage. On they galloped, skirting Penzoy Pound and the army sleeping in utter unconsciousness of the fate that was creeping stealthily upon it out of the darkness and mists across the moors; they clattered on past Langmoor Stone and dashed straight into the village, Richard never drawing rein until he reached the door of the cottage where Feversham was lodged.

They had come not only at a headlong pace, but in a headlong manner, without quite considering what awaited them at the end of their ride in addition to their object of finding Ruth. It was only now, as he drew rein before the lighted house and caught the sound of

Blake's raised voice pouring through an open window on the ground floor, that Richard fully realised what manner of rashness he was committing. He was too late to rescue Ruth from Blake. What more could he look to achieve? His hope had been that with Wilding's help he might snatch her from Sir Rowland before the latter reached his destination. But now – to enter Feversham's presence and in association with so notorious a rebel as Mr Wilding were a piece of folly of the heroic kind that Richard did not savour. Indeed, had it not been for Wilding's masterful presence, it is more than odds he had turned tail, and ridden home again to bed.

But Wilding, who had leapt nimbly to the ground, stood waiting for Richard to dismount, impatient now that from the sound of Sir Rowland's voice he had assurance that Richard had proved an able guide. The young man got down, but might yet have hesitated had not Wilding caught him by the arm and whirled him up the steps through the open door, past the two soldiers who kept it, and who were too surprised to stay him, straight into the long, low-ceilinged chamber where Feversham, attended by a captain of horse, was listening to Blake's angry narrative of that night's failure.

Mr Wilding's entrance was decidedly sensational. He stepped quickly forward, and taking Blake, who was still talking, all unconscious of those behind him, by the collar of his coat, he interrupted him in the middle of an impassioned period, wrenched him backwards off his feet, and dashed him with a force almost incredible into a heap in a corner of the room. There for some moments the baronet lay half dazed by the shock of his fall.

A long table, which seemed to divide the chamber in two, stood between Lord Feversham and his officer and Mr Wilding and Ruth – by whose side he had now come to stand in Blake's room.

There was an exclamation, half anger, half amazement, at Mr Wilding's outrage upon Sir Rowland, and the captain of horse sprang forward. But Wilding raised his hand, his face so composed and calm that it was impossible to think him conceiving any violence, as indeed he protested at that moment.

"Be assured, gentlemen," he said, "that I have no further rudeness to offer any so that this lady is suffered to withdraw with me." And he took in his own a hand that Ruth, amazed and unresisting, yielded up to him. That touch of his seemed to drive out her fears and to restore her confidence; the mortal terror in which she had been until his coming dropped from her now. She was no longer alone and abandoned to the vindictiveness of rude and violent men. She had beside her one in whom experience had taught her to have faith.

Louis Duras, Marquis de Blanquefort, and Earl of Feversham, coughed with mock discreetness under cover of his hand. "Ahem!"

He was a comely man with a long nose, good low-lidded eyes, a humorous mouth, and a weak chin; at a glance he looked what he was, a weak, good-natured sensualist. He was resplendent at the moment in a blue satin dressing-gown stiff with gold lace, for he had been interrupted by Blake's arrival in the very act of putting himself to bed, and his head – divested of his wig – was bound up in a scarf of many colours.

At his side, the red-coated captain, arrested by the General's sardonic cough, stood, a red-faced, freckled boy, looking to his superior for orders.

"I t'ink you 'ave 'urt Sare Rowland," said Feversham composedly in his bad English. "Who are you, sare?"

"This lady's husband," answered Wilding, whereupon the captain stared and Feversham's brows went up in surprised amusement.

"So-ho! T'at true?" quoth the latter in a tone suggesting that it explained everything to him. "T'is gif a differen' colour to your story, Sare Rowlan'." Then he added in a chuckle, "Ho, ho – *l'amour!*" and laughed outright.

Blake, gathering together his wits and his limbs at the same time, made shift to rise.

"What a plague does their relationship matter?" he began. He would have added more, but the Frenchman thought this question one that needed answering.

"*Parbleu!*" he swore, his amusement rising. "It seem to matter somet'ing."

"Damn me!" swore Blake, red in the face from pale that he had been. "Do you conceive that if I had run away with his wife for her own sake I had fetched her to *you*?" He lurched forward as he spoke, but kept his distance from Wilding, who stood between Ruth and him.

Feversham bowed sardonically. "You are a such flatterer, Sare Rowlan'," said he, laughter bubbling in his words.

Blake looked his scorn of this trivial Frenchman, who, upon scenting what appeared to be the comedy of an outraged husband overtaking the man who had carried off his wife, forgot the serious business, a part of which Sir Rowland had already imparted to him. Captain Wentworth – a time-serving gentleman – smiled with this French general of a British army that he might win the great man's favour.

"I have told your lordship," said Blake, froth on his lips, "that the twenty men I had from you, as well as Ensign Norris, are dead in Bridgwater, and that my plan to carry off King Monmouth has come to ruin, all because we were betrayed by this woman. It is now my further privilege to point out to your lordship the man to whom she sold us."

Feversham misliked Sir Rowland's arrogant tone, misliked his angry, scornful glance. His eyes narrowed, the laughter faded slowly from his face.

"Yes, yes, I remember," said he; "t'is lady, you have tole us, betray you. Ver' well. But you have not tole us who betray you to t'is lady"; and he looked inquiringly at Blake.

The baronet's jaw dropped; his face lost some of its high colour. He was stunned by the question as the bird is stunned that flies headlong against a pane of glass. He had crashed into an obstruction so transparent that he had not seen it.

"So!" said Feversham, and he stroked the cleft of his chin. "Captain Wentwort', be so kind as to call t'e guard." Wentworth moved to obey, but before he had gone round the table Blake had looked behind him and espied Richard shrinking by the door.

"By Heaven!" he cried, "I can more than answer your lordship's question."

Wentworth stopped, looking at Feversham.

"*Voyons*," said the General.

"I can place you in possession of the man who has wrought our ruin. He is there," and he pointed theatrically to Richard.

Feversham looked at the limp figure in some bewilderment. Indeed, he was having a most bewildering evening – or morning, rather, for it was even then on the stroke of one o'clock. "An' who are *you*, sare?" he asked.

Richard came forward, nerving himself for what was to follow. It had just occurred to him that he held a card which should trump any trick of Sir Rowland's vindictiveness and the prospect heartened and comforted him.

"I am this lady's brother, my lord," he answered, and his voice was fairly steady.

"*Tiens!*" said Feversham, and, smiling, he turned to Wentworth.

"Quite a family party, sir," said the captain, smiling back.

"*Oh! mais tout-à-fait*," said the General, laughing outright, and then Wilding created a diversion by leading Ruth to a chair that stood at the far end of the table, and drawing it forward for her. "Ah, yes," said Feversham airily, "let Madame sit."

"You are very good, sir," said Ruth, her voice brave and calm.

"But somewhat lacking in spontaneity," Wilding criticised, which set Wentworth staring and the Frenchman scowling.

"Shall I call the guard, my lord?" asked Wentworth crisply.

"I t'ink yes," said Feversham, and the captain gained the door, and spoke a word to one of the soldiers without.

"But, my lord," exclaimed Blake in a tone of protest, "I vow you are too ready to take this fellow's word."

"He 'as spoke so few," said Feversham.

"Do you know who he is?"

"You 'af 'eard 'im say – t'e lady's 'usband."

"Aye – but his name," cried Blake, quivering with anger. "Do you know that it is Wilding?"

The name certainly made an impression that might have flattered the man to whom it belonged. Feversham's whole manner changed; the trivial air of persiflage that he had adopted hitherto was gone on the instant, and his brow grew dark.

"T'at true?" he asked sharply. "Are you Mistaire Wildin' – Mistaire Antoine Wildin'?"

"Your lordship's most devoted servant," said Wilding suavely, and made a leg.

Wentworth in the background paused in the act of reclosing the door to stare at this gentleman whose name Albemarle had rendered so excellently well known.

"And you to dare come 'ere?" thundered Feversham, thoroughly roused by the other's airy indifference. "You to dare come 'ere – into my ver' presence?"

Mr Wilding smiled conciliatingly. "I came for my wife, my lord," he reminded him. "It grieves me to intrude upon your lordship at so late an hour, and indeed it was far from my intent. I had hoped to overtake Sir Rowland before he reached you."

"*Nom de Dieu!*" swore Feversham. "Ho! A so great effrontery!" He swung round upon Blake again. "Sare Rowlan'," he bade him angrily, "be so kind to tell me what 'appen in Breechwater – everyt'ing!"

Blake, his face purple, seemed to struggle for breath and words. Mr Wilding answered for him.

"Sir Rowland is so choleric, my lord," he said in his pleasant, level voice, "that perhaps the tale would come more intelligibly from me. Believe me that he has served you to the best of his ability. Unfortunately for the success of your choice plan of murder, I had news of it at the eleventh hour, and with a party of musketeers I was able to surprise and destroy your cut-throats in Mr Newlington's garden. You see, my lord, I was to have been one of the victims myself, and I resented the attentions that were intended me. I had no knowledge that Sir Rowland had contrived to escape, and, frankly, it is a thing I deplore more than I can say, for had that not happened much trouble might have been saved and your lordship's rest had not been disturbed."

"But t'e woman?" cried Feversham impatiently. "How is she come into this *galère*?"

"It was she who warned him," Blake got out, "as already I have had the honour to inform your lordship."

"And your lordship cannot blame her for that," said Wilding. "The lady is a most loyal subject of King James; but she is also, as you observe, a dutiful wife. I will add that it was her intention to warn me only when too late for interference. Sir Rowland, as it happened, was slow in…"

"Silence!" blazed the Frenchman. "Now t'at I know who you are, t'at make a so great difference. Where is t'e guard, Wentwort'?"

"I hear them," answered the captain, and from the street came the tramp of their marching feet. Feversham turned again to Blake.

"T'e affaire 'as 'appen' so," he said, between question and assertion, summing up the situation as he understood it. "T'is rogue," and he pointed to Richard, " 'ave betray your plan to 'is sister, who betray it to 'er 'usband, who save t'e Duc de Monmoot'. *N'est-ce pas?*"

"That is so," said Blake, and Ruth scarcely thought it worth while to add that she had heard of the plot not only from her brother, but from Blake as well. After all, Blake's attitude in the matter, his action in bringing her to Feversham for punishment, and to exculpate himself, must suffice to cause any such statement of hers to be lightly received by the General.

She sat in an anguished silence, her eyes wide, her face pale, and waited for the end of this strange business. In her heart she did permit herself to think that it would be difficult to assemble a group of men less worthy of respect. Choleric and vindictive Blake, foolish Feversham, stupid Wentworth, and timid Richard – even Richard did not escape the unfavourable criticism they were undergoing in her subconscious mind. Only Wilding detached in that assembly – as he had detached in another that she remembered – and stood out in sharp relief a very man, calm, intrepid, self-possessed; and if she was afraid, she was more afraid for him than for herself. This was something that, perhaps, she scarcely realised just then; but she was to realise it soon.

Feversham was speaking again, asking Blake a fresh question. "And who betray you to t'is rogue?"

"To Westmacott?" cried Blake. "He was in the plot with me. He was left to guard the rear, to see that we were not taken by surprise, and he deserted his post. Had he not done that, there had been no disaster, in spite of Mr Wilding's intervention."

Feversham's brow was dark, his eyes glittered as they rested on the traitor.

"T'at true, sare?" he asked him.

"Not quite," put in Mr Wilding. "Mr Westmacott, I think, was constrained away. He did not intend…"

"*Tais-toi!*" blazed Feversham. "Did I interrogate you? It is for Mistaire Westercott to answer." He set a hand on the table and leaned forward towards Wilding, his face very malign. "You shall to answer for yourself, Mistaire Wildin'; I promise you you shall to answer for yourself." He turned again to Richard. "*Eh, bien?*" he snapped. "Will you speak?"

Richard came forward a step; he was certainly nervous and certainly pale; but neither as pale nor as nervous as from our knowledge of Richard we might have looked to see him at that moment.

"It is in a measure true," he said. "But what Mr Wilding has said is more exact. I was induced away. I did not dream any could know of the plan, or that my absence could cause this catastrophe."

"So you went, eh, *vaurien*? You t'ought t'at be to do your duty, eh? And it was you who tole your sistaire?"

"I may have told her, but not before she had the tale already from Blake."

Feversham sneered and shrugged. "Natural you will not speak true. A traitor I 'ave observe' is always liar."

Richard drew himself up; he seemed invested almost with a new dignity. "Your lordship is pleased to account me a traitor," he inquired.

"A dam' traitor," said his lordship, and at that moment the door opened, and a sergeant, with six men following him, stood at the salute upon the threshold. "*A la bonne heure!*" his lordship hailed them. "Sergean', you will arrest t'is rogue and t'is lady," – he waved his hand from Richard to Ruth – "and you will take t'em to lock-up." The sergeant advanced towards Richard, who drew a step away from him. Ruth rose to her feet in agitation. Mr Wilding interposed himself between her and the guard, his hand upon his sword.

"My lord," he cried, "do they teach no better courtesy in France?"

Feversham scowled at him, smiling darkly. "I shall talk wit' you soon, sare," said he, his words a threat.

"But, my lord…" began Richard. "I can make it very plain I am no traitor…"

"In t'e mornin'," said Feversham blandly, waving his hand, and the sergeant took Richard by the shoulder. But Richard twisted from his grasp.

"In the morning will be too late," he cried. "I have it in my power to render you such a service as you little dream of."

"Take 'im away," said Feversham wearily.

"I can save you from destruction," bawled Richard, "you and your army."

Perhaps even now Feversham had not heeded him but for Wilding's sudden interference.

"Silence, Richard!" he cried to him. "Would you betray…?" He checked on the word; more he dared not say; but he hoped faintly that he had said enough. Feversham, however, chanced to observe that this man who had shown himself hitherto so calm looked suddenly most singularly perturbed.

"Eh?" quoth the General. "An instan', Sergean'. What is t'is, eh?" and he looked from Wilding to Richard.

"Your lordship shall learn at a price," cried Richard.

"Me, I not bargain wit' traitors," said his lordship stiffly.

"Very well, then," answered Richard, and he folded his arms dramatically. "But no matter what your lordship's life may be hereafter, you will never regret anything more bitterly than you shall regret this by sunrise if indeed you live to see it."

Feversham shifted uneasily on his feet. "What you say?" he asked. "What you mean?"

"You shall know at a price," said Richard again.

Wilding, realising the hopelessness of interfering now, stood gloomily apart, a great bitterness in his soul at the indiscretion he had committed in telling Richard of the night attack that was afoot.

"Your lordship shall hear my price, but you need not pay it me until you have had an opportunity of verifying the information I have to give you."

"Tell me," said Feversham after a brief pause, during which he scrutinised the young man's face.

"If your lordship will promise liberty and safe conduct to my sister and myself."

"Tell me," Feversham repeated.

"When you have promised to grant me what I ask in return for my information."

"Yes, if I t'ink your information is wort' it."

"I am content," said Richard. He inclined his head and loosed the quarrel of his news. "Your camp is slumbering, your officers are all abed with the exception of the outpost on the road to Bridgwater. What should you say if I told you that Monmouth and all his army are marching upon you at this very moment, will probably fall upon you before another hour is past?"

Wilding uttered a groan, and his hands fell to his sides. Had Feversham observed this he might have been less ready with his sneering answer.

"A lie!" he answered, and laughed. "My fren', I 'ave myself been tonight, at midnight, on t'e moor, and I 'ave 'eard t'e army of t'e Duc de Monmoot' marching to Bristol on t'e road – what you call t'e road, Wentwort'?"

"The Eastern Causeway, my lord," answered the captain.

"*Voilà!*" said Feversham, and spread his hands. "What you say now, eh?"

"That that is part of Monmouth's plan to come at you across the moors, by way of Chedzoy, avoiding your only outpost, and falling upon you in your beds, all unawares. Lord! sir, do not take my word for it. Send out your scouts, and I dare swear they'll not need go far before they come upon the enemy."

Feversham looked at Wentworth. His lordship's face had undergone a change.

"What you t'ink?" he asked.

"Indeed, my lord, it sounds so likely," answered Wentworth, "that…that… I marvel we did not provide against such a contingency."

"But I 'ave provide'!" cried this nephew of the great Turenne. "Ogelt'orpe is on t'e moor and Sare Francis Compton. If t'is is true, 'ow can t'ey 'ave miss Monmoot'? Send word to Milor' Churchill at once, Wentwort'. Let t'e matter be investigate' – at once, Wentwort' – at once!" The General was dancing with excitement. Wentworth saluted and turned to leave the room. "If you 'ave tole me true," continued Feversham, turning now to Richard, "you shall 'ave t'e price you ask, and t'e t'anks of t'e King's army. But if not…"

"Oh, it's true enough," broke in Wilding, and his voice was like a groan, his face overcharged with gloom.

Feversham looked at him; his sneering smile returned.

"Me, I not remember," said he, "that Mr Westercott 'ave include you in t'e bargain."

Nothing had been further from Wilding's thoughts than such a suggestion. And he snorted his disdain. The sergeant had fallen back at Feversham's words, and his men lined the wall of the chamber. The General bade Richard be seated whilst he waited. Sir Rowland stood apart, leaning wearily against the wainscot, waiting also, his dull wits not quite clear how Richard might have come by so valuable a piece of information, his evil spirit almost wishing it untrue, in his vindictiveness, to the end that Richard might pay the price of having played him false and Ruth the price of having scorned him.

Feversham meanwhile was seeking – with no great success – to engage Mr Wilding in talk of Monmouth, against whom Feversham harboured in addition to his political enmity a very deadly personal hatred; for Feversham had been a suitor to the hand of the Lady Henrietta Wentworth, the woman for whom Monmouth – worthy son of his father – had practically abandoned his own wife; the woman with whom he had run off, to the great scandal of court and nation.

Despairing of drawing any useful information from Wilding, his lordship was on the point of turning to Blake, when quick steps and the rattle of a scabbard sounded without; the door was thrust open without ceremony, and Captain Wentworth reappeared.

"My lord," he cried, his manner excited beyond aught one could have believed possible in so phlegmatic-seeming a person, "it is true. We are beset."

"Beset!" echoed Feversham. "Beset already?"

"We can hear them moving on the moor. They are crossing the Langmoor Rhine. They will be upon us in ten minutes at the most. I have roused Colonel Douglas, and Dunbarton's regiment is ready for them."

Feversham exploded. "What else 'ave you done?" he asked. "Where is Milor' Churchill?"

"Lord Churchill is mustering his men as quietly as may be that they may be ready to surprise those who come to surprise us. By Heaven, sir, we owe a great debt to Mr Westmacott. Without his information we might have had all our throats cut whilst we slept."

"Be so kind to call Belmont," said Feversham. "Tell him to bring my clot'es."

Wentworth turned and went out again to execute the General's orders. Feversham spoke to Richard.

"We are oblige', Mr Westercott," said he. "We are ver' much oblige'."

Suddenly from a little distance came the roll of drums. Other sounds began to stir in the night outside to tell of a waking army. Feversham stood listening. "It is Dunbarton's," he murmured. Then, with some show of heat, "*Ah, Pardieu!*" he cried. "But it was a dirty t'ing t'is Monmoot' 'ave prepare'. It is murder; it is not t'e war."

"And yet," said Wilding critically, "it is a little more like war than the Bridgwater affair to which your lordship gave your sanction."

Feversham pursed his lips and considered the speaker. Wentworth re-entered, followed by the Earl's valet carrying an armful of garments. His lordship threw off his dressing-gown and stood forth in shirt and breeches.

"*Mais dépêche-toi, donc, Belmont!*" said he. "*Nous nous battons! Il faut que je m'habille.*" Belmont, a little wizened fellow who understood nothing of this topsy-turvey-dom, hastened forward, deposited his armful on the table, and selected a finely embroidered waistcoat, which he proceeded to hold for his master. Wriggling into it, Feversham rapped out his orders.

"Captain Wentwort', you will go to your regimen' at once. But first, ah – wait. Take t'ose six men and Mistaire Wilding. 'Ave 'im shot at once; you onderstan', eh? Good. *Allons*, Belmont! my cravat."

Chapter 22

THE EXECUTION

Captain Wentworth clicked his heels together and saluted. Blake, in the background, drew a deep breath – unmistakably of satisfaction, and his eyes glittered. A muffled cry broke from Ruth, who rose instantly from her chair, her hand on her bosom. Richard stood with fallen jaw, amazed, a trifle troubled even, whilst Mr Wilding started more in surprise than actual fear, and approached the table.

"You heard, sir," said Captain Wentworth.

"I heard," answered Mr Wilding quietly. "But surely not aright. One moment, sir," and he waved his hand so compellingly that, despite the order he had received, the phlegmatic captain hesitated. Feversham, who had taken the cravat – a yard of priceless Dutch lace – from the hands of his valet, and was standing with his back to the company at a small and very faulty mirror that hung by the overmantel, looked peevishly over his shoulder.

"My lord," said Wilding, and Blake, for all his hatred of this man, marvelled at a composure that did not forsake him even now, "you are surely not proposing to deal with me in this fashion – not seriously my lord?"

"*Ah ça!*" said the Frenchman. "T'ink it a jest if you please. What for you come 'ere?"

"Assuredly not for the purpose of being shot," said Wilding, and actually smiled. Then, in the tones of one discussing a matter that is grave but not of surpassing gravity, he continued: "It is not that I fail to recognise that I may seem to have incurred the rigour of the law; but these matters must be formally proved against me. I have affairs to set in order against such a consummation."

"Ta, ta!" snapped Feversham. "T'at not regard me. Wentwort', you 'ave 'eard my order." And he returned to his mirror and the nice adjustment of his neckwear.

"But, my lord," insisted Wilding, "you have not the right – you have not the power so to proceed against me. A man of my quality is not to be shot without a trial."

"You can 'ang if you prefer," said Feversham indifferently, drawing out the ends of his cravat and smoothing them down upon his breast. He faced about briskly. "Give me t'at coat, Belmont. His Majesty 'ave empower me to 'ang or shoot any gentlemens of t'e partie of t'e Duc de Monmoot' on t'e spot. I say t'at for your satisfaction. And look, I am desolate' to be so quick wit' you, but please to consider t'e circumstance. T'e enemy go to attack. Wentwort' must go to his regimen', and my ot'er officers are all occupi'. You comprehen' I 'ave not t'e time to spare you – *n'est-ce-pas?*"

Wentworth's hand touched Wilding on the shoulder. He was standing with head slightly bowed, his brows knit in thought. He looked round at the touch, sighed and smiled.

Belmont held the coat for his master, who slipped into it, and flung at Wilding what was intended for a consolatory sop. "It is *fortune de guerre*, Mistaire Wilding. I am desolate; but it is fortune of t'e war."

"May it be less fortunate for your lordship, then," said Wilding dryly, and was on the point of turning, when Ruth's voice came in a loud cry to startle him and quicken his pulses.

"My lord!" It was a cry of utter anguish.

Feversham, settling his gold-laced coat comfortably to his figure, looked at her. "Madame?" said he.

But she had nothing to say. She stood, deathly white, slightly bent forward, one hand wringing the other, her eyes almost wild, her bosom heaving frantically.

"Hum!" said Feversham, and he loosened and removed the scarf from his head. He shrugged slightly and looked at Wentworth. "*Finissons!*" said he.

The word and the look snapped the trammels that bound Ruth's speech.

"Five minutes, my lord!" she cried imploringly. "Give him five minutes – and me, my lord!"

Wilding, deeply shaken, trembled now as he awaited Feversham's reply. The Frenchman seemed to waver.

"*Bien,*" he began, spreading his hands. And in that moment a shot rang out in the night and startled the whole company. Feversham threw back his head; the signs of yielding left his face. "Ha!" he cried. "T'ey are arrive'." He snatched his wig from his lacquey's hands, donned it, and turned again an instant to the mirror to adjust the great curls. "Quick, Wentwort'! T'ere is no more time now. Make Mistaire Wilding be shot at once. T'en to your regimen'." He faced about and took the sword his valet proffered. "*Au revoir, messieurs! Serviteur, madame!*" And, buckling his sword-belt as he went, he swept out, leaving the door wide open, Belmont following, Wentworth saluting and the guards presenting arms.

"Come, sir," said the captain in a subdued voice, his eyes avoiding Ruth's face.

"I am ready," answered Wilding firmly, and he turned to glance at his wife.

She was bending towards him, her hands held out, such a look on her face as almost drove him mad with despair, reading it as he did. He made a sound deep in his throat before he found words.

"Give me one minute, sir – one minute," he begged Wentworth. "I ask no more than that."

Wentworth was a gentleman and not ill-natured. But he was a soldier and had received his orders. He hesitated between the instincts of the two conditions. And what time he did so there came a clatter of hoofs without to resolve him. It was Feversham departing.

"You shall have your minute, sir," said he. "More I dare not give you, as you can see."

"From my heart I thank you," answered Mr Wilding, and from the gratitude of his tone you might have inferred that it was his life Wentworth had accorded him.

The Captain had already turned aside to address his men. "Two of you outside, guard that window," he ordered. "The rest of you, in the passage. Bestir there!"

"Take your precautions, by all means, sir," said Wilding; "but I give you my word of honour I shall attempt no escape."

Wentworth nodded without replying. His eye lighted on Blake – who had been seemingly forgotten in the confusion – and on Richard. A kindliness for the man who met his end so unflinchingly, a respect for so worthy an enemy, actuated the red-faced captain.

"You had better take yourself off, Sir Rowland," said he. "And you, Mr Westmacott – you can wait in the passage with my men."

They obeyed him promptly enough, but when outside Sir Rowland made bold to remind the captain that he was failing in his duty, and that he should make a point of informing the General of this anon. Wentworth bade him go to the devil, and so was rid of him.

Alone, inside that low-ceilinged chamber, stood Ruth and Wilding face to face. He advanced towards her, and with a shuddering sob she flung herself into his arms. Still, he mistrusted the notion to which she was a prey – dreading lest it should have its root in pity. He patted her shoulder soothingly.

"Nay, nay, little child," he whispered in her ear. "Never weep for me that have not a tear for myself. What better resolution of the difficulties my folly has created?" For only answer she clung closer, her hands locked about his neck, her slender body shaken by her silent weeping. "Don't pity me," he besought her. "I am content it should be so. It is the amend I promised you. Waste no pity on me, Ruth."

She raised her face, her eyes, wild and blurred with tears, looked up to his.

"It is not pity," she cried. "I want you, Anthony. I love you, Anthony, Anthony!"

His face grew ashen. "It is true, then!" he asked her. "And what you said tonight was true! I thought you said it only to detain me."

"Oh, it is true, it is true!" she wailed.

He sighed; he disengaged a hand to stroke her face. "I am happy," he said, and strove to smile. "Had I lived, who knows…?"

"No, no, no," she interrupted him passionately, her arms tightening about his neck. He bent his head. Their lips met and clung. A knock fell upon the doors. They started, and Wilding raised his hands gently to disengage her pinioning arms.

"I must go, sweet," he said.

"God help me!" she moaned, and clung to him still. "It is I who am killing you – I and your love for me. For it was to save me you rode hither tonight, never pausing to weigh your own deadly danger. Oh, I am punished for having listened to every voice but the voice of my own heart where you were concerned. Had I loved you earlier – had I owned it earlier…"

"It had still been too late," he said, more to comfort her than because he knew it to be so. "Be brave for my sake, Ruth. You can be brave, I know – so well. Listen, sweet. Your words have made me happy. Mar not this happiness of mine by sending me out in grief at your grief."

Her response to his prayer was brave indeed. Through her tears came a faint smile to overspread her face so white and pitiful.

"We shall meet soon again," she said.

"Aye – think on that," he bade her, and pressed her to him. "Goodbye, sweet! God keep you till we meet!" he added, his voice infinitely tender.

"Mr Wilding!" Wentworth's voice called him, and the captain thrust the door open a foot or so. "Mr Wilding!"

"I am coming," he answered steadily. He kissed her again, and on that kiss of his she sank against him, and he felt her turn all limp. He raised his voice. "Richard!" he shouted wildly. "Richard!"

At the note of alarm in his voice Wentworth flung wide the door and entered, Richard's ashen face showing over his shoulder. In her brother's care Wilding delivered his mercifully unconscious wife. "See to her, Dick," he said, and turned to go, mistrusting himself now. But he paused as he reached the door, Wentworth waxing more and more impatient at his elbow. He turned again.

"Dick," he said, "we might have been better friends. I would we had been. Let us part so at least," and he held out his hand, smiling.

Before so much gallantry Richard was conquered almost to the point of worship; a weak man himself, there was no virtue he could more admire than strength. He left Ruth in the high-backed chair in which Wilding's tender hands had placed her, and sprang forward, tears in his eyes. He wrung Wilding's hands in wordless passion. "Be good to her, Dick," said Wilding, and went out with Wentworth.

He was marched down the street in the centre of that small party of musketeers of Dunbarton's regiment, his thoughts all behind him rather than ahead, a smile on his lips. He had conquered at the last. He thought of that other parting of theirs, nearly a month ago, on the road by Walford. Now, as then, circumstance was the fire that had melted her. But the crucible was no longer – as then – of pity; it was the crucible of love.

And in that same crucible, too, Anthony Wilding's nature had undergone a transmutation; his love for Ruth had been purified of that base alloy of desire which had driven him into the unworthiness of making her his own at all costs; there was no carnal grossness in his present passion; it was pure as a religion – the love that takes no account of self, the love that makes for joyous and grateful martyrdom. And a joyous and grateful martyr would Anthony Wilding have been could he have thought that his death would bring her happiness or peace. In such a faith as that he had marched – or so he thought – blithely to his end, and the smile on his lips had been less wistful than it was. Thinking of the agony in which he had left her, he almost came to wish – so pure was his love grown – that he had not conquered. The joy that at first was his was now all dashed. His death would cause her pain. His death! Oh, God! It is an easy thing to be a martyr; but this was not martyrdom; having done what he had done he had not the right to die. The last vestige of the smile that he had worn faded from his tight-pressed lips – tight-pressed as though to endure some physical suffering. His face greyed, and deep lines furrowed his brow. Thus he marched on, mechanically, amid his marching escort, through the murky, fog-laden night, taking no heed of the stir about them, for all Weston Zoyland was aroused by now.

Ahead of them, and over to the east, the firing blazed and crackled, volley upon volley, to tell them that already battle had been joined in earnest. Monmouth's surprise had aborted, and it passed through Wilding's mind that to a great extent he was to blame for this. But it gave him little care.

At least his indiscretion had served the purpose of rescuing Ruth from Lord Feversham's unclean clutches. For the rest, knowing that Monmouth's army by far outnumbered Feversham's, he had no doubt that the advantage must still lie with the Duke, in spite of Feversham's having been warned in the eleventh hour.

Louder grew the sounds of battle. Above the din of firing a swelling chorus rose upon the night, startling and weird in such a time and place. Monmouth's pious infantry went into action singing hymns, and Wentworth, impatient to be at his post, bade his men go faster.

The night was by now growing faintly luminous, and the deathly grey light of approaching dawn hung in the mists upon the moor. Objects grew visible in bulk at least, if not in form and shape, by the time the little company had reached the end of Weston village and come upon the deep mud dyke which had been Wentworth's objective – a ditch that communicated with the great rhine that served the King's forces so well on that night in Sedgemoor.

Within some twenty paces of this Wentworth called a halt, and would have had Wilding's hands pinioned behind him, and his eyes blindfolded, but that Wilding begged him this might not be done. Wentworth was, as we know, impatient; and between impatience and kindliness, perhaps, he acceded to Wilding's prayer.

He even hesitated a moment at the last. It was in his mind to speak some word of comfort to the doomed man. Then a sudden volley, more terrific than any that had preceded it, followed by hoarse cheering away to eastward, quickened his impatience. He bade the sergeant lead Mr Wilding forward and stand him on the edge of the ditch. His object was that thus the man's body would be disposed of without waste of time. This Wilding realised, his soul rebelling against this fate which had come upon him in the very hour when he most desired to live. Mad thoughts of escape crossed his mind – of a leap across the dyke, and a wild dash through the fog. But the futility of it was too appalling. The musketeers were already blowing their matches. He would suffer the ignominy of being shot in the back, like a coward, if he made any such attempt.

And so, despairing but not resigned, he took his stand on the very edge of the ditch. In an irony of obligingness he set half of his heels over the void, so that he was nicely balanced upon the edge of the cutting, and must go backwards and down into the mud when hit.

It was this position he had taken that gave him an inspiration in that last moment. The sergeant had moved away out of the line of fire, and he stood there alone, waiting erect and with his head held high, his eyes upon the grey mass of musketeers – blurred alike by mist and semi-darkness – some twenty paces distant along the line of which glowed eight red fuses.

Wentworth's voice rang out with the words of command.

"Blow your matches!"

Brighter gleamed the points of light, and under their steel pots the faces of the musketeers, suffused by a dull red glow, sprang for a moment out of the grey mass, to fade once more into the general greyness at the word, "Cock your matches!"

"Guard your pans!" came a second later the captain's voice, and then: "Present!"

There was a stir and rattle, and the dark, indistinct figure standing on the lip of the ditch was covered by the eight muskets. To the eyes of the firing party he was no more than a blurred shadowy form, showing a little darker than the encompassing dark grey.

"Give fire!"

On the word Mr Wilding lost the delicate, precarious balance he had been sustaining on the edge of the ditch and went over backwards, at the imminent risk – as he afterwards related – of breaking his neck. At the same instant a jagged, eight-pointed line of flame slashed the darkness, and the thunder of the volley pealed forth to lose itself in the greater din of battle on Penzoy Pound, hard by.

Chapter 23

MR WILDING'S BOOTS

In the filth of the ditch, Mr Wilding rolled over and lay prone. He threw out his left arm, and rested his brow upon it to keep his face above the mud. He strove to hold his breath, not that he might dissemble death, but that he might avoid being poisoned by the foul gases that, disturbed by his weight, bubbled up to choke him. His body half sank and settled in the mud, and seen from above, as he was presently seen by Wentworth – who ran forward with the sergeant's lanthorn to assure himself that the work had been well done – he had all the air of being not only dead but already half buried.

And now, for a second, Mr Wilding was in his greatest danger, and this from the very humaneness of the sergeant. The fellow advanced to the captain's side, a pistol in his hand. Wentworth held the light aloft and peered down into that six feet of blackness at the jacent figure.

"Shall I give him an ounce of lead to make sure, Captain?" quoth the sergeant. But Wentworth, in his great haste, had already turned about, and the light of his lanthorn no longer revealed the form of Mr Wilding.

"There is not the need. The ditch will do what may remain to be done, if anything does. Come on, man. We are wanted yonder."

The light passed, steps retreated, the sergeant muttering, and then Wentworth's voice was heard by Wilding some little distance off.

"Bring up your muskets!"

"Shoulder!"

"By the right – turn! March!" And the tramp, tramp of feet receded rapidly.

Wilding was already sitting up, endeavouring to get a breath of purer air. He rose to his feet, sinking almost to the top of his boots in the oozy slime. Foul gases were belched up to envelop him. He seized at irregularities in the bank, and got his head above the level of the ground. He thrust forward his chin and took great greedy breaths in a very gluttony of air – and never came Muscadine sweeter to a drunkard's lips. He laughed softly to himself. He was alone and safe. Wentworth and his men had disappeared. Away in the direction of Penzoy Pound the sounds of battle swelled ever to a greater volume. Cannons were booming now, and all was uproar – flame and shouting, cheering and shrieking, the thunder of hastening multitudes, the clash of steel, the pounding of horses, all blent to make up the horrid din of carnage.

Mr Wilding listened, and considered what to do. His first impulse was to join the fray. But, bethinking him that there could be little place for him in the confusion that must prevail by now, he reconsidered the matter, and his thoughts returning to Ruth – the wife for whom he had been at such pains to preserve himself on the very brink of death – he resolved to endanger himself no further for that night.

He dropped back into the ditch, and waded, ankle deep in slime, to the other side. There he crawled out, and gaining the moor lay down awhile to breathe his lungs. But not for long. The dawn was creeping pale and ghostly across the solid earth, and a faint fresh breeze was stirring and driving the mist in wispy shrouds before it. If he lingered there he might yet be found by some party of Royalist soldiers, and that would be to undo all that he had done. He rose, and struck out across the peaty ground. None knew the moors better than did he, and had he been with Grey's horse that night, it is possible things had fared differently, for he had proved a surer guide than did Godfrey the spy.

At first he thought of making for Bridgwater and Lupton House. By now Richard would be on his way thither with Ruth, and Wilding was in haste that she should be reassured that he had not fallen to the muskets of Wentworth's firing-party. But Bridgwater was far, and he began to realise, now that all excitement was past, that he was utterly exhausted. Next he thought of Scoresby Hall and his cousin Lord Gervase. But he was by no means sure that he might count upon a welcome. Gervase had shown no sympathy for Monmouth or his partisans, and whilst he would hardly go so far as to refuse Mr Wilding shelter, still Wilding felt an aversion to seeking what might be grudged him. At last he bethought him of home. Zoyland Chase was near at hand; but he had not been there since his wedding-day, and in the meantime he knew that it had been used as a barrack for the militia, and had no doubt that it had been wrecked and plundered. Still, it must have walls and a roof, and that, for the time, was all he craved, that he might rest awhile and recuperate his wasted forces.

A half-hour later he dragged himself wearily up the avenue between the elms – looking white as snow in the pale July dawn – to the clearing in front of his house.

Desertion was stamped upon the face of it. Shattered windows and hanging shutters everywhere. How wantonly they had wrecked it! It might have been a church, and the militia a regiment of Cromwell's iconoclastic Puritans. The door was locked, but going round he found a window – one of the door-windows of his library – hanging loose upon its hinges. He pushed it wide, and entered with a heavy heart. Instantly something stirred in a corner; a fierce growl was followed by a furious bark, and a lithe brown body leapt from the greater into the lesser shadows to attack the intruder. But at one word of his the hound checked suddenly, crouched an instant, then with a queer, throaty sound bounded forward in a wild delight that robbed it on the instant of its voice. It found it anon and leapt about him, barking furious joy in spite of all his vain endeavours to calm it. He grew afraid lest the dog should draw attention. He knew not who – if any – might be in possession of his house. The library, as he looked round, showed a scene of wreckage that excellently matched the exterior. Not a picture on the walls, not an arras, but had been rent to shreds. The great lustre that had hung from the centre of the ceiling was gone. Disorder reigned along the bookshelves, and yet there and elsewhere there was a certain orderliness, suggesting an attempt to straighten up the place after the ravagers had departed. It was these signs made him afraid the house might be tenanted by such as might prove his enemies.

"Down, Jack," he said to the dog for the twentieth time, patting its sleek head. "Down, down!"

But still the dog bounded about him, barking wildly. "Sh!" he hissed suddenly. Steps sounded in the hall. It was as he feared. The door was suddenly thrown open, and the grey morning light gleamed upon the long barrel of a musket. After it, bearing it, entered a white-haired old man.

He paused on the threshold, measuring the tall disordered stranger who stood there, his figure a black silhouette against the window by which he had entered.

"What seek you here, sir, in this house of desolation?" asked the voice of Mr Wilding's old servant.

He answered by one word. "Walters!"

The musket dropped with a clatter from the old man's hand. He sank back against the doorpost and leaned there an instant; then, whimpering and laughing, he came tottering forward – his old legs failing him in this excess of unexpected joy – and sank on his knees to kiss his master's hand.

Wilding patted the old head, as he had patted the dog's a little while ago. He was oddly moved; there was a knot in his throat. No home-coming could well have been more desolate. And yet, what home-coming could have brought him such a torturing joy as was now his? Oh, it is good to be loved, if it be by no more than a dog and an old servant!

In a moment Walters was himself again. He was on his feet, scrutinising Wilding's haggard face and disordered filthy clothes. He broke into exclamations between dismay and reproach, but these Wilding interrupted to ask the old man how it happened that he had remained.

"My son John was a sergeant in the troop that quartered itself here, sir," Walters explained, "and so they left me alone. But even had it not been for that, I scarcely think they would have harmed an old man. They were brave fellows for all the mischief they did here, and they seemed to have little heart in the service of the Popish king. It was the officers drove them on to all this damage, and once they'd started – well, there were rogues amongst them saw a chance of plunder, and they took it. I have sought to put the place to rights; but they did some woeful, wanton mischief."

Wilding sighed. "It's little matter, perhaps, as the place is no longer mine."

"No…no longer yours, sir?"

"I'm an attainted outlaw, Walters," he explained. "They'll bestow it on some Popish time-server, unless King Monmouth can follow up by greater victories tonight. Have you aught a man may eat or drink?"

Meat and wine, fresh linen and fresh garments did old Walters find him; and when he had washed, eaten, and drunk, Mr Wilding wrapped himself in a dressing-gown and laid himself down to sleep on a settle in the library, his servant and his dog on guard.

Not above an hour, however, was he destined to enjoy his hard-earned rest. The light had grown, meanwhile, and from grey it had turned golden, the heralds of the sun being already in the east. In the distance the firing had died down to a mere occasional boom.

Suddenly old Walters raised his head to listen. The beat of hoofs was drawing rapidly near, so near that presently he rose in alarm, for a horseman was pounding up the avenue, had drawn rein at the main entrance.

Walters knit his brows in perplexity, and glanced at his master, who slept on utterly worn out. A silent pause followed, lasting some minutes. Then it was the dog that rose with a growl, his coat bristling, and an instant later there came a sharp rapping at the hall door.

"Sh! Down, Jack!" whispered Walters, afraid of rousing Mr Wilding. He tiptoed softly across the room, picked up his musket, and, calling the dog, went out, a great fear in his heart, but not for himself. The rapping continued, growing every instant more urgent, so urgent that Walters was almost reassured. Here was no enemy, but surely someone in need. Walters opened at last, and Mr Trenchard, grimy of face and hands, his hat shorn of its plumes, his clothes torn, staggered with an oath across the threshold.

"Walters!" he cried. "Thank God! I thought you'd be here, but I wasn't certain. Down, Jack!"

The hound was barking madly again, having recognized an old friend.

"Plague on the dog!" growled Walters. "He'll wake Mr Wilding."

"Mr Wilding?" said Trenchard, and checked midway across the hall. "Mr Wilding?"

"He arrived here a couple of hours ago, sir…"

"Wilding here? Oddsheart! I was more than well advised to come. Where is he, man?"

"Sh, sir! He's asleep in the library. You'll wake him, you'll wake him!"

But Trenchard never paused. He crossed the hall at a bound, and flung wide the library door. "Anthony!" he shouted. "Anthony!" And in the background Walters cursed him for a fool.

Wilding leapt to his feet, awake and startled. "Wha… Nick!"

"Oons!" roared Nick. "You're choicely found. I came to send to Bridgwater for you. We must away at once, man."

"How – away? I thought you were in the fight, Nick."

"And don't I look as if I had been?"

"But then…"

"The fight is fought and lost; there's an end to the garboil. Monmouth is in full flight with what's left him of his horse. When I quitted the field, he was riding hard for Polden Hill." He dropped into a chair, his accents grim and despairing, his eyes haggard.

"Lost?" gasped Wilding, and his conscience pricked him for a moment, remembering how much it had been his fault – however indirectly – that Feversham had been forewarned. "But how lost?" he cried a moment later.

"Ask Grey," snapped Trenchard. "Ask his craven, numskulled lordship. He had as good a hand in losing it as any. Oh, it was all most infernally mishandled, as has been everything in this ill-starred rising. Grey sent back Godfrey, the guide, and attempted in the dark to find his own way across the rhine. He missed the ford. What else could the fool have hoped? And when he was discovered and Dunbarton's guns began to play on us – hell and fire! we ran as if Sedgemoor had been a racecourse.

"The rest was but the natural sequel. The foot, seeing our confusion, broke. They were rallied again; broke again; and again were rallied; but all too late. The enemy was up, and with that damned ditch between us there was no getting to close quarters with them. Had Grey ridden round, and sought to turn their flank, things might have been – oh, God! – they would have been entirely different. I did suggest it. But for my pains Grey threatened to pistol me if I presumed to instruct him in his duty. I would to Heaven I had pistolled *him* where he stood."

Walters, at gaze in the doorway, listened to the bitter tirade. Wilding, on the settle, sat silent a moment, his elbows on his knees, his chin in his hands, his eyes set and grim as Trenchard's own. Then he mastered himself, and waved a hand towards the table where stood food and wine.

"Eat and drink, Nick," he said, "and we'll discuss what's to be done."

"It'll need little discussing," was Nick's savage answer as he rose and went to pour himself a cup of wine. "There's but one course open to us – instant flight. I am for Minehead to join Hewling's horse, which went there yesterday for guns. We might seize a ship somewhere on the coast, and thus get out of this infernal country of mine."

They discussed the matter in spite of Trenchard's having said that there was nothing to discuss, and in the end Wilding agreed to go with him. What choice had he? But first he must go to Bridgwater to reassure his wife.

"To Bridgwater?" blazed Trenchard, in a passion at the folly of the suggestion. "You're clearly mad! All the King's forces will be there in an hour or two."

"No matter," said Wilding. "I must go. I am dead already, as it happens." And he related his singular adventure in Feversham's camp last night. Trenchard heard him in amazement. If any suspicion crossed his mind that his friend's love affairs had had anything to do with rousing Feversham prematurely, he showed no sign of it. But he shook his head at Wilding's insistence that he must first go to Lupton House.

"Shalt send a message, Anthony. Walters will find someone to bear it. But you must not go yourself."

In the end Mr Trenchard prevailed upon him to adopt this course, however reluctant he might be. Thereafter they proceeded to make their preparations. There were still a couple of nags in the stables, in spite of the visitation of the militia, and Walters was able to find fresh clothes for Mr Trenchard above stairs.

A half-hour later they were ready to set out on this forlorn hope of escape; the horses were at the door, and Mr Wilding was in the act of drawing on the fresh pair of boots which Walters had fetched him. Suddenly he paused, his foot in the leg of his right boot, and sat bemused a moment. Trenchard, watching him, waxed impatient.

"What ails you now?" he croaked.

Without answering him, Wilding turned to Walters. "Where are the boots I wore last night?" he asked, and his voice was sharp – oddly sharp, considering how trivial the matter of his speech.

"In the kitchen," answered Walters.

"Fetch me them." And he kicked off again the boot he had half drawn on.

"But they are all befouled with mud, sir."

"Clean them, Walters; clean them and let me have them."

Still Walters hesitated, pointing out that the boots he had brought his master were newer and sounder. Wilding interrupted him impatiently.

"Do as I bid you, Walters." And the old man, understanding nothing, went off on the errand.

"A pox on your boots!" swore Trenchard. "What does this mean?"

Wilding seemed suddenly to have undergone a transformation. His gloom had fallen from him. He looked up at his old friend and, smiling, answered him. "It means, Nick, that whilst these excellent boots that Walters would have me wear might be well enough for a ride to the coast such as you propose, they are not at all suited to the journey I intend to make."

"Maybe," said Nick with a sniff, "you're intending to journey to Tower Hill?"

"In that direction," answered Mr Wilding suavely. "I am for London, Nick. And you shall come with me."

"God save us! Do you keep a fool's egg under that nest of hair?"

Wilding explained, and by the time Walters returned with the boots Trenchard was walking up and down the room in an odd agitation.

"Odds my life, Tony!" he cried at last. "I believe it is the best thing."

"The only thing, Nick."

"And since all is lost, why…" Trenchard blew out his cheeks and smacked fist into palm. "I am with you," said he.

Chapter 24

JUSTICE

It has fallen to my lot in the course of this veridical chronicle of Mr Anthony Wilding's connection with the Rebellion in the West, and of his wedding and post-nuptial winning of Ruth Westmacott, to relate certain matters of incident and personality that may be accounted strange. But the strangest yet remains to be related. For in spite of all that had passed between Sir Rowland Blake and the Westmacotts on that memorable night of Sunday to Monday on which the battle of Sedgemoor was lost and won, towards the end of that same month of July we find him not only back at Lupton House, but once again the avowed suitor of Mr Wilding's widow. For effrontery this is a matter of which it is to be doubted whether history furnishes a parallel. Indeed, until the circumstances are sifted it seems wild and incredible. So let us consider these.

On the morrow of Sedgemoor, the town of Bridgwater became invested – infested were no whit too strong a word – by the King's forces under Feversham and the odious Kirke, and there began a reign of terror for the town. The prisons were choked with attainted and suspected rebels. From Bridgwater to Weston Zoyland the road was become an avenue of gallows, each bearing its repulsive gemmace-laden burden; for the King's commands were unequivocal, and hanging was the order of the day.

It is not my desire at this stage to surfeit you with the horrors that were perpetrated during that hideous week of July, when no man's life was safe from the royal butchers. The awful campaign of Jeffreys and his four associates was yet to follow, but it is doubtful if it could compare in ruthlessness with that of Feversham and Kirke. At least, when Jeffreys came, men were given a trial – or what looked like it – and there remained them a chance, however slender, of acquittal, as many lived to prove thereafter. With Feversham there was no such chance. And it was of this circumstance that Sir Rowland Blake took the fullest and the cowardliest advantage.

There can be no doubt that Sir Rowland was a villain. It might be urged for him that he was a creature of circumstance, and that had circumstances been other it is possible he had been a credit to his name. But he was weak in character, and out of that weakness he had developed a Herculean strength in villainy. Failure had dogged him in everything he undertook. Broken at the gaming-tables, hounded out of town by creditors, he was in desperate straits to repair his fortunes, and, as we have seen, he was not nice in his endeavours to achieve that end.

Ruth Westmacott's fair inheritance had seemed an easy thing to conquer, and to its conquest he had applied himself to suffer defeat as he had suffered it in all things else. But Sir Rowland did not yet acknowledge himself beaten, and the Bridgwater reign of terror dealt him a fresh hand – a hand of trumps. With this he came boldly to renew the game.

He was as smooth as oil at first, a very penitent, confessing himself mad in what he had done on that Sunday night – mad with despair and rage at having been defeated in the noble task to which he had turned his hands. His penitence might have had little effect upon the Westmacotts had he not known how to insinuate that it might be best for them to lend an ear to it – and a forgiving one.

"You will tell Mr Westmacott, Jasper," he had said, when Jasper told him that they could not receive him, "that he would be unwise not to see me, and the same to Mistress Wilding." And old Jasper had carried his message, and had told Richard of the wicked smile that had been on Sir Rowland's lips when he had uttered it.

Now Richard was in many ways a changed man since that night at Weston Zoyland. A transformation seemed to have been wrought in him as odd as it was sudden, and it dated from the moment when with tears in his eyes he had wrung Wilding's hand in farewell. Where precept had failed, Richard found himself converted by example. He contrasted himself in that stressful hour with great-souled Anthony Wilding, and saw himself as he was, a weakling, strong only in vicious ways. Repentance claimed him; repentance and a fine ambition to be worthier, to resemble as nearly as his nature would allow him this Anthony Wilding whom he took for pattern. He changed his ways, abandoned drink and gaming, and gained thereby a healthier countenance. Then in his zeal he overshot his mark. He developed a taste for Scripture-reading, bethought him of prayers, and even took to saying grace to his meat. Indeed – for conversion, when it comes, is a furious thing – the swing of his soul's pendulum threatened now to carry him to extremes of virtue and piety. "O Lord!" he would cry a score of times a day, "Thou hast brought up my soul from the grave; Thou hast kept me alive that I should not go down to the pit!"

But underlying all this remained unfortunately the inherent weakness of his nature – indeed, it was that very weakness and malleability that made this sudden and wholesale conversion possible.

Upon hearing Sir Rowland's message his heart fainted, despite his good intentions, and he urged that perhaps they had better hear what the baronet might have to say.

It was three days after Sedgemoor Fight, and poor Ruth was worn and exhausted with her grief – believing Wilding dead, for he had sent no message to inform her of his almost miraculous preservation. The thing he went to do in London was fraught with such peril that he foresaw but the slenderest chance of escaping with his life. Therefore, he had argued, why console her now with news that he lived, when in a few days the headsman might prove that his end had been but postponed? To do so might be to give her cause to mourn him twice. Again he was haunted by the thought that, in spite of all, it may have been pity that had so grievously moved her at their last meeting. Better, then, to wait; better for both their sakes. If he came safely through his ordeal it would be time enough to bear her news of his preservation.

In deepest mourning, very white, with dark stains beneath her eyes to tell the tale of anguished vigils, she received Sir Rowland in the withdrawing-room, her brother at her side. To his expressions of deep penitence he found them cold; so he passed on to show them what disastrous results might ensue upon a stubborn maintaining of this attitude of theirs towards him.

"I have come," he said, his eyes downcast, his face long-drawn, for he could play the sorrowful with any hypocrite in England, "to do something more than speak of my grief and regret. I have come to offer proof of it, by service."

"We ask no service of you, sir," said Ruth, her voice a sword of sharpness.

He sighed, and turned to Richard. "This were folly," he assured his whilom friend. "You know the influence I wield."

"Do I?" quoth Richard, his tone implying doubt.

"You think that the bungled matter at Newlington's may have shaken it?" quoth Blake. "With Feversham, perhaps. But Albemarle, remember, trusts me very fully. There are ugly happenings in the town here. Men are being hung like linen on a washing-day. Be not too sure that yourself are free from all danger." Richard paled under the baronet's baleful, half-sneering glance. "Be not in too great haste to cast me aside, for you may find me useful."

"Do you threaten, sir?" cried Ruth.

"Threaten?" quoth he. He turned up his eyes and showed the whites of them. "Is it to threaten to promise you my protection; to show you how I can serve you? – than which I ask no sweeter boon of heaven. A word from me, and Richard need fear nothing."

"He need fear nothing without that word," said Ruth disdainfully. "Such service as he did Lord Feversham the other night…"

"Is soon forgotten," Blake cut in adroitly. "Indeed, 'twill be most convenient to his lordship to forget it. Think you he would care to have it known that 'twas to such a chance he owes the preservation of his army?" He laughed, and added in a voice of much sly meaning, "The times are full of peril. There's Kirke and his lambs. And there's no saying how Kirke might act did he chance to learn what Richard failed to do that night when he was left to guard the rear at Newlington's!"

"Would you inform him of it?" cried Richard, between anger and alarm.

Blake thrust out his hands in a gesture of horrified repudiation. "Richard!" he cried in deep reproof, and again, "Richard!"

"What other tongue has he to fear?" asked Ruth.

"Am I the only one who knows of it?" cried Blake. "Oh, madam, why will you ever do me such injustice? Richard has been my friend – my dearest friend. I wish him so to continue, and I swear that he shall find me his, as you shall find me yours."

"It is a boon I could dispense with," she assured him, and rose. "This talk can profit little, Sir Rowland," said she. "You seek to bargain."

"You shall see how unjust you are," he cried with deep sorrow. "It is but fitting, perhaps so after what has passed. It is my punishment. But you shall come to acknowledge that you have done me wrong. You shall see how I shall befriend and protect him."

That said, he took his leave and went, but he left behind him a shrewd seed of fear in Richard's mind, and of the growth that sprang from it Richard almost unconsciously transplanted something in the days that followed into the heart of Ruth. As a result, to make sure that no harm should come to her brother, the last of his name and race, she resolved to receive Sir Rowland, resolved in spite of Diana's outspoken scorn, in spite of Richard's protests – for though afraid, yet he would not have it so – in spite even of her own deep repugnance of the man.

Days passed and grew to weeks. Bridgwater was settling down to peace again – to peace and mourning; the Royalist scourge had spread to Taunton, and Blake lingered on at Lupton House, an unwelcome but an undeniable guest.

His presence was as detestable to Richard now as it was to Ruth, for Richard had to submit to the mockery with which the town-rake lashed his godly bearing and altered ways. More than once, in gusts of sudden valour, the boy urged his sister to permit him to drive the baronet from the house and let him do his worst. But Ruth, afraid for Richard, bade him wait until the times were more settled. When the royal vengeance had slaked its lust for blood it might matter little, perhaps, what tales Sir Rowland might elect to carry.

And so Sir Rowland remained and waited. He assured himself that he knew how to be patient, and congratulated himself upon that circumstance. Wilding dead, a little time must now suffice to blunt the sharp edge of his widow's grief; let him but await that time, and the rest should be easy, the battle his. With Richard he did not so much as trouble himself to reckon.

Thus he determined, and thus no doubt he would have acted but for an unforeseen contingency. A miserable, paltry creditor had smoked him out in his Somerset retreat and got a letter to him full of dark hints of a debtor's gaol. The fellow's name was Swiney, and Sir Rowland knew him for fierce and pertinacious where a defaulting debtor was concerned. One only course remained him: to force matters with Wilding's widow. For days he refrained, fearing that precipitancy might lose him all; it was his wish to do the thing without too much coercion; some, he was not coxcomb enough to think – coxcomb though he was – might be dispensed with.

At last one Sunday evening he decided to be done with dallying, and to bring Ruth between the hammer and the anvil of his will. It was the last Sunday in July, exactly three weeks after Sedgemoor, and the odd coincidence of his having chosen such a day and hour you shall appreciate anon.

They were on the lawn taking the cool of the evening after an oppressively hot day. By the stone seat, now occupied by Lady

Horton and Diana, Richard lay on the sward at their feet in talk with them, and their talk was of Sir Rowland. Diana – gall in her soul to see the baronet by way of gaining yet his ends – chid Richard in strong terms for his weakness in submitting to Blake's constant presence at Lupton House. And Richard meekly took his chiding and promised that, if Ruth would but sanction it, things should be changed upon the morrow.

Sir Rowland, all unconscious – reckless, indeed – of this, sauntered with Ruth some little distance from them, having contrived adroitly to draw her aside. He broke a spell of silence with a dolorous sigh.

"Ruth," said he pensively, "I mind me of the last evening on which you and I walked here alone."

She flashed him a glance of fear and aversion, and stood still. Under his brow he watched the quick heave of her bosom, the sudden flow and abiding ebb of blood in her face – grown now so thin and wistful – and he realised that before him lay no easy task. He set his teeth for battle.

"Will you never have a kindness for me, Ruth?" he sighed.

She turned about, her intent to join the others, a dull anger in her soul. He set a hand upon her arm. "Wait!" said he, and the tone in which he uttered that one word kept her beside him. His manner changed a little. "I am tired of this," said he.

"Why, so am I," she answered bitterly.

"Since we are agreed so far, let us agree to end it."

"It is all I ask."

"Yes, but – alas! – in a different way. Listen now."

"I will not listen. Let me go."

"I were your enemy did I do so, for you would know hereafter a sorrow and repentance for which nothing short of death could offer you escape. Richard is under suspicion."

"Do you hark back to that?" The scorn of her voice was deadly. Had it been herself he desired, surely that tone had quenched all passion in him, or else transformed it into hatred. But Blake was playing for a fortune, for shelter from a debtor's prison.

"It has become known," he continued, "that Richard was one of the early plotters who paved the way for Monmouth's coming. I think that that, in conjunction with his betrayal of his trust that night at Newlington's, thereby causing the death of some twenty gallant fellows of King James's, will be enough to hang him."

Her hand clutched at her heart. "What is't you seek?" she cried. It was almost a moan. "What is't you want of me?"

"Yourself," said he. "I love you, Ruth," he added, and stepped close up to her.

"Oh God!" she cried aloud. "Had I a man at hand to kill you for that insult!"

And then – miracle of miracles! – a voice from the shrubs by which they stood bore to her ears the startling words that told her her prayer was answered there and then.

"Madam, that man is here."

She stood frozen. Not more of a statue was Lot's wife in the moment of looking behind her than she who dared not look behind. That voice! A voice from the dead, a voice she had heard for the last time in the cottage that was Feversham's lodging at Weston Zoyland. Her wild eyes fell upon Sir Rowland's face. It showed livid; the nether-lip sucked in and caught in the strong teeth, as if to prevent an outcry; the eyes wild with fright. What did it mean? By an effort she wrenched herself round at last, and a scream broke from her to rouse her aunt, her cousin, and her brother, and bring them hastening towards her across the sweep of lawn.

Before her, on the edge of the shrubbery, a grey figure stood erect and graceful, and the face, with its thin lips faintly smiling, its dark eyes gleaming, was the face of Anthony Wilding. And as she stared he moved forward, and she heard the fall of his foot upon the turf, the clink of his spurs, the swish of his scabbard against the shrubs, and reason told her that this was no ghost.

She held out her arms to him. "Anthony! Anthony!" She staggered forward, and he was no more than in time to catch her as she swayed.

He held her fast against him and kissed her brow. "Sweet," he said, "forgive me that I frightened you. I came by the orchard gate, and my coming was so timely that I could not hold in my answer to your cry."

Her eyelids fluttered, she drew a long sighing breath, and nestled closer to him. "Anthony!" she murmured again, and reached up a hand to stroke his face, to feel that it was truly living flesh.

And Sir Rowland, realising too by now that here was no ghost, recovered his lost courage. He put a hand to his sword, then withdrew it, leaving the weapon sheathed. Here was a hangman's job, not a swordsman's, he opined – and wisely, for he had had earlier experience of Mr Wilding's play of steel.

He advanced a step. "O, fool!" he snarled. "The hangman waits for you."

"And a creditor for you, Sir Rowland," came the voice of Mr Trenchard, who now pushed forward through those same shrubs that had masked his friend's approach. "A Mr Swiney. 'Twas I sent him from town. He's lodged at the 'Bull,' and bellows like one when he speaks of what you owe him. There are three messengers with him, and they tell of a debtor's gaol for you, sweetheart."

A spasm of fury crossed the face of Blake. "They may have me, and welcome, when I've told my tale," said he. "Let me but tell of Anthony Wilding's lurking here, and not only Anthony Wilding, but all the rest of you are doomed for harbouring him. You know the law, I think," he mocked them, for Lady Horton, Diana, and Richard, who had come up, stood now a pace or so away in deepest wonder. "You shall know it better before the night is out, and better still before next Sunday's come."

"Tush!" said Trenchard, and quoted, " 'There's none but Anthony may conquer Anthony.' "

" 'Tis clear," said Wilding, "you take me for a rebel. An odd mistake! For it chances, Sir Rowland, that you behold in me an accredited servant of the Secretary of State."

Blake stared, then fell a prey to ironic laughter. He would have spoken, but Mr Wilding plucked a paper from his pocket, and handed it to Trenchard.

"Show it him," said he, and Blake's face grew white again as he read the lines above Sunderland's signature and observed the seals of office. He looked from the paper to the hated smiling face of Mr Wilding.

"You were a spy?" he said, his tone making a question of the odious statement. "A dirty spy?"

"Your incredulity is flattering at least," said Wilding pleasantly as he repocketed the parchment, "and it leads you in the right direction. I neither was nor am a spy."

"That paper proves it!" cried Blake contemptuously. Having been a spy himself, he was a good judge of the vileness of the office.

"See to my wife, Nick," said Wilding sharply, and made as if to transfer her to the care of his friend.

"Nay," said Trenchard, " 'tis your own duty that. Let me discharge the other for you." And he stepped up to Blake and tapped him briskly on the shoulder. "Sir Rowland," said he, "you're a knave." Sir Rowland stared at him. "You're a foul thing – a muckworm – Sir Rowland," added Trenchard amiably, "and you've been discourteous to a lady, for which may Heaven forgive you – I can't."

"Stand aside," Blake bade him, hoarse with passion, blind to all risks. "My affair is with Mr Wilding."

"Aye," said Trenchard, "but mine is with you. If you survive it, you can settle what other affairs you please – including, belike, your business with Mr Swiney."

"Not so, Nick," said Wilding suddenly, and turned to Richard. "Here, Richard! Take her," he bade his brother-in-law.

"Anthony, you damned shirk-duty, see to your wife. Leave me to my own diversions. Sir Rowland," he reminded the baronet, "I have called you a knave and a foul thing, and faith! if you want it proving you need but step down the orchard with me."

He saw hesitation lingering in Sir Rowland's face, and he uncurled the lash of the whip he carried. "I'd grieve to do a violent thing before the ladies," he murmured deprecatingly. "I'd never respect myself again if I had to drive a gentleman of your quality to the ground of honour with a horsewhip. But, as God's my life, if you don't go willingly this instant, 'tis what will happen."

Richard's newborn righteousness prompted him to interfere, to seek to avert this threatened bloodshed; his humanity urged him to let matters be, and his humanity prevailed. Diana watched this foreshadowing of tragedy with tight lips, pale cheeks. Justice was to be done at last, it seemed, and as her frightened eye fell upon Sir Rowland she knew not whether to exult or weep. Her mother – understanding nothing – plied her meanwhile with whispered questions.

As for Sir Rowland, he looked into the old rake's eyes agleam with wicked mirth, and rage welled up to choke him. He must kill this man.

"Come," said he. "I'll see to your fine friend Wilding afterwards."

"Excellent," said Trenchard, and led the way through the shrubbery to the orchard.

Ruth, reviving, looked up. Her glance met Mr Wilding's; it quickened into understanding, and she stirred. "Is it true? Is it really true?" she cried. "I am being tortured by this dream again!"

"Nay, sweet, it is true; it is true. I am here. Say, shall I stay?"

She clung to him for answer. "And you are in no danger?"

"In none, sweet. I am Mr Wilding of Zoyland Chase, free to come and go as best shall seem to me."

He begged the others to leave them a little while, and he led her to the stone seat by the river. He set her at his side there and told her the story of his escape from the firing-party, and of the inspiration that had come to him on the morrow to make use of the letter in his boot which Sunderland had given him for Monmouth in the hour of panic. Monmouth's cavalier treatment of him when he had arrived in Bridgwater had precluded his delivering that letter at the council. There was never another opportunity, nor did he again think of the package in the stressful hours that followed. It was not until the following morning that he suddenly remembered it lay undelivered, and bethought him that it might prove a weapon to win him delivery from the dangers that encompassed him.

"It was a slender chance," he told her, "but I employed it. I waited in London, in hiding, close upon a fortnight ere I had an opportunity of seeing Sunderland. He laughed me to scorn at first, and threatened me with the Tower. But I told him the letter was in safe hands and would remain there in earnest of his good behaviour, and that did he have me arrested it would instantly be laid before the King and bring his own head to the block more surely even than my own. It frightened him; but it had scarcely done so, sweet, had he known that that precious letter was still in my boot, for my boot was on my leg, and my leg was in the room with the rest of me.

"He surrendered at last, and gave me papers proving that Trenchard and I – for I stipulated for old Nick's safety too – were His Majesty's accredited agents in the West. I loathed the title. But…" – he spread his hands and smiled – "it was that or widowing you."

She took his face in her hands and stroked it fondly, and they sat thus until a dry cough behind them roused them from their joyous silence. Mr Trenchard was sauntering towards them, his left eye tucked farther under his hat than usual, his hands behind him.

" 'Tis a thirsty evening," he informed them.

"Go, tell Richard so," said Wilding, who knew naught of Richard's altered ways.

"I've thought of it; but haply he's sensitive on the score of drinking with me again. He has done it twice to his undoing."

"He'll do it a third time, no doubt," said Mr Wilding curtly, and Trenchard, taking the hint, turned with a shrug, and went up the lawn towards the house. He found Richard in the porch, where he had lingered fearfully, waiting for news. At sight of Mr Trenchard's grim, weather-beaten countenance he came forward suddenly.

"How has it sped?" he asked, his lips twitching on the words.

"Yonder they sit," said Trenchard, pointing down the lawn.

"No, no. I mean… Sir Rowland."

"Oh, Sir Rowland?" cried the old sinner, as though Sir Rowland were some matter long forgotten. He sighed. "Alas, poor Swiney! I fear I've cheated him."

"You mean?"

"Art slow at inference, Dick. Sir Rowland has passed away in the odour of villainy."

Richard clasped nervous hands together and raised his colourless eyes to heaven.

"May the Lord have mercy on his soul!" said he.

"May He, indeed!" said Trenchard, when he had recovered from his surprise. "But," he added pessimistically, "I doubt the rogue's in hell."

Richard's eyes kindled suddenly, and he quoted from the thirtieth Psalm, " 'I will extol thee, O Lord; for Thou hast lifted me up, and hast not made my foes to rejoice over me.' " Dumfounded, wondering, indeed, was Westmacott's mind unhinged, Trenchard scanned him narrowly. Richard caught the glance and misinterpreted it for one of reproof. He bethought him that his joy was unrighteous. He stifled it, and forced his lips to sigh "Poor Blake!"

"Poor, indeed!" quoth Trenchard, and adapted a remembered line of his play-acting days to suit the case. "The tears live in an onion that shall water his grave. Though, perhaps, I am forgetting Swiney." Then, in a brisker tone, "Come, Richard. What like is the muscadine you keep at Lupton House?"

"I have abjured all wine," said Richard.

"A plague you have!" quoth Trenchard, understanding less and less. "Have you turned Mussulman, perchance?"

"No," answered Richard sternly, "Christian."

Trenchard hesitated, rubbing his nose thoughtfully. "Hum," said he at length. "Peace be with you, then. I'll leave you here to bay the moon to your heart's content. Perhaps Jasper will know where to find me a brain-wash." And with a final suspicious, wondering look at the whilom bibber, he passed into the house, much exercised on the score of the sanity of this family into which his friend Anthony had married.

Outside, the twilight shadows were deepening.

"Shall we home, sweet?" whispered Mr Wilding.

The shadows befriended her, a veil for her sudden confusion. She breathed something that seemed no more than a sigh, though more it seemed to Anthony Wilding.

Rafael Sabatini

Captain Blood

Captain Blood is the much-loved story of a physician and gentleman turned pirate.

Peter Blood, wrongfully accused and sentenced to death, narrowly escapes his fate and finds himself in the company of buccaneers. Embarking on his new life with remarkable skill and bravery, Blood becomes the 'Robin Hood' of the Spanish seas. This is swashbuckling adventure at its best.

The Gates of Doom

'Depend above all on Pauncefort', announced King James; 'his loyalty is dependable as steel. He is with us body and soul and to the last penny of his fortune.' So when Pauncefort does indeed face bankruptcy after the collapse of the South Sea Company, the king's supreme confidence now seems rather foolish. And as Pauncefort's thoughts turn to gambling, moneylenders and even marriage to recover his debts, will he be able to remain true to the end? And what part will his friend and confidante, Captain Gaynor, play in his destiny?

'A clever story, well and amusingly told' – *The Times*

Rafael Sabatini

The Lost King

The Lost King tells the story of Louis XVII – the French royal who officially died at the age of ten but, as legend has it, escaped to foreign lands where he lived to an old age. Sabatini breathes life into these age-old myths, creating a story of passion, revenge and betrayal. He tells of how the young child escaped to Switzerland from where he plotted his triumphant return to claim the throne of France.

'...the hypnotic spell of a novel which for sheer suspense, deserves to be ranked with Sabatini's best' – *New York Times*

Scaramouche

When a young cleric is wrongfully killed, his friend, André-Louis, vows to avenge his death. André's mission takes him to the very heart of the French Revolution where he finds the only way to survive is to assume a new identity. And so is born Scaramouche – a brave and remarkable hero of the finest order and a classic and much-loved tale in the greatest swashbuckling tradition.

'Mr Sabatini's novel of the French Revolution has all the colour and lively incident which we expect in his work' – *Observer*

Rafael Sabatini

The Sea Hawk

Sir Oliver, a typical English gentleman, is accused of murder, kidnapped off the Cornish coast, and dragged into life as a Barbary corsair. However Sir Oliver rises to the challenge and proves a worthy hero for this much-admired novel. Religious conflict, melodrama, romance and intrigue combine to create a masterly and highly successful story, perhaps best-known for its many film adaptations.

The Shame of Motley

The Court of Pesaro has a certain fool – one Lazzaro Biancomonte of Biancomonte. *The Shame of Motley* is Lazzaro's story, presented with all the vivid colour and dramatic characterisation that has become Sabatini's hallmark.

'Mr Sabatini could not be conventional or commonplace if he tried'
– *Standard*

7164368R0

Made in the USA
Lexington, KY
26 October 2010